Praise for author Lynette Eason

"[A] suspenseful mystery and a great love story of personal discovery."

—*RT Book Reviews* on *A Silent Fury*

"Eason's third Santino sibling [story] has a wonderful mystery and plenty of suspense."

—*RT Book Reviews* on *A Silent Pursuit*

"Fast-paced scenes and a twist...keep the reader engaged."

—*RT Book Reviews* on *Her Stolen Past*

Praise for *USA TODAY* bestselling author Laura Scott

"A page turning combination of suspense and second chances."

—*Harlequin Junkie* on *Primary Suspect*

"*Primary Suspect* by Laura Scott is truly enjoyable from start to finish... An excellent choice for fans of law enforcement heroes, medical drama, and run-for-your-life romantic suspense!"

—*Reading Is My Superpower* blog

W9-BNX-726

TOO CLOSE TO HOME

LYNETTE EASON

Previously published as *Hide and Seek*
and *Secret Agent Father*

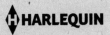

Recycling programs for this product may not exist in your area.

ISBN-13: 978-1-335-40636-1

Too Close to Home
First published as Hide and Seek in 2013.
This edition published in 2021.
Copyright © 2013 by Lynette Eason

Secret Agent Father
First published in 2010. This edition published in 2021.
Copyright © 2010 by Laura Iding

This edition published by arrangement with Harlequin Books S.A.

For questions and comments about the quality of this book, please contact us at CustomerService@Harlequin.com.

Harlequin Enterprises ULC
22 Adelaide St. West, 40th Floor
Toronto, Ontario M5H 4E3, Canada
www.Harlequin.com

Printed in U.S.A.

CONTENTS

Lynette Eason is a bestselling, award-winning author who makes her home in South Carolina with her husband and two teenage children. She enjoys traveling, spending time with her family and teaching at various writing conferences around the country. She is a member of Romance Writers of America and American Christian Fiction Writers. Lynette can often be found online interacting with her readers. You can find her at Facebook.com/lynette.eason and on Twitter, @lynetteeason.

Books by Lynette Eason

Love Inspired Suspense

Holiday Homecoming Secrets

True Blue K-9 Unit

Justice Mission

Wrangler's Corner

The Lawman Returns
Rodeo Rescuer
Protecting Her Daughter
Classified Christmas Mission
Christmas Ranch Rescue
Vanished in the Night
Holiday Amnesia

Military K-9 Unit

Explosive Force

Classified K-9 Unit

Bounty Hunter

Visit the Author Profile page at Harlequin.com for more titles.

HIDE AND SEEK

Lynette Eason

Look at the birds of the air; they do not sow or reap or store away in barns, and yet your heavenly Father feeds them. Are you not much more valuable than they?

—*Matthew* 6:26

To my wonderful Savior, who lets me write for Him.
I also want to dedicate this book to my sweet niece,
Willow Dorris, and my nephews, Jonah Dorris and Liam
Dorris. Thanks for being such great kids and good
friends as well as cousins to my kids. You guys rock!

Acknowledgments

Thanks to my family for all their support. This is
my fifteenth Love Inspired Suspense book. I'm so
thankful that you understand about deadlines and the
desperation of pulling a plot and scenes from thin air—
or your lives. (I suppose I should thank you for your
forgiveness in this regard.) I love you all so much.
I thank God for blessing me with you.

Thanks to Emily Rodmell, my Harlequin editor, for
all her hard work on every single book I've written
for Love Inspired. We made it to fifteen!

Thanks to Officer Jim Hall, who critiques and corrects
all of my police procedural. If there's anything wrong
in here, it's not his fault! Jim, you're awesome. So glad
God dropped you into my life when you were living
in North Carolina. God bless you!

Thank you to the ACFW Romantic Suspense loop and
all of you who brainstormed this book and the next
one with me. Thanks to Mary Lynn Mercer, Michelle Lim,
Terri Weldon, Beth Ziarnik, Misty Kirby, Jeff Reynolds
and Jessica Patch. You guys gave me some fabulous
ideas, and even if I didn't use them all, you gave me
some direction and inspiration. God bless each of
you in your own personal writing journey.

Chapter 1

Searching for a crack house had not been in Erica James's plans for the evening. However, Detective Katie Randall had uttered the one sentence that could send her into one of the worst neighborhoods in the city.

"We've found new evidence in Molly's disappearance."

Erica let the words ring through her mind as she drove, looking for the address of the crack house that had been raided two days ago.

New evidence. *New evidence.*

"It's been three years," Erica exclaimed. "What possibly could have come to light now?" she'd asked, hating the shakiness in her voice, the desperate hope that she knew was carved on her face.

Detective Katie Randall had shown her a photograph of a crime scene. Even now, Erica's fingers curled around the steering wheel as she remembered the little outfit clearly pictured amidst the trash and rubble.

The outfit three-year-old Molly had been wearing when she'd disappeared from the day-care field trip to the zoo. Erica touched the picture with a shaking finger.

"That's her hair bow."

"We got a fingerprint from it. A girl by the name of Lydia Powell. Her prints are in the system for a shoplifting charge two years ago."

"So what does she say? Did you ask her about Molly?"

"We haven't been able to find her," Katie admitted.

"Then I will."

Now, two days later, on a cold Tuesday evening, Erica glanced at the sky. The sun would set in about ten minutes and she still hadn't found the address.

In this dark, dank part of town.

Drug deals on one corner, the selling of bodies and souls on the other. Her heart shuddered at the thought of her child being in the middle of all of this. And yet at the same time, her heart ached for the innocents trapped in this cycle of crime and abuse. For those who wanted out, but didn't know how to accomplish that. Or were too young to try.

Narrowed, suspicious eyes followed her progress down the trash-strewn street. The sun crept lower and her pulse picked up a notch.

As daylight disappeared so did the people on the street. One by one, everyone in a yard or on a porch made their way behind a closed, locked door.

She hadn't counted on it being dark by the time she got here. Then again, she hadn't counted on the place being so hard to find, either. Her GPS had led her down one street and up another until she was so twisted around she'd never find her way back out.

For the first time since Katie had told her the news, fear started to replace the hope she'd allowed herself to feel. She'd taken the information and run with it. Straight into one of the most dangerous parts of town.

What was she doing? Was she crazy?

After another hesitant second, she picked up the phone and dialed her brother, Brandon. Nerves on edge, she watched the street as she waited for him to answer. Finally, she heard, "Hello?"

"I think I've gone and done something stupid."

"Who, you? You're kidding." He didn't sound concerned—or surprised.

With good reason, she had to silently admit. She bit her lip. "No, Brandon, this time I'm serious."

That got his attention. "What is it? What's wrong?"

The mechanical voice from the GPS told her, "Turn left and your destination will be on the right." Erica rolled to a stop and looked to her left.

Brandon said, "Where are you?"

"Five sixty-seven Patton Street."

"Patton Street! Are you crazy?"

Now she heard the concern. "Yes, I think so. If I stay in my car and wait, will you meet me here?" Uneasy and on alert, she glanced around, felt unseen eyes watching her every movement. "Because while I'm not comfortable here, I'm not leaving yet, either."

She heard him muttering and thought she heard the words "crazy woman" in there somewhere. "I'm getting you home and then you're going into a safe occupation like accounting or—"

As Brandon continued his tirade, Erica chewed her bottom lip and tuned him out. Brandon worked with her at Finding the Lost, an organization dedicated to finding missing children she'd started after Molly disappeared. Erica, Brandon and Jordan—Brandon's best friend who'd needed a job and came highly recommended—worked together to find children who disappeared either through criminal activity such as kidnapping, or because they ran away.

Erica glanced in the rearview mirror and saw two rough-looking characters headed her way. Her stomach flipped. She whispered, "Oh, yeah, bad idea. Bad, bad idea." She had her self-defense training and her weapon, but—

"Bad idea is right. What made you decide to go there?" he demanded.

"New information about Molly's disappearance," she said with her eyes still on the rearview mirror.

Brandon paused then sighed, a small breath of understanding. "Ah."

Erica had to admit having a good working relationship with several police officers afforded her information she'd otherwise have trouble getting. Katie was her friend and Erica had proved herself trustworthy over the past couple of years. Which was why she now found herself in a possibly very bad situation.

A police cruiser rolled past on the street perpendicular to hers and the two figures behind her took off. She blew out a relieved breath, looked at her GPS one more time and turned left. And there it was.

"Give me about fifteen minutes," Brandon said. "Stay put."

The house she wanted loomed ahead on her right. She pulled to the curb two houses down and cut her engine, then her lights. The street lay empty, quiet as a tomb. She had a perfect view of the front of the house.

Night approached, sneaking in as though even it was reluctant to be found in this area of town.

"Erica? Did you hear me?"

"I heard you. I'll be waiting. A cop drove by and scared away the riffraff."

"If you're determined to stay, stay in the car with the doors locked. I mean it."

"Okay."

She had every intention of staying hunkered down in the front seat and waiting for Brandon to get there.

Until she caught a glimpse of a slim figure in a hoodie, hunched over and slinking down the street toward the deserted house.

Erica's stomach twisted. She reached for the weapon she'd earned the right to carry in a concealed holster, but on second glance, the person didn't look to be a threat. Male or female? She couldn't tell.

Erica glanced at the clock, then back. The figure shot a look over a thin shoulder every so often. Finally, under one of the few working streetlights, Erica caught a glimpse of a pale face and scared eyes that flicked in every direction, watchful and jumpy. She looked to be about fifteen or sixteen and walked with quick jerky steps, shoulders bowed, arms crossed protectively across her stomach as though she wanted to make herself as small as possible.

Excitement spun inside Erica. This girl looked familiar. Could it be Lydia?

Did she need help? She kept looking over her shoulder. Was someone behind her? Following her?

Erica watched for a few minutes until the girl disappeared around the side of the house. She put her hand on the door handle. If that was Lydia, she couldn't let her get away. She started to get out of the vehicle and stopped when she caught sight of another figure who had emerged from the shadows. He trailed the young girl, his steps quick and hurried.

Dread centered itself in the middle of her stomach. This didn't look good. Her fingers tightened on the handle, everything in her wanting to leap from the car. But she'd promised Brandon she'd wait.

When a shrill scream rent the night air, she could wait no longer. Erica threw open the door and raced toward the dark house.

Private investigator Max Powell shifted his eyes toward the older-model Ford Taurus parked on the street and leaned forward over the steering wheel as though that would give him a better view.

The car's open door and empty driver's seat set his nerves on edge. That didn't bode well. His gut tensed. Was his sister in that house? He'd gotten word from one of his street sources that she'd been here last night and would probably be back tonight. Max had rushed over to see if he could intercept her.

Max got out of his truck and peered inside the empty Ford. Relieved to see no evidence of foul play, he walked toward the house, his head swiveling in all directions, trying to discern whether there was a threat nearby or just someone who'd broken down and went looking for help.

Neither was a good option for the owner in this neighborhood.

Two feet away from the front porch steps, he stopped and checked the area one more time. The hair on the back of his neck stood at attention and adrenaline shot through his veins. He didn't have a good feeling about this—at all.

The brief thought that he should call one of his cop buddies flashed through his mind. But he wanted to find Lydia first, have a chance to talk to her before they found her.

He'd take his chances on going in alone.

He pulled his weapon and headed toward the front door.

Erica turned the corner around the back of the house and stopped. The door hung on one hinge, the darkness yawning beyond it now silent. In fact, it was so quiet, Erica wondered if it was possible she'd imagined the scream.

No. That had been real enough. Erica pictured the young girl she'd seen walking down the street. Her destination had been this house. Had that been her scream?

Her heart kicked into overdrive, pounding hard enough to make her gasp.

She swallowed hard and looked around. She couldn't just stand here waiting for Brandon. Where was he? What if the girl needed help?

Nausea swirled in the pit of her stomach as she

looked back at the house and thought about her precious baby being held in such a place.

A crack house.

One that kept its secrets hidden, maybe forever lost, her daughter's whereabouts never to be revealed. Had Molly cried for her, expecting her mama to come rushing in to save her?

The girl in the hoodie was someone's baby. And she might need help.

Tears clogged her throat even as she put one foot in front of the other to enter the black hole of a doorway. She hadn't been able to save Molly, but maybe she could help someone else's child.

She slipped just inside and moved to the left. The kitchen. The rancid smell of unwashed bodies, rotten food and…other odors she couldn't identify assaulted her.

Doing her best to ignore the offense to her nose, she listened. And heard nothing but her own ragged breathing. Erica moved farther inside. The moonlight sliced through the kitchen window to her left, casting shadows on the walls. Shadows that danced and mocked her. Should she call out?

Just as she opened her mouth, a creaking sound reached her ears. A thump sounded from down the hall, a scuffle. A muffled curse.

"Help!" a high scared voice called.

Erica dashed through the kitchen and into the hall. She tripped over the debris on the floor and managed to catch herself before she fell. Glass crunched beneath her feet, but she didn't stop. Light pierced the darkness behind her, illuminating the filth surrounding her.

"Hey! Who's in here?"

The deep male voice coming from behind her penetrated Erica's fear even as she rounded the corner into the nearest bedroom only to come to a screeching halt.

A male in his midthirties had the girl by the throat with his left hand, a knife in his right. The girl's fingers clawed at his hand.

"Stop it!" Erica yelled. "Get away from her!"

Running footsteps sounded behind her. Erica moved and placed her back to the wall so she could see who entered the room, but she didn't want to take her eyes off the scene in front of her.

The attacker froze then shoved the crying young woman away from him and stepped toward Erica, knife raised, his eyes darting toward the door then back to her.

Adrenaline flowed, fear pulsed and she swallowed hard as she felt for the weapon in the holster just under her left arm.

In all the situations she'd found herself over the past three years, never once had she been forced to pull her gun.

It looked like tonight might be the night.

In the moonlight, she could make out the man's harsh features: glittering dark eyes and a scar that curved from the corner of his right eye to his jaw.

She shivered, notched her chin and demanded, "Leave her alone!"

"Stay outta this, lady, or you'll be sorry," he snarled.

"Drop the knife! Now!"

Erica whirled to see a man, weapon drawn and aimed at the young man in the torn jeans and black sweatshirt.

Blue lights flickered and flashed against the walls

as backup arrived. The attacker licked his lips, shifted his feet.

"Drop it!" the man yelled again. The knife clattered to the floor. Erica nearly wilted with relief. "Up against the wall!" he shouted.

More footsteps sounded in the hallway as the man spoke into his cell phone. Erica's head spun as she watched the young girl's terrified eyes snap to the man then to the window.

Before Erica could call out, the young teen ran to the window and climbed out.

"No! Lydia! Come back."

The man's shout hung on the empty air. Erica raced for the window, the breeze blowing back her blazer.

"Police! Hands in the air!"

She spun, shocked to see an officer's weapon trained on her.

Chapter 2

Max spotted the concealed weapon under the woman's blazer and knew his pal, Officer Chris Jiles, had his gun on her. Her eyes, wide with shock, simply stared. Max brushed past her, careful to stay out of Chris's line of fire, and stopped at the window. Lydia was nowhere to be seen.

Max slapped a hand against the wall and spun as Chris said to the woman, "Put your hands on your head."

She finally blinked and said, "My name's Erica James. I… I have a concealed weapons permit."

"We'll get to that in a moment. Hands on your head." The woman complied and Chris stepped forward to remove her weapon from her holster. "Now show me some ID."

Max knew Chris had the situation under control, and

he turned and dashed from the room. He raced down the hall and out the door. "Lydia!"

He spun to the left, then back to the right.

She was gone.

Heart heavy, he returned to the scene to find Chris's partner, Steve Shepherd, had the attacker on his knees. The man's hands were bound behind him and his cries of innocence fell on deaf ears.

Two other officers had gone after Lydia. Two more had cleared the rest of the house.

Max looked into the woman's face across from him. *Beautiful* pretty well summed her up—huge green eyes and curly red hair pulled back in a ponytail that accentuated high cheekbones. She had a fragile appearance that made Max want to offer his protection. Right after he questioned her and found out everything she might know about what just went down.

Chris ordered, "Let me see the permit."

"It's in my purse." She frowned. "Which is still in my car. Hopefully."

Chris looked at Max. "What are you doing here?"

"You have to ask?"

Chris scowled. "Right." Then he motioned for the woman to walk. Max followed them down the hall and out the front door. As they exited, Max heard, "Erica!"

Erica stopped and waved at the man, who looked like he was ready to start pounding the officers holding him back. "I'm all right, Brandon." Brandon gave her a fierce frown as she said, "Thanks for being willing to come to my rescue, but I didn't need you, after all."

His brows shot north. "What did you stumble into now?"

While she retrieved her license and showed it to Chris, she gave the man she'd called Brandon an abridged version of the events, which Max thought was still too long. She must have sensed his impatience because she finally said, "Go on back home, Brandon, I'll be all right now."

"I'm not leaving until I know you're home safe."

Max said, "I'll see to it she gets there."

Brandon rubbed his nose. "And you are?"

Max held out a hand. "I'm Max Powell. Former cop. Currently a private investigator."

Brandon shook Max's hand with a glare at Erica. "I'm Brandon Hayes, Erica's long-suffering older brother."

A sigh escaped her, and Max felt protective instincts surge to the surface once again. He couldn't help but wonder at his strange reactions to this woman. Maybe he was just stressed out and overly tired.

Erica stiffened, and Max saw her start to say something then stop. Finally she seemed to decide on her words. "Brandon, I'm fine. Go home. I'm sorry I called you out here on a false alarm."

The man wilted. "Aw, Erica…" He leaned over to give her a hug then shot a look at Max. "You're sure?"

Max nodded.

"Go, Brandon. Jordan's probably wondering where you are," Erica said.

"Your boyfriend will be fine without me," Brandon said, giving Max a pointed look. The disappointment that shot through Max at the mention of Erica's boyfriend was just one more emotional surprise today.

"Knock it off, Bran. Just because you want him to be my boyfriend doesn't make it so. Now go home. I'll text you when I'm behind locked doors." She shot a look at Chris, who still held her license. "Hopefully they won't have bars on them."

Chris handed her wallet back to her. She spun away to stuff it into her purse as her brother got in his car.

He said, "I'll be checking on you."

"I'm sure you will."

Brandon pulled away just as the officers who had gone after Lydia returned—empty-handed. Anxiety twisted inside Max. Would he never be at the right place at the right time?

"Do you know the girl?" Erica asked.

He hedged. "Do you?"

"No."

Max watched as Steve led Lydia's attacker to the nearest cruiser and stuffed him in the back.

He felt her eyes on him. "But you do," she said.

"Why do you say that?"

She shot him a look full of exasperation. "Because you called her Lydia."

He nodded. "Yeah, I know her."

"I'm looking for a girl named Lydia, too."

Max stilled, tense. "Why's that?"

"Because she's a suspect in the kidnapping of my daughter three years ago."

The breath left his lungs. "You're Molly's mother?"

She paled. "You know who Molly is?"

"Of course I do. I've been following the story since I saw Lydia's face on the news."

"So who is she to you?"

Max blew out a deep breath and rubbed a hand over his head. "My sister."

* * *

Erica rolled with the shock wave. Of course. Lydia Powell, Max Powell. "Your sister?" she said. Anger swelled inside her. "Your sister had something to do with my daughter's kidnapping."

His eyes flashed. "She wasn't involved. She wouldn't do something like that. When I saw her face on the news, it floored me. To hear that she was wanted for questioning about kidnapping a three-year-old?" He shook his head. "She wouldn't. There's got to be some explanation."

Erica tucked her purse back behind her seat, thankful the car was exactly as she'd left it. She supposed having several police vehicles next to it had helped. "Well, I'd sure like to hear that explanation. And so would the cops."

His lips tightened and he narrowed his eyes. "What are you doing here?" he asked.

Erica lifted her chin, struggling a little to keep it together. "This is the house where my daughter was kept right after she was taken. When they did the raid last week, they found the clothes she was wearing when she disappeared. Along with the hair clip that had your sister's fingerprint on it. I couldn't believe that stuff was still here after three years. So I came to see… I hoped…" Tears clogged her throat as her failure hit home.

Max swiped a hand across his eyes but not before she saw the brief flash of sorrow in them. He sighed. "Let's get this wrapped up here, and we'll talk. I want to know what you know about Lydia."

"And I want to know what you know." She slid into the driver's seat.

He spoke to the officers, and she focused on slowing her rapidly beating heart. Her emotions were on overload. She had accomplished nothing with her impulsive trip to the crack house.

No, that wasn't completely true. She'd found Lydia's brother. Maybe that was the first step in finding Lydia. She closed her eyes and leaned her head back against the headrest. *Oh, baby girl, where are you? Please Lord, help me find her.*

Sobs threatened once again as the helplessness overwhelmed her. With an effort, she focused on what she had to do next. The next step in the plan.

"I'll follow you home." She recognized Max's voice and opened her eyes.

She sighed. "It's all right. I can manage."

His jaw firmed. "It's late and you're in the toughest neighborhood in Spartanburg. Plus, I promised your brother I'd make sure you got home safe."

"I thought we were going to talk."

"We are." He tapped the hood of her car. "But you need some rest and I'm not through with my search for Lydia tonight." He paused and glanced at his watch. "Would you be able to meet for breakfast?"

Erica mentally went through her calendar. She had two appointments she could delegate. "What time?"

"Eight thirty?"

"Sure." She cranked her car.

Max pointed to the weapon that had been returned to her. "What made you feel the need to carry that?"

Erica felt a wry smile cross her lips. "A job that brings me into neighborhoods like this."

Curiosity lifted his brow. "What kind of job is that?"

"I find missing people. Children mostly." Sadness filled her. "I have a great track record, too. Mostly."

"Then why the sad eyes?"

She started, surprised he'd noticed. "It seems I can find everyone's child but my own."

He looked away for a brief moment, but not before she caught another flash of raw grief in his blue eyes. "Yeah. I know what you mean."

"Lydia?"

He nodded.

"She ran from you," she said softly. Even though she thought Lydia had something to do with Molly's disappearance, Max didn't. He obviously believed in his sister, and Erica's heart hurt for him. "I'm sorry."

He swallowed hard. "At least I know she's still alive. As of tonight anyway."

"Who was the guy attacking her?" Erica asked.

He frowned. "He's a punk who preys on young girls."

"A pimp?"

"That, and more."

She shuddered. "I'm sorry."

With another shake of his dark head, he straightened and gripped the door, ready to close it. "Which is why we need to talk. Tomorrow."

"Right." She let him shut the door and waited for him to get into his vehicle.

Relief that she'd survived this night swirled as her phone rang. She glanced at the caller ID. Jordan. She frowned. "Hey, is everything all right? Did Brandon get home okay?"

"Yeah. He told me what you'd been up to. I wanted to make sure *you* were okay."

"I'm fine." She was really tired of that phrase.

"Glad to hear it, but you're not home yet. I've been sitting on your front porch for the last few minutes and Mrs. Griffin is giving me the evil eye from her window across the street."

Mrs. Griffin. The street busybody who kept her nose in everyone's business, but was a sweet woman. "Why are you on my porch?"

Max flashed his lights to tell Erica he was ready, and she pulled away from the curb and made her way out of the neighborhood. She lived about ten minutes away, on the opposite side of town, and right now, all she wanted to do was get home, crawl into bed and sleep for a week.

But she couldn't. Not if Jordan was there.

Jordan was saying, "Because I care about you, Erica. Brandon does, too. He shouldn't have left you alone."

"I'm not alone." She grimaced. A sigh slipped out. "Look, go home." Those words were getting old, too.

Jordan paused. "All right. I'll just wait until you get here. Make sure you get inside safely."

"A P.I. is following me home. I'll be—" She refused to say it again. "All the drama is over." *Please don't add to it,* she finished silently.

"Okay." He didn't hang up. At this rate, he'd still be there when she pulled into the drive.

"So go."

"Right. I'll just be going."

Erica frowned. He sounded weird. "What's wrong with you?"

"Nothing. Nothing. I was just—"

"Just what?"

"Nothing. I'll talk to you tomorrow."

Erica hung up and glanced in the rearview mirror. Seeing Max following behind her was comforting in an odd sort of way, even though she knew he had questions for her. That was fine—she had questions for him. And she would not notice his blue eyes again. Even though she had a feeling she could get lost in them, wondering what was going on behind them. Wondering what it would feel like to see them soften and sparkle for her. But she wouldn't do that. She couldn't. She wasn't interested in getting to know the brother of the girl who'd helped kidnap Molly. And she'd keep telling herself that as long as she had to in order to make herself believe it.

A few minutes later, she turned into her drive.

Jordan was gone and she breathed a sigh of relief. He'd been hovering like a mother hen lately—she couldn't figure out what was going on with him. And Brandon calling him her boyfriend just added to the confusion. Why would he say that? Jordan was a nice guy, but he was like a brother to her, and Brandon knew that.

Max pulled up against the curb and rolled the window down. Erica got out of her car and walked up to him. "Thanks for the escort."

"You want me to check out your house?"

"No thanks. No need."

"So. Tomorrow morning?"

"Yes." Her heart did a funny pitter-patter thing as

his lips curved in a gentle smile. Shocked, she swallowed hard. She hadn't felt an attraction for a man in such a long time, she almost didn't realize what it was when it hit her. Ever since her husband had left her, she'd gone out of her way to avoid men. And now, in this crazy situation, she was finding herself attracted to a man she just met?

She shook it off and said, "We never picked a place."

"Where's your office?"

"On East Main Street in the same complex as the post office."

"How about the café?"

"I'll be there."

"You have your phone?"

Erica lifted a brow and pulled it out.

He gave her his number. "Call me if you need anything, or if something changes and you can't make it." She punched in the number and heard his phone ring. When she hung up, he nodded toward her house. "Now go inside while I'm watching. And lock the door."

"I always do." Irritated by his bossy manner, Erica turned and made her way into the house, twisting the dead bolt after shutting the door. The lamp on the end table next to her sofa gave off a soft light that reached into the foyer, casting friendly shadows on the wall beside her.

Much friendlier than the ones in the crack house.

Erica glanced out the window and watched Max drive away. Without his distracting presence, images from the night bombarded her and she shivered. "So close," she whispered to the empty room. So close to some answers, and once again they'd slipped away from her grasp.

Erica crossed to the mantel and picked up her favorite picture of Molly, the one taken the day before she disappeared. As always, the tears threatened, but she couldn't look away from Molly's bright smile, her unruly red hair pulled up into a ponytail and her green eyes glinting with good-humored mischief.

Well, the answers may have slipped away tonight, but at least she had a name to follow up on, thanks to Katie, and now she'd seen Lydia's face up close and personal. She would recognize her again when she saw her, even if she was still trying to hide beneath that hoodie.

Erica set Molly's sweet picture back on the mantel and turned to flip the lamp off.

Darkness covered her and for a moment she just stood there, nearly drowning in her grief. It had been three years and still sometimes the pain of missing her child made her go weak.

Erica forced herself to head for her bedroom. She needed her rest. She would be no good for anyone if she let herself get to the point where she couldn't sleep again. Thankfully, she no longer needed medication most nights.

Tonight might not be one of those nights.

In her bedroom, she flipped on the closet light and let the warm light filter into the room. She wasn't in the mood for the strong overhead light tonight.

Just as she started for the bathroom to get ready for bed, she heard the distinctive click of the front door closing.

Chapter 3

Max sat in his den staring at the file in front of him, wondering why he couldn't get Erica James off his mind. Her story touched him. Her fragile beauty drew him to her. But her accusations made him angry. The fact that she thought Lydia was involved with Molly's kidnapping made him more determined than ever to find his little sister and prove her innocent.

He ignored the little niggling of concern at the back of his mind that Erica might have a reason to be throwing her accusations out there.

Which was why he'd made a point of doing his homework on her.

Erica was twenty-eight years old, and had, by all appearances, been happily married until her daughter's kidnapping three years ago. Her husband had left and moved overseas about a year later.

Erica had pulled herself together and started her own business working as a skip tracer, learning how to use specialized equipment and unique skills to locate missing people—or in Erica's case, missing children. He remembered the sadness in her eyes, and what she'd said about being able to find other people's children and yet not Molly.

Thanks to his contacts at the police station, acquiring Molly's case notes hadn't been a problem. He flipped to the evidence section.

A witness had reported seeing a woman with red curly hair, large sunglasses and a long coat at the zoo that day. Another witness claims he saw a man following the preschool group. Too many reported seeing nothing unusual.

Curly red hair. Erica had curly red hair. But she had an airtight alibi. She'd been working another missing persons case and had even had a police officer with her.

And then there was the matter of that pain in her eyes. No, she hadn't had anything to do with her daughter's disappearance.

It had been a chilly day in November when Molly had gone missing. This month would be a tough one for Erica.

And now she was looking for Lydia. Max felt anger surface again. Twenty-one years old, his sister could pass for thirteen or thirty, depending on how close one looked. He supposed the drugs and sporadic eating could do that to a person. His heart ached for her. If only…

An idea hit him, and Max hauled himself out of the recliner and made his way into the kitchen to get his phone. He grabbed it only to frown as he saw an unfamiliar number listed, indicating he'd missed a call.

He dialed the number and listened to it ring.

When the phone went to Erica's voice mail, he hung up and felt the heat climbing into his face as he realized she'd called him earlier, when he'd given her his number. And here he was, calling her at nearly midnight. He shrugged. If she asked, he'd explain.

Then again, he couldn't help but wonder why she hadn't answered. Was she all right? Or had something happened?

He clenched his jaw.

He had no reason to think that anything had happened to her.

Just like he'd had no reason to think anything had happened to Tracy. His throat tightened at the thought of his fiancée, dead because he hadn't worried enough.

He'd ignored his instincts and she'd died.

Max grabbed his keys.

Erica's pulse pounded as she stood frozen, unsure what to do.

When the door had clicked, she'd raced into the bathroom and twisted the lock.

Leaving her cell phone on the end table in her bedroom.

She listened to it ring and put her hand on the knob. When it stopped, she bit her lip and looked around.

The only window in the bathroom was stained glass and didn't open. That cold hard knot in the pit of her stomach turned to granite as she realized what she'd done.

She'd trapped herself.

Desperately, she tried to control her ragged breaths so she could listen.

She pressed her ear against the door and heard nothing.

Except her phone ringing again.

Should she stay and assume whoever had entered her house would get what he was looking for and then leave?

Or should she try to slip into the bedroom and grab the phone?

Indecision warred with her fear. By the time she decided to stay put, the phone had stopped again.

How had her intruder come in the front door—the one she remembered locking? Mentally, she ran through a list of people who had a key to her house. Her brother, Brandon; her best friend Denise Tanner, who'd moved to New Mexico; her parents, although they'd only used the key one time in the past three years; another friend, Ginny Leigh, and…

Footsteps sounded outside the bathroom door. She gasped and pulled back. He was in her bedroom. What would she do if he tried to get in the bathroom? Frantic, she cast her gaze around, looking for something she could use as a weapon.

A razor, a can of hair spray, the towel bar.

Then the steps receded. Faded. Stopped.

Was he gone?

Did she dare open the door? She waited. And listened.

Still nothing. Just the pounding of her heart.

The minutes ticked by.

Silence.

Her shaky fingers twisted the lock. She gripped the

doorknob and turned it slowly, then pulled the door open a crack.

The door exploded inward and she cried out as the edge of it caught her on the chin. She fell to her knees as a tall figure reached down to grab her by the arm. "I knew you were in there."

"Let me go!" She twisted, kicking out and catching a shin.

Her captor grunted.

"Hey! Let her go!"

She froze once again. "Peter?" Disbelief made her dizzy. "What are you doing?" she cried. Peter approached her, his hands replacing her captor's on her arms.

Erica hit him in the chest to push him away from her, but he kept his grip on her upper arms. It didn't hurt, but she didn't like it.

"Hey, chill, sis. We just need some cash, okay?" His foul breath made her grimace.

"Let. Me. Go." She kept her voice low and did her best to rein in her fury and fear. Peter—her younger brother, the black sheep, the ne'er-do-well. Whatever one wanted to call him, he had also once been a suspect in Molly's disappearance but had been cleared when there'd been no evidence to support his involvement. He released her and she backed away from him until the back of her knees touched the bed. "Where did you get the key?"

"Let's get the cash and get out of here." Erica swiveled toward the man who'd grabbed her when she'd exited the bathroom. Menace dripped from his gaze.

Real fear clutched her. "Who's he?" she asked Peter.

Peter advanced. He stopped in front of her, but he didn't attempt to grab her again. His sullen, bloodshot eyes slid from hers, and she reached for the cell phone on the end table. "It's late, Peter, and I'm tired," she said, trying to sound normal. "I don't have any cash on me."

And she wouldn't give it to him if she did.

He was twenty-four and in spite of the drugs he pushed into his body, still looked young and innocent. He shot his buddy a black look. "I told you to wait outside."

"I got tired of waiting. You were looking in the wrong place." Drug-addled green eyes lingered on her and he licked his lips.

Peter stepped between her and the other intruder. "Back off, Polo. That's not what you're here for."

Polo leered. "Says you."

Peter stood tall and straightened his shoulders. "Yeah. I do. Now get out of here."

Erica blinked at Peter's defense of her. All of a sudden, she had a glimpse of the man he could have been.

Polo shrugged and backed down. "I'll be outside." He gave Erica one last look and she shuddered with distaste when he finally turned his back.

"Peter, get rid of that loser, then give me back my key." She paused for a moment, knowing she probably shouldn't say what she was about to say. "You can stay in the guest room tonight."

Peter lifted his hands and raked them through his hair. They trembled. He paced from one end of the room to the other, glancing at the door as though expecting Polo to return. "I need you to give me some cash. I'll give it to him, and he'll leave you alone."

What was he coming down from? His drug of choice was usually cocaine or heroin.

He shook his head. "I'm so tired." He sighed and rubbed his eyes. "Look, Erica, I'm sorry about all this."

She lifted a brow. "You're sorry?"

"Yeah. I'm—" He waved a hand. "I wish…"

"Wish what, Peter?"

Erica took his arm and tried to lead him from the room but he jerked away from her. "What are you doing?"

"Police! Anyone here?"

Peter froze like a deer caught in the headlights. "You called the cops?" he snarled.

"No! I didn't." She turned and yelled, "We're back here! Everything is fine."

Had they seen Polo?

Footsteps sounded on her hardwood and for the second time that night she faced the officers Max seemed to know personally, with their weapons drawn. She held her hands where they could see them. "Why are you here?" she asked.

"Everything all right?" The officer in front stepped forward, his narrowed eyes taking in the scene before him.

Erica nodded. "Yes. Fine."

The officers exchanged glances and the first one holstered his weapon. The second only lowered his.

"Who called you?" Erica asked.

"Your neighbor said she saw a suspicious man hanging around your front door. He was on his way over to see if you needed help when he heard you scream. Decided to call the cops instead." He motioned to the bruise on her chin. "Want to explain that?"

Erica looked at her brother as she reached up to touch her chin. "He surprised me and I got banged with the door."

Peter looked contrite. "I'm sorry. I didn't mean for you to get hurt."

Was he sorry? Or was he sorry he wasn't going to get what he came here for? She honestly didn't know what to think of him anymore. She just knew she wanted to help him, couldn't give up on him.

He was her brother, plain and simple.

The cop nodded, suspicion still written on his face. "What's he coming off?"

Pete glared at the officer and Erica sighed. "I have no idea, but I'll take care of him."

"You're not helping him by covering for him."

"I know." Weariness invaded her as she looked at her little brother. How had he become this stranger she didn't know anymore? Someone she didn't trust and was afraid of some of the time, like when he came into her apartment with a creep and tried to shake her down for cash? "He had someone with him. A guy named Polo."

Peter winced and the officer's eyes shot wide. "Polo Moretti?"

She grimaced. "I didn't get a last name." She looked at her brother. "Peter?"

"I just met the guy," Peter muttered. "I don't know his last name."

"Who is he?" Erica asked.

The two officers exchanged a glance. Then one said, "He's involved in all kinds of nasty stuff. You don't want to mess around with him."

Erica drew in a quick breath. "Peter, what are you involved in?"

"Erica?"

She frowned—she knew that voice. She shot a look at Peter to let him know the conversation wasn't over. "Max?"

Max stepped into the hall and greeted the officers by name. Then he looked at her. "What's going on? I kept calling but you didn't answer."

"So you drove over here?" Erica felt a thrill in the pit of her stomach that she couldn't explain but didn't want to think about.

"Yeah. It's not that far." Pain flashed in Max's gaze for a brief moment—long enough for her to wonder about it— until his gaze shifted to her brother, a question on his face.

Peter's eyelids drooped. He didn't seem so dangerous now. In fact he reminded her of the sleepy little brother she used to put to bed. Erica said, "Look, let me get Peter settled and we'll talk in the den."

Max and the other two officers left the room. "Go on in the bedroom. I'll take care of this," she said to Peter.

For once, he didn't argue with her, just shuffled his way down the hall with one last look toward the front door, probably wondering where his friend went.

If Peter stayed here, would that Polo guy come back looking for him?

She felt sick at the thought.

The guest room door shut with a decisive click. Erica stood staring at the door for a brief moment then shut her eyes as she fought the weariness that threatened to make her keel over. *Oh, Peter.* What was she going to do with him?

Voices from the den grabbed her attention. She'd worry about Peter later.

Erica made her way back into the den where she found Max sitting on her couch and the other officers standing in front of her fireplace looking at Molly's picture.

Max said, "This is Chris and Steve. You remember them from earlier tonight?"

Erica nodded, shook their hands and said, "Sorry for all the trouble. Peter's going through a rough patch and…" Her voice trailed off. What could she say? Peter's actions, the company he was keeping and his appearance spoke for themselves. She refused to make excuses for him anymore.

Chris nodded and said, "Just give us a holler if you need any more help with him." He paused. "But I'll caution you. Don't trust him."

She sighed. "I know."

After Chris and Steve asked her a few more questions and finally left, Max rose. "Guess I'd better be going, too." He glanced down the hall. "I'd feel better if he wasn't here."

So would she, but Erica wasn't going to tell him that. "Peter will sleep awhile and so will I. I'll talk to him in the morning, see if he's open to a plan—or rehab. Again."

Max nodded. "Okay." He rubbed his chin. "I talked to the detectives who handled Molly's case."

She lifted a brow. "Lee and Randall."

"Yes. Good detectives."

"Not good enough." The words left her lips before she could stop them.

He stuffed his hands into the front pockets of his jeans. "I can see why you would think that. But I work with them on a regular basis. And I'll tell you, not a week goes by that Katie—Detective Randall—doesn't review Molly's case. She keeps it fresh in her mind and is always ready for something to break. She's the one who recognized Molly's dress at the crime scene."

"Really? She didn't tell me that." Erica reached up to rub the rocklike muscles at the base of her neck. "Well, it's good to know they really do care," she said softly. She truly was touched to know that Katie reviewed Molly's case on a regular basis. Katie had become a friend during the nightmarish days and then months following Molly's disappearance. Erica had checked in with Katie regularly, but the woman had had nothing more to tell her.

Until the raid had unearthed Molly's dress and bow.

Erica watched Max walk over to her mantel and pick up the picture of Molly. "She looks like you."

Tears threatened, but Erica held them back. "Yes. She does."

He placed the picture back and looked at the others. "Your parents?"

"They live across town." Erica snagged the family portrait that had been taken at Christmas almost four years ago. "This is the brother you met tonight at the crack house—Brandon. He has a town house on East Main near our office. And this is Peter during one of his better times." She sighed. "He lives in our grandparents' old home on the west side of town. He doesn't have to pay rent so at least he has a place to sleep at night when he runs out of money." She reached out to trace a finger over Molly's image. "This is the last picture we had taken with all of us."

"And this one?" He pointed to the small silver and blue frame in the line.

Erica gave a sad smile. "That's Denise Tanner, my best friend. She and I were inseparable from third grade to graduation. We were even roommates before I got married. She lives in New Mexico now but we talk at least once a week."

Max placed a hand on her shoulder. "You've moved on. You haven't forgotten Molly or given up hope, but it hasn't broken you."

She could feel the warmth of Max's hand through her heavy sweater, and the sudden desire to lean into him and let him take a share of her burden nearly overwhelmed her. She resisted, but barely. "I didn't exactly have a choice and it hasn't been easy. But that's a story for another time." She really needed him to go or she was going to be a blubbering mess.

He gave the family photo another look. "You seem like a close family."

A snort slipped out before she could stop it. At his surprised look she shook her head. "Looks can be deceiving. We're not close. It's been months since I've seen or talked to my parents. Things changed after Molly was taken."

He lifted a brow. "I'm sorry."

"Don't be. It is what it is. Maybe one day things will be different." *Only if you make an effort to change them,* said that little voice that was always right about such things. She cocked her head. "And maybe one day I'll tell you about it."

Max nodded and made his way to the door. "I'll see

you in the morning. Sleep lightly and be careful," he said before he left.

She knew what he meant. He was worried about Peter.

Erica got that—she was worried, too.

I'll sleep with one eye open.

Not to mention with my bedroom door locked and my gun close by.

Chapter 4

Max glanced at his watch for the third time in as many minutes. Was she coming? He sipped the cup of coffee he'd ordered and stared at the door, wondering if her brother or his "friend" had caused her any more trouble last night.

He frowned and shifted in his seat. How was he going to convince Erica that Lydia had nothing to do with Molly's kidnapping?

He finally concluded that he wasn't going to be able to convince her—not with words, anyway. He would have to show her who Lydia was, help her see his sister the way he saw her.

The mixture of smells in the café, such as cinnamon and coffee, tantalized him, making his stomach growl. The bagel and cream cheese in front of him was going to be too much temptation to resist if he had to wait on her much longer.

Max pulled out his phone, ready to punch in Erica's number when the door finally opened and she stepped inside, bundled against the frigid November wind.

She spotted him and smiled.

He waved her over.

Erica settled into the seat across from him and he said, "Any trouble last night?"

She shook her head. "He was gone when I got up this morning. I heard him leave around five o'clock." And she hadn't asked him to stay.

"Does he show up like that very often?"

"Every once in a while. That was the first time in about three months."

And Peter had never brought anyone with him before—the appearance of Polo Moretti was new. Erica wasn't sure what to make of that yet.

"You want some coffee?"

"Yes, I'll be right back."

Max sat back to study her as she headed to the counter to order. He decided he could look at her for a long while without growing bored. Very pretty, with auburn curls and green eyes. She was also tall. He put her at around five feet eight inches or so.

Within minutes, she had her coffee and a pastry, and she settled back into her seat with a sigh. "It was a long night, but we survived."

"Indeed." He rested his elbows on the table and clasped his fingers together in front of him. "Do you mind if I say a blessing?"

Erica set her coffee cup down. "Of course not."

Max bowed his head and thanked God for the food and for His guidance in finding Lydia and Molly. Short but effective. He saw Erica blink away tears and take a deep breath.

His heart ached for her loss. He couldn't even imagine what it must be like to have someone steal your child. Not knowing where his sister was nearly ate him alive, but if it was his child...

Erica took a bite of her pastry, which dripped with chocolate sauce, and said, "Do you mind telling me about your sister?"

Max sighed and said, "It's not a pretty story." Of course, in telling her about Lydia, he would also be opening himself up and revealing information he didn't share with just anyone. She must have seen this on his face because she reached across the table and placed her hand over his.

"Please," she said.

Max felt his stomach twist at her touch.

She thinks Lydia had something to do with her daughter's kidnapping, he reminded himself.

He drew his hand away and snagged his coffee cup. Her face flushed and she clasped her fingers in her lap. Guilt hit him. He hadn't meant to make her feel awkward.

"Look, Lydia's not perfect by any stretch of the imagination. And I know she's a suspect, but I really don't think she would have anything to do with kidnapping."

Erica gave a small shrug and her lips tightened. "I don't know your sister, of course. I only know that her fingerprint was found on the bow Molly was wearing when she disappeared. That makes me want to find her and talk to her. And if she didn't have anything to do with it, why is she running?"

He had to admit that running didn't look good, but that was typical Lydia. She ran from problems instead of facing them whether she was guilty of causing them or just in the wrong place at the wrong time. "I want to find her, too, give her a chance to explain."

Erica took a sip of her coffee and studied him. She finally asked, "Can we work together?"

He paused. Work with her? Maybe. Keep an eye on her? Definitely. "I think we can. But you have to understand I'm looking to prove she didn't have anything to do with the kidnapping."

Erica nodded. "I'm not looking to prove her guilty of anything—I'll leave that to the cops. I just want to talk to her, find out what she knows. Ask her why her fingerprint was on my daughter's bow."

He could live with that. For now. Plus, keeping her close and under his watchful eye would be better than having her go off on her own and finding Lydia before he could.

"All right," Max said, "I'll tell you Lydia's story."

Erica waited while Max gathered his thoughts. Her nerves danced and her heart pounded. She wasn't sure if it was due to the man seated across from her or what he was about to say. She reluctantly admitted it was probably a combination of both.

Max had dark good looks, and his no-nonsense attitude matched her own. She liked that he was willing to work with her even though he knew she thought it was very possible Lydia had something to do with Molly's kidnapping.

She liked him. Period. And for the first time in a long time, she wanted to see if she would still like him the more she got to know about him.

But for now, Lydia was her priority. Erica couldn't afford to have romantic feelings, not when there was a new lead in Molly's case.

"The short version," Max said, "is that Lydia and I grew up in the neighborhood you found yourself in last night."

Erica hadn't expected that one. "Oh wow."

"Yes. It was a bad situation. Our parents were also products of that neighborhood. I'm eight years older than Lydia so by the time she came along, I was already a seasoned pro at staying out of the way of the fights and the drug dealers." He shrugged. "I felt like I had to protect her, but for an eight-year-old that was a lot."

"No eight-year-old should face a responsibility like that," she whispered, appalled and yet amazed he'd survived to become the man he was today. "Why are you different? How did you get out?"

He gave her a rueful smile. "Foster homes. One of them anyway. I learned that the world was not just pain and drugs and abuse. I learned about love and God, and that if I wanted to climb out of the hole that was my life, I could do it as long as I wasn't afraid of hard work." He rubbed his chin. "You want to hear something silly?"

"Sure." Her fingers curled into her palms as she fought the urge to offer comfort.

"I watched a lot of movies growing up, and I saw these families portrayed as loving, kind to one another. Not perfect, but definitely not like my family." He gripped his knife and looked at it, then laughed—a sad, derisive sound. "I used to picture my family sitting around me at Thanksgiving or Christmas while I carved the turkey."

"And you wanted a family like that?"

"Yeah." He flushed and shook his head. "I don't know why I told you that."

"It's okay," she said softly. This time she didn't fight her feelings. Erica reached over and squeezed his hand. "I know exactly what you mean."

He shook his head. "So anyway, I guess you see that we didn't have a great childhood."

"But you rose above it. So many people don't. What happened with Lydia?"

Pain flashed in his eyes. "I lost touch with her for a while. When I turned eighteen, she was ten and a ward of the state. I didn't find her again until she was sixteen. She's the reason I quit the force and turned to private investigating. I could spend more hours on tracking her down as a P.I. than I could as a cop. When I finally found her, I asked her to come live with me, but she was pretty happy with her foster mother, a woman named Bea Harrison. So I didn't push the issue. The next time I went to visit her, though, she was gone." His mouth tightened at the memory and his eyes flashed.

"Did you find her again?" She knew Lydia was alive as of last night, but she still tensed as she waited for his answer.

He took a bite of his bagel and nodded. "Yes. Turns out our mother had gone through some kind of program and completed it successfully. And the court gave Lydia back to her."

Erica gaped. "What?"

"I couldn't believe it, either. I was furious. I went to the house and found Lydia high and my mother passed out on the couch. Alcohol and drugs were everywhere." He swallowed hard. "I called DSS and the cops and waited for them to get there. They took her back into the system, and Lydia has been mad at me ever since."

Erica swallowed hard. This was the girl Molly had possibly been with? What had her child experienced while with her? Erica shut off that line of thought. She just couldn't go there.

Max was saying, "I finally got custody of her about two months before she turned eighteen, but she refused to stay with me. The court sent her back to Bea, and Lydia agreed to that arrangement as long as I wouldn't come around. The only time she talks to me now is to beg money for a hit." He paused. "I had hoped things were turning around when she agreed to let me take her out on her eighteenth birthday. Things were definitely looking better between us, but about a month later, she was back to her distant, I-hate-Max self."

Her heart ached for him. "I'm so sorry."

Max ran a hand down his face. "She was stabbed around that time and ended up in the hospital. I never found out what the circumstances were, but she almost died. I sat with her day and night, hoping to show her how much I loved her, but once she was released, she disappeared again. Over the last three years, we've had minimal contact." He grimaced at Erica. "There—you have the whole ugly story. You sure you don't want to run screaming in the other direction?"

"No, your story doesn't scare me. It makes me hurt for you and Lydia, but it doesn't scare me."

She thought she saw relief in his eyes before he glanced out the window.

"I hate to point this out, Max, but Lydia's lifestyle makes it more likely that she would be involved in something like Molly's kidnapping than not."

His jaw hardened and she could tell he didn't like her statement. "You don't know her. I do."

"Do you really? You said yourself you two have been estranged, and she will hardly even talk to you. How can you claim to know her?"

Max's nostrils flared. "You'll just have to trust me on this."

Erica bit her lip. "I'm not deliberately pushing you, but surely you can understand where I'm coming from. Her fingerprint was found on the bow."

He nodded. "I get that. But I'm sure there's an explanation for it. Which is why I want to find her. To help her. Because the police aren't going to care about helping her." He brought his intense gaze back to Erica. "I'd really like to find her first."

I'm sure you do, Max. And I plan to be there when it happens.

"You said you'd gotten custody of Lydia before she turned eighteen. Does she still have a room at your house?"

He lifted a brow. "Yes."

"Do you mind if I take a look at it?"

"She doesn't stay there." He looked away. "I keep it for her, hoping one day she'll show up and want to work things out."

"You didn't do anything wrong."

"Maybe not, but maybe I could have handled it differently. Instead of calling DSS, I could have just taken her out of there and…" He shrugged.

"And maybe not. If there's anything I've learned over the past three years, it's that we can't avoid making mistakes, and when we do, we should learn from them. Unfortunately, you can't rewrite the past."

"I know." He offered her a sad smile.

"So what happened to your parents?"

"My dad was killed in a car accident about seven years ago. After I called the cops on her, my mom went back to jail for possession. When she got out, she went right back to drugs and died from an overdose."

Erica gasped. "How awful, Max. I'm so sorry." She couldn't seem to find any other words. No child should have to live the way he and Lydia had, scrambling and scraping to survive.

He sighed. "I couldn't help her, but I'm going to do my best to help Lydia."

"I understand. That's how I feel about Peter." She paused. "I still want to see Lydia's room. Do you mind?"

He shook his head. "She's only stayed there a handful of times. Mostly when Bea caught her doing something wrong. Since I actually had custody, it wasn't something her social worker worried about. And after she turned eighteen she was out of the system anyway."

If Lydia had been in that room for even one minute, Erica wanted to see it. "Do you mind if I ride with you, or do you want to take me to my car?"

"I don't mind driving. Come on."

Erica's mind clicked with renewed hope. Seeing Lydia's room was a great start. Something the cops hadn't had access to three years ago—simply because they hadn't known about it. Praying the room would lead somewhere, she got into the car.

On the drive to his house, Erica checked in with her office. Rachel Armstrong, Erica's cousin, answered the phone. "Hey, Rachel, anything I need to know about?"

"No, it's kind of slow right now," Rachel replied. "You've got two calls to return, though—the parent of a runaway and someone who wants a status update."

"Okay." Erica gave instructions for the update and then said, "Give the parent of the runaway to Jordan. I'm working on this lead we've got on Molly."

"A lead on Molly? Really?"

"Yes." The hope mingled with sadness in Rachel's voice tugged at her. Rachel had loved Molly like her own. "I'll be praying it pans out."

Rachel, along with other family members, had given up hoping that Molly would ever be found. Erica didn't hold it against any of them, but she refused to join ranks. She hoped, she believed, she prayed and she searched. And she'd never give up. Ever.

As a result of her obsession with finding Molly, she'd pushed a lot of her family away, including her own parents. With a start, she saw the parallels between her life and Denise's. When Denise's husband had left her, she'd also pushed away her family and friends and focused on her job. Denise allowed her work to consume her. Erica had allowed finding Molly to do the same.

Acting on impulse, Erica said, "What are you doing tomorrow night, Rachel? Want me to bring over some Chinese and we'll play Scrabble until we can't think straight?"

"Seriously?" The stunned tone in Rachel's voice caused Erica to wince.

"We haven't done that in forever. It'll be like old times."

"Oh, I'd love to, Erica. That sounds like a ton of fun, but I already have plans tomorrow. What about another time?"

"Sure, you let me know when," Erica said. "But soon, okay? I need some girl time."

"You bet."

Erica hung up and chewed her bottom lip. Was she too late to reconnect with her cousin? She hoped not. She hoped Rachel was simply busy and not avoiding her. Vowing to do better at reaching out to the people in her life, she stared out the window.

Cutting into her thoughts, Max asked, "How many people do you have working for you?"

"We're a crew of four right now." Erica tucked the phone in her jacket pocket. "There's me and Brandon, who was a detective on the police force but gave it up to help me put this business together. And then Brandon's best friend Jordan joined us. He was with the FBI, but he quit." She shot him a sidelong glance. "I still don't know the whole story. Maybe one day he'll feel like he can share it."

"You've got a lot of skills and resources at your disposal. What about Rachel?"

"She's my cousin. She's also the administrator—she answers the phones and does whatever office work needs doing. She and I used to be much closer than we are now." She sighed. "It's time to do something about that." The last sentence was more for her than for him.

"Sounds like quite a team."

"I don't mind bragging a little—it really is an amazing—"

Max slammed his foot on the brakes and Erica's seat belt locked hard as she rocked forward, crushing it against her chest. Tires squealed, horns blared—and Erica screamed as a green car came straight at her.

Max turned the wheel a split second before the other vehicle hit, managing to avoid the worst of the collision. Like fingernails on a chalkboard, the green car scraped down the passenger side and Erica felt herself thrown against the seat belt once again.

Max brought his truck to a shuddering stop.

"What happened?" Erica gasped.

"That guy ran a red light," he said. He reached out and grasped her arm. "Are you all right?"

"I think so."

The green car quickly backed up and spun into a three-point turn. "He's leaving," Erica warned.

Max grabbed his phone. "I have a hit-and-run to report. License plate is NRV444." He looked at her. "Are you sure you're all right?"

Erica took a moment to gather her wits and make sure she was still in one piece. "Yes. Yes, I'm fine. Are you?"

He nodded. "It looks like the only real damage is to the car, thank goodness."

A knock on her window made her jump. She tried to roll the window down but she couldn't. Next she tugged on the door handle. "I can't open the door, Max. It's stuck."

He opened his door and she crawled across the seat,

letting him help her out onto the asphalt. Questions from the bystanders and witnesses started instantly. The police arrived, and Erica felt her head begin to pound.

There was something about that green car….

An officer approached her. "Hey, you look really pale. Do you need to sit down? Do you need an ambulance?"

She felt Max take her arm and lead her away from the cop to the curb, where he helped her sit. "Take a minute and get your breath."

She looked up at him. "I think I know who hit us."

"You saw the driver?" Max asked.

"No. But I saw the car."

His eyes narrowed. "And you recognized it?"

"Maybe."

"Who does it belong to?"

"Well, I didn't get a good look, but I'm pretty sure it was my brother Peter's."

Chapter 5

Erica waited while Max shared all the information he could with the officers and they promised to get a BOLO—a Be On the Lookout—on the vehicle and find Peter for questioning. He looked at Erica, who had risen from the curb to pace. "Do you want me to take you home?"

"I think we need to find Peter."

"The cops are going to be looking for him."

"I know. Which is why I want to find him first."

"Where do you think he is?"

She sighed. "He has a job doing construction. When he's sober, he's working but it's a different job every week. But if that was him in the car…"

"You want to try his house first?"

"Okay."

"Then let me tell the officers we're leaving and we'll

head over to see if Peter's at home. I'm pretty sure my truck is drivable."

She nodded. "I'll see if I can reach him on his phone. Depends on if he has any minutes or not."

While she tried Peter, Max let the officers know they were leaving and to contact him if they needed anything else.

As they drove, Erica tried Peter again. "He's not answering his phone. Who knows where he is?" She chewed her bottom lip.

"We'll find him." He glanced at her. "You're going to be sore. You really flew into that seat belt."

"I'll be all right. I'll take something if I need to."

They rode in silence for the first few minutes then he asked, "So how do you fit in?"

She blinked at the out-of-the-blue question. "What do you mean?"

"With your company. You told me all about everyone who works there. What about you?"

Erica sorted through what to tell him, then decided to just lay it out there. "After Molly disappeared, I spent all my money trying to find her. At least all the money I could get my hands on. My husband…" She gave a heavy sigh. "My marriage fell apart. We tried counseling, but by that time…" She waved a hand. "Anyway, I just couldn't give up on finding Molly. I had to be doing something, not just waiting for the phone to ring. So I picked the career that would allow me to do that. I became a skip tracer and I specialize in finding missing children."

"While you keep searching for Molly."

"Yes." She pointed. "Turn here."

Max turned into Peter's subdivision and followed her directions until she motioned to the one-story house on the corner. "It's nice."

Her lips quirked into a wry smile at his surprise. Junkies didn't usually have nice places to sleep. "I pay for someone to do the yard each week. I don't want the neighbors complaining." She frowned. "I don't recognize the car at the curb."

Max had noticed the black Mustang, too.

"He may have company." She hesitated. "Inside is pretty bad most of the time. Every once in a while I'll come over to check on him and clean up some. It's been a week since I've been here so no guarantees about what it looks like in there."

He nodded. "I've seen worse, I'm sure."

She knocked on the door and waited. Then knocked again.

Max was ready to concede Peter wasn't home when the lock clicked. The door swung open and Peter stood there blinking in the sunlight, unshaven and offensive to Max's nose.

Erica acted as though she didn't notice. "May we come in?"

"Why?"

Impatience tightened her features. "Because we need to talk to you before the cops get here."

That seemed to wake him up a bit. "Cops? Why'd you call them? I thought all that was straightened out last night. I just needed some cash."

"For a hit." Erica glared at him. "Looks like you found some."

Pain flashed in his eyes for a brief moment then a silly smile crossed his dry, cracked lips. "Yeah. I did. Polo hooked me up. He's got this friend named Sandy—"

Erica pushed her way inside. Peter stopped his explanation and didn't protest, so Max kept his mouth shut and followed.

And wished he'd volunteered to wait outside.

Body odor and spoiled food assaulted his nose. Erica gagged and walked into the kitchen to the right. She shook her head and came back into the tiny foyer. "I'm not going to lecture."

"Good. 'Cuz I'm not going to listen."

Polo stumbled from the rear of the house. "Who is it?"

Peter sighed and rubbed his bleary eyes. "My sister and her friend. Let me take care of this."

Polo eyed Erica. Then his gaze slid to Max. "She belong to you?"

"Yeah," Max said before Erica could answer. He stared Polo down until the man gave a short nod.

"Bummer." He looked at Peter. "Get 'em outta here. We got business."

"Cops are on the way. You better vanish. Business can wait."

With a glare at Erica and Max, Polo slipped out of the house. Within seconds, they heard the roar of the motor and the squeal of tires as he pulled away from the curb. Erica looked at Peter. "Were you at the corner of Henry and East Main earlier today? Like about an hour and a half ago?"

Peter squinted. "No, man. I was asleep. I haven't left the house since I got home from Sandy's."

Knowing junkies sometimes got their facts skewed, Max asked, "What time was that?"

A shrug. "I don't remember. Probably around eight o'clock this morning."

"And you didn't leave again?"

"I said no."

"When did your friend show up?"

"About ten minutes before you did. He woke me up."

"Where's your car?"

He gave her a puzzled look. "In the garage where I always keep it when I'm not using it. What's with the third degree?"

Max said, "Your car sideswiped us this morning."

"What?" He laughed. "Not possible." Peter shook his head and walked through the kitchen. He opened a door that probably led to the garage.

And gaped.

He spun. "It's not there." He paced to the sink and back to the door again. "Where's my car?"

"That's what we want to know," said Max's cop buddy from the front door where he stood next to his partner. "Peter Hayes?"

Peter held his hands up. "I wasn't driving. I swear."

"Can anyone give you an alibi?"

He swallowed hard. "I was asleep. I didn't even know my car was missing."

Chris and Steve exchanged a glance, then looked at Max. "What are you doing here?"

"The same thing you are."

"We got the hit-and-run you called in."

Max gestured to Erica. "She recognized the car."

"But he wasn't driving it?"

Erica shook her head. "I don't think so."

"I wasn't!" Peter said. "I want to report a stolen car." He ran a hand through his greasy hair. "I can't believe someone stole my car."

Max snorted as Peter muttered a few more dire threats on the head of the person responsible for the missing vehicle. He looked at Chris. "This the first time this has happened?"

"Yeah. I checked to see if he was a repeat, but he's not." Max was surprised. A missing car was a common call from drug addicts. They often loaned their vehicle to their addict friends and when the friend didn't bring it back, they filed a stolen vehicle report.

Erica managed to calm her brother down enough to sit on the sagging couch.

Chris pulled out his notebook and said, "Tell me, in detail, where you were this morning and who would have taken your car?"

"I don't know! That's why you're here, right? To find out?"

The man truly looked distressed. Max began to wonder if he wasn't telling the truth.

Chris continued. "Who has the keys?"

"The keys were probably in it," Peter mumbled.

"Uh-huh. And what crackhead did you loan it to?"

"I didn't loan it to anyone." Peter sighed and ran a dirty hand through his greasy hair. Max saw Erica wince and turn her face from the man's odor.

"All right, give me the description of the vehicle, the tag number, make and model, color and all that."

As Peter provided the information, Erica massaged her sore shoulder, and Max said, "Come on. We can't do anything else here. Let's get you some Ibuprofen then we can head to my house and I'll show you Lydia's room."

They left Peter to fill out his stolen car report and to retell his story to the officers. Max wondered if they'd believe him, but as of right now, they didn't have any proof to refute the story. Max knew Chris and Steve would continue to investigate the accident. He just hoped for Erica's sake that her brother wasn't lying.

Erica looked at the modest brick two-story from Max's driveway. "Very nice."

"I bought this house about four years ago." Pride echoed in his words. "I'd never owned anything in my life. I lived mostly in apartments while trying to go to school and just keep my head above water financially, but when I decided to get custody of Lydia, I wanted someplace special to bring her."

Together they walked toward his front door. Erica couldn't help a glance over her shoulder, wondering at her feeling of being watched. She forced herself to brush it aside. Once inside the house, her uneasiness disappeared and she gasped in delight. "It's beautiful. Did you decorate this yourself?"

A flush crept up into Max's cheeks. "Well, I did the woodwork, the molding and the painting. A friend of mine helped me out with the decorating aspect."

A friend? Erica couldn't help wondering if that friend was more than just a "friend." A little dart of jealousy shot through her and she stood still, shocked by the feeling. Not wanting to dwell on it, she turned back to admiring his home. Shiny hardwood floors made her pause. "Should I take off my shoes?"

He laughed. "No. You're fine."

A simple, classy chandelier hung overhead. Stainless steel appliances and granite graced the kitchen to the right. "It's truly lovely."

He motioned toward the steps. "Lydia's room is upstairs."

Erica followed him up the steps, her fingers trailing over the banister. At the top, he turned left and entered the first room on the right. Erica stepped inside and was once again impressed. "I can't believe she didn't want to stay here. It's charming, but simple enough she could put her own stamp on it if she wanted to."

Max gave her a warm yet sad smile. "Yeah, well, I'm still not her favorite person so—" He shrugged, and she could tell his heart was heavy.

She laid a hand on his arm. "Maybe she'll come around soon."

"Maybe."

Even though she felt sorry for Max and the angst his sister was putting him through, she still couldn't get past the fact that the evidence pointed to Lydia's guilt. She removed her hand.

"What if she's staying away because she's guilty and she's afraid you'll turn her in to the cops?"

He sighed and dropped his head. "It's more likely that she's staying away because she believes that I think she's guilty. That's one of the reasons I have to find her. I have to convince her that I believe in her."

"Do you have to convince her? Or yourself?"

Max stared at her. "You've already got her tried and convicted."

"And you've bypassed the evidence and are letting your emotions get in the way."

Max held up a hand. "We've agreed to disagree. Can we please not argue about it?"

Erica sighed and looked at the closet. "May I?"

"Sure."

She opened the door and saw a few outfits and several shoe boxes lined up on the shelf. She went through them, hoping to find anything that might lead her to Lydia. Disappointment spiked when she only found shoes that would appeal to a young woman. "Did you buy this stuff for her?"

"Yes."

"You've got good taste."

He gave a short laugh and pulled open the top drawer of the dresser. "I've searched her room each time she's stayed and never found anything." He rummaged through the next drawer. "I think she figured I'd search and just didn't bother bringing anything here."

Erica planted her hands on her hips. "You could have told me that."

His sad smile speared her. "You needed to see for yourself."

He was right. She gave a slight nod of acknowledgment, and they finished the search together in silence.

They came up empty.

Erica ran a weary hand over her face. "Well, it was worth a try. Thanks for letting me look." She thought for a moment then said, "Do you have time to go to Bea Harrison's house?"

He glanced at his watch. "I can call her and see if she's home."

"That would be great."

As Max called, Erica stepped outside in the chilly afternoon air.

From the corner of her eye, Erica noticed a green car rolling down the street. "Max, I think that's my brother's—"

A gunshot cracked and wood from the porch roof rained down on them.

Chapter 6

Erica screamed and ducked. Max grabbed her against him, shielding her with his body as he fell back inside his house and kicked the door shut. "Get behind the sofa and crouch down."

He peered out the window. The vehicle sat in the middle of the street in front of his house. His blood pounded through his veins as he saw the barrel of a rifle appear in the open passenger window.

He ducked back down. Another burst of gunfire erupted. Windows shattered as he hunkered beside the front door. Max winced as flying glass grazed his face. Heart thudding, he waited.

He could hear Erica on the phone with a 911 operator, giving a status report in a shaky voice.

Tires squealed on the street out front and Max peered

through the broken window. The green car shot down the street and the sudden quiet echoed in his ears.

People peered from behind pulled curtains. Doors opened and curious neighbors with stunned expressions stepped out onto their porches once they realized the threat was gone.

"Erica," Max called, "are you all right?" He rushed into the den to find her still on the floor behind the couch, phone pressed to her ear.

Pale and shaken, she looked up and nodded. "Are you?"

"Yeah."

"The cops are on the way."

He helped her up and felt her pulse jumping under his fingers. "That was pretty close."

She swallowed hard. "Too close." She searched his face. "So is someone after me? Or you?"

He lifted a brow and pursed his lips. "That's a really good question."

"You have some enemies you need to tell me about?"

He smirked. "The list is endless."

"I've made a few people mad in my line of work, too."

He shook his head. "I really can't think of a way to narrow the list, but I'll call Chris and see if he'll look into it. I can think of four or five characters I've arrested who've made threats to get even. We'll see what they're doing now."

"And I'll get Jordan or Brandon to look into the same thing on my end." She chewed her lip. "Although I have to say I really think this is somehow related to this search for your sister."

He wanted to protest, but he didn't have any proof that she was wrong, so he didn't argue. And he couldn't say the thought hadn't crossed his mind.

Sirens sounded as law enforcement descended. Chris bolted from his cruiser as Max stepped outside. Chris shook his head. "I recognized your address over the radio. You okay?"

"Yeah. Just a drive-by with lousy aim, fortunately."

Chris eyed him with a frown. "Man, I've seen you more in the past twenty-four hours than I ever did when we actually worked in the same precinct. What have you got going on? Someone tries to take you out in a hit-and-run this morning, then this?"

"I know." Max knew the two incidents were related. There was no doubt it was the same car, thanks to the scrape alongside the passenger-side door. "I'm looking for Lydia. That's the only thing I can think of."

"Someone doesn't want you to find her?"

"Lydia doesn't want me to find her, but I don't think she'd shoot at me."

"And I don't believe Peter would try to run us off the road," Erica said.

Max looked doubtful and asked Chris, "Do we have a location on Peter while this shooting was going on?"

Chris shook his head. "We left soon after you did. We're not ruling him out. He's still a suspect and it's very possible he's hiding the car, but right now there's no evidence. Although the plate I got this morning was definitely registered to Peter. We're going to keep looking into this and keep an eye on him."

"Great." He glanced at Erica. "Because the car that

was involved in the drive-by was the same one from this morning."

"What? Peter's?"

"Yeah." Max drew in a deep breath. "Looks like we need to ask him some more questions."

Max watched the officers question neighbors and put up the crime scene tape. The crime scene unit started looking for the bullets.

An hour later when they'd talked to everyone they could find that might have seen something, the officers left.

Erica gave him a weary smile and glanced at her watch. "I need to get going."

"I'll drive you. Where to?"

"I volunteer at the community church on Main Street serving meals to the homeless."

Max gave her a hard look. "The homeless? Why would you want to be around people like that?"

She blinked. "People like that?"

"A lot of them are criminals. They'll take advantage of you the moment your back is turned. Or kill you."

Shock made her blanch, then her face turned red. "Really? That's what you think about the homeless? How sad." She shot him a look full of anger mixed with pity. "Forget the ride. I'll get someone else to drive me."

Max watched her stomp off and winced. He'd obviously offended her, but she was just such an innocent when it came to watching out for herself. Someone had to do it. Right?

Possibly, but he could have phrased his concerns better. Been less blunt. Just because his experience with the homeless hadn't been ideal didn't mean he could push his feelings on Erica.

He'd have to apologize and explain his strong reaction. She still had her stiff back toward him. That is, he'd explain if she gave him a chance.

Erica sat at her desk and stared out the window. Twice today her life had been in danger. And twice today, she'd been involved in giving statements to the police.

Of course Max could say the same. She thought about his negative reaction to her charity work and tightened her jaw. She had to forget about that for now and focus.

She wanted to find Lydia.

Max had called to say that Bea Harrison hadn't answered her phone but that he'd keep trying, and let Erica know when he reached her. His words had been stilted, but not rude. She'd kept her attitude chilly but polite. She supposed she should apologize.

She grimaced.

But there was another issue that wouldn't leave her alone. Max thought the homeless people who came to be served a free meal at the church were dangerous criminals. That said a lot about his character.

She suddenly found herself on the verge of tears. What was going on?

If she really thought about it, Erica had to admit that she found Max…attractive. In a way that she hadn't found anyone attractive in a very long time. Maybe she'd been hoping that at some point, after this was all over—if it was *ever* all over—there might be something between them.

But that wasn't going to happen. Not after that comment.

It had been all she could do to hold her tongue when he'd said that.

"What's going on with you?" Brandon demanded as he entered her office.

Erica jumped, startled. "What do you mean?"

He leaned over the desk opposite her, his green eyes fiery with concern. "First the car wreck, then getting shot at?"

She sighed and looked at her brother. A handsome man with the same auburn hair and green eyes she had, he was just two years older than her twenty-eight years.

On the outside, he exuded charm and confidence. Underneath, she knew he was hurting, his self-esteem suffering from the blow of his fiancée ditching him for another man. And yet the experience had brought them closer together. They'd both been left by people they'd loved, and Erica was able to help him with his pain.

"I'm not sure what's going on, Brandon." She spun a pen between her fingers. "I was chasing down a lead on Molly when this all happened." She paused and looked in his eyes. "It was Peter's car, Brandon."

"What?" He frowned and slid into the chair opposite her desk.

"But I don't think it was Peter driving. The first incident, where his car sideswiped us, I might be able to put the blame on him. He's irresponsible and not thinking straight these days. But the gunfire…" She shook her head. "No way."

"Peter's been acting crazy for the past several months, but you're right, he wouldn't shoot at you. What reason would he have?"

"I don't know. I would have thought if he was going to shoot me, it would have been three years ago when I named him as a possible suspect in Molly's kidnapping." Pain at the memory made her shudder. She cleared her throat. "I'm hoping the cops can find his car and figure out who stole it."

"This is scary, sis. I don't want you going anywhere by yourself until this is resolved."

"But that's the problem. I don't know what *this* is. If I don't even know what—or who—I'm fighting, how can I win?"

"Good point." He stretched his neck and sighed. "The best thing you can do right now is to make sure you do the smart thing." He paused. "Like don't go into dangerous neighborhoods. By yourself."

She flushed. "I know that was dumb. I'm not going to do anything like that again."

"Good." He clasped his hands in front of him and leaned forward. "I got an anonymous tip on that seven-year-old kidnapped by her dad. I raided the cash box and I'm going to follow up on the tip."

She frowned. "Be careful and take Jordan with you." Sometimes tipsters were willing to meet in person if they needed some cash but it wasn't the safest way to do business.

"What time are you leaving?"

She shrugged. "You know me. I don't keep set hours."

"I'll be back by five thirty to pick you up. If you want to leave earlier, call me. If I'm not ready, I'll make arrangements."

"Fine." She rolled her eyes at her brother but she supposed letting him pick her up was the smart thing to do.

Jordan knocked on the door. "I wasn't invited to the meeting?"

Brandon motioned him in and then filled him in on the events of the morning. Erica watched the two men. Jordan was a mystery—a man with a mysterious past, but a man she'd come to trust. Even Brandon, who'd gone to high school and later college with Jordan, didn't know the secrets that haunted his friend's gray eyes.

Erica didn't press the issue. Jordan was trustworthy and good at his job, and that was all that mattered to her.

Right now, a red flush covered his cheeks and his narrowed eyes shot sparks. "Who'd want to shoot at you?"

"I was just telling Brandon I have no idea." She rubbed her eyes. "And it could have been Max the person was aiming for. He was with me for both incidents."

"You definitely need to take extra precautions," Brandon said.

"I'm planning on it."

"And if this Max guy is a trouble magnet, you need to stay away from him."

Erica pointed toward the door. "Go meet your informant. I'll keep you posted on what time I want to leave."

The two men left, muttering about how they were going to come up with a plan to protect her, and Erica turned back to her computer. She was concerned, of course, and would take precautions, but she wasn't going to let anything stop her from doing her job.

Or finding her daughter.

Time passed as she worked. Her growling stomach

finally reminded her she hadn't eaten a whole lot today and it was well past supper time. Thunder rumbled in the distance and she figured there'd be rain soon.

Rachel popped into the office. "I'm out of here. There's a storm brewing out there."

"I know… I heard the thunder. I'll be fine. See you tomorrow."

"Sure." Rachel started to leave, then came back, her brow creased. Erica tilted her head. "Something on your mind?"

Rachel played with the hem of her shirt, then said, "I'm just concerned about you."

"About what?"

Rachel stared at her. "About the fact that you were in a car wreck? And you were shot at? Does the list go on?"

"Oh. That."

"Yes. That."

"I'm okay, Rachel. Really."

Rachel eyed her, doubt in her eyes. Rachel finally sighed. "Is someone making sure you get home safe?"

"Brandon said he'd be back around five thirty." She glanced at the clock and frowned. "He's late. Has he called?"

"No."

Erica waved her cousin on. "I'll call him and let him know I'll be ready to leave around six thirty." Still Rachel hesitated. "What is it, Rach?"

"I saw your mom yesterday."

Erica froze. "You did?"

"Yes. I ran into her at the grocery store."

"How was she?"

Rachel shrugged. "She seemed fine. Still working long hours at the hospital."

"Did she ask about me?"

"Yes. Said she wants to see you."

Erica felt a pang of something she couldn't identify. She and her mother had never been close—in fact, Erica had never truly felt that she mattered to her mother that much. But things had gotten worse since Molly's disappearance, and Erica knew that was her fault. She'd pulled away from her family after Molly disappeared. Her obsession with finding her daughter had been her priority. She regretted that now. "What does she want to see me about?"

"Something about putting her family back together."

"You're sure?" Erica asked, stunned.

Rachel shrugged. "That's what she said. I told her I'd tell you to call her."

"Right." And she would call her. Just like she did once or twice a month. And she'd leave a message her mother might or might not return. Just like she did once or twice a month. Her mother harbored anger with Erica and her choices and that was her way of letting Erica know it. "Well, thanks for the message."

"Sure." Rachel still hovered in the doorway. "Are you working on Molly's case tonight?"

"I am."

"Do you want me to stay and help?"

Erica shook her head. "No, I don't know how much more I'm going to be able to do anyway."

"Okay." Rachel still hesitated.

"What's up with you, Rachel? Is there something we need to talk about?"

Her cousin blinked and gave a nervous laugh. "What do you mean?"

She'd been thinking about their relationship for a while. She missed the closeness they'd shared as teens and even adults before she'd married and had a child.

"I mean ever since Molly disappeared, things have been a little strained between us. Why?"

Rachel lifted her chin a notch. "Because you pushed me away."

Erica stared, openmouthed. "I did?"

Her cousin's face hardened. "It doesn't matter now."

Erica stood. "Yes, it does. Tell me."

Finally, Rachel blurted, "You were so determined to find Molly, and I understood that. I wanted to help. I hounded you about helping and you tossed aside my offers like they weren't important, and yet for those three weeks after Molly disappeared, you spent hours upon hours with Denise Tanner. I'm family... I wanted to help. Denise was just a friend, and it seemed to me she wasn't helping as much as she was hindering, keeping you from family who wanted to—" She stopped herself and waved a hand.

Erica blinked as she processed what her cousin was saying. And then gulped when she realized she couldn't refute it. She stood. "Oh, Rachel, I didn't realize... I didn't know. I'm so sorry you felt that way."

Rachel grimaced. "I'm going home before I say anything else. I just want to see you happy, not crushed when new leads lead nowhere." For the first time in forever, Rachel wrapped her arms around Erica and gave her a squeeze. "Have a good night."

Erica cherished the embrace for a few moments then

pushed back to look into her cousin's eyes. "Let's start over. Can we do that?"

Rachel sniffed then sighed. "Maybe." A smile trembled on her lips. "I want to."

"Then let's get some girl time on the calendar soon."

Rachel nodded. "Get this mess with Lydia and Max wrapped up, and we'll see what we can do."

She left, and Erica tossed the pen onto the desk and swiveled around to look out the window. She felt lighter, less burdened at the new beginning with Rachel. Erica knew Rachel was worried about her and her obsession with finding Molly, but there was nothing she could do to ease her cousin's mind in that respect. This was her life now, and until Molly came home, it would continue to be her life.

However, Rachel's revelations did resonate within her.

Rachel had been jealous of Erica's time with Denise. Erica remembered that now, although she wasn't sure it had quite registered at the time. She could see Rachel's point about how she'd pushed her away, and now Erica wondered who else felt that way. Maybe Peter? Her parents definitely did. She'd have to think about that later. Right now, she was on emotion overload.

November in Spartanburg, South Carolina, meant darkness fell early. The blackness beyond the window didn't bother her. She welcomed it. Darkness had become a friend in a strange way, because it was only in the dark of the night that she allowed herself to break, to cry, to wail out her grief and beg God to bring Molly home.

She swallowed the lump in her throat and turned

back to her computer. She was so close to locating a father who'd taken his five-year-old child and fled after a bitter custody battle that he'd lost. So close.

Just like she'd been so close to finding Lydia and possibly some answers about Molly's disappearance.

With a sigh, she picked up her phone and dialed her mother's number.

And left a message for her to call.

Erica kept working. By six forty-five, she was ready to go home, and wondering where her brother was.

Her phone rang and she jumped. "Hello?"

"Stop looking for her."

Erica froze. "Who is this?"

"Stop looking for her or I'll kill her."

Chapter 7

Max snapped a picture of two men meeting in the restaurant across the street. His client was convinced his partner was stealing from him and passing on bid numbers so the competition could come in just under and steal the job. From the looks of things, the client might be right.

As he focused the camera and zoomed in on the handshake, his mind went to Erica James. Just thinking about her made his pulse jump a little faster. Apparently this attraction he had for her—which he'd been trying to ignore—wasn't going to just disappear.

And before he'd learned about her work with the homeless, he hadn't really wanted it to. But two facts remained: she worked with the kind of people who were responsible for his fiancée's death, and she thought Lydia had something to do with Molly's kidnapping.

He had no doubt Erica would turn Lydia in to the cops the minute she tracked her down.

But Max had other plans.

Which meant putting any kind of feelings he had for Erica on hold. Maybe permanently.

Thunder rumbled and he glanced at the dark sky. He needed the rain to hold off just a little while longer.

Max lifted the camera once again and snapped as the men ordered and continued their conversation. No money had been exchanged, but he could be patient.

He had all night.

His phone rang and he grabbed it, hoping to see Lydia's number on the screen.

No such luck. "Hey, Chris."

"Hey, you got a minute?"

"Or two."

"I looked into some of your past cases like you asked. You've got quite a history here, don't you?" he said, sounding impressed.

Max had been the star player in his two years at the precinct. He didn't let it go to his head. Some of his busts had been due to dumb luck. Or divine guidance. "I was just doing my job, Chris. What do you have for me?"

Papers rustled. "There were a couple of possibilities that I checked out and came up empty on. The only real thing that stands out is the time you busted the daughter of Judge Terrell Brown for DUI and then wouldn't be bought off."

"I'd forgotten about that."

"Brown hasn't. Neither has the daughter. I asked him about you, and it wasn't pretty."

"Can you look into that a little more?"

"I've got feelers out on his location when your incidents went down. Should know something tomorrow." He paused.

"What is it?" Max asked.

"While Brown's a candidate, I'm not seeing his hand on this one."

"Why not?" Max looked through the viewfinder and clicked.

"Instinct. It's been three and a half years since you've been on the force. Doesn't make sense for him to all of a sudden come after you now."

Max lowered the camera as his phone beeped. He looked at the called ID—it was his client, Carl Rogers. "I have to take this call, Chris. Thanks for going to the trouble."

"Sure. Let me know if you need anything else."

"Will do."

Max clicked over to the other line. "Hi, Carl."

"Anything?"

"You may have reason to suspect Klein's selling your bids."

A curse ripped through the line and Max grimaced. "I knew it," Carl said. "There wasn't any other explanation for why we kept losing jobs. What an idiot. Did he think I wouldn't catch on?"

"I don't have irrefutable proof, but you'll have some pictures to show Klein and ask for an explanation."

"I'll be looking for them."

Max hung up and glanced at the clock. As he lifted his camera, his thoughts went right back to Erica—before he remembered that he'd decided to put his feelings on hold.

It was going to be a long evening.

Erica couldn't move. Her brain almost couldn't process the call.

Then she flew into action.

Fingers clicked on the keyboard, activating the tracing software. She might be able to pull the number. And once she had the number she would know where it came from. Minutes later, she had it. And a few more clicks told her the location.

The caller had used a pay phone. A pay phone across the street from her office.

She jumped up and made it to the door before she stopped. Even though she had her gun with her, she couldn't go barreling out there.

One moment, she felt sure the caller had been talking about Molly, the next moment she was full of doubt. Was the caller one of the many pranksters who had complicated the investigation with false sightings and bogus reports? Or was the caller making a legitimate threat?

Or was the call even about Molly? It could be about Lydia.

Despite her fear, hope flamed anew. If the call *was* about Molly, then Molly was still alive.

She grabbed the nearest phone and called Katie. After hearing Erica's story, the detective said, "I know how much you want to believe she's still alive. I do, too, but the fact of the matter is, with the resurgence of publicity about Molly's kidnapping, we're getting the crazies calling again."

Erica bit her lip. "I know, but this was different. The person just said to stop looking for her or he would kill her. Katie, that means she might still be alive."

"If that person was for real." Katie paused. "I'll look into it, but please, Erica, don't get your hopes up."

"My hope is in the Lord, Katie. You know that."

The detective sighed. "I know. And that's exactly where it needs to be. But…"

"It's okay. Just see if you can figure out who called me."

"I'll get right on it. Was the voice male or female?"

"I thought it was male, but I don't know. It was low, harsh, like the person was using something to disguise it."

"All right, let me see what I can find out."

When she hung up, Erica dialed Brandon's number.

No answer. Jordan's number went to voice mail, too. She frowned. Where were those guys? Worry bit at her.

Max. She should call Max.

She grimaced at the thought. After his reaction to her volunteer work, she wasn't sure she wanted to see him again just yet. Then again, she didn't want to leave the office alone and possibly place herself in danger. And he *was* a P.I. If anyone could help her figure out who had called her, it was probably him.

He answered on the second ring. "Hello?"

"Hi, Max, I'm at my office. Alone. I just got a very strange call and don't want to—" She sighed. "How far are you from my office? I sure could use some help."

"I'm about fifteen minutes away. A strange call?

What kind of strange call?" His concern touched her, his tone conveying that he held no grudge toward her. And she found she held none toward him. He just needed to be educated.

"Brandon was supposed to meet me at five thirty and he hasn't shown up. I'm a little worried about him, but I promised I wouldn't leave the office by myself because of everything that's happened. I know it's a bit of an inconvenience, but—"

"I'll be right there."

Relief washed over her as she heard his engine starting up. "Thanks."

She headed back to her office to try to reach Brandon or Jordan again. As she sat at her desk, she listened to the creaks and groans of the building. The heating unit hummed quietly and rain pattered against her window.

Still, neither Brandon nor Jordan answered her calls.

She stared at the phone and whispered a prayer for their safety. Then her mind went back to the anonymous caller who wanted her to stop searching for Molly.

It had to be Molly, right?

No, not necessarily. It could actually be about any of the cases she was working right now. She mentally ran down her list. The call could easily be about the little girl whose father had snatched her three weeks ago. Her heart dipped a bit at the thought, but her gut was telling her the call had to do with Molly.

Was that just because she desperately wanted to believe?

Erica rubbed the heels of her palms against her eyes and sighed. *Please, God...*

A crack of thunder made her jump. The lights flickered then went out.

Eerie silence surrounded her. Her heart pumped faster. "It's just the storm, Erica." She stepped to the window and let her eyes adjust to the darkness. She could see the lightning flashing, hear the rain coming harder. "Come on, Max, where are you?"

Erica saw headlights in the distance. They passed her office. She grabbed her purse and moved to the front door.

Lightning flashed again, illuminating a dark silhouette standing in front of the glass door. Erica screamed and dropped her purse.

The figure at the door ducked before Erica could get a glimpse of a face and hurried from the building. Erica gasped, breathless from fear. Shaky fingers checked the lock, and then Erica slid to the floor, her legs refusing to hold her anymore.

Headlights cut through the lobby, and Erica felt her pulse speed even faster. Then she recognized Max's truck and allowed herself to wilt back against the wall for a brief moment of thanks.

With effort, she rose and unlocked the door.

Max was already out of the truck, running toward her through the drenching rain. "Are you okay? Why were you sitting on the floor?"

To her surprise, she found she wanted nothing more than for Max Powell to wrap his arms around her and let her simply rest her head on his very broad shoulder. Only the memory of his reaction to her volunteer work held her back. That, and the fact that she'd only known him a short time.

And his sister possibly having something to do with Molly's kidnapping.

Erica straightened her shoulders, took a step back and told herself to be strong. She allowed him to escort her to the truck as he held his jacket above her head to keep her from getting wet, and then help her up into the seat. "It's a long story."

He climbed into the driver's side, slammed the door and turned to her. "What happened?"

"The lights went out. I was watching for you from my office window and saw your headlights. I went to wait for you in the lobby and when the lightning flashed—" she swallowed hard "—there was someone standing in front of the door. Nearly gave me a heart attack."

"Did the person say or do anything?"

"No. When I screamed, he ran."

"Ran? Did he get in a car?"

"No. Just ran through the rain toward the street. It was weird."

A frown creased his forehead. "Everything that's happening is weird."

"And now Brandon and Jordan aren't answering my calls. I'm worried something's wrong." She ran a hand over her hair. "Could you pull into that convenience store across the street? That's where the call originated from."

He lifted a brow. "How do you know?"

"I have tracing software."

"Handy," he said as he pulled out of the parking lot. A minute later, he turned right into the convenience store, and Erica jumped out of the vehicle.

She found the pay phone in the back toward the restrooms. A security camera attached to the side of the building gave her a rush of hope—could it be that easy to figure out who had called her? She stepped inside the store and approached the clerk, a young woman who looked to be in her early twenties.

"Help you?" The woman snapped her gum and swiped the counter with a cloth. Her tag read Doreen.

"Yes. I have a strange request, Doreen."

"Probably not so strange. You wouldn't believe some of the stuff that goes on around here."

"I'd like to see the security video of the pay phone and restrooms back there."

Doreen lifted a brow. "Okay, now that's strange enough. What for?"

"I got a threatening phone call and it came from that pay phone."

"You a cop?"

"I specialize in finding people. I could probably get a court order to look at the video but I really don't want to do that."

"Well, I'd show it to you, but it's broke."

"Broken?"

"Yep, got hit by lightning last night. Waiting on the repair guy to come sometime tomorrow. Sorry."

Of course. "What about the one that monitors the gas pumps. I could see who came into the store, right?"

"I reckon."

"You know how to work the video?"

"Sure. Someone tried to rob the place about three months ago and I had to show the cops the tape." Uncertainty creased the girl's brow. "But I can't leave the front untended."

"What time do you close?"

She snickered. "We don't."

Erica did her best to rein in her impatience. "Could you just put a sign on the door and say you'll be back in ten minutes?"

The young woman hesitated. In desperation, Erica said, "I'll give you twenty bucks."

"Make it fifty and you've got a deal."

"Everything all right?"

Erica turned to find Max. "Yes, Doreen here is going to show us the video footage from around the time the call was made." She passed the money to the woman who quickly slid it in her pocket.

Doreen locked the doors and put a sign in the window, and Erica and Max followed her to the back room. "What time do you need to see?"

Erica said, "Try around seven fifteen."

Doreen clicked on the computer and within seconds had the video rolling. Erica leaned in and watched. At seven twenty-two, a figure in a hoodie walked into the store. The figure immediately reminded her of Lydia, but she didn't want to jump to conclusions. They watched a few more minutes, but Erica knew this was the person who'd made that call. "Can you back it up?"

She watched the footage again and Max said, "Can't tell anything about him."

"Or her," Erica murmured.

He shot her a dark look. "According to where he hit on the height of the door, he's around five foot five or six. It's hard to tell by body build—he's hunched over, avoiding the camera. Which means he might be quite a bit taller, too."

Erica had Doreen rewind and she watched again.

Max sighed. "I don't think you're going to get anything else from this. We need to find another camera." She told him about the nonworking camera. He shook his head. "Doreen, did you notice anything about this individual?"

She shrugged. "Nothing that caught my eye. Noticed he kept his hood pulled low and he was kinda skinny. Like a junkie. He just used the pay phone and went on his way. Didn't even come inside."

Max sighed. "Then I'd say we're done here."

Erica agreed. She thanked Doreen and followed Max to the door.

The rain had slackened to a drizzle by the time they headed back to Max's truck. She pulled out her phone once more. "I need to try Brandon—"

Her phone rang just as the words left her lips. "Brandon, are you all right?"

"Actually, this is Jordan, and yeah, Brandon's all right. He's in the hospital, though, getting patched up."

"What? What happened?"

"His informant was followed, and Brandon caught a bullet."

Erica gasped. "Where were you?"

"Grabbing the kid."

Her heart jumped. "So she's safe?"

"And back with her mama in an emergency shelter. The cops are talking to Christine there now."

Christine. The sweet young mother who'd been terrorized by her husband. When she'd left him, he'd tracked her to a hotel room and nearly killed her. He'd snatched their seven-year-old daughter and gone on the run. Now, after three months, mother and daughter were reunited and hopefully could rest assured that the terror was over.

Erica closed her eyes and breathed a brief prayer of thanks. "And Brandon's going to be all right?"

"Yeah. It's just a flesh wound. Shouldn't slow him down much."

Erica swallowed hard. "Okay, thanks for the update. I'll be at the hospital in a few minutes."

"You don't need to come. We're almost done here."

"He's my brother. I'm coming."

"You need me to pick you up?"

"No. I'm with Max."

He paused. "You're seeing a lot of him, aren't you?"

"We're looking for Molly, Jordan." Max glanced over at her, and she said, "Look, I've got to go. I'll be there shortly. Would you please put Brandon on the phone?"

Max made a U-turn to head for the hospital. Her heart gave a grateful thud at his thoughtfulness. She waited for Brandon to pick up the phone, feeling sick to her stomach with worry.

"Hey, sis, I'm all right."

"You got shot, Brandon." She hated the shakiness in her voice, but the thought of him being in danger scared her. "I know you're talking to me, but are you sure you're all right?"

"Once again, I'm fine. I'll be out of here in a few minutes. Jordan will drive me home. Sorry I didn't answer the phone, I was a little preoccupied."

"I know. I'm on the way to the hospital. We'll talk about that when I get there."

"What? No way. Don't waste your time. I'm almost ready to walk out of the door."

"But—"

"I said no, sis."

She bit her lip. "Brandon, you got shot. I can't just go home and sleep."

"That's exactly what you're going to do. You can check on me tomorrow. I'm going to take a painkiller and go to bed."

"Jordan's going to be with you, right?"

"Probably wouldn't be able to pry him from my side with a crowbar," he muttered. "He's worse than a mother hen."

She almost smiled. Almost. "All right. I'll check on you tomorrow then." She hung up with Brandon and said to Max, "You can do another U-turn." He did.

"I'm glad he's all right," Max said.

"I am, too. He didn't want me coming to the hospital."

"Doesn't want to be mothered, I guess."

She pursed her lips, trying not to be overwhelmed by emotion as she thought of her brother in the hospital with a gunshot wound.

Max didn't say anything, just reached over and grasped her cold fingers.

They rode in silence until they reached her driveway.

When he released her hand, she wanted to grab it back, to hold on to the security and warmth he offered. Instead, she curled her fingers around the handle. "Thanks for the ride."

"Anytime."

Weariness eating at her, Erica opened the car door and stopped as Max placed a hand on her arm.

"I'm also glad you called me tonight."

She lifted her gaze to his. "Even after I bit your head off earlier?"

"Even after."

"So what *was* that all about?"

He dropped his head for a moment. When he looked up, he said, "I've had more than one bad experience with the homeless. I'm embarrassed to admit this, but I suppose I'm a bit prejudiced against them." He gripped the steering wheel until his knuckles turned white. "It's not something I'm proud of. In fact, I really don't like that part of myself, but I'm not sure how to get past it."

"I…see." She didn't really. Didn't most cops have run-ins with homeless people on a regular basis? "Sounds personal."

"Very."

She closed her door. "Want to tell me about it?"

His lips tightened. "Two years ago, my fiancée was killed by a homeless man."

Erica felt her anger toward him dissolve. "Oh, no! I'm so sorry."

"Ever since then—" He shook his head as though to dislodge the memory. "I know it's wrong to lump people into one category because of one person's actions, but I can't seem to stop doing it. Tracy was a trusting woman. A woman who never met a stranger and was kind to everyone who crossed her path." He glanced at her. "Kind of like you."

Erica swallowed. "I don't know what to say," she whispered. "My heart breaks for you."

"I've let Tracy go. She's with the Lord. And while I selfishly wish she wasn't, it is what it is. I'm still here and I still have a life to live." He traced a finger down her cheek and she shivered. He smiled but it didn't reach his eyes. "Anytime you need something, don't hesitate, all right?"

She nodded and blinked back tears. "All right."

"Good. Now what time should I pick you up in the morning?"

She stared as her brain scrambled to switch gears. "Oh, my car. Right. How about eight?"

"I'll be here."

"Do you think Mrs. Harrison would let us see Lydia's room first thing in the morning?"

"Lydia doesn't have a room there anymore, but I'll ask if she minds me bringing you by and introducing you."

"Great." Erica looked at her dark house and shivered. She'd forgotten to leave some lights on. Again.

"You want me to walk you in?"

She gave a breathless little laugh that sounded more scared than confident. "No. I'll be all right. I'm just a little spooked after everything that's happened in the last twenty-four hours."

"Who could blame you?"

In the close quarters of the car, she looked him in the eye. "Thanks again for coming to the rescue, Max."

His eyes dropped to her lips then rose back to meet her gaze. Thanks to the streetlight, she could make out the hue of a red flush on his cheeks. "Sure. I'll just wait here until you get inside."

On impulse, she leaned in and gave him a quick hug. "I'll see you in the morning."

She opened the door and raced for the cover of her front porch. From the rocker to her left, a shadow rose. Erica stepped back with a scream.

Chapter 8

Max bolted from the car as he snatched his weapon from his shoulder holster and trained it on the figure that had stepped toward Erica from the shadows. "Hey! Back away!"

The shadow froze, and Erica darted back into the rain toward Max.

"Erica! It's me, Peter."

Max grabbed her hand and led her back onto the porch, out of the rain. "Are you crazy? Scaring her like that?"

Peter held his hands up as though in surrender. "I thought she saw me."

"Nobody saw you," Max growled.

"I'm sorry. I was practically asleep when you drove up."

"What are you doing here?" Erica asked. Max could feel the tension vibrating from her.

Her brother swiped a hand down his face. "The cops think I had something to with crashing into you today. They think I was responsible for that hit-and-run, and the shooting."

"They said they didn't have any proof," Erica said.

"They don't." The man fidgeted, fingers tapping against his leg. "But they're looking for it. It's only a matter of time."

"Only a matter of time before what?" Max felt himself leaning toward Peter as if to drive him back, away from Erica. He told himself to cool it. He put his protective instincts on hold and said, "I thought you had an alibi."

Peter snorted and sank back onto the rocker, his leg jiggling up and down. "I did, but my alibi seems to have suffered some memory loss." Sarcasm dripped from his words. He grabbed Erica's hand. "Erica, you've got to believe I didn't have anything to do with that. I would *never* hurt you." His vehemence was almost believable.

Erica sighed and unlocked the door. "Let's get inside where it's warm. It's freezing and you're soaking wet."

Peter bolted to his feet as though sitting was too much for him. They stepped inside and he hesitated. "Can I have a towel?"

Max noticed the shivers trembling through the man's body. Erica set her purse on the small table just inside the foyer and went to the bathroom off the hall. Lips tight, she handed Peter the towel. "How did you get here?"

"I walked."

Erica flinched and Max raised a brow. She said, "That's a good ten miles, Peter. Are you crazy?"

The man shrugged.

Max asked, "Where were you tonight around seven?"

"On the way here. Why?"

"It wasn't him," Erica said to Max.

"What wasn't me?" His gaze darted from Max to Erica. Max thought his eyes looked clear. He wasn't high right now, but he was jittery, constantly moving.

"Someone scared Erica at the office tonight."

Peter frowned. "Well you're right, it wasn't me." He looked toward the back bedroom then said to Erica, "Do you still have some of my clothes here?"

"Yes. Go take a shower and warm up. I'll fix some coffee."

"Decaf, okay?" He started down the hall then turned back. "Oh, I meant to tell you, I saw Denise Tanner today."

Erica blinked. "You did? When?"

His brow crinkled. "Right before I left to come over here. I was at the gas station trying to get someone to buy me a soda and she pulled in." He rubbed his head and smirked. "I think she tried to avoid me, but I didn't let her. Stepped right in front of her and asked her what she was doing in town."

"And you wonder why she never cared much for you. You constantly antagonized the woman."

He shrugged his apathy. "She always looked down her nose at me. She was the bossiest thing ever, and I didn't like her. But apparently her father is on his death-bed. Not expected to live much longer."

"Oh, no. I knew he was sick, but I didn't know that he was close to death." Erica frowned. "Why didn't she call me and let me know?"

"I don't know." He raised a shaky hand. "She didn't look all that great, though. Must be taking a toll on her." He turned again and went to the room down the hall.

"Denise Tanner?" Max asked.

"I can't believe this. I just talked to her last week. She said her father was declining, but she didn't say anything about coming this way."

"Maybe it was really sudden." Max saw her glance at her phone and figured she wanted to call her friend. "I'll get out of here. Are you sure you'll be all right with him here?"

"Yes. Peter's not the one after me."

Max pursed his lips and thought about it. "We don't know that for sure."

Erica placed her hands on her hips. "Well, I do."

Max gave a slow nod. "Just like I know Lydia wouldn't be involved in a kidnapping." Erica's face flushed. "Call me if you need anything else tonight, promise?"

She nodded. "I promise. I really appreciate your help."

"Anytime." He stepped onto the porch. "At least the rain's stopped."

As Max walked down the steps, movement to his right caught his attention. He froze and squinted toward the dark shadows. "Who's there?"

The shadow darted around the corner of the house. Max chased after it.

"Max?" He could hear Erica calling after him, but had no time to stop and fill her in.

"Stay in the house!"

Within a second, Max was around the side of the

house and staring into inky blackness. The neighborhood streetlights didn't reach back far enough to illuminate the area behind the house and the quarter moon wasn't any help, either.

The light drizzle turned to a downpour again. Old cop instincts humming, Max pulled his weapon from his holster and clicked the safety off. Moving forward, eyes probing, he listened. A footstep to his left? He whirled, gun ready.

A figure slithered behind a tree. He moved toward it, rounding the tree with his gun outstretched. Nothing.

Heart hammering with adrenaline coursing through him, he placed his back against the tree and waited. Silence. The cold began to settle in his bones. His toes turned numb. For ten minutes, he stood in the dark, listening, hearing nothing but the night sounds.

In his mind, he pictured the person using the same strategy—holding still and silent, waiting for Max to make the first move.

"Max?"

Erica.

He kept the gun in his hand but lowered it as he heard her approaching. "Max, are you all right? Answer me."

Max kept his eyes glued to the area around him. He saw nothing. Heard nothing.

"I'm here, Erica."

He ground his teeth in frustration and walked toward her, keeping his senses tuned to anything out of the ordinary. As he approached, he saw the weapon in her hand. "He's gone."

"Who's gone? You scared me when you took off like that."

"I told you to stay in the house."

"And I don't sit back and wait very well when someone's in danger because of me." Together, they walked back to the house. Max glanced over his shoulder, feeling like he and Erica were one big bull's-eye.

Once they reached the porch, she asked, "What did you see?"

He pointed. "Someone was trying to look in that window."

She spun to her left. "That's my bedroom window."

He opened the door. "Is Peter still here?"

"I'm still here." Peter walked out, fresh from the shower. He looked much better, and seemed entirely oblivious to what had just happened. "I'm going to get something to eat if that's all right."

"Yeah. Sure." She waved him into the kitchen.

Once Peter disappeared around the corner, Max asked, "Do you have an alarm system?"

"Yes."

"Turn it on, okay?"

"Of course." She crossed her arms in a self-hug and shivered. "I think Peter's going to end up staying here tonight."

Max reached out and rubbed her arms, trying to chase away her chill. Then he surprised himself by pulling her into a gentle hug. And she surprised him by letting him do it. The feel of her in his arms felt right. Like something that was meant to be. Without letting go, he asked, "You think Peter'll be sober enough to help you if you need it?"

She pulled away from him and blew out a breath as

she glanced out into the night. "I don't know. Maybe whoever it was won't be back."

Max wasn't sure he agreed and mentally reviewed a plan to make sure Erica was safe tonight. In the meantime, he'd hold on to the memory of what it felt like to hold her next to his heart—and pray he had the opportunity to do it again.

Erica shut the door, her hand still on the knob, the feel of Max's embrace a strong sensation. Within the circle of his arms, she'd felt safe. Comforted. She wanted to beg him not to go, ask him to hold her and—

She heard Peter in the kitchen. Wanting something she couldn't have would get her nowhere. Max was off-limits.

At least for now.

She walked into the kitchen. "Are you staying here tonight?" She wasn't quite sure whether she wanted him to or not.

He looked up from the refrigerator, an apple in his left hand. "Do you mind?"

"No." She bit her lip then said, "I want to help you, Peter."

"Why? You still think I had something to do with Molly's disappearance." His bitterness filled the air. "Why would you want to help someone who could do such an awful thing?"

Erica blinked. "No, I don't. You were cleared."

"But you doubted," he said. "You really thought I would do something so vile as to kidnap my own niece—" He waved a hand and a deep sadness entered his eyes. "Never mind."

"Well, what was I supposed to think?" she demanded. "You came to me only a few weeks before, begging for money to shoot up your arm or snort up your nose. You shoved me against the wall when I refused and you raided my wallet for a lousy twenty bucks." Anger at the memory crested. She stepped forward and jabbed a finger in his chest. He flinched while she continued. "And you told me if I didn't give you what you wanted, you'd find a way to get it. What was I supposed to think?"

She couldn't stop the sob that broke free.

Erica whirled and went into the den. She sank onto the couch and tried to get a grip on her emotions even as tears ran freely down her cheeks.

Peter followed her, jaw tight, eyes narrowed. "I don't remember that."

"Well, you were high. It's not surprising you don't remember." She swiped the tears and sniffed.

"I'm going to go." He started for the door.

"That's right, Peter. Run away. Because that's always worked so well for you."

He turned on her. "Look, Erica, you don't understand…you…" He stopped and dropped his head. "This isn't why I came here tonight. I wanted to apologize for earlier."

"For what?"

"For letting Polo follow me here the other night. For whatever's going on that would make someone steal my car and try to frame me for hurting you. For—" he threw his hands out "—for whatever I need to apologize for."

Erica stared at her brother. "What is this, Peter? You're acting strange."

His eyes changed, hardened, yet the conflicted sadness remained. "Because I offered you an apology? What do you want from me?"

"I want you to go to rehab and quit destroying your life!"

"Maybe I want to destroy it so you'll quit trying to run it." He took a deep breath and closed his eyes. When he opened them, she thought she saw a sheen of tears there. But before she could question him, he strode to the front door, opened it and walked out into the night.

"Peter, wait!"

But he was already heading down the street, his phone pressed to his ear, shoulders hunched against the cold. "Come back!" He ignored her. Within five minutes, a car pulled up beside him and Peter climbed in. The vehicle roared to the stop sign at the end of the street and turned right. She had no hope of getting him to come back now.

Erica dropped her face into her hands and let the sobs come.

Two minutes later, a knock disrupted her crying jag. Rising to her feet, she snagged the gun from the top drawer of the desk and peered out the window.

Max.

She opened the door. "Why did you come back?"

His eyes swept her face. "I never left. I thought you might need me." He shut the door.

Her lower lip trembled. "I'm fine." She set the gun on the foyer table and gave her wet face an angry swipe.

"Sure you are."

His sympathy undid her. The sobs broke free once again and he pulled her into his arms. At first Erica wasn't quite sure what to think, but the blessed feeling of comfort washed over her and she hung on to it until she was able to rein in the tears.

When she opened her eyes, she found herself snuggled against Max's chest and sitting on the couch. Embarrassed that she didn't realize he'd led her there, she pulled away and scrubbed her eyes. "I'm so sorry."

"What for?"

"For blubbering all over you. I barely know you." She hiccuped and sniffed. "But thanks for the shoulder. I needed it."

He smiled. "Jordan is outside watching your house. He and I are taking shifts. Brandon tried to insist on helping, but the pain meds were kicking."

"Poor Brandon." The ever-present guilt tugged at her.

"He'll be all right. I asked for the four-to-eight shift so I could take you to get your car in the morning." He paused. "And talk you into breakfast again."

Erica sighed and pressed her fingertips against her eyelids, hoping to relieve some of the pressure. "Thanks. I appreciate that."

For the second time that night, Max moved to the door. "See you in a few hours. Get some rest if you can."

Erica nodded. "I'll do my best."

Erica leaned against the door as she turned the lock. A quick check out the window showed Max driving away and Jordan on guard.

She shook her head at the thought that someone wanted to hurt her. Who? A disgruntled spouse who was sitting in jail for kidnapping because she'd caught up with him? An angry ex-spouse who now had to pay child support? Any number of people had a bone to pick with her, but no one really stood out in her mind.

Stop searching for her or I'll kill her. The caller's words still echoed in her ears and Erica couldn't help but wonder, if she kept searching for her daughter, would that lead to Molly's death?

Would it lead to her *own* death?

Chapter 9

At eight o'clock Thursday morning, Max felt a dart of pleasure at the sight of Erica stepping out of her house and walking toward him. In jeans and a sweater, with her auburn hair pulled up in a neat ponytail, she looked comfortable, peaceful.

He wished he could say the same for his nerves. They were on edge. Probably from the gallon of coffee he'd drunk over the last three hours.

She slipped into the passenger seat. "Morning."

"Hey." He handed her a cup of coffee and a bagel. "Compliments of Brandon. He stopped by about thirty minutes ago."

"What?" She grimaced. "I wish he wouldn't push himself so hard."

"He cares about you."

"I know. He's a good brother. I just wish he would take it easy sometimes."

"Yeah. Like you do, right?"

She stuck her tongue out at him and he laughed. He swallowed a bite of the bagel and took a sip of coffee. "Bea agreed to meet us at eight thirty. She has a doctor's appointment at ten."

"That works for me. Did you get any rest last night?"

"A bit. You?"

"A bit."

Which meant not much. "Did you get hold of your friend, Denise?"

She winced. "No. I didn't even try. I plan to as soon as we're finished with Mrs. Harrison."

Max kept his mouth shut, but thought if a woman Erica considered her best friend hadn't bothered to call and let her know she was in town, then maybe she needed a new best friend. Like him, maybe.

"I appreciate you arranging this."

He shrugged. "I've been by to see Bea several times in the last few days and the story is always the same. She hasn't seen Lydia but will call if she does."

Erica played with her napkin, and he could almost see her thinking. "Well, I haven't talked to her," she said. "I want to see what she has to say to me."

He had a feeling it wouldn't be anything new, but he supposed she needed to hear it herself. "What makes you think she'll tell you anything different than what she's told me?"

"I don't think she will, necessarily. But I won't know until I try."

He finished off the bagel and cranked the car. "Then let's do it. She's expecting us anytime now." As he pulled away from the curb, he said, "I did some research on Lydia's calls."

"What do you mean?"

"I bought her a cell phone not too long ago and I get the bill. I went through the latest one and found something interesting."

Erica lifted a brow. "What'd you find?"

"Lydia made several phone calls to a construction company and got one return call from the same business."

"Why is that weird?"

"For someone living on the streets and doing drugs, it just struck me as kind of strange."

She nodded. "Okay, so did you call the number?"

"I did."

"And?"

"I got voice mail. We'll try again a little later. I want to know what kind of business Lydia had with them."

"Won't the cops have questioned them already?"

He shook his head. "I'm not sure. If they did, Katie didn't mention it."

"Okay, sounds good to me."

Max looked in the rearview mirror. No one followed. At least no one obvious. His mind worked the puzzle of his sister's ability to hide so well when he knew most of her hiding places.

She may have found a new one. At least, he hoped she did. Otherwise, her disappearance didn't bode well. Had Lydia escaped her attacker two nights ago only to fall into the wrong hands?

He sent up a brief prayer and a desperate plea for the Lord to keep the girl safe.

Erica watched Max's strong hands grip the wheel. She inhaled, liking his fresh, clean scent. He smelled… good. Really good. He must have showered before coming over in the wee hours of the morning. She wondered if he'd done that for her.

She thought about his loss. A fiancée. Someone he'd loved enough to want to spend the rest of his life with her.

She must have been a special woman.

And she'd been killed by a homeless person. Her heart ached for him even as it thumped a little harder at his nearness.

Her attraction to him made her frown as she watched him drive. What was she going to do with this pull she felt for him?

What *could* she do with it?

A plan formed in her mind. What if she invited him to spend some time with her at the shelter? Introduced him to some of the regulars and let him see that the man who killed his fiancée was an aberration? That the homeless man's act of murder was not the norm?

She felt sure he knew this in his head, but had a feeling his heart needed to learn it.

She watched him. He was as lost in his own thoughts as she. Warmth settled in her belly as she remembered his sweet care when she'd cried on his shoulder. Longing swept through her—oh, to have that on a daily basis. To have someone next to her, someone in her life to support and offer support in return.

That would be so wonderful.

But she couldn't have that with Max. What if his sister *was* guilty of having something to do with Molly's kidnapping? What would happen then?

She knew the answer to that.

Max would do everything in his power to help the girl stay out of jail; he would fight for her no matter what.

And Erica would be just as determined to see Lydia Powell pay for whatever part she played in the crime that had broken her heart.

Max's sister was too big of a barrier to get past.

She bit her lip and looked out the window. Max Powell might be good-looking and make her pulse pound a little faster when she was around him, but that didn't mean she could fall for him. Because when his sister was charged, he would be forced to choose sides.

And Erica had no doubt which side he would choose.

For her own sake, she needed to guard her heart.

Lydia may be innocent, a little voice whispered.

Erica ignored it. Lydia was the first thing in three years that looked like a solid lead and there was no chance she was going to let her feelings for Max Powell get in the way.

Erica would find Lydia, and find out what she knew.

No matter what.

Max pulled up to the curb of Bea Harrison's home. "She was old when Lydia lived here," he told Erica. "At least it seemed that way to me. I think she's around seventy now."

"Seventy's not that old these days." She shot him an amused glance.

He gave her a wry grin. "I have to admit, the older I

get, the younger seventy seems. It wasn't too long ago I thought thirty was the equivalent of having one foot in the grave. Now I'll be thirty in three months." He shook his head and looked up to see Bea standing at the screen door. "Come on, she's waiting on us."

They climbed from the vehicle and Max hunched his shoulders against the chill. Thanksgiving would be here soon. He swallowed at the thought. Another holiday without a family of his own. This time of year sent his emotions spinning.

Anger over his childhood and grief over his fiancée surged to the surface often. Technically, he still had Lydia, but who knows if she would show up for a meal?

Or if she would even be able to come. If she was sitting in jail, or on the run, a happy family celebration would most likely be out of the question.

He sighed at his sarcasm. Focus on the positive, right?

Pushing the depressing thoughts aside, he stepped inside the warm house and introduced Erica. The two women greeted each other and Max said, "I'm still looking for Lydia, Bea. Have you seen or heard from her?"

"Have a seat, you two." The rail-thin yet spry woman didn't look seventy. Energy radiated from her and he could see Erica was drawn to her. Bea asked, "Would you like something to drink? Eat?"

Erica shook her head. "I don't care for anything, thanks."

Impatience tugged at him. He forced it away. This woman had been able to reach a part of his sister no one else had touched. He supposed he should be jealous. But he wasn't, he was just glad Lydia had someone she trusted. "Me, either, Bea. We don't have a lot of time, but I wanted to introduce Erica to you."

Bea's sharp eyes homed in on Erica. "You're Molly's mother, aren't you?"

Max saw Erica flinch, but she nodded. "Yes."

"I recognize you from your picture on the news recently. I also followed your story three years ago." She clucked her tongue. "I just couldn't believe a child could disappear from the zoo on a field trip." Her lips pursed. "I've had close to a hundred children come through my home in the last thirty years and none of 'em went missing on my watch." She narrowed her eyes. "Well, Lydia might be the exception to that. But I always knew she'd come back."

Max interrupted, hating the pain in Erica's eyes. "I know you told me on the phone that you haven't seen Lydia." He leaned forward. "Please, Bea, this is for Lydia's own good. You've been around the system enough to know that protecting her isn't going to be good for her in the long run. We need to find her."

For the first time, doubt creased her brow and she sighed. "Max, I've never had a biological child, but if I did, she would have been just like Lydia. Lydia's like my own." She paused. "I didn't get her young enough. I would have raised her better than what she had. Deep down Lydia has a good heart. She just can't seem to stop making stupid decisions."

"I know."

"And while she has her faults, she's good to me." She nodded toward her ankle, which was wrapped up in a brace. "She came by a day after I fell about a month ago and bought me this. Said I should go to the doctor, but I don't have any insurance. Yep, she's good to me."

"And you're good to her. Maybe too good." He took her hand. "You know I'd pay for any doctor visit you needed."

She flushed and waved him off. "I know that, but I knew it was just a sprain and would heal in time."

Max leaned back. "Look at it this way. We want to find Lydia because we want to help her. Someone may be after her, and I want to find her first." He gripped her hand. "Please, Bea, tell me what you know."

The woman twisted her fingers together. "What do you mean someone's after her and wants to hurt her?" He told her about the attack they'd saved her from the other night. Bea listened, eyes wide. "You really think she's still in danger?"

"I don't know, but we're trying to find her before it's too late."

Bea closed her eyes for a moment then stood and said, "All right, I'll be right back."

As she disappeared down the hall toward the bedrooms, Erica asked in a low voice, "What makes you think Lydia is in danger, other than the attack the other night?" She shot a glance toward the hall. "I thought that was just a random thing of Lydia being in the wrong place at the wrong time."

He shrugged. "Just a feeling."

Bea's sprightly steps echoed on the hardwood as she returned to the kitchen. She set a shoe box on the table and heaved a sigh. "You're sure she's in danger? Because I promised Lydia I'd guard this with my life."

"What's in it?"

"I don't know." She huffed in indignation. "I didn't look. I just made her promise it wasn't drugs or anything that could get me arrested. She swore it wasn't."

Max lifted a brow. "And you believed her?" It wasn't like Bea to have her head in the sand. She'd had enough kids who were hooked on drugs come through her house to know how it worked. You couldn't trust them. Period. He would have looked the minute Lydia walked out the door.

Which was probably why she left the box with Bea.

Bea was nodding. "Yes. Strangely enough I did believe her about this. She said it was a memory box. She'd come by to visit it every once in a while."

They all looked at the box for a moment, and then Max reached for the lid, wondering what he was about to find, and knowing it probably wasn't going to be anything good.

Erica desperately wanted to snatch the box from the table and just dump out the contents. Instead, she curled her fingers into fists and held on to her unraveling patience as Max removed the lid.

He stared down into the box, his expression unreadable, and then pulled out a photo. Erica scooted forward to see. "That's you, isn't it?"

"Yeah." Surprise tinged his voice. "This was taken on Lydia's eighteenth birthday. She was sober and being civil to me. I took her out to eat at her favorite restaurant and the server snapped the picture." He ran his fingers over his sister's face, and Erica's heart cramped at the pain etched on his features.

He shook himself and set the picture aside to pull other items out. A cheap necklace with a heart pendant, a pack of cards, a college application. "She has dreams," Erica whispered.

"Yeah. She's wanted to be an architect for as long as I can remember." Max cleared his throat and held up a small piece of paper. "A business card." He read it and looked up. "Kenneth Harper, Brown and Jennings Construction. It's the same company that called her cell phone."

"Then they're next on the list," Erica said.

He pulled out the last item—a thick envelope. He opened the flap and reached in.

Erica gasped as he withdrew a stack of money.

Max set it on the table and stared at it. "Whoa."

"Where would she get that?" Erica asked Bea.

Bea shook her head, the dumbfounded expression leaving no doubt she was just as surprised. "She never said anything about it."

Max counted the bills. "Twenty fifty-dollar bills."

"A thousand bucks?" Erica lifted a brow.

He sat back and crossed his arms. "I have no idea where she would have gotten this kind of money."

Erica picked up another picture. "Who's this?"

Max took the picture from her and flipped it over. "It just says, 'Me and Red.'"

"Who's Red?"

Bea said, "She was in rehab with Lydia at that place across town."

"Billings Rehab Center," Max said. "I went to visit her while she was there, but she wouldn't see me. That was when she was first sent there. After I kept going back, she finally understood I wasn't going to give up and started letting me visit."

Bea nodded and told Erica, "She was court ordered to go to Billings after she was kicked out of high school for having drugs on her. She spent four months there."

Max looked at Erica, disappointment evident on his face. "It seemed to help. For a while. She started talking to me and we were working on our relationship, but then—" He shrugged. "After she got out and celebrated her eighteenth birthday, things went downhill fast."

"Do you think Red would know where Lydia is?" Erica asked.

Bea sighed. "Red's probably your best chance. She and Lydia were real close. Probably still are."

"Do you know where we can find her?"

"No. All I know is she goes by Red. I don't know her real name or where she's from. Nothing."

Max stood. "I can probably get her name from the rehab center."

"That's protected information, isn't it?" Bea frowned.

Max smiled and met Erica's eyes. "We have our ways." The smile slipped as he looked at the money. "Just keep this here for now, okay? Until we find out where she got it."

Erica shook her head. "There's no way a drug addict would have a thousand dollars tucked away. It would be gone in a split second."

"You think it's not hers?" Bea asked.

"I don't know. If it is, the reason she's holding on to it has got a stronger hold on her than the drugs."

Hope flashed in Max's eyes. "Yeah. True." He slapped the lid back on the box and stood. "Let's go see if we can find that reason."

Chapter 10

As Max walked around to the driver's side of his truck after opening Erica's door for her, he found himself checking the road. When he settled behind the wheel, he glanced in the rearview mirror. Something was making him uneasy, but he couldn't say what. He felt watched, and he didn't like that he didn't see anyone doing the watching.

"I think that was productive," Erica said.

"Definitely." With one more glance in the mirror, he grabbed his phone and called the number for Brown and Jennings Construction. "I'll see if we can stop by and talk to Kenneth Harper."

Erica nodded. "After we talk to him, I need to go in to the office for at least a couple of hours. Rachel's already left three messages on my voice mail and it's only ten thirty."

Max drove, his mind mulling over the thousand dollars cash in the box. Where would Lydia have gotten that much money? And a thousand even? All fifty-dollar bills. He looked in the mirror. Nothing alarming caught his attention. A blue Toyota behind him. A white Honda next to him.

The phone continued to ring. Just as he was about to hang up, a harried voice answered, "Brown and Jennings."

"Could I speak to Kenneth Harper?"

"He's out at a site giving an estimate." Papers rustled in the background. "Looks like he'll be back here around lunchtime."

"He have a cell phone?"

"Who is this?"

"I'm a private investigator trying to track down a young woman named Lydia Powell. Do you know her?"

"Nope, sorry. Name doesn't ring a bell." There was a pause, and then, "Wait a minute. Yes, it does. Isn't she the girl the cops are looking for?"

"Yes."

"Yeah, I remember seeing her name on the news. Why are you looking for her here?"

"I found your company's business card in some of her things."

"Oh. Wow. You'll have to talk to Ken. He's the owner, and if Lydia talked to anyone around here, it was probably him."

"Okay, thanks." Max hadn't held too much hope that this woman would know something, but it had been worth a shot. "So may I have the cell number?"

"Sure." She rattled it off and Max repeated it so Erica could write it down.

He hung up and tried the number. No answer. He left a message and then drove Erica to her office. Several cars filled the parking lot, including hers.

"You mind if I come in?" he asked.

"Of course not." She climbed from the truck, and then glanced behind him. "I don't think we were followed, do you?"

"I didn't see anyone, but I was wondering the same thing at Bea's house." He thought for a moment. "I'm going to call her and tell her to be on the alert."

Alarm crossed her features. "You don't think someone would try to hurt her, do you?"

"If they thought she knew something about Lydia, they might." He frowned. "I was careful—very careful—about being followed."

"But not careful enough?"

"I'm not a hundred percent sure, and I don't like that."

He made a call to Bea, who said everything was fine but she'd keep her eyes open, and another to a buddy named Nick Kirby, who was still on the force and still a good friend. He explained what he needed and said to Erica, "Nick's going to hang out and watch Bea's house for the rest of the day and night."

Relief crossed her face. "Good. I would hate to be the reason trouble arrives on her doorstep."

He followed her into the building, trailing a few steps behind her, eyes roaming, senses tuned to the area around them. He wouldn't mind seeing her office, but the main reason he wanted to go in was to make sure there wasn't a bad surprise waiting inside for her.

He was probably just being paranoid.

But that was all right.

Inside, the warmth hit him and he shed his coat to hang it on the rack. Erica turned to the young woman at the desk and said, "Rachel, this is Max Powell."

He shook hands with the pretty receptionist and thought he saw a bit of a family resemblance. Cousins, Erica had said. "Nice to meet you."

She eyed him curiously. "You, too."

He looked around. "So, this is it, huh?"

"Yep." She smiled. "This way to my office."

"I put your mail on your desk," Rachel said.

"Thanks." Erica turned into the office three doors down. Max stepped up to help her slip her coat off. As he did, his fingers accidentally slid across the back of her neck, touching her soft skin.

She shivered and turned to look at him, surprise on her face. He cleared his throat. "Where do you want me to hang this?"

Erica blinked and nodded to a coat rack behind the door. He hung the jacket up for her. "Nice office," he said. He practically groaned at the lameness, but right now he needed to get his mind off the way her skin had felt. Because in that moment, all of his arguments about why he should ignore his attraction to this woman had flown out the window.

"Thanks. It's nothing much, but it serves its purpose." She shifted through the messages and the mail. With a frown, she pulled an envelope from the stack. "This is weird."

"What is it?"

"It's addressed to me, but there's no return address or stamp." Erica slid her letter opener under the tab and pulled out a sheet of paper. Her face went pale and she dropped into the chair behind her desk.

"What is it?" Max asked. He stepped forward and took the paper from her. It said, "I warned you. Stop looking for her or she dies."

"The same message as my phone call last night." She rubbed a shaky hand over her eyes. "It has to be about Molly, right?"

"Or Lydia."

"But the person is warning me. You haven't gotten anything about not searching for Lydia, have you?"

He rubbed his chin. "No."

Excitement darkened her green eyes. "Molly's still alive, Max." Her throat worked and deep joy filled her face. "If she's alive, I have a chance to get her back. You can't imagine the horrible thoughts I've had about who might have taken her," she whispered.

"I can imagine. But you have to keep fighting those thoughts, praying against them." He reached over and took her hand. The fragile strength brought his protective instincts surging to the surface.

"I know. I do every day."

"And keep believing you can get her back." As soon as the words left his lips, he wondered if he should encourage her to continue hoping. Three years was a long time. Odds were completely against Erica being reunited with her child.

Odds he was sure she could quote him.

She pulled her hand from his and reached for the note and he held it aloft with thumb and forefinger. "Let's see if Katie can get anything off this."

"Fingerprints. Yes, of course. You're right." She took

a deep breath and rubbed a hand down her face. "I usually think a little more clearly. It's just…"

"I get it."

She reached for the phone. He noticed she didn't have to look up Katie Randall's number. She hung up. "She's on her way over to pick it up."

As they waited, Max decided to ask Erica a question he'd had on his mind for a while. "What made you volunteer at the homeless shelter?"

She flushed. "Well, if I'm going to be honest, I'll have to admit my motives weren't completely pure at first."

Intrigued, he leaned forward. "Why do you say that?"

She picked up Molly's picture. "One of the first tips that came in was that she'd been seen at the shelter eating a free meal. No one remembered who she was with, just that she was there. The police got several calls about her being seen there so we all felt it was a legitimate tip."

"So you went there."

"I did. Of course no one would talk to me. But I noticed the rapport between the servers and the homeless. I signed up to serve the next day. It took time, but they came to trust me. I learned that Molly was there two days after she was kidnapped, but I didn't learn anything else over the next few weeks. I developed a relationship with the people there and—" she shrugged "—I stayed." She eyed him. "They're not all criminals."

"Realistically, I know that." He rubbed his chin and eyed her. "But what about the ones who are?"

She said, "I won't say I don't take precautions. Of

course I do. But I've come to care for these people.
I've listened to their stories. And shared mine. I'm not
homeless, but 'there but for the grace of God, go I,'
you know?"

"Yeah. I know." And he did. He understood what
she meant.

"Why don't you come with me? Help me serve? Meet
the people?"

An outright refusal hovered on his tongue, but the
look on her face kept him from expressing it.

A knock on the door made them both jump. Relieved
he didn't have to answer right away, Max turned to see
Brandon in the doorway. Erica hopped to her feet and
rushed to her brother. "Are you all right? What are you
doing here?"

"I'm all right. Feeling a bit rough, but I had a new
case I wanted to get the paperwork on." He held up a
hand to halt her protests. "I can't just sit around doing
nothing."

Jordan stepped into the room behind his friend and
lifted his brow when he caught sight of Max. "You're
becoming a regular fixture, aren't you?"

Max remembered that when they'd first met, Brandon had made a reference to Jordan as Erica's boyfriend. And while Erica quickly set the record straight,
it appeared that Jordan might have a different take than
Erica.

He was surprised by the spike of jealousy he suddenly felt.

Max met Jordan's stare head-on. "I'm doing what I
can to help."

Rachel entered the crowded office. "Detective Randall is here."

Hope flared in Erica's eyes. "Show her in, please."

"What's she doing here?" Brandon asked as Rachel went to get the detective. His color had paled just since entering the office. Erica must have noticed as she waved him into a chair. "Sit down before you fall down."

Brandon didn't argue.

Jordan took the other seat and left Max standing.

"Katie's here because someone sent a letter with a rather cryptic message," Erica explained. "I want her to take a look at it."

"What kind of message?" Brandon asked.

Max's phone buzzed and he pulled it from his pocket. "It's the guy from the construction company," he told Erica. "I'll take this outside."

Jordan watched Max very closely as he left the room. Yup, the guy definitely had his own ideas about Erica.

Ideas that Max had to admit he didn't like one bit.

Erica was torn. She wanted to hear the conversation between Max and the man on the phone, yet she knew her obligation was to Katie. She forced a smile. "Come on in."

"Good to see you again, Erica."

"You, too." Erica stepped back into her office. Jordan and Brandon both rose and offered the detective a seat. Katie took one look at Brandon and chose Jordan's. When her brother simply sat back down without protest, Erica knew he was in pain.

"What's this about someone leaving you a nasty note?" asked the detective.

Erica filled the group in on the phone call and the note. Brandon's jaw tightened as Jordan scowled. "Should have told us about this earlier."

"I didn't have time." She looked at Katie. "I think this means that Molly could still be alive. Don't you?" She could hear the desperation in her voice, but didn't care.

Katie frowned. "But, Erica, you've been actively searching for Molly since she disappeared. What's different about the search now?"

"I think this means I must be getting closer. Somebody must be feeling more threatened than they have in the past."

"About what?" Katie asked.

"Lydia Powell, maybe? I think she may know something and someone doesn't want me to find her. Maybe they're warning me off trying to find Lydia." She hated to say the words out loud, especially since Max thought his sister was completely innocent. And yet, what else was she supposed to think?

Max came back into the office and leaned against the wall. Erica picked up the note and handed it to Katie. "Will you see if you can get any prints off this?"

Katie pulled a glove from her back pocket and snapped it onto her hand. She slid the note from the envelope, read it, then returned it. "I'll see what I can do. No promises, though."

"I know."

Katie paused, looked at Erica and said, "It's okay to hope, but don't pin your emotions on this, okay?"

Erica pursed her lips then nodded. She knew Katie

was right. But still, it was hard to squash that little seedling of wild hope that wanted to sprout like a wildflower.

Katie left and Brandon said, "I think you need to cool it on the search for Molly. Let Jordan and me take over."

Erica snorted. "Not likely."

"Seriously, sis. This person may not be fooling around. What if you keep searching and Molly ends up dead?"

Erica bit her lip. It was that very question that had been tearing her up. "I think if the person wanted Molly dead, he would have killed her long before now."

"Assuming the person we're talking about is Molly," Brandon said.

Erica sighed and rubbed her eyes. "Exactly."

Max asked, "Are you up to visiting the construction site?"

"Yes, of course. When?"

He glanced at his watch. "Around two this afternoon."

"I can do that."

"We can grab a bite in the meantime."

"I can't. Unless you want to help me at the homeless shelter—I'm serving lunch today."

He stared at her for a moment. "I'll take a rain check."

Sadness pressed in on her but she forced a smile. Maybe Max just wasn't ready yet. "I understand."

"I'll sit outside and make sure you're safe while you're there."

Jordan stepped forward and put a hand on Erica's

arm. "Let me go with Max to the construction site. No need to put yourself through the stress of it."

"No." She moved away from Jordan. "Molly's my daughter. If you want to help find her, I welcome it, but I won't stop searching myself. You know I've got to go to the site." She softened her tone. "But thanks for the offer."

Jordan's nostrils flared, but he backed away. He studied her for a moment longer, compassion in his angry gaze.

At least she hoped it was compassion and not pity. As Erica walked from the office, she felt Max's gentle hand on her lower back, ushering her down the hall. She also felt Jordan's stare like two lasers boring into the back of her head.

Jordan didn't like Max, and that concerned Erica a bit because she respected the man. But she had a feeling his dislike was more about Max's proximity to Erica than about Max himself. And the bottom line was, Max was going to help her find Molly, and right now, that was all that mattered.

Max felt awful. He couldn't get Erica's disappointed look out of his mind.

He'd followed her to the shelter simply to ensure her safety, walking her inside to make sure everything looked normal, in her eyes at least. Now he stood against the wall and watched her interact with person after person, smiling encouragement with each dip of her serving ladle.

He could understand her wanting to help the shelter's children, but the adults all looked shifty and lazy to his experienced eye. And yet he felt convicted for judging. He'd had a rough childhood, but he'd never been homeless. Was he wrong to judge them all against Tracy's killer?

Yes.

He shifted, uncomfortable with the prodding of his heart, his spirit.

He kept his phone close and his weapon closer. And yet he felt compelled to pray. *Lord, I may be wrong here. Help me change my heart.*

The delicious aroma of the food couldn't quite mask the odor of unwashed bodies. Max noticed it didn't seem to bother Erica.

Max's gaze landed on two men at a table in the far corner. They both leaned forward, their conversation quiet. Max's cop instincts hummed. He was willing to let God change his heart, but that didn't mean he wasn't going to be on the alert for trouble.

The one on the left sported a shaggy black beard and a long, dirty, tan overcoat. The one across from him looked a little better. At least he'd found a razor sometime in the past couple of days.

Together they watched Erica.

Max watched them.

When Erica walked over to their table, he straightened and moved closer to hear their conversation.

"Hello, Jed. Anything else I can get you gentlemen?"

They shook their heads and she moved on to the next table, treating the patrons like they were in a high-class restaurant. Her kindness floored him; her compassion for others stirred his heart in a way he couldn't name.

Max looked back at the two men in the corner. They

were tracking Erica with their eyes. Finally, the one on the left rose and sauntered from the building. Max watched him go, suspicion crawling all over him. If he'd still been a cop, he would have called for someone in the area to follow him just to allay his concerns.

The other man stood and also slipped out the door. Max relaxed a fraction, then tensed again.

Would they be waiting for her when she left the shelter?

What if she ended up just like Tracy?

He stepped outside and scanned the area. Nothing seemed out of place. Nothing alarming. No men waiting to ambush Erica on her way to her car.

Nothing to worry about.

And yet he did.

He didn't like the way the two men had paid such close attention to her.

He went back inside.

"Well? What do you think?" Erica asked him.

Max shrugged, unable to admit he might have been wrong, especially in light of what he'd just seen. "Everyone seems calm, friendly, glad to have a hot meal to put in their bellies."

She smiled. "They are. For the most part. They may begrudge the fact they get that meal at the shelter, but they're not going to turn it down."

He paused, then asked, "Who were those two men sitting in the corner? The one with the beard and the one with the red ball cap?"

She frowned. "I'm not sure who the guy in the red cap was, but that was Jed Barnes with the beard. Why?"

He shrugged. "Just wondering."

Erica nodded in the direction of a young family. "That's Bill and Mary Lawson, and their daughter Claudette. He lost his job eight months ago. She never graduated high school, but was working on her GED when they were foreclosed on. They take turns taking care of Claudette while the other person hunts for a job. They come here to eat, to hear any news of possible job leads and to regroup."

He had to admit the little family looked about as dangerous as Erica herself.

Erica nodded to her left. "And see those two women? They're sisters who were evicted from their apartment when they couldn't pay the bills anymore. They lost their husbands within days of each other. Neither woman has worked a day in their lives because they stayed home with their children. Children who won't have anything to do with them now."

She went on, pointing out different individuals and giving him background. Against his will, he felt himself softening. And he also felt his heart opening up to Erica in a way that felt out of his control.

Erica touched his arm. "Tessa is waving to me. Let me see what she wants and then I'll be ready to leave."

She started to turn and he grabbed her hand. She looked up at him, a question in her eye. "I know we're on opposite sides of the fence as far as Lydia is concerned, but I want you to know that I think you're a very special woman."

A bright flush appeared on Erica's cheeks. "Well… thank you." He smiled at her flustered thanks and released her hand.

As he watched her walk away, he had to resist the

urge to grab her back, wrap his arms around her and keep her from harm.

Erica twisted the tie on the last garbage bag and opened the back door of the shelter's kitchen. She stepped outside to place the bag in the can, and the door slammed shut behind her.

She whirled and grabbed the knob. Locked. "Of course," she muttered. She knocked and waited.

Most of the volunteers had already left, but she and Tessa and a couple of others had stayed to clean up the dining area and the kitchen. She pounded on the door this time. "Hey! Let me in, will you?"

Where was Max?

"Tess?" she called, her voice starting to sound panicked even to her own ears.

Gravel crunched behind her.

She spun and saw nothing but the back alley with the tall fence. The Dumpster loomed to her left.

Her stomach dipped. She was outside, alone. Normally that wouldn't have fazed her. However, with all of the incidents that had happened over the past couple of days, she would have rather had someone with her.

"Is someone there?"

She sucked in a deep breath. She'd just have to walk around to the front of the building. Simple, right?

A figure stepped out from behind the Dumpster. Shoulders hunched, a black beard touching his chest, he shoved a hand into his coat pocket. Erica froze.

The door opened behind her. "Erica?"

She spun. "Max." Relief filled her. She turned back to the man who still stood beside the Dumpster.

"What's going on?" His tight voice was directed at the stranger.

Erica said, "I'm not sure." She stepped forward, feeling safe now that she had Max at her back. "Jed, you scared me for a minute there."

"Sorry about that."

"Get your hands out of your pockets," Max demanded, shoving Erica behind him.

"Max…"

"Now."

The man complied. He held a small box in his left hand. "I just wanted to give this to Erica."

Her fear beginning to dissipate, Erica stepped around Max. "What is it?"

"A…a gift." He cleared his throat.

Uneasy again, she watched him. An alcoholic and a drug addict, he'd never been physically abusive to Melissa, but the emotional damage he'd done to the woman had been painful to see. "What are you doing out here?"

"I was going to leave, but wanted to catch you alone."

Max kept his protective stance and said, "Erica, why don't you go back on inside and let me take care of Mr. Barnes."

She considered it for all of a split second. "It's all right, Max."

Jed didn't smile. "You told my wife to leave me."

Max stiffened. "Erica…"

"I didn't tell her to leave you, Jed. I told her she needed a break from the stress of your abuse or she was going to have a nervous breakdown." She would never tell someone to leave a spouse. But take a break? Yes.

"Well, she left me."

Erica's heart hurt. "I hate that it came to that."

"I do, too, but…" His shoulders slumped.

"But?"

"It was the best thing she could have done. The only thing."

Erica relaxed a fraction. Max's defensive posture slackened slightly. "What do you mean?"

"I mean, it forced me to take a good hard look at myself, and I didn't like what I saw so I got help. I've been clean for six months. Melissa said she'd go to counseling with me."

Relief and gladness filled her. "Oh, Jed, I'm so glad."

"Me, too."

Max released a breath and she felt his tension ease. Jed held out the gift to Erica, setting the small box on her palm. "This was my grandmother's. I want you to have it."

"What? Oh, no, I can't—"

"Please. I've been coming in here just about every day for the past three months. After I got out of rehab, I'd look for a job and come here to eat and sleep and work on getting my life in order." He shuffled his feet and ducked his head. When he looked up, tears were in his eyes. "You encouraged me that I could change. That I could be the man that Melissa and my kids needed. I never had anyone do that for me before." He nodded. "I started to believe you after a while. This is just a small way to say thanks. And maybe when you look at it you'll remember that some of us do want help. We just don't know where to get it until someone like you comes along."

"Jed, I… I don't know what to say."

"Don't have to say anything." He gave a half smile. "I'll be seein' you." He turned and walked down the alley to disappear around the corner.

Erica shook her head and silently thanked God for the way He worked.

"What is it?" Max asked. He settled his hands on her shoulders and she breathed in his spicy scent. A scent that was becoming as familiar as her own. One she liked. A lot.

She lifted the top of the box to find a tiny cross pin nestled on the velvet fabric. "Oh, it's beautiful." She drew in another deep breath. "Goodness, I can't keep this."

"I think you have to." She looked up to see him staring toward the end of the alley. "I think he needed to give that to you. It was like he was doing something his grandmother would approve of, and that was important to him."

Erica closed the box and slipped the treasure into her pocket. "This is one of the reasons I do what I do, Max."

"Yeah." The cryptic look on his face didn't tell her anything about what he was thinking. He stared at her for so long, she shifted under his hands. "What is it?"

His eyes grew tender. "Like I said before, you're incredibly special, Erica." He lifted a hand to her cheek.

Her heart thumped at his words, at the feel of his touch, at the look in his eyes.

"I—"

"What about Lydia?" she interrupted, turning away.

He sighed. "Lydia. Right." He hadn't forgotten about her, but he couldn't deny that a part of him wanted to move forward with a relationship with Erica, regardless of their different opinions about Lydia. "I know it looks bad for her, and I don't want to believe she's guilty, but I've come to the conclusion that whatever she's done, she's done. And if she hasn't done anything, that will come out, too. Whatever the result, I don't want it to keep us apart."

Erica's eyes widened in shock. "But—"

Before she could finish, he leaned over and pressed a kiss to her lips. A sweet, gentle kiss that sparked a flame inside her. Her heart and her mind battled it out while she wrapped her arms around him and kissed him back.

After what seemed like forever, he lifted his head, eyes glittering. "I care about you, Erica."

"I know," she whispered. "I care about you, too."

"After we find Lydia—"

She pressed her fingers to his lips. "Don't say anything. Don't make promises. Let's just find her."

Disappointment flashed in his eyes, but he nodded. His jaw looked tight, as though he wanted to say something more, but he held the words back. Finally, instead of saying what was in his eyes, he said, "Come on, let's go talk to Kenneth Harper and see what he knows about Lydia."

Chapter 11

Max couldn't help feeling relieved as the homeless shelter disappeared from view. He had mixed emotions. The people he'd met weren't like the ones he'd arrested as a cop. At least not all of them. Most of the residents were, if not exactly peaceful, at least calm.

Granted, there'd been a few moments with Jed that had stressed him out, but once again, he was reminded not to judge a person by his appearance. He would pray for Jed and his wife, Melissa.

Max glanced at Erica. She had her phone pressed to her ear. "Denise, this is Erica. Peter told me you were back in town. Give me a call and let's catch up. I'll try to get to the hospital to see your father soon. Call me, hon." She hung up with a frown. "I wish she would have called me when she got in town."

"She's probably busy with her father."

"I know, but still…" She sighed. "Denise has been so good about keeping in touch since she left. We've talked on the phone almost every week since she moved."

"I'm sure she'll return your call soon."

"I suppose I could just go up to the hospital."

"Do you want me to drop you off?"

"No, I want to be there for Denise if she wants me to, but right now Molly comes first."

As they drove to the construction site, his mind whirled with other questions he wanted answers to. Starting with Jordan. And if he and Erica were going to have any sort of romantic relationship, Max needed to know those answers. If she would tell him.

"Jordan's not a very friendly guy, is he?"

She shot him a sideways glance he caught from the corner of his eye. "Jordan's all right. He's just hard to get to know."

"He makes it hard."

"I suppose he does."

She wasn't going to say anything about the man, negative or otherwise. Max appreciated her tact but at the same time found it frustrating. He looked at her. "Did you two date?"

"No." A smile curved her lips. He turned his attention back to the road, but all he wanted to do was watch her. He decided he could spend hours just watching her.

"So…is there a history there? A story?" He knew he was pushing but he couldn't seem to stop himself.

At first she didn't answer. About a mile later, she finally said, "Jordan is a unique person. He has a history, but I'm not part of it. All I know is he and Brandon were roommates and best friends in college. About a year ago, Jordan showed up and needed a place to crash. Brandon then talked him into joining Finding the Lost shortly thereafter." She looked at Max and added, "He's very good at what he does."

Max pulled into Brown and Jennings Construction and parked. He didn't really want to hear any more about Jordan. And he didn't enjoy the admiration in Erica's voice when she talked about him.

Jealousy was a new emotion for Max. He seemed to be feeling it a lot lately, and he didn't like it. He opened his door. "Let's go see what we can find out."

Erica nodded, and he chose to ignore the somewhat amused look on her face.

At the desk, Max flashed his private investigator credentials and the young receptionist's eyes widened. "What do you need?"

"To speak with Kenneth Harper."

She got on the phone. When she hung up, she said, "Go through that door to the left. He's waiting for you."

Max appreciated the fact that Erica was allowing him to take the lead on this. As she walked from the car to the office, he could feel her impatience ramping up again. No one else would probably notice, but having spent most of the past thirty-six hours in her presence, he'd learned to read her pretty well.

Kenneth was a short round man with a bald head and blue eyes that flitted between Max and Erica. "Have a seat. What can I do for you?"

"I found your business card in my sister's belongings," Max said. "I wondered what she wanted from you."

Kenneth scratched his head. "We had advertised at

some of the local restaurants that we were looking to hire a receptionist. She came in for an interview."

Max sat still, trying to process the information. "An interview?"

"Yeah, but she was just too young and inexperienced. She was up front and honest about the fact that she'd been through rehab, but you can see this place—it's crazy. I needed someone with experience. There just wasn't time to train anyone." He looked at Erica. "You look like the type who would know how to run an office. Want to apply?" The flirty tone in his voice grated on Max.

"How did she react when you turned her down?" Max asked.

Still looking at Erica, Ken said, "She said she understood, but I could tell she was disappointed. I felt kind of bad about it. Then I saw her name on the news."

"Did you call the cops and let them know she'd been here?" Erica asked.

He flushed and rubbed his chin. "No."

Max lifted a brow. "Why not?"

Finally, the man's eyes met his. "You're not a cop, right?"

"Not anymore."

Ken shrugged. "I didn't have the time to mess with them coming out and asking a bunch of questions I don't have the answers for. Simple as that. If I thought I could have helped them, I would have called, but she was in and out, and I have no idea where she was going once she walked out my door."

"Did you notice how she got here for her interview?"

Ken pursed his lips. "Came in a little white car.

Someone else was driving. I remember because the car was blocking one of my trucks and I had to wave it out of the way."

"Male or female driver?"

"Couldn't tell." Another shrug. "Didn't look."

"And when was this?"

"About two weeks ago."

"You got security video?"

"Yeah, but it's only good for a week. Then we start over."

Of course.

Max stood. This was getting them nowhere. Erica rose, too, and held out her hand. Ken eagerly took it.

And held on way too long.

Max put a hand on her shoulder and steered her toward the door, forcing the man to release her. "Thanks for your help."

Thanks for nothing.

Kenneth looked disappointed at Max's possessiveness with Erica, and Max felt a dart of satisfaction shoot through him.

Once outside, Erica planted her hands on her hips. "What was that Tarzan routine about?"

He blinked. "He was flirting with you. I thought I'd get you out of there."

She lifted her chin and he braced himself. "I've had men flirt with me before. I can handle it myself, thanks."

What had he done?

His bewilderment must have been stamped on his face because her eyes softened. She dropped her hands from her hips and said, "Just because you kissed me once doesn't give you the right to do this kind of thing."

Kissed her once? He pulled her to him and kissed her thoroughly. He felt her still, held her a bit longer, then set her back from him and said, "Now we've kissed twice. Have I earned that right yet?"

She sputtered and he grinned, enjoying her discomfiture. Finally, she tossed her hands up and shook her head. "I just mean that I can take care of myself in some situations, okay?

"Sure." He paused. "How am I supposed to know the difference between the situations?"

"I'll let you know."

"Right."

Friday morning, Erica woke early and climbed out of bed around five thirty. She'd finally fallen asleep last night out of sheer exhaustion, prayers for Molly's return and Lydia's safety on her lips.

With her bedroom door locked, her gun in the drawer of her end table and Jordan and Max taking shifts playing bodyguard, she'd felt safe.

Safe enough to grab a few hours of much-needed sleep.

After a quick shower and some time with her Bible and her Lord, she dressed and looked out the window to spot Max sitting in his truck, sipping coffee from a thermos top, eyes narrowed and watchful, taking in the area around him. She grabbed her purse and walked out of the house toward him.

When he spotted her, he smiled, yet it didn't reach his eyes, which darted from one end of the street to the

Hide and Seek

other, then back to her. She shivered, the hair on her neck spiking at the danger she sensed could be lurking in the morning shadows. She slipped into the passenger seat. "You can't do this much longer. You're going to wear yourself out."

"I'm a private investigator. I do this all the time."

"Maybe so, but still…"

"It was quiet last night."

She found herself looking at the strong fingers holding the thermos top in a gentle grasp. Just then, her phone rang. It was Denise. Finally calling her back. "Hello?"

"Erica, I'm so sorry it's taken me this long to call you. I guess Peter told you about my dad."

"Yes. Why didn't you let me know you were coming to town? You know I would have been there for you, sat with your father, whatever you needed."

A sigh came over the line. "I know. And I'm sorry. I guess the only-child syndrome kicked in, and I just figured I would handle it myself. And you're busy with your business. I didn't want to impose."

"Impose? Denise. Come on. We're friends."

"I know, I know. Forgive me, please. You're welcome to come help as much as you want." Another quiet sigh. "But truly there's not much to do. The cancer has riddled his body so now we're just waiting for the end. They've upped his morphine, so…"

It was just a matter of time. "I'm so sorry, Denise. What can I do?"

Max shot her a concerned look and she gave a helpless shrug.

"Nothing right now," Denise said, "but I'll let you know if I need something."

"Okay." Erica frowned.

"On a different note, I noticed Peter wasn't looking so great. He's still using?"

"Afraid so."

Denise paused. "Did he ever say anything about Molly?"

Pain seared her. "No. We've discussed this, Denise. I don't think he had anything to do with her disappearance."

"So you say, but after his threats, you have to admit he seemed like the most likely suspect."

"Yes, it seemed so at that time." She left it at that.

"The doctor just walked in. I'd better run."

"Keep me updated."

"Sure," Denise replied, and Erica hung up.

Max looked at her and raised a brow. She shook her head. "Denise has never given up on the idea that Peter was behind Molly's kidnapping." She told him how Peter had come asking for money for a hit and how she'd refused him. "He grabbed me and pushed me into the wall then stole the money out of my purse. It wasn't much and he threatened to get the money one way or another. Molly disappeared about a week later."

He pursed his lips.

"Sounds like she has reason to believe he had something to do with the kidnapping."

"I know. And I'm ashamed to say that I even entertained the thought for a while, but…"

"But?"

"I don't anymore."

"Any proof?"

"Nope. No proof he did it, and no proof he didn't do it. I choose to believe he didn't. Just like you choose to believe Lydia in spite of the evidence against her. So. Are we going to sit here all day or go find some answers?"

He smiled. "I made an appointment to see Red at eleven. She's back at the rehab facility."

"Well, that was easy. I think that's the first thing that's gone our way since all of this started." He cranked the car and pulled away from the curb.

Erica bit her lip then asked a question that had been bugging her. "Has Lydia ever accused you of wanting to control or run her life?"

"Yes, that was every other sentence for a while when she was talking to me. Why?"

"Peter said something along those lines the other night."

"It's a manipulation tactic. The addict tries to throw the guilt back on the person who cares for him, make that person feel guilty for not 'helping' him enough. And then when your help isn't the kind he wants, you're being controlling."

She grunted. "It's rather effective." She nibbled on a thumbnail. "Did it work on you? When Lydia used it?"

"The first few times. Until I caught on." He smirked. "And the crazy thing was, I had studied that stuff in law enforcement, seen it in the families of addicts when I worked the streets. It wasn't until a buddy of mine pointed it out to me that I saw it with Lydia."

Erica sighed and leaned her head back. "I don't want to control his life. I want him to grow up and live his life. I want him to have the life God created him to have."

"I know." He reached over and took her hand in his. The feel of his warm fingers wrapped around hers chased some of the chill from her bones. "The problem is, he has to want that, too."

"Yeah," she whispered, then fell silent.

She was glad Max didn't let go of her hand until he had to put the car in Park. Having someone to talk to, someone to hold her made all the difference in the world to her. She just prayed that when they finally found Lydia, her budding happiness wouldn't come crashing down.

Chapter 12

Red wasn't happy to see them, but Max hoped she'd come around. He and Erica sat across from her on a love seat—the family room had several for visitors. Max had chosen this room for its less-threatening atmosphere.

Staring at Red, he had a feeling not much threatened her. She stared back, measuring, watching.

Erica said, "Thanks for meeting with us."

The girl shrugged. "Got nothing better to do. So what's this about anyway?"

"Lydia Powell," Max said.

Red froze, leaned forward and took another look at Max. Recognition burned across her gaze. She stood. "I got nothing to say to you."

"Wait! Please!" Erica jumped up and raced after Red. She touched her arm and Red spun, but her eyes landed on Max.

"Lydia told me how you called DSS on her and got her taken away from your mother. She told me she never wanted to see you again. So if she's off your radar then good for her." She turned back toward the hall.

Erica blurted, "She's in trouble and you may be the only one who can help."

Red stopped. She turned and this time looked at Erica. "What kind of trouble?"

"You haven't seen the news?"

"No." A frown puckered the skin between her brows. "The news is boring and depressing." Her eyes flicked back and forth between them.

"Lydia's wanted for questioning in a kidnapping," Erica told her.

"Kidnapping!" Red's eyes widened. "She'd never do anything like that."

Satisfaction and relief filled Max at Red's spontaneous outburst. "I know. But the cops don't. That's why I need to find her."

Erica's lips went tight and he could see she didn't agree with him. Or Red. Renewed sadness hit him that Erica truly believed Lydia had something to do with Molly's disappearance. He'd just have to keep working to prove her wrong.

"She doesn't want you to find her," Red snapped.

"Look, Red," Erica intervened. "Lydia may have some answers we desperately need to find this missing child. But it appears that someone doesn't want Lydia found."

Just like with Bea, they told the story of Lydia being attacked at the crack house. And like Bea, concern filled Red's eyes. As painful as it was for Max to think about his sister's difficult journey, it was good for him to know that she'd met people who cared for her, and worried about her. Just like he did.

"I don't know where she is. I saw her about a week ago and she was acting a little weird. I just thought she was back on the dope."

"But she wasn't?"

"I don't know. It would have surprised me because she was so determined to stay clean. She talked about getting a job and proving to you that she isn't the loser you think she is."

Max winced. "I don't think she's a loser."

Red ignored him. "Now that I know all this, she could have been jittery 'cuz she was scared."

Max's phone rang and he grabbed it to shut it off. Then he saw the number. "Excuse me a second." He stepped from the room, leaving Erica and Red staring after him. "Chris, have you found her?"

"No, but we've got a good idea where she was about four o'clock this morning."

"Where?"

"At Erica's office."

"Please, Red," Erica pleaded, trying to keep one eye on Max, "if there's anything else you know, tell me now."

"I'll think about it." The attitude had returned along with the curled lip, and Erica knew she was done here. Erica thought the young woman might know more than she was sharing, but figured she wanted to talk to Lydia before she told too much.

Max waved her over urgently. Erica said goodbye to Red, and told her to call them if she thought of anything. The look on the woman's face made it clear that that probably wasn't going to happen.

In the car, she asked Max, "Can we monitor her calls?"

"I've already thought of that." He waved his phone at her. "Katie's working on getting a court order and I've got her counselor stalling on letting her use the phone until they can get it set up. Katie wants to question Red, but agreed to hold off and see if she makes any phone calls in the next few hours."

"Does she even have that privilege?"

"Yes, she's been good since she's been here."

Erica nodded. "I'd like to go to the hospital to check on Mr. Dougherty."

"Denise's father?"

"Yes."

"So, Tanner is her married name?"

"Denise was married for a brief time, but her husband left her for another woman."

He winced. "When was that?"

"About a year after I was married." She shook her head. "They seemed so happy. I never would have thought he'd do something like that."

"Jerk."

"Definitely. It changed her, of course." Erica sighed. "She cried on my shoulder and I did my best to help her." She bit her lip. "But it was still a terribly hard time. In order to get through it, she focused on her job and ended up pulling away from everyone, including her family—and me. She'd been offered a promotion at one point, but had turned it down because her husband didn't want to move. After he left, there was no reason for her to say no the second time they offered it. And she left. I think it was a huge relief for her. Even though I missed her, I could tell it was the right thing for her."

He shook his head. "It's good you could remain close in spite of the physical distance between you." He took his eyes off the road for a second and studied her. "You look like you could use a bite. Are you hungry?"

"A little," she said, startled that he'd been able to read her needs just by looking at her. It had been a long time since a man other than her brother could do that.

"How about a burger?"

She grimaced. "How about a salad?"

With a grin, he found a drive-through that served a variety of palates and ordered the food.

"We can eat at my office if you want."

"Sounds good."

Five minutes later, he turned left into the office parking lot. "So you think you'll get together with Denise?"

She nodded. "Of course." She gave a small shrug. "Everything fell apart around the same time three years ago. Molly disappeared, then three weeks later, Denise had to leave. She hated it, but had put off going when Molly was kidnapped. She couldn't wait any longer and I had to encourage her to go. She left. My husband didn't seem to care that his daughter was missing…." Her throat wouldn't work. She cleared it. "Let's just say it was a really bad time in my life and I felt all alone."

Max put the car in Park and looked at her, stunned. "Didn't care she was missing? Why not?"

Erica leaned her head back and closed her eyes. Why had she opened that can of worms? She looked at him. "He never wanted her. Not really. Oh, he put on a good show in public, but at home, he basically ignored her. Children didn't fit in with his philosophy of 'life's a party.'"

He blinked. "Why did you marry him?"

She groaned. "I've asked myself that question a million times. We were high school sweethearts. He was handsome and rich and…"

"And?"

She shrugged. "He wanted me. *Me.*" She tapped a finger to her chest. "I'd never had anyone chase after me, make me feel like I was a big deal, like I was special, and I fell hard for that—and him."

Max frowned and she could see his mind spinning. "But what about your brothers? And your parents? You come from a good home."

"My parents provided everything we needed and even a few things people consider luxuries. But they were so consumed with working to make ends meet that they didn't really have time for us kids. Mom was a nurse and took any extra shift she could. Dad was a mechanic and practically lived at his shop." She sighed. "They still work like that. It's crazy." She sniffled and rubbed her eyes. "It wasn't a horrible childhood. I just felt…invisible. Andrew noticed me." She gave another shrug. "I will say this for my parents—they love Molly and have dug into their savings to help try and get her back."

He squeezed her hand and said, "Sounds like your childhood wasn't anything to brag about, either."

She shook her head. "I had it easy compared to you, but you're right—it left some scars. And left me open to Andrew James sweet-talking me and making me feel special. And mistaking that for love. I found out what love was when Molly was born."

"What about Andrew's family?"

"Once he left me, I never heard from them again." She shrugged. "I wasn't good enough for him and neither was Molly. They never really had much to do with us."

"Unbelievable."

Rachel waved from the door and Max released her hand. "Come on. Let's see if we get an inkling of why Lydia would show up at your office in the middle of the night."

As she followed Max into the office, Erica found herself surprised at how easy it had been to talk about Andrew to Max. It wasn't just that he was a good listener—although he was that—it also had to do with the fact that she was finally healing from Andrew's betrayal. Finally letting herself open up to another man. She took a deep breath and offered up a silent prayer. *Please Lord, let this be the right thing to do. Letting Max in my heart means being vulnerable to hurt and disappointment—and I just don't know if I'm strong enough for that. If this isn't what I'm supposed to do, let me know. Soon. Please.*

Max stared at the letter left on the front door. He'd used gloves to pull it from the glass.

Taped there by Lydia.

On Erica's computer, the video footage showed Lydia's face clearly. She wasn't trying to hide. She wanted them to see it was her.

STOP LOOKING FOR ME. LEAVE ME ALONE. I DON'T KNOW ANYTHING ABOUT THAT KIDNAPPING.

"She's scared," Erica whispered. "Look at her face, her eyes."

Erica was right. Lydia's eyes never stopped darting. Her fingers shook as she taped the note to the door.

Max said, "Paranoia is a side effect of the drugs. Could be she thinks someone is after her but no one really is."

"Look at her eyes when she stares at the camera with that pleading look. They're clear, her pupils are normal."

He saw that. "She moved in close. She did that on purpose," he said. "She wanted whoever looked at this video to see she wasn't high."

Erica looked at him. "So if she's innocent, why won't she come in? She knows we're looking for her."

"You saw. She's scared."

"Or, like you pointed out, she's just paranoid because of the drugs."

Max shook his head. "I don't think so."

"Come on, Max, you need to wake up," Erica said, her voice sharp, cutting into him. "She's just like Peter."

Max flinched and stared. "Maybe so, but just like you're not giving up on Peter, I'm not giving up on Lydia."

She snapped her lips shut and closed her eyes. Took a deep breath. "You're right. I'm sorry."

"Apology accepted." He rubbed a hand down his face. "The truth of the matter is, we won't know anything until we find her."

"Then let's hope this video is a step in the right direction."

While Max took a phone call, Erica called Katie and asked about the note that had been mailed to her, the note that had warned Erica to stop searching.

Katie said, "I was going to call you. There were a few prints on the envelope—yours, Max's and Rachel's—but that's all. Whoever wrote the note and put it in the envelope wore gloves. Traces of latex were found as well as powder that's common to rubber gloves."

"So you're saying that's a dead end."

"Unfortunately."

Erica sighed. "Okay, thanks for checking for me. You did that fast, too. I appreciate it."

"I want to find her, too, Erica."

"I know you do."

For some reason, Katie was very attached to Molly's case. She'd worked tirelessly during the first few days and weeks after Molly's disappearance. And she was crushed when she had to move on to other cases when the trail ran cold. Yet she still worked on the case on her own time. Erica figured there was a story there, but Katie had never shared it. And Erica hadn't asked.

"I've got the court order. We're waiting for Allison Redmond—Red—to make a phone call. When she does, we'll trace it."

"Okay, thanks."

"Oh, and I saw Brandon coming out of the police station a while ago. I gave him a file you'll be interested in."

"Perfect. Talk to you soon."

Erica hung up with Katie just as Max stepped into her office. "Anything on Lydia?" she asked.

"Nothing."

"And Bea's all right?"

"Yes. She said everything has been normal."

Erica frowned. "I'm glad."

"So why the frown?"

"My head is spinning. I'm having a hard time figuring out what to do next."

Brandon rapped on the door. She waved him in and he slapped a file on her desk. Then he nodded to her salad. "You need protein."

"It has chicken, Brandon," Erica said, with a warning in her voice.

He grunted and she saw Max duck his head to hide a smile. She grabbed the file. "Is this the file Katie sent?"

"Yes."

Erica opened it. She studied it for a moment then looked up. "Another missing child."

"Yeah. She's making a referral. Said they were at their wits' end and maybe you would have some luck with it."

Erica sighed. "I don't have the time. I'm consumed with this new lead on Molly."

"Want me to take it?"

"You feel up to it?"

He rolled his eyes and snagged the file back from her. "I feel up to it." He glanced back at her. "What are we doing for Thanksgiving?"

"Our usual, I suppose. Have you talked to Mom or Dad?"

He grimaced. "No. Not lately."

"Everyone can come to my house," she said. "It needs some cheering up."

He nodded and she saw Max watching them, his eyes following their volley. When Brandon left, he stood.

"You're good at what you do." She lifted a brow and

Max shrugged. "Brandon and Jordan both respect you. They listen to you."

"You mean underneath the rolling of the eyes and overprotective instincts?"

A small smile played around the corners of his mouth. "Yeah."

She returned the smile. "You're right, they do." She spread her hands. "I'm a delegator. I see past the forest to the individual trees."

"And yet you see the big picture, too."

"Most of the time." She let out a sigh. "And sometimes I can't see anything but a big impenetrable brick wall."

"Finding Molly?"

"Finding Molly."

Silence sat between them for a moment before Rachel stuck her head in the door. "Someone here to see you."

"Who?"

"Me."

Denise Tanner stepped from behind Rachel and gave Erica a wide smile. Joy rushed through her, and she quickly crossed the office to give her friend a tight hug. "Oh, Denise, I'm so glad to see you."

"I hoped you wouldn't mind me stopping by."

"Of course not." She turned to Max and introduced him.

"This is Max Powell. He's a private investigator… and a good friend. He's helping me track down a new lead on Molly."

"A new lead?" Denise leaned forward, eyes intent.

"Yes. Have you seen the news?"

"No. I've been so busy with Dad I haven't had a moment to do anything normal like watch TV or catch up with friends."

Erica told her about the new evidence, and Denise brushed away tears. "Oh goodness, that's the craziest thing ever. I'm praying it pans out. Do the police have anything else at all besides this girl, Lydia?"

"No. That's why we need to find her."

"You'll find her. I have no doubt about that." She turned to Max. "Erica's like Midas, you know. Everything she touches turns to gold. It's a quality I've envied for years." She gave a light laugh.

Erica tilted her head. "Why would you say that?"

Denise shrugged. "It's true. I always wanted to be like you when we were in high school."

Shocked, Erica stared at her friend. "What? You're kidding. But you're super successful."

"I am now, but when we were growing up, I was always in your shadow." She stood. "But I have you to thank for my success. Wanting to be like you made me work extra hard. You were a huge influence in my life."

Denise's words floored her. She gaped. Max laughed. "I think you've managed to make her speechless."

"I've needed to say those words for a long time now." She wiped a tear. "Okay, enough with the mushy stuff. I won't keep you any longer. I just took a break and ran over here to see you."

Erica gave her friend another hug. "I'm so glad you did. Please let me know if I can do anything for you."

"I will." She shrugged. "Right now it's just hurry up and wait. It's sad, but it's his time and I think I've finally accepted that." Denise smiled at Max. "Nice to meet you."

"You, too."

After Denise left, Erica dropped into her chair. "Well. That was interesting."

Max stepped over and sat across from her. "See? You never know whose life you're going to impact. I'm not surprised she had such great things to say. I've come to discover just how wonderful you really are."

She felt the flush climb up her neck, but forced herself to meet his eyes. "I think you're pretty wonderful, too, Max."

He reached across the desk and snagged her fingers. Just as he opened his mouth, her phone rang. Shooting him an apologetic glance, she checked the number. "It's Katie."

He sat back. "You'd better take it."

Erica snatched the phone. "Hello?"

"Red called a pay phone located at the mall."

Excitement zipped along her spine. "Are you on the way?"

"We are. And we've got the stores pulling video even as we speak. Detective Lee is on Red at the rehab center."

Erica chewed on her lip. "You think you'll get there in time?"

"I don't know. We're trying to be subtle, go in quiet and see if we can spot her."

"Okay, call me as soon as you know something."

"I will."

Erica hung up and looked into Max's expectant face. "They traced the call."

"Then let's go."

Erica stood. "I'm worried if Lydia's been watching the news, she may recognize Katie or Detective Lee. If she sees them, she'll run."

He ran a hand over his face and pinched the bridge of his nose. "If she sees me, she'll run for sure."

Erica hesitated only a second. "Let's chance it."

He nodded and she followed him out the door.

Chapter 13

The drive to the mall took about ten minutes. Erica shifted on the seat, impatient to be doing something, anything. She was so tired of waiting on someone else to call with news. She wanted to find Lydia herself.

And yet she didn't want to do anything that would send the girl running. But how could she convince Lydia to talk to her if she couldn't even make contact?

Her phone rang and she snatched it. Denise said, "Are you still willing to help?"

"Of course."

"It was so good seeing you. I've missed you."

"I've missed you, too." Her friend paused. Erica asked, "What do you need, Denise?"

"Do you think we could meet for dinner tonight?"

"Sure." Why would Denise hesitate over asking that question? "You want me to come to the hospital?"

"If you don't mind."

Erica could hear the tears in Denise's voice and her heart broke for her friend. She'd been particularly close to her father, and this had to be killing her. "No problem. What time?"

"Five thirty in the cafeteria?"

"I'll be there." She hung up and looked at Max. "Denise wants me to meet her for dinner."

"I'm glad you two will have a chance to catch up a little."

"I am, too. I'm glad she finally asked me to do something, offered a way for me to help her."

"You're a good friend, Erica."

Max parked and they walked into the food court. Erica pushed the phone call with Denise aside as her nerves hummed. Would this be the day she finally found Lydia and learned what happened to Molly?

With her throat tight and her stomach cramped, Erica ignored her anxiety and scanned the crowd as they walked from the car into the food court. People sat at tables and chatted, others stood in the long lines waiting to order. Erica simply wanted to see Lydia's face.

"She used a pay phone over there," Max said after consulting his phone.

"Have they spotted her yet?"

"No."

Erica felt her hopes start to disintegrate. It was too late. There was no way Lydia would still be hanging around the mall.

"Security has her picture," Max said as his eyes probed the area. Erica could feel the tension, the hope, radiating from him.

"We need to find her."

"I know."

Max's phone rang. He listened for a brief second then his eyes caught hers. "That was Chris. They found Peter's car abandoned on the outskirts of town in an old barn. Guy who owns the place found it and called it in."

"Then it probably wasn't Peter driving it. Or shooting at us."

He shrugged. "There's a good possibility it wasn't him. Then again, he could be the one who abandoned the car."

"I really don't think it was."

He gave her a sad smile. "And I really don't think Lydia was involved with the kidnapping. I hope we're both right."

His words hurt, and she grimaced. Just because they'd grown close in this search for his sister and her daughter didn't mean he had to change his mind to her way of thinking. And she'd better remember that if she didn't want to wind up with a broken heart. Lydia came first for him. And that's the way it probably should be. She couldn't help the small selfish wish that she'd come first for someone.

His phone rang again. He listened, and hung up. "They think they spotted her over near the arcade."

Erica pushed aside her pity party and checked the mall map. She headed in the direction of the arcade, Max following close behind. Security descended and Erica clenched her jaw. "I thought they were going to be subtle."

"I did, too." He didn't look pleased. "Stay with me."

"Wouldn't it be better if we split up?"

He grasped her fingers. "I don't want to take a chance on losing you."

Losing her? A tingle shot through her in spite of the circumstances. She didn't want to lose him, either. But what if Lydia *was* involved? How would he feel about her then? And how would she feel about him?

She pulled away. "Don't be silly. Security's all over this area." She looked around. "Which is why she wouldn't stay here."

Max sucked in a deep breath. Katie broke away from a group of teens and walked toward them. "She was here. As recently as fifteen minutes ago."

Hope leaped. "Then we have a chance of finding her."

Max's eyes narrowed. "Is there a back door to this place?"

Katie nodded. "I've got officers on it."

"She saw security coming toward her and took off." She nodded toward the officer who stood near the entrance. "He said she acted like she was waiting on someone."

"Red?" Erica asked.

Katie shook her head. "Red can't leave the rehab center. If she does, leaves before she completes the program, her parents take a loss on what they've paid for her to be there."

"Doesn't mean she wouldn't do it," Max muttered.

"True, but I already called and they said Red was in the social room playing a game of chess with her grandfather."

"So if not Red, who?"

Max sighed and shook his head. "I have no idea."

Katie's radio buzzed and she listened. Her eyes snapped to Erica. "Go to the nearest exit and get out."

"Why?"

"We've got a bomb threat."

Erica gasped. Max grabbed her hand. He asked, "Where?"

"The caller didn't say. We're trying to get a trace on where the call came from." She motioned toward the door. "Security will be evacuating the mall immediately."

No sooner had she spoken than the mall intercom came on announcing the building was closing due to a gas leak. "Please leave in an orderly fashion through the nearest exit."

"Gas leak?" Erica asked.

"Saying there was a bomb threat would cause a stampede," Max said. He cast a glance around. "This isn't a coincidence."

"I know." Katie frowned at him. "You were followed."

"Possibly."

They fell in with the moving crowd, and Erica glanced behind her. "We can't leave yet. We have to find her."

"She's not here any longer," Max stated with certainty.

"You don't know that."

"Yeah, I do."

"You can't." Erica stepped to the side, desperation urging her onward. She simply couldn't leave yet. Not yet. She pushed her way through the throng of people to go in the opposite direction.

"Erica!"

Max's frustrated shout made her grimace, but she couldn't leave without searching for the girl who might have answers about Molly.

She didn't believe there was a bomb.

But what if there was? Was she acting irresponsibly?

Max finally caught up with her as she caught a glimpse of Katie searching the arcade area. Erica rushed toward the detective. "Anything?"

Katie spun. "What are you still doing here?"

"There's no bomb, Katie. It's a trick."

"Doesn't matter. You need to get out." Her eyes flashed. "Get her out of here, Max."

He grasped her upper arm. "Come on, Erica."

"But Lydia—"

"We'll find her. Just not like this." Concern hardened into determination.

And Erica realized something. He was just as determined to find Lydia as she was, and he wasn't going to leave her behind. If there was a bomb, she wasn't only risking her life, but his, as well. She couldn't do that. The thought of him being hurt because of her insistence that they stay in the midst of danger nearly smothered her with fear. "Let's go."

She let him pull her back into the crowd heading for the exit.

"Why would someone call in a—" she glanced around at the listening ears nearby "—gas leak?"

He understood her question and shook his head. "I don't know. Unless it was to smoke Lydia out, but the person wouldn't have any idea where she was in the mall or which door she would leave by."

The crowd shoved and pushed toward the exit. Erica grabbed Max's arm to keep her balance. He steadied her and she was grateful for his support.

"Erica?"

She twisted to see who was calling her.

"What's wrong?" Max asked.

"I thought I heard someone call my name."

Max looked behind her, but she didn't think he'd be able to spot anyone in this mess.

"Erica! Stop!"

This time he heard it. He swiveled his head and looked behind them.

"Do you see anyone?"

"No. Let's get outside and we'll see if we can figure out who's calling you." He turned back, keeping an arm around her shoulders, and she realized he was doing his best to protect her from the smothering press of bodies.

Just a few more feet and they'd be out the door.

A sudden stinging sensation in her lower back had her spinning and losing her balance.

"What is it?" Max asked as he righted her.

"Something stung me."

His eyes narrowed. "What?"

"My back. It hurt. I—" Dizziness hit her, her throat tightened. Awareness and fear struck at the same time. She gasped, "EpiPen."

He caught on fast. "Where?"

"Purse," she managed to squeak out as her airway closed and darkness took over.

Max had known fear in his life, but it was nothing compared to what he felt at the sight of the blue tinge appearing around Erica's lips. She went limp and he caught her. His heart pounded. He had to get her help and fast.

Pushing his way through the crowd, apologizing for shoving and trampling on toes, he made it to the sidewalk, dropped to his knees and laid her down. He grabbed her purse from her shoulder and dumped the contents beside her.

"Sir? You need to move—" The officer stopped. "What's wrong with her?"

"Not sure." He snatched the EpiPen from the concrete. "Call an ambulance."

"Got one standing by. You'll have to get her to it. I can't let them down here with a bomb threat."

Max nodded. "I know." The officer got on the radio while Max uncapped the EpiPen and jabbed Erica in the thigh.

Within seconds, the wheezing eased and a bit of color came back into her cheeks. Her eyes opened, but looked glazed and unfocused. "Erica, hang in there, honey. I've got to get you out of here. EMTs are waiting, okay?"

She gave him no response other than to shut her eyes. He threw the contents of her purse back into the bag. The officer grabbed it while Max picked her up. Sweat rolled down his back in spite of the chilly temperatures as he rushed toward the ambulance waiting a safe distance away.

Heart pounding, legs pumping, Max reached the ambulance as Erica began to stir. "What—?"

"Hold still. You passed out."

"Bees," she mumbled. "Allergic."

The sting she said she'd felt on her back.

He motioned for the EMT to roll her to her side. With

gentle fingers, he lifted the edge of her shirt to look at her lower back. "There." He pointed to a red-and-white welt that looked like a bee sting.

The paramedic frowned as they rolled her back into place. "It's November. And cold. Shouldn't be any bees around here."

Max's blood whooshed through his veins. He had a bad feeling about the whole bee-sting emergency.

The EMT placed the oxygen tubing in her nose and cranked the air. "Let's get her to the hospital. She needs to be monitored for the next few hours."

Max nodded. "I'll ride with her. I need to call her brother, too."

While he watched the paramedic work on Erica, making sure she continued to breathe, Max called Brandon.

The man answered on the third ring. "Hello?" He sounded out of breath.

"This is Max. I'm on the way to the hospital with Erica."

"What happened?" Worry coated Brandon's question.

"A bee sting."

Brandon gave a snort. "In this weather?"

"Yeah. Weird, right? We'll figure it out after we know she's all right."

"I'll meet you there."

Max rubbed a hand down his face and said a prayer for Erica. The ambulance pulled into the Emergency entrance and within minutes Erica had been whisked away behind secure doors. Max filled out as much of the paperwork as he could, but had to admit relief when Brandon burst through the door. Max waved him over.

"How is she? Where is she?"

"Looks like she'll be all right. I was worried there for a few minutes." Worried sick. Scared he'd failed her. Maybe he didn't need to worry about her working with the homeless. Maybe he needed to worry more about her being with him while he was looking for Lydia.

A sigh slipped out as he settled back to wait. And ponder the next step in the investigation. They needed to figure something out and fast. Erica had almost died. Whoever was targeting her was getting more bold. The thought terrified him.

He looked over at Brandon, who sat beside him. Quiet. Lost in his own thoughts.

"How's the gunshot wound?" Max asked.

Brandon shrugged. "It's healing. I turn the wrong way and I pay for it, but other than that…" He paused. "Do you mind if I ask you a question?"

"Shoot…er…go for it."

Brandon gave a wry grin then turned serious again. "What's with you and Erica?"

Max looked toward the door that had swung shut behind her. "I…she's…we're…"

"Friends?"

"Yes." Max jumped on that.

"More than friends?"

"Yes," he admitted more slowly. He looked Brandon in the eye. "I like her. A lot. And—" he rubbed his suddenly sweaty hands down his thighs "—I think I could love her."

Brandon didn't look surprised. "She's easy to love, but she can drive you crazy."

Max smiled. "Yeah."

Brandon let out a slow whistle. "You've got it bad, don't you?"

The door that led to the E.R. opened and a woman in a white lab coat stepped through, saving Max from having to answer that one. "Brandon?"

Brandon jumped to his feet. "That's me."

Max stood more slowly, trying to read the doctor's face. Brandon asked, "How is she?"

The woman hesitated for a moment. "She's going to be fine."

"But…?" Max asked.

The doctor tilted her head, motioning the men to follow her into a small conference room. "I'm Doctor Caroline Watson. Erica had a reaction to what appears to be a bee sting."

"She's been allergic since she was a kid," Brandon said.

Dr. Watson nodded. "Good thing she carried that EpiPen with her or she wouldn't be here with us."

Max's stomach dropped to his toes. Brandon's face paled. The doctor went on. "I have a real concern about this."

"What's that?"

"I've examined the wound site carefully." She shook her head. "I may be wrong, but it looks like she was injected with bee venom. There's a clear needle puncture in the middle of the welt—it's not a sting from a bee itself." Her eyes took in both men. "That means some-one did this to her. On purpose."

Brandon exhaled and caught Max's eye. Max felt a little nauseous at hearing his suspicions voiced. Dr. Watson asked, "You might want to find out if she's involved in something she shouldn't be involved in."

That was a given.

"We'll take care of it."

"I'll have to file a police report."

"Of course. We'll talk to them, too." Max swallowed hard.

"We're going to keep her overnight for observation, but she should be all right to go home in the morning."

Brandon said, "I'll get Rachel to come stay with her."

"Not your mother?" Max asked.

Brandon's eyes shuttered. "No."

Max realized he should have kept his mouth shut. "Right."

The doctor's brow lifted but she didn't ask. Instead, she said, "You want to see her?"

"Yes."

The word flew from Max's lips.

He chose to ignore Brandon's amused look and answered his ringing phone.

Chapter 14

Erica groaned. Her head throbbed and her mouth felt dry as wool. As she gathered her thoughts, memory returned. She'd been stung. By something.

Her memory stopped there.

A knock on the door forced her to drag her eyes open. Darkness greeted her. It was nighttime?

"Erica?"

Brandon.

"Come in." She heard the croak in her voice but couldn't seem to turn up the volume. Brandon pushed the door open and stepped inside. Max followed, and Erica tried to sit up a little. When her muscles simply wouldn't cooperate, she gave up and studied them. Two men she cared for very much.

They both looked drawn and worried. Weary.

Max stepped to the side of her bed and gripped her

fingers. Her heart picked up speed to match the pounding in her head. The feel of his hand wrapped around hers gave her comfort. And even felt like a possible lifeline in the midst of everything. He asked, "How are you feeling?"

"Like I've been hit by a truck."

"You've been out for a while."

She tilted her head. "And you've been busy. Did you find Lydia?" Strength returned at the thought.

"No. But Katie called. She watched the mall video and got a pretty good shot of someone working their way through the crowd to get behind you."

She frowned. "Okay. Who?" Brandon and Max exchanged a look. "Who?" she demanded.

"Peter," Max finally said.

"Peter?" she whispered. "But why?" She remembered thinking someone had called her name. "He was there?"

"Yes. Clear as a bell, and it was obvious he was trying to get close to you. As soon as he did, that's when you cried out and said something stung you." Max sighed. "I was so busy trying to get you out the door and keep you from getting trampled, I didn't see him."

"But he's on the video."

"Yes."

"What about Lydia?"

Brandon nodded. "We watched the video of the arcade room. She was definitely there and it looked like she was waiting for someone." He ran a hand over his eyes. "And Peter was there, too."

Max squeezed her fingers. "Erica, someone definitely injected you with bee venom."

She swallowed hard, grateful she could. The sensation of her throat closing up was one of the worst she'd ever experienced. "Then that means whoever did this is someone who knows me pretty well and knows that I'm allergic to bees."

"Which means it could be Peter."

"No." She shook her head. "He wouldn't do that. He has no reason to kill me." Another exchanged look between the men grated on her nerves. Brandon looked torn, not wanting to believe it, either, but he was a black-and-white personality. He'd seen the video, and she knew he wasn't convinced Peter was innocent. "Where *is* Peter?"

"We don't know. We're looking for him."

"Seems like we're looking for everyone without much success," she muttered.

No one argued with her.

The knock on the door made her jump. Max took a defensive stance and Brandon moved to open it.

It took Erica a moment to process whom she was seeing. "Mom?" she gasped.

Brandon stood with his mouth open.

Shelby Ann Hayes stood five feet five inches tall. She had her auburn curls pulled away from her face with two clips. Erica thought she spotted some gray at the temples.

The woman smiled and approached the bed. "Saw your name on the chart and thought I'd come see how you were doing."

Erica tried to remember the last time she'd seen her mother. At least a year, maybe longer. "What are you doing here?" She blurted the words, then wanted to re-call them.

Shelby stopped, her confident expression fading to uncertainty. "Like I said, I just wanted to see how you were doing."

Max stepped to the side like he might slip out the door. Erica grabbed his hand. For some reason, she wanted—no, needed—his support. Brandon still gaped like he couldn't find enough oxygen. Then his mouth snapped shut and his face reddened. "Since when do you care?"

Her mother sighed and said softly, "I care, Brandon. So does your father. We did the best we could."

And Erica thought maybe they had. Her parents had just been too young to have kids. At sixteen Shelby Hayes should have been a cheerleader, not a mother.

"It's a little late," Brandon growled.

"No. It's not," Erica countered. She met her mother's eyes, suddenly sick of the distance, the roller-coaster emotions associated with her parents. And Erica had been the one who pulled away after Molly went miss-ing—she couldn't blame her parents for that.

Her mother had offered an olive branch of sorts. Erica decided to take it. "I'm doing all right. I'll prob-ably go home tomorrow."

"Do you need anything?"

"No. But thanks."

Her mother looked uncertain, nervous and agitated. She kept shooting glances at Brandon, then at Max. Erica introduced him while Brandon glared.

"Well." Shelby backed toward the door, which Bran-don didn't waste any time opening. "I guess I'll check on you later. Or in the morning...or sometime."

"Sure, Mom. You do that." The woman turned to leave and Erica called, "Wait!" Her mother looked back over her shoulder and Erica shifted forward on the bed. "Do you know where Peter is?"

Shelby's shoulders slumped in defeat. "No. I've tried to call him several times over the past couple of months. He hasn't called me back."

"If you hear from him, will you call me?"

"I'll call."

Erica felt the shock set in after her mother had left the room. Brandon stepped toward her. "Why are you being nice to her?"

She stared at him. "I'm tired of being mad at her."

"Mad? You should hate her."

Erica looked at Max. "For what, Brandon? Working all the time to support us? At least she was never on drugs, we had warm beds to sleep in and she occasionally hugged us." She swallowed hard. "She wasn't a great mother, and Dad wouldn't win any Father of the Year awards, but they were kids when they had us. They didn't want children, Brandon, but they didn't give us up or separate us or abuse us."

His jaw never softened. "Maybe we would have been better off if they had. Given us up, I mean."

"I refuse to dwell on it. The past is the past."

He stared at her, suspicious and curious. "This seems awfully sudden."

Erica picked at the blanket. "They were crazy about Molly. You saw that yourself. At Christmas they overspent. They treated her like they never treated us. I don't understand it, but maybe it's because they're finally grown up and want to make amends."

"You do what you want. I don't want them back in my life."

"Let go of the anger, Brandon. It won't do you any good."

He grunted. "I'm going to get a cup of coffee." He strode out the door without looking back.

End of discussion.

Erica shook her head then looked at Max. "I need to call Denise and tell her I'm not going to be able to meet her at five thirty."

"Yeah." He shoved his hands in his pockets. "What was all that about letting the past be the past?"

She sighed and leaned her head back against the pillow. "I'm just tired of being angry with them. Sometimes you just have to let things go."

Max nodded, a pensive look on his face. "Yeah, I guess sometimes you do."

"What is it?"

He shrugged. "At least she cares."

Erica stared at him. Her mother would win Mother of the Year award compared to his. "She does, and it's time for Brandon and me—and Peter—to understand and forgive." If Peter wasn't the one trying to kill her. Pain shot through her at the thought, but almost instantly, she realized she didn't believe it. "I want to talk to Peter."

"I know."

"I don't believe he would try to hurt me."

"I know that, too." He leaned over and placed a soft kiss on her lips. "You're an amazing woman."

Erica placed a hand on the back of his neck and pulled him in for another kiss. Then she smiled at him. "You're pretty amazing yourself."

Max cleared his throat and stepped toward the door. "I'd better let you get some rest."

"I'm not sleepy." She yawned and he laughed.

"Right. I won't be gone long."

Erica nodded and closed her eyes. Maybe she would just rest her eyes for a bit.

Just a short nap while she felt safe and the person who wanted her dead couldn't get to her.

Max watched Erica sleep, his emotions in turmoil. Someone had tried to kill her. Just like someone had killed Tracy. His heart shuddered at the memory, and his fingers curled into fists.

But the person after Erica wasn't someone she'd worked with at the homeless shelter.

This was worse.

This was someone she knew.

But who?

He didn't know her well enough to mentally make a list of people close to her who would know about her allergy.

But he thought it odd her mother would decide to pay her a visit. It was such an out-of-the-blue thing. And yet, maybe not. After all, the woman worked at the hospital and she really did care about her children.

And then there was Peter.

A light rap on the door caught his attention. He rose to open it and found Denise Tanner. She frowned, as if surprised to find him in Erica's room. "I got your message. Is Erica okay?"

"She's all right, but she's sleeping right now." Max stepped out into the hall and shut the door behind him.

Denise twisted her fingers together. "My dad's taken

a turn for the worse, but I wanted to run up and check on Erica."

"It could have been a lot worse. But she'll make a full recovery."

Denise placed a hand over her heart. "Oh, thank goodness."

"I'll tell her you came by. And I'm sorry about your father, Denise."

She nodded. "Thanks. I'm going back down to be with him, but please call me if you need anything."

Max thanked her and she left.

He went back to Erica. He'd stay with her until Rachel arrived to spend the night. After the doctor had filed her report with the police, and Max had spoken with Chris, an officer was posted at Erica's door. She would have protection tonight.

Her auburn curls lay spread around her, looking like they could set the pillow on fire at any moment. Long, pale lashes lay against her cheeks. She looked peaceful. Untroubled.

He ran a finger down her arm. *Please keep her safe, Lord. My heart's in too deep. If something happens to her, I don't think I'll recover.*

Max vowed to stick as close to her as possible and catch the person responsible for the chaos that had become their lives.

No matter who it was.

The next morning Max beat Brandon to the hospital and into Erica's room by mere seconds. He flashed his ID to the officer standing outside her room, glad to see he was still on duty. As he knocked and pushed open the door, Brandon rounded the corner.

He held the door for the man then stepped in at Erica's welcome. She sat on the bed looking much better than the night before. In fact, she looked great. Alive. Whole. Healthy.

Beautiful.

He wanted to grab her into his arms and never let her go.

She looked up and gave him a wan smile as he stepped in. Rachel sat in the chair frowning. "I'm trying to talk Erica into going home," Rachel said. "But she wants to work her shift at the homeless shelter."

Max felt his heart hit his toes. Holding on to Erica might not be an option. Not if she insisted on continuing her work with the homeless.

Maybe that was selfish, but how could he forget the past and move on? Tracy had gone to work at the shelter that evening, just like she did every Thursday night. Max had been working and when she didn't call to let him know she was home, he'd wondered, but had been knee-deep in a drunk driving accident and hadn't had time to call her until two hours later.

She hadn't answered. Chris Jiles had been called to the scene of her murder then had been the one to break the news to Max.

The investigation had found that Tracy's murderer had followed her from the shelter. He was one of the regulars. He'd also been in need of a fix. At the trial, he'd wept. He hadn't meant to kill her, but she'd fought him when he'd tried to rob her. He'd pushed her down and she'd cracked her head on the sidewalk. She'd died from a broken neck.

Every time Erica walked out the door, he'd wonder if she'd be back. He couldn't live like that. And it wasn't that he still thought every person at the shelter was a criminal or a murderer. It was just his memories of Tracy and how she didn't make it home, memories that still haunted him. It seemed the closer he got to Erica, the more he thought about what had happened to Tracy, and how he was sure he could never go through something like that again.

He tried to hide his reaction to Rachel's announcement. "Why don't you get some rest first? If you collapse at the shelter you won't be doing anyone any good." He paused. "And besides, who's to say your attacker doesn't know your schedule? He could be waiting at the shelter."

"Or he could be down in the lobby waiting for me to walk out the front door. I have no doubt he knows I'm here."

"You have an officer on this room," Max argued, feeling his protective instincts kicking in. "When you leave here, you won't have police protection."

She bit her lip and her forehead creased. Her cousin nodded. "He's right, Erica. You need to stay safe and stay away from the shelter until you find out who's behind all this."

This time Erica scowled. "You don't like me working there, either."

Rachel sighed and shrugged. "Just think about it."

"I have." She rubbed her face and looked at Rachel. "Will you call and tell them I'm not coming?"

"Sure." Rachel pulled her cell phone from her pocket and excused herself from the room.

Max couldn't deny the rush of relief he felt at her sensible response. But what about the next time? What about after her attacker was caught and she didn't have to worry so much about her safety?

Brandon spoke for the first time since entering the room. "I think not going to the shelter is a wise decision. You need to go home and rest, Erica."

"But there's so much to do. Lydia's still missing. And Peter. And Molly." Tears welled in her eyes and Max had to hold himself back from taking her in his arms right there. Instead, he reached for her hand.

Squeezing her fingers, he said, "The cops are looking for Peter. They'll find him. And we'll find Lydia. I've got calls in all over the place and friends are looking for her. She can't stay hidden forever."

"It feels like she can," Erica said.

From the door, Rachel said, "I forgot."

Erica looked at her. "Forgot what?"

"Peter called, looking for you yesterday. I told him you were heading for the mall. That's how he knew how to find you."

"Did he say what he wanted?"

"No. And I didn't ask." She cast her eyes toward the floor then back up. "I figured he just wanted money."

Erica swallowed hard, and Max wanted nothing more than to take her in his arms and hold her. But since he couldn't do that, he did the one thing he could.

"Come on and I'll take you home."

Brandon lifted a brow. "Well, since I'm not needed as a taxi, I'll check all of Peter's known drug connections."

"And you'll let me know as soon as you know something?" Erica asked.

"Of course."

She sighed. "Then all right. I'll go home."

Max saw her frustration, felt her impatience. After Brandon left, he sat on the edge of the bed and took her hand in his once again. "Everyone is fighting hard to make sure you stay safe."

Her eyes softened and she nodded. "I know and I appreciate it."

He leaned in and placed his forehead against hers. "I don't want anything to happen to you."

Erica met his gaze then shifted so she could give him a light kiss. Max raised a hand to cup her chin and deepened the kiss, needing to tell Erica how he felt about her without words. Then he pulled back and gathered her close.

He relished the moment with her in his arms. But he couldn't help but wonder how long she would stay home before thoughts of Molly sent her searching once again—and right into the arms of danger.

Chapter 15

Erica woke in her own bed with a start. Heart pounding, she listened. Footsteps, the hardwood creaking, a drawer closing. Anger surged.

Peter.

How had he gotten past the officer sitting outside watching her house? Max had dropped her off so he could continue searching for Lydia. And Peter.

Only it looked like Peter had come to find her before Max could find him.

Erica snagged her weapon from her bedside table and shoved it in the back of her sweatpants. She had no intention of shooting her brother, but if he was high, there was no telling what kind of trouble he'd be.

Maybe the gun would be enough to scare him.

On silent, bare feet, she padded down the hall toward the noise, ignoring the slight dizziness and residual weakness she felt.

At the entrance to the den, she paused. Listened.

And heard voices.

Her rushing adrenaline slowed, but her pulse skittered as she recognized the first voice. Max.

Then Brandon and Jordan.

Erica leaned against the wall and closed her eyes as her blood pressure returned to normal.

It wasn't Peter.

She took a deep breath and ran a hand through her curls. Then did it again and again until she felt presentable. Max didn't need to see her with the rat's-nest, just-rolled-out-of-bed look. Then she felt heat invade her cheeks and wondered why she cared.

But she knew exactly why. There was no denying it.

In spite of their conflicting interests in finding his sister and his issues with the homeless shelter, she had feelings for Max Powell. And she wanted to look nice. She turned and walked back down the hall to her room where she changed into a pair of denim capris and a green shirt she knew brought out the color of her eyes.

With one final look in the mirror and an eye roll at her vanity, she headed back to the den.

Max sat on one end of the couch and Jordan on the other. Brandon sat in the recliner. He looked up when she walked in. "You decided to join us?"

"Didn't know there was anyone to join."

"You were snoring pretty good in there," Brandon teased.

She resisted the urge to revert to her childhood habit of sticking her tongue out and simply rolled her eyes at him. "What's with the good-morning welcoming committee?"

"Wanted to make sure you were safe," Jordan said.

"So all three of you had to come over?" She crossed her arms. "What gives?"

Max quirked a smile at her. "We got a lead on Lydia."

Erica dropped her arms. "Then what are we waiting for? Let's go get her."

"Bea called and said Lydia got in touch with her and is going to come by her house," Max said.

"When?"

"In a couple of hours."

"So what's the plan?"

"We just finished setting that up," Jordan said and stood. "I'm going to Bea's house. I'll let you know when I have Lydia."

Jordan walked right out of the room without another word as Erica gaped. "Wait a minute. What's going on?" She looked at Max. "Aren't we going?"

He shook his head. "You and I are being watched. Brandon, Jordan and I discussed this and we think it's best if the two of them grab her. I don't want to take a chance on leading anyone to Bea's house."

"And you don't think someone will follow Jordan?"

Brandon stood. "That's where I come in. I'm going to make sure he's not followed."

Erica swallowed. "And you'll call the minute you have her?"

"Of course."

She nodded. "All right. I don't like it, but I have to admit it might work. She won't be looking for you guys."

"Exactly." Brandon leaned over and kissed her forehead. "Take care."

"You be careful. You're still healing from one gunshot wound—you don't need another."

He grinned at her and flexed his arm. "Good as new." But she caught the slight grimace before he turned his back.

"I mean it, Brandon."

"I know you do." He looked at Max. "Keep her safe."

Max nodded and Brandon left.

Erica slumped onto the couch next to Max. "I hate this waiting. It reminds me so much of the first few weeks after Molly disappeared."

He wrapped an arm around her shoulders and leaned in to place a kiss on the top of her head. "I know. But hopefully this time it's going to pay off."

"I miss her so much," she whispered. "Even after three years, I miss her with an ache that feels like it'll never heal."

Max pulled her close so that she could rest her cheek against his chest. He smelled good. Woodsy and spicy all at the same time. She appreciated his attempt to comfort her. She looked up to find him gazing at her. Their noses touched and she drew in a deep breath. Then his lips were on hers. She reveled in the softness, the comfort he was trying to express. When he lifted his head, she wanted to pull him back. Instead she sighed and snuggled against him.

His hand stroked her hair and they sat in silence for several minutes. Then he said, "I noticed your Bible on the end table by the recliner."

"Mmm-hmm."

"Is that how you've stayed strong through everything?"

"Yes." She picked at a piece of nonexistent lint on his shirt. "I don't understand why God allowed Molly to be kidnapped. At first I thought maybe it was because I wasn't a good enough mother, that I was doing something wrong and that He was punishing me by taking her away from me."

His arms tightened. "I'm sorry."

"I kept reading the Bible, trying to find out how I could make things right. How I could make God love me again so that He would send Molly back to me." She felt a tear slide across her nose. She sniffed.

"What did you find?"

"I found that God didn't take Molly away because I'd done something wrong or been a bad mother." She raked a hand through her hair. "And I learned that if God loved me enough to send His son to the cross before I was even born, then He loved me unconditionally."

"How long did it take you to discover that?"

"It took about a year for me to believe it. Especially after Andrew walked out."

"What finally convinced you?"

She smiled against his chest then pulled back to look into his eyes. "One of the most well-known verses in the Bible. John 3:16."

"'For God so loved the world that He gave His only Son…'"

"'…that whoever believes in Him will never die, but have everlasting life,'" she finished. "It hit me that He died for me before I was even born. For me. Molly's disappearance didn't take God by surprise. Could He have stopped it? Yes. But He didn't and I have to admit, that hurts. I don't always understand his ways, but I choose to believe Him when He says He has a plan for everyone. And that includes Molly."

"What if she's…"

"Dead?"

"Yeah."

Erica heaved a sigh. "I know it's possible. It's possible she died the day she disappeared." She swallowed past the lump in her throat. "I'm not out of touch with reality. I know the statistics when it comes to missing children. So…if she's dead, then I'll have to figure out how to move on. Somehow, I'll have to let God be my strength, because I'm not strong enough to do it on my own." The last sentence was a mere whisper. She wasn't even sure she'd said it aloud.

He pressed a kiss to the top of her head and said, "I want to be here for you, too, Erica."

Longing gripped her. "I want that, too, Max." She leaned back from his embrace, immediately missing his warmth. "But let's see what happens with Lydia before we go any further."

"I don't know that I want to do that."

She stared at him. "Well, I think we have to. We have no idea how this is all going to turn out, and I don't want to put you in the position of having to choose between Lydia and me."

Max pulled her back against him while he thought about what Erica had said. Even as he held her, he wondered what he'd do if it came down to making that choice.

He couldn't abandon Lydia. He wouldn't give up on her.

And he couldn't give up this woman who had so

filled his heart in such a short time that he was almost willing to call his feelings for her *love*.

Which scared him, for a whole bunch of reasons.

Lord, I'm going to need Your help.

"I don't think it's going to come to that," he finally said.

She gave him a sad smile. "Let's hope not."

Her phone rang and she pulled it from her pocket. She listened for a moment then sat straight up. "You did? When?" Her eyes locked onto his. "I'll be right there."

"What?"

"Someone saw Lydia eating breakfast at the shelter."

Max felt his gut twist. He knew what her next move was going to be. He reached for his keys even as she stood and shoved her feet into the shoes she'd kicked off.

She looked at him. "You're not going to try and talk me out of going?"

"Nope."

"Good decision."

"I figured." He opened the door and followed her out as he called Brandon's number. "I'll drive."

She didn't argue.

Max drove them to the shelter with a familiar tightness in his belly. He hated that place and all it represented. He'd avoided it for the past four years, refusing to drive past it if at all possible. Now in the span of two days he was making yet another visit.

He'd lost his mind.

Or fallen really hard.

Or both.

Ten minutes later, he pulled into the parking lot and

told his racing heart to slow down. Erica was out of the truck and bolting for the door.

"Erica, wait!"

She paused for a slight second, her impatience clear. He caught up fast and they entered together. The smells hit him again. Just like before, a mixture of fried chicken, pine cleaner, unwashed bodies and air freshener.

But he also noted the atmosphere of calm once again. It wasn't a cheerful, homey place, but it wasn't a cold institution, either. Patrons sat at picnic tables in a large cafeteria, eating and chatting.

He processed the information as his eyes scanned the area, desperately searching.

And not seeing the one person he wanted to see.

"Where is she?" Erica asked. He didn't answer. Instead, he pulled out Lydia's picture and began going table to table, asking people if they'd seen her.

He saw Erica make a beeline toward the rotund black woman in the pink warm-up suit. Tess, if he remembered correctly.

The two hugged, and Max went back to showing Lydia's picture. Finally, a young woman with a toddler in her lap said, "I saw her a few minutes ago." She looked around. "She was sitting by herself and looked real sad."

Hope leaped inside him. "Did you see where she went?"

"She left when you walked in." The woman pointed. "Went right out the back."

Max bolted for the back door.

"Max?"

Erica's questioning voice stopped him for a fraction of a second. "She went out the back a few minutes ago."

Erica left her friend's side and followed him.

They pushed through the back door of the kitchen and Erica glanced around, disappointment washing over her. "She managed to disappear again."

"But she's around here somewhere."

Erica stood still as half an idea came to her. "We need to stop chasing her."

"What?" Max spun toward her, disbelief on his face.

She shook her head. "We need to give her a reason to come to us."

Max appeared to think that over. "Okay. How do you propose we do that?"

"I haven't worked out all the details, but…what if we…" She paused. "No, it'll have to be just you."

"What?"

"What if you go on the news and make a plea for her to come home?"

"What if she doesn't see it? And to be honest, she probably wouldn't care if she did."

Erica chewed on her bottom lip. "I feel sure she's watching the news every chance she gets." She pursed her lips. "When you're one of the top stories, you can't help yourself. And I bet Lydia will care more than you think about seeing you making such a public plea."

He swiped a hand down his face. "I suppose it's worth a try." He pulled out his phone. "Let me make some calls."

Erica's phone vibrated. "Hello?"

After a pause, Erica heard, "Hi, it's Denise."

"Denise? Are you okay?"

"He's gone." Sorrow thickened her friend's voice. "His pain is over. All the arrangements have been made. I'm going home now. I just need to…think. Be alone."

"I'll come over right now." Lydia was gone, Max was working on the plan and Denise needed her.

"No. It's okay. Really."

"I'll be there soon."

She hung up and felt Max watching her. "You take care of getting on the news. I'm going to be with Denise for a few hours."

"You can't be alone, Erica."

She sighed and closed her eyes. "Brandon and Jordan are at Bea's house."

"I'll take you to Denise's. I can make these calls while I wait on you."

"You're sure?"

"I'm sure."

Erica wanted to weep. They'd missed Lydia by a few minutes. She couldn't believe it. Hopelessness tore at her, but she refused to give in to the feeling. They had a plan, a plan that might actually work.

God, I don't know why this is happening, but I sure wish You'd at least let me talk to the girl.

She rode in silence as she pondered what Max should say on his plea on the news, but her frustration was making it hard to think clearly. Visiting with Denise would be good for her—she would focus her energy on her heartbroken friend, instead of constantly thinking about herself and her situation. She prayed she could offer Denise some real comfort.

Max pulled up to the house. She started to get out and he placed a hand on her arm. "Hold on a second."

"What is it?"

"I just want to watch and listen for a few minutes."

Puzzled, she stared at him as she settled back into the seat. "Okay."

For the next five minutes, he kept the window down and watched the street. Finally, he said, "All right. You can go. I don't see anything that rings my alarm."

Of course. He was worried they'd been followed. "I won't stay too long. She said she wanted to be alone, but—" she shrugged "—I want to check on her."

"It's fine." He held up his phone. "I have plenty to keep me occupied. And I'll be watching the house."

"Okay. Thanks, Max."

He leaned over and planted a quick kiss on her lips. She felt a real, genuine smile on her face and realized it had been a while since she'd actually grinned. "What was that for?"

"You're growing on me."

She reached up and touched his face. "The feeling's mutual."

"Good, because I learned something today."

"What's that?"

"I've been petty and judgmental since Tracy's death." He swallowed hard. "Being at that homeless shelter was very hard at first…then as I began talking to people, I started to see them as individuals, not as a group." He sighed. "They're not all bad people."

"No. They're not." She paused. "Some fit into that 'bad' category, but the majority are there through no fault of their own. Most of them just want a bed to sleep in, food to eat and the opportunity to make their lives better."

He nodded. "I saw a little bit of that yesterday. And even more today." He reached up and put his hand on hers. "You made me see that. And I've been praying for God to change my heart." He smiled. "I think He's answering that prayer."

"I'm glad, Max. I'm so sorry about Tracy. It was a horrible experience, I'm sure. But don't let it keep you from giving people a chance."

"Yeah." He nodded toward the porch where Denise stood. She must have just noticed them and stepped outside. "She's waiting on you."

Erica turned to see Denise, hands on her hips, shoulders stooped with weariness. She asked Max, "Are you coming in?"

"Maybe in a little bit. I'm going to make those calls and check in with Brandon and Jordan. Go be with your friend."

"Okay. Thanks."

She got out of the car and walked toward Denise.

"You didn't have to come, Erica." Tear tracks stained Denise's cheeks, and her mascara had smudged under her eyes.

Erica wrapped her arms around Denise's stiff form. "Of course I did." Why was Denise so resistant to her?

Denise finally offered her a pat on the back and said, "I'm cleaning out Dad's house. You sure you want to tackle that?"

"If you're feeling up to it and ready for the bombardment of memories, I'll be glad to help."

"I'm not ready, but I have to get it done and get home."

"Then let me help you."

Denise dropped her arms, seeming to lose the will to fight Erica's insistence. "Okay, I appreciate it."

Erica followed Denise into the house and noted the boxes everywhere. "You don't want to move back here, Denise?"

"No. Never. I'm quite happy where I am. As soon as Dad's buried, I'm going home."

Erica didn't realize until that moment that she deeply missed her friend and had been hoping she'd return, but she supposed she understood. Denise had made a life for herself in a new place with a great job—and probably good friends. She wouldn't be selfish and wish otherwise. "Where do you want me to start?"

A sigh slipped from Denise's lips. "I don't care. Everything has to go. The house goes on the market next week."

Erica blinked. "My. You've been busy."

Denise shrugged. "I didn't have anything else to do while I was sitting in the hospital waiting for him to take his last breath. I figured it was better to be productive rather than to be in denial."

Erica was a little taken aback, but that was Denise. Blunt and to the point. "All right, why don't I tackle the kitchen?"

Denise stared at her a moment, then her face crumpled. "I already miss him," she gasped. "I can't believe he's gone."

Erica moved to take her friend in her arms. "I know," she whispered against her hair. "It'll be all right."

"No, it won't. It really won't." She blinked and reached up, grasping her hair with her hands in despair. "I killed him."

Erica was stunned. "Of course you didn't kill him. Why would you say that?"

Denise let out a harsh sound that was half chuckle, half sob. "I'm sorry. I'm not making any sense."

"What do you mean you killed him?"

Denise pulled away and swiped her eyes. "He's never forgiven me for leaving. My choice to leave was something he couldn't get over, and now he's gone."

"But you always talked about how you enjoyed his visits. He flew out there a couple of times a year to see you. If he hadn't forgiven you, he wouldn't have bothered." She rubbed her friend's arm.

Denise shook her head. "Never mind. I'm just…"

"Grieving," Erica finished for her. "Come on, let's get busy. Maybe some physical activity will help."

Denise's grief-stricken face returned to normal. "Yes, of course, you're right. I was working in his bedroom. I figure if I can get through that, I can make it through the rest of the house."

"Do you want me to do that for you?"

"No. I need to. You finish the kitchen. It's almost done anyway."

Erica picked up one of the boxes leaning against the wall and a roll of packing tape. "All right, the kitchen it is."

"The bubble wrap is on the table."

"Got it."

Erica moved into the kitchen and taped the box together. Several boxes already sat stacked next to the back door. It wouldn't take much to finish. Just the pantry and the few dishes stacked on the counter.

For the next thirty minutes, Erica worked quietly, thinking. As she packed, she realized a startling fact.

No one was here for Denise. Her father had just died and no one had come by. She couldn't remember if the man had been a member of a church or not. She thought so, but maybe not.

Erica frowned as she pulled the tape across the top of the last box. Where were Denise's other friends and family? She tried to think of other family in the area.

An uncle. A cousin or two she remembered from childhood but hadn't kept up with so had no idea if they still lived in town or not. "Strange," she muttered. Then shrugged. She was glad she'd come to support her friend. Perhaps Denise hadn't kept in touch with anyone when she'd left. But that didn't explain why no one else was mourning her father.

Finished with the kitchen, Erica walked to the window and looked out.

Max still sat in his truck, the phone pressed to his ear. A lump rose in her throat. "Please, Lord," she whispered. "Let us find Lydia and Molly. Show us where to look next. And keep them both safe."

The prayer echoed in her mind, filling her heart. But she just couldn't quell the uneasy feeling that time was running out.

For everyone.

Chapter 16

The more Max thought about it, the more he felt they were missing something. Something that was as plain as the nose on his face, only he couldn't see it. Mentally, he ran down a list of everyone in Erica's life that he could think of. Unfortunately, he didn't know whom he might be missing. But those he did know…

Who would know she was allergic to bees?

And who would even have access to the venom? Anyone doing an online search, probably.

Peter was the obvious suspect. But Max didn't like the obvious. Everything that had happened with Peter could have been set up. From stealing his car to luring him to the mall.

And then there was Rachel. She had some jealousy over Erica and Denise's friendship, but was it a motive to kidnap her own niece? And if so, where had she kept the child all this time? Assuming Molly was still alive. If Rachel was the kidnapper, the cold knot in his belly told him Molly was dead.

Please let her be alive, God.

He pulled the file on Molly from under his seat and opened it. One thing kept nagging at him. One of the witnesses said she saw a woman that looked like she could be with the group but wasn't. He read the witness's statement. "I only noticed her because she seemed so alone. Lonely. I felt sorry for her. The next time I turned around, she was gone and I really didn't think anything more about her until Molly disappeared and you started asking me questions."

Katie had questioned the woman further, but had gotten only a brief description. Curly red hair pulled up in a ponytail, large sunglasses, thin, kept her hands in her coat pocket. The police had written her off as a visitor because no one reported seeing Molly leave with her.

The more Max thought about it, the more he was convinced the woman had something to do with the kidnapping.

He pulled out the sketch the artist had created based on the witness's description. Unfortunately, it wasn't a very good one.

"Curly red hair," he muttered. Rachel? An idea hit him. He grabbed his phone and called Brandon.

"Any luck with Lydia?" he asked when Brandon answered.

"No. Just sitting here watching the house, drinking coffee and trying to figure out who could be after Erica."

"I have an idea and I need your help."

"What do you need?"

He glanced at the window he'd seen Erica looking out of a few minutes ago. "I need you to get me into Erica's house."

"Why don't you just ask Erica?" Max was glad Brandon seemed curious, rather than suspicious. Maybe the man trusted him.

"Denise's father died."

"Oh. I'm sorry to hear that."

"Erica's over here at Denise's father's house. She's helping her pack it up. I don't want to bother her until I figure out if I'm right or not."

"Right about what?"

"I'll explain when I see you. I'm going to call Chris and see if he can take over for me."

"This can't wait?"

"No."

Chris arrived within fifteen minutes, pulling up behind Max's truck in his squad car. Max got out and shook hands with the man. "Nothing's going to happen to Erica while I'm watching out for her."

"If she sees you out here and asks what's going on, just tell her I'm following up on a lead and I'll be back soon, all right?"

"Of course."

Max climbed back in his truck and took off for Erica's house. Within minutes, Max was in her drive. Brandon pulled up behind him. "What's this bright idea?"

"I need pictures of everyone in Erica's life at the time of the kidnapping."

Brandon blinked. "That's a lot of people."

"Okay, not everyone, but anyone who was especially close to her."

"She's got an album inside that has tons of pictures from the time Molly was born to the time she disappeared. Erica never looks at it anymore, but I know where it is. Come on."

Brandon turned the alarm off and led the way inside. Max waited for the man to get the album. Brandon handed it to him. "What are you going to do with it?"

"Show it to someone. Come on."

Erica was halfway through the china cabinet in the dining room when Denise walked in. "You're making good progress." Surprise tinted her voice.

"Well, it's a no-brainer kind of job." Denise had pulled her dark hair into a ponytail. The dark circles under her eyes tugged at Erica's heartstrings. "I'm sorry you're going through all of this."

Denise shrugged. "It's the way it is. It's not fair, but whatever."

"I owe you an apology," Erica said.

Denise's brow rose. "Whatever for?"

"For not being there when Todd left you."

Her friend's jaw tightened. "That was a pretty bad time in my life."

"I know." Erica dropped her head. "I was so consumed with my own marriage and Molly that I wasn't there for you like I should have been."

Denise sighed. "I don't know that it would have helped if you had been. You couldn't have done anything." She shook her head. "I wasn't exactly there for you when Andrew walked out."

"You let me cry on your shoulder many times in the three weeks before you had to leave."

Denise grabbed her hand. "I just want you to know that was one of the hardest things I've ever done in my life."

Erica gave her a soft smile. "I understood." She drew in a deep breath. "So…should I finish up the china cabinet?"

"Sure. I'm going to see what I can do about that bathroom in the hall upstairs."

Erica turned back and within minutes finished packing up the cabinet. She took another box and the tape and went down the hall to the guest bedroom and stepped inside.

She could hear Denise upstairs on the phone once again as she set the box on the floor. Denise's belongings lay strewn around the room. Erica was turning to leave, figuring Denise would want to take care of this room herself, when her eye landed on a photo album on the bedside end table.

Curious, she picked it up and sat on the bed.

She'd wondered about Denise's life ever since the woman had moved to New Mexico. In their weekly conversations, Denise had talked about her job, the friends she'd made and the fact that she didn't miss anything about her hometown except her best friend.

Erica opened the album and stared down at her daughter's face.

Max found the witness from the zoo at a church potluck dinner in the gym, also known as the Family Life Center. It had taken them only about thirty minutes to track the woman down, and then Brandon had returned to join Jordan at the stakeout at Bea's house.

Max stood at the door and scanned the crowd.

A woman in her late fifties stepped away from the food line. "You look exactly like you described yourself."

He smiled, anxiety tightening his gut. If his suspicions were correct, Erica would be devastated.

"Mrs. White?"

"Yes."

"I appreciate your being willing to do this."

"It's not a problem. That day has haunted me." She pressed a hand to her lips. "They never found the little girl, did they?"

"No, ma'am."

They found a couple of chairs and Max handed her the photo album. Mrs. White settled in and opened it in her lap. "I remember watching the news, praying they'd find her. Eventually, the news stopped running the story." She looked up. "They ran something the other day about it, didn't they?"

"Yes, ma'am."

She nodded and went back to the album, flipping pages all the way to the end. Max's heart stopped when she didn't point to anyone. It had been a long shot, but he'd hoped...

"Nothing?"

She shook her head but didn't hand the album back to him. Instead, she closed her eyes. "The woman I saw that day was all alone. She looked lonely and kind of sad. I never really saw her face, but I remember her specifically because of her coat."

"Her coat?"

She nodded and opened the album to one of the pages in the beginning. "I have one almost just like it. It seemed like every time I turned around that day, I was seeing this woman in my coat."

"Why would you have seen her so much? You weren't with the day care."

"I was with another school. We were all following the same guide around the zoo."

"What about the man that was spotted?" He pointed to a picture of Peter. "Did you ever see him there?"

She shook her head. "I didn't notice him." She pointed to a photo. "This looks like the coat the woman was wearing that day. In fact, I'm pretty sure it's the same one."

She turned the album around and showed him the photo. She was pointing to a picture of Denise.

"But you said the woman had curly red hair. This one has brown hair."

"She did. But that coat and those sunglasses look identical to the ones I saw. The only thing different is the hair color." She tapped the picture. "This is her, I know it."

"A wig," he whispered. "She wore a wig." So it wasn't Rachel, the cousin she trusted. But the person's identity and subsequent betrayal would still be devastating to Erica.

A cold ball of fear centered itself in the pit of his stomach. He thanked the woman and called Erica's number as he rushed to his car. Her phone rang four times, then went to voice mail. He hung up and tried again. Same thing.

His phone rang, distracting him for a moment. He ignored it, slipped behind the wheel and called Chris. As soon as the man came on the line, he said, "Denise kidnapped Molly. Get Erica out of there. Play it cool if you can—don't tip Denise off. I've got backup on the way coming in silent."

As soon as he hung up with Chris, his phone rang. He pulled out of the church parking lot even as he answered.

"We've got Lydia," Brandon said. "She's scared out of her wits. I've called Rachel to come stay with us, hoping a female presence will calm her down."

"Good idea." He should have thought of that. He filled Brandon in on where he was headed and why. "The witness picked her out of the photo album, Brandon."

"Denise!" The shout made his ears ring.

"I've got law enforcement on the way there now. Chris is going to get her out of the house, hopefully with no problem."

"That's not good."

"Tell me about it."

"I'll be there as soon as Rachel gets here. Jordan can handle this."

An idea hit him. "Let me talk to Lydia." He turned left, then right. Almost there.

"She refuses to take the phone."

Anger infused Max. "Put her on speakerphone. She has to hear this."

"Go."

"Listen to me, Lydia. I don't know if you had anything to do with this kidnapping or not, but a woman is in danger because of the person who took Molly. I need your cooperation, not your silence. Hate me if you want, but help me save Molly's mother."

A sob sounded.

"Lydia? Talk to me. Help us. If you don't, you could find yourself in jail, and I don't think I could handle seeing my baby sister in that awful place."

"Oh, Max. I'm sorry." She was crying.

And in that horrible moment, Max had to face the facts: his sister *had* had something to do with Molly's disappearance. But what? What had been her role?

He forced his emotions away. He'd deal with them later. Right now, he had to do everything he possibly could to get Erica away from Denise.

"Get yourself together and help me. I need to know whatever you can tell me about Denise's state of mind."

"At first, she was so nice. I thought she was helping me. I thought I was helping her. But then I saw that the little girl I was babysitting was really Molly James. I was going to take her back to her mother, but then they left town and Denise said she'd kill me if I said anything."

She was crying so hard now it was difficult to understand her. "The men with you are going to bring you to me, okay? I may need you."

"No! I'll tell you everything, but you gotta just let me leave, okay?"

"Let's see how it all plays out, Lydia."

He couldn't just let her leave, but he wasn't going to tell her that. Not now.

"Max, she tried to kill me twice already."

"Yeah," Max hardened his jaw. "There's been a lot of that going around."

"I thought if I could just disappear, she'd leave me alone. Then they put my face on television and everyone started looking for me."

"You should have come in, honey."

"I couldn't! Even in jail, she could get to me. I'm just so tired." Sobs broke through, and Max heard Brandon come back on the line.

"We'll be there shortly."

"I'm going to check back in with Chris and make sure he's got her out of there."

He hung up and dialed Chris's number once again as he did his best to beat the cops to Denise's father's house.

Erica wasn't sure how long she sat there and stared at that photo.

Shock bombarded her. Molly was alive.

Her blood pounded in her veins as her heart beat so hard she thought it might explode. She flipped the pages. Pictures of Molly. From infancy to now, at the age of six.

How did Denise have this? Why?

Her hands shook. She started at the beginning of the album again, staring at the first picture. It was Molly as an infant, a photo Erica had taken and given to Denise.

She flipped to the last picture. Molly—older, but Molly all the same.

Her baby.

In this photo album on Denise's nightstand.

She felt frozen. Disconnected from reality.

And then time sped up. She had to call Katie. And Max.

Max. He was right outside, still patiently waiting for her to come out. She snapped the album shut and replaced it on the nightstand as her brain scrambled to put everything together. She stood and turned to find Denise in the doorway.

"What are you doing in here?"

Erica's blood hummed as she bit back the desire to scream at her former friend and demand to know where Molly was. Instead, she took a deep breath. She couldn't blow this, couldn't let Molly slip through her fingers once again.

"I… I thought I'd see what else I could pack up for you. I didn't realize this was the room you'd been using." She picked up the box and the tape. "I was just going to check out the den area. Make sure you got everything."

Denise nodded and smiled. "I have to return a couple of phone calls. Don't worry about this room…it's mostly my stuff. Why don't you help me with the garage?"

"Sure," Erica managed, nearly choking on the word. "I can do that."

Denise turned and left.

Erica swallowed hard. How long had Denise been standing there? Had she seen her looking at the album? Her phone was in her purse on the kitchen table, and Max was outside. She would be fine. She tried not to dwell on the fact that Denise—her best friend—had tried to kill her. Several times.

The betrayal cut deeper than Erica could have ever imagined. This woman had stolen her child and tried to kill her. Anger churned with the fear as she moved toward the bedroom door.

She had one goal: getting her daughter back. All she had to do was get out of the house safely without tipping Denise off that she knew what the woman had done.

On shaky legs she stepped out of the bedroom. The hall stretched before her, empty.

Where was Denise? She said she had to make some phone calls, yet Erica didn't hear her talking. Her stomach twisted itself into knots, perspiration dotting her brow. *I'm coming, Molly. I'm coming.*

Erica listened, trying to pinpoint where Denise might be. But she still heard nothing. Had she already gone into the garage to make her phone calls while she packed?

Or was she waiting for Erica so she could ambush her?

Nausea swirled, her heart pounded.

No. Stay calm. Denise didn't know she'd seen the pictures.

Or did she? She'd been in the doorway when Erica put the album back on the end table. How long had she been standing there?

Erica had to get out of the house. She couldn't confront Denise, not this way, not all alone with no one realizing she was in the house with a killer.

A knock sounded on the front door.

Erica made a beeline for it.

As she passed the living room, a blur moved to her right, pain lanced up the back of her head and down her neck and then blackness reached out to snatch her.

Chapter 17

Max pulled up to the curb two doors down from the house and parked. He hopped out of the vehicle and saw Chris on the front porch standing to the side and knocking on the door. Foreboding set in. He shouldn't still be knocking. What was taking so long?

"Chris?"

The man turned, his eyes flashing. "I can't get either of them to come to the door. Denise told me to hang on, but that was the last thing I heard."

Max followed Chris's example and stood to the side of the door. He raised his knuckles and rapped. "Erica?"

No answer.

Chris growled, "We need backup."

"It's on the way. This neighborhood is off the beaten path—it's going to take them a bit to get here. I got here fast because I was just a few miles away." He knocked again. "Erica? Denise?"

"Just a minute! I'm in the middle of a phone call."

He heard the impatience in Denise's voice. Why wouldn't Erica answer him? What was taking so long? Why wouldn't Denise open the door?

He realized he needed the answer to those questions. And now.

"She has no reason to suspect we know anything, right?" Chris asked quietly.

Max thought for a second. "No. But what if she has reason to suspect that Erica knows something?"

He looked at Chris, whose narrowed eyes and tense jaw said he wasn't happy about that possibility. Chris asked, "You want to knock it down?"

Max hesitated. He hadn't heard anything from the inside that caused him concern—other than Erica's lack of response.

"Might be better to ask for forgiveness rather than permission in this case. If she does suspect something by the time backup arrives, things could get ugly." He glanced at the still-empty road. "Will you check and see what their ETA is? I'm going to see if there's an unlocked door or window I can slip in."

Chris nodded and pulled his phone from his pocket as he leaned forward slightly and peered through the window. He jerked back with a grim frown. "She's got a gun."

"What?" Max's mouth went dry with fear for Erica.

"I just caught a glimpse of it." He shifted to look in again. "I can't see anything else. Just her back now."

"Where's Erica?"

"I can't see her."

Max felt his heart start to thud double time. Erica

was in danger. Again. "Then we don't want to kick the door in—yet. Denise doesn't know we know anything. I'll try one more time—try to keep her talking until backup gets here."

Prayers on his lips, he lifted his fist and knocked.

Erica groaned. Why did her head feel like it was going to explode? She tried to open her eyes, but it seemed like lead weights pressed down on them.

The pounding continued.

"Go away!" A shrill voice cut into Erica's brain. She winced at the pain.

"Let me in! I need to talk to Erica!"

Max?

"She's in the bathroom!"

Erica tried to block the pounding and shouting. With her eyes closed, she concentrated on keeping her stomach settled.

"Wake up, Erica," the voice hissed.

Fear shot through her, but she couldn't figure out why.

Nausea swirled harder.

The pounding on the door continued.

Something nudged her side. She ignored it. A sharp jab in her ribs made her gasp, and she opened her eyes. Debilitating pain sliced through her brain, and she gagged.

"A headache, huh?"

Denise. Her best friend. Her confidante. Her shoulder to cry on.

Her…daughter's kidnapper.

"Denise…why?"

"I need you awake. I've got some guy pounding on the door asking about you. That man, Max, I think. I need you to tell him everything's all right and get him to leave."

Erica's eyes finally focused. They landed on the weapon in the woman's left hand. "Why didn't you just kill me?"

She'd almost prefer it to the pain in her head.

"Are you not listening? Get him out of here then go in the garage and get in the car. We're leaving. Now get up."

With a gasp and a groan, Erica forced herself to roll to her side. She got on all fours and pushed herself up. Dizziness hit her; nausea won out.

Erica raced to the kitchen trash can and lost what little food she had in her stomach. She sank to the floor and held her head in her hands, praying for relief.

"Denise, I need to talk to Erica." Max sounded firm and in control. Calm and detached.

"Hold on, she's coming!"

Erica took a deep breath and watched the woman from the corner of her eye.

Denise wasn't quite as calm and in control as she wanted Erica to believe. Her hands shook, her eyes darted and Erica knew she was thinking, trying to work out a plan that would allow her to escape. She also knew that if Max wasn't outside pounding on the door, she'd be dead.

And Denise would be gone.

If Denise managed to disappear, Erica would never find Molly. She shut her eyes and prayed while Denise paced and Max continued to insist on talking to her.

"Get over there and get rid of him." Her eyes were cold. "Or I'll make sure you never see your little girl again."

"Hold on, Max! I'm coming." Erica managed to say the words above a normal volume, but she paid for it with another wave of nausea. Bending over, she closed her eyes and waited for it to pass as she wondered if he'd heard her.

The pounding on the door stopped. Her head was another matter.

She made her way to the door. "Max, there's…um…so much stuff blocking the door. You'll…um…have to just hang on a second while we move it."

"Then let me in the back door."

"Too much stuff there, too. Just…give us a minute." She met Denise's eyes. Satisfaction gleamed there.

Erica's legs gave out and she sank to the floor once again. She dropped her head and cradled it in her hands while she spun scenarios. "Can you at least get me a bag of ice for my head?"

"No," Denise hissed. "Into the garage and in the car. You drive."

"Denise, I'm seeing double. I can't drive."

Erica felt Denise move in front of her. She cracked her eyes and saw feet. She looked up. Denise's upraised fist, curled around the gun, made her flinch. "Get up," the woman ordered.

"I can't." She licked her lips. "And if you hit me again, I'll be down for the count."

Denise pointed the gun in Erica's face. "Then I'll kill you now."

Erica knew if she got up, she'd black out again.

And who knew what Denise would do at that point. "I thought you needed me," she said.

Denise's frustration was evident on her face. "I do." She walked to the window and looked out. "I can't believe this. This wasn't supposed to happen. Just one more day and I would have been gone." She turned back. "Only now if you don't answer the door, they're going to know something's wrong."

"I'm pretty sure they already know." So why weren't they knocking the door down? "Where's Molly?"

"I don't know. She was kidnapped, remember?"

Erica's fingers balled into a fist—it was all she could do not to use her last bit of strength to plant it right in the woman's face. That wouldn't help. She had to stay calm and in control if she wanted to see her daughter again.

"You just threatened that if I didn't do what you wanted, I'd never see her again. Don't bother denying that you took her."

"She should have been mine in the first place." Denise opened the door in the kitchen that led to the garage. "Get in the car."

"If you'd get me some ice, it might help. But if I move now, I'll just pass out."

Denise blinked at the change of subject. Erica had done a brief course on hostage negotiation. She'd taken it out of curiosity when she'd become a skip tracer. Now she did her best to remember everything from the class. Unfortunately, she was having trouble focusing. Her vision dimmed.

No, no passing out. Stay awake.

Cold filled her palm. She looked down at the ice pack

Denise had fixed for her. Guess she didn't want Erica passing out after all.

Erica placed the ice against the back of her head and winced. It hurt and felt wonderful all at the same time. "You said you killed him. He knew, didn't he?" she whispered.

"What?" Denise stumbled back like Erica had jolted her with a Taser.

"Your father. He knew what you'd done. And the secret killed him."

Bitterness hardened Denise's eyes, and she lowered herself into the chair behind her. "He found out on his first visit. It wasn't like I could hide her. He was horrified." Her lips thinned. "But I convinced him Molly was much better off with me. I told him how her own father didn't want her and how you were too messed up to be a good mother." A slight smile curved her lips. "When Dad saw how wonderful Molly and I were together, he let it go. He fell in love with her just like I did and was the best grandfather ever."

Was she crazy? Erica looked into her eyes and saw no sign of insanity. Just anger that she'd been caught, and a desperation to escape that sent shards of fear slamming through Erica. Desperation was not a good thing for a woman with a gun in her hand.

Gun.

Erica stilled. Her gun was in her purse. Her head still throbbed, but the debilitating nausea had passed. However, Denise didn't need to know that.

The pounding on the front door resumed. "Erica? Come on. What's taking so long? Are you all right? Open the door. I need to talk to you."

Denise jumped and cursed.

"I'm coming," Erica called, looking at Denise as she stood on wobbling legs. Would Denise really shoot her?

"Hey," Max yelled, "you've got me worried, you two. Open the door or I'm going to kick it in." She heard the fear in his voice.

Denise aimed the gun at the door, and Erica screamed, "Max, she's got a gun!"

The bullet pierced the wooden door and Erica dropped to the floor in case Denise decided to swing the gun around in her direction. Pain throbbed through her, blackness threatened once more and she closed her eyes, fighting desperately to hang on to consciousness.

"Denise!" Max called. "Put the gun down."

"Go away!"

"It's all over. We know you took Molly. The cops are pulling in now."

Denise panicked. "No! No. No. No." She fired the gun again and again into the door, bullets sending wood fragments flying. "Go away! I'll kill her! Go away!"

Erica rolled into the kitchen and under the table to the opposite side.

Max kicked the door down and spun into the foyer as Denise pulled the trigger again. Erica moved from her position under the table and tried to scramble toward Max. "Stay still!" Denise screamed at her. She slammed the end of the barrel against Erica's head, sending another wave of lightning through her brain. A cry escaped her and she sank back to the floor.

Max rolled into the next room, taking refuge behind the wall.

Erica felt sick wondering what she should do, desperate to figure out how she could help Max help her. If her head would quit pounding, maybe she could think.

"Denise, put the gun down," Max said.

"Move to the other end of the table and sit," Denise ordered Erica, holding her weapon against Erica's temple. Erica swallowed hard as she moved at a slow, deliberate pace. She could see Max's foot in the mirror above the fireplace. She couldn't believe he'd burst through the door like that. He could have been shot.

The phone rang.

Denise jumped. She kept the weapon trained on Erica as she backed up two paces and grabbed the handset. Erica noticed how she held the gun like she knew how to use it, and that she kept Erica between her and Max's line of fire should he come around the corner of the door.

"I want to leave," Denise said into the phone. "I have my car in the garage. We're going to get in it and leave."

Did she really think the police would just let her drive off? That Max wouldn't stop her? "Denise. It's over."

Her former friend stared at her and snapped, "Stay still."

Erica obeyed, cradling her head, acting weaker than she felt. She needed time to build her strength while making Denise think she was still wobbly. She also needed to come up with a plan.

"What are you going to do, Denise?" Max called from the den.

"I'm thinking." She stopped at the window and peered out from the side. "They probably have snipers ready to shoot me the minute they get a clear shot, don't they?"

"Probably," Max said. "That's standard procedure."

"They won't shoot if you surrender," Erica said softly.

"Surrender? Not a chance. My little girl is waiting on me."

Erica swallowed the sob that threatened and bit her lip. She drew in a steadying breath as she inched her fingers toward her purse on the table.

Max sat on the other side of the kitchen wall and prayed. Prayed for Erica's safety and for the wisdom to know what to do with the woman holding Erica hostage. He sent a text to Katie telling her the layout of the house, the situation in the kitchen and the fact that he didn't have a plan but was thinking.

Katie texted him back.

Sit tight. Negotiator coming. For now it's U and me.

Sit tight? Not likely.

He kept his eyes on the mirror that gave him a pretty good view of the kitchen. He could see Denise still had the gun on Erica, but he couldn't see the table where Erica sat.

Erica would be all right. She had to be.

His phone vibrated.

Give me more details on the layout.

The home phone rang until Denise grabbed it and disconnected it. She tossed it on the table almost within reach of Erica.

Then Denise's cell phone started up.

He texted Katie back everything he could see.

Katie wrote, She won't talk to me.

Max called, "Denise. Will you please talk to the detective?"

"No. I won't listen to another word from her. She's just trying to stall me and keep me from getting out of here."

He sent another text to Brandon, asking him to get the police in New Mexico to check on Molly at Denise's residence. He wouldn't put it past Denise to have Molly moved even as she was involved in a hostage situation.

"Will you at least talk to me?" He wanted her talking, not working on a plan.

"There's nothing to talk about. I need to think so I need you to shut up."

He paused for a moment, praying for the right words. "All I want is for Erica to be safe. I'm not a cop. I'm not a negotiator. And I really don't care if you get away as long as Erica's safe. Will you let me help you? Can we help each other?"

For a moment she didn't answer. He moved slightly to his left, hoping for a better visual, even though it meant putting himself closer to the line of fire.

With the shift, he could see more of the kitchen. And he could see Denise. She held the gun steady on Erica. All he needed was a distraction. If he could get her to move the gun away from Erica even for a split second, he might be able to get a shot.

And it would have to be the best shot he'd ever made.

Chapter 18

Erica glanced at the clock as her fingers crept toward her purse. Her first two attempts had been interrupted. But she had to do something. Distract Denise. Get her gun. *Something.* She managed to hang the phone up, but so far it had remained silent. The waiting dragged across her nerves like nails on a chalkboard.

"How does Lydia fit in with all of this?" she asked.

Denise scowled. "That brat. I tried to help her out. I paid her to do something worthwhile, and she betrayed me."

"Betrayed you? How?"

"She figured out who Molly was and was going to go to the police. I could see it in her eyes."

The phone rang, cutting into Erica's confusion.

Denise snatched the handset. "Stop calling me!"

Erica could suddenly hear Katie's voice—Denise

must have hit the speaker button. "Denise, we have to talk or we won't be able to resolve this," Katie said. Erica nearly wilted hearing her friend's calm voice.

Denise tensed up, a vein in her forehead jumping. "You either arrange for me to leave here with a live hostage or you get to clean up two dead bodies. Your choice."

A slight pause. "I'll have to talk to my superior about that."

"Then I suggest you start talking. You have thirty minutes. If you don't give me the answer I want at that time, then it's over." She hung up. Denise screamed, "Get out of my house, Max! Get out!"

"I'm not going anywhere."

"You want me to shoot her? I'll shoot her right here and right now!"

"If you do that, you have no chance of ever seeing Molly again," Max said. "None."

Erica swallowed hard as she watched Denise lose hold of some of her control. She needed her to get it back before she did something even crazier than what she was already doing. "Denise."

The woman looked at her. "What?"

"Why? Just tell me why. What did I do to make you hate me?"

Tears sprang to Denise's eyes, and hope burned in Erica's chest that the woman might still have some feelings of warmth toward her.

"Because you had it all, and I got squat."

Erica's hope dissipated. Confused, she shook her head. "I don't understand. What do you mean I had it all? My parents worked 24/7—you had parents at home who loved you. For me, money was always tight, but you never seemed to lack—"

"At school," Denise hissed as she shook the gun in Erica's face. Erica prayed it wouldn't go off during the rant she could see coming. "You were the popular one, voted most likely to succeed, voted prom queen, had the best grades." She contracted her empty hand into a fist. "I was nothing next to you. The boys didn't notice me, the teachers compared the rest of the students to you and then Andrew asked you out…" She stopped and dropped her head, but the gun never wavered. "It was just too much."

"So you stole my child?" Erica stared at her. The conversation was working. Denise seemed to have forgotten about Max. Erica dared a glance at the door and saw nothing.

The woman's head snapped up. Eyes blazing, she asked, "Do you know why my husband left me?"

Erica blinked at the sudden change in topic. She racked her brain to remember what Denise had said about the man she'd been married to for such a short time and why he'd left. "I guess I assumed it was another woman." She frowned. "But now that I think about it, I don't think you ever said."

"Because it was too shameful. Too…awful." Erica simply looked at her. Denise waved the gun toward the ceiling, then let her hand drop to her side. "I can't have children. That's why he left me."

Erica swallowed hard. She hadn't known that. Even as the reality of what had happened sank in, she was nearly overwhelmed with gratitude. Molly was alive. She'd been with a woman who loved her.

Loved her enough to commit murder for her.

"They know you have her, Denise. It's only a matter of time. The only way this is going to end well is if you let me go." She swallowed hard and forced the next words out. "I'll push for leniency. We'll prove you were in a depression, that you weren't thinking clearly. I won't press charges."

Denise stared at her. "You would do that?"

"Yes," Erica lied. "Yes, I'll do that if you'll just put the gun away. We'll walk out of here together."

"No." Denise shook her head. "You're lying."

"Denise, in all the years you've known me, have I *ever* lied to you? Ever?"

Denise hesitated as she thought. Then she swallowed. "No. I really don't think you have."

"Well, I sure wouldn't start now."

A tear rolled down Denise's cheek. "I thought after a while, you would stop looking for her. That you would get back to a life without her." Denise lifted the gun to Erica's head again. "Why couldn't you just let her go?"

Max felt his heart stop in his chest at the sight of that gun against Erica's head once again.

They were running out of time.

He held his phone out with the camera option on and, although, it was awkward, managed to snap a picture. He pulled it back in and looked at it. He texted the picture to Katie.

Her immediate reply:

Can Denise see front door?

Not at moment. Can u hear?

Yes. We have ears. Erica's doing good. Working on a distraction.

I can give u that.

What do u have in mind?

He answered in four short words.
She responded, Too dangerous.

Only choice. Get ready.

Don't do anything stupid.

He almost smiled. It was too late. In an incredibly short period of time, he'd fallen in love with a woman he could probably never have. But he planned to do his best to convince her she needed him in her life. Because he sure needed her.

That is, if they both got out of this mess alive.

Motion at the front door caught his eye. A uniformed SWAT member nudged the front door open with his foot.

"This is ridiculous." In the mirror, he saw Denise move toward the kitchen door, giving her a perfect view of the front door, too.

He held up a hand to the SWAT member. The man froze.

Max shifted. Now that Denise had moved, he could get a better view of the kitchen. Denise stood next to the garage door. Erica still sat at the table between them. He could get off a shot, but if he hit Denise and her finger pulled the trigger, she wouldn't miss Erica.

He kept his hand up, silently telling the SWAT members to stay back. If Denise saw them, she'd panic.

A scraping sound from the kitchen drew his attention away from the phone.

"What are you doing?" Denise sounded frantic, worried. "Sit down."

"I'm not sitting here anymore." Erica sounded calm. Too calm. "I'm walking out that door and going to get my daughter."

"Sit down!" the woman hissed. "I've already sent a text to the person who has her and he's moving her. You'll never see her. Never!"

Max peered around the corner, his heart pounding out his fear for Erica. What was she doing?

Almost faster than he could blink, Erica grabbed her purse by the strap and swung it at the weapon in Denise's hand as she dropped to the floor.

Max yelled, jerking Denise's attention from Erica. She spun toward him, eyes wide with fury. A crash from behind him made him duck as Denise pulled the trigger. He fired back in her direction.

Two more shots sounded and then there was a brief second of eerie silence before chaos erupted and the SWAT team swarmed in. One of them kicked the weapon away from Denise, who groaned and coughed as she was cuffed.

"Clear the rest of the house," the man ordered.

In a few short minutes it was deemed clear, and EMTs were allowed to enter.

The second he was allowed to move, he flew to Er-

ica's side and helped her out from under the table. Pale
and trembling, she leaned against him. "She has Molly.
She took my baby."

"I know, but we're going to get her back." Shielding
her from the sight of Denise and the paramedics working on her, he tried to lead her from the room.

Erica resisted, pulling away from him. "What is it?"
he asked her.

She didn't answer. Instead, she walked over to the
woman who'd betrayed her in a way that he couldn't
fathom. Denise was conscious, but her breathing was la-
bored. She looked up at Erica and grimaced. She gasped
out again, "Why couldn't you just let her go?"

Erica's fingers curled into fists and Max wondered if
he'd have to step in to keep her from belting the woman
lying bleeding on the floor.

But Erica simply said, "If you thought I could do
that, you didn't know me at all."

Erica's head still throbbed but joy bubbled inside her.

Her nightmare was over. She would get her daughter back.

She looked up at Max and linked her fingers with
his. This time she let him lead her out into the chilly
afternoon.

She shivered and he gave her fingers a squeeze. Just
that small gesture conveyed his compassion, his sympathy. She gave him a weary smile, hoping he could
see the gratitude she felt all the way down to her soul.

Katie strode up to her. "Are you all right?"

Erica nodded and winced. "I will be if I can remember not to move my head."

"Let's get you checked out." Katie waved several EMTs over.

"I will later. I want to find Molly." She needed to wrap her arms around the little girl, hear her voice. She'd have to take time to get to know her again, and allow Molly to know her. There was so much to do to repair the damage.

"First things first, Erica," said Max. The closest EMT approached her and shone a light into her eyes. She blinked.

"Pupils are even."

She grimaced. "I have a hard head."

"It's still bleeding some. Let me get that cleaned up for you." He reached for a box containing his medical supplies.

"Erica?" She looked up to see Brandon and Jordan standing next to the ambulance. Brandon broke away and raced over to wrap her in a bear hug. "You okay?"

"Yeah," she whispered against his cheek.

He let her go and said, "I've got some great news. Molly's on her way home." He looked up and caught Max's eye. "She lands tomorrow morning at eleven."

Tears flowed from her. This time it was Max who wrapped her in a hug. She clung to him and sobbed. Then she laughed, trying to ignore the pain in her head. "My baby's coming home, Max."

"I know." He gave her a quick kiss that was over much too soon, in her opinion. She caught him before he pulled away and said thank-you by planting his lips back on hers. He chuckled, deepened the kiss and lifted her off the ground.

When he let her go, his smoky eyes said they'd be talking. About everything.

Jordan cleared his throat and Max looked up from the sweetness of Erica's lips, wondering if he was going to have a fight on his hands. But the man's eyes conveyed a resigned sadness. He gave Max a small smile that said more than any words could have.

Max nodded. Message received.

"Max?"

He turned to see Lydia standing next to Rachel, uncertainty in her eyes. She looked fragile, breakable. His heart constricted and he held out his arms. She burst into tears and Max didn't hesitate to transfer his hug from Erica to his baby sister. "It's going to be all right, Lydia."

"No, it's not," she wailed. "It's never going to be all right again."

He could feel Erica beside him as he gripped Lydia's upper arms and pushed her away to stare into her eyes. "Look at me, Lydia." She sniffed. Stringy blond hair hung in her eyes. He pushed it away from her face and tilted her chin up. "It's really going to be okay." He nodded to Katie, who came over. "I need you to take her downtown and Mirandize her."

"What?" Lydia gasped and jerked away from him, eyes accusing and scared.

"This has got to be done right for when this goes to court," he explained. "I need you to look at a lineup of pictures and tell us which one is the woman who paid you to babysit Molly." He wanted a positive identification just for his own peace of mind. The last thing he wanted was for Denise to get off on a technicality—if she survived.

Her attention caught, she stopped crying. "Who?" She drew in a shuddering breath.

"Let's go downtown and let Katie walk you through everything."

Katie took an unhappy Lydia over to her unmarked vehicle and helped her into the backseat. Max turned to Erica. "We'll follow them downtown and see what Lydia says, okay?" Erica nodded.

Once she was bandaged and declared concussion free, she climbed into his truck and they headed for the police station.

Max gripped the wheel, so tense he thought he might snap it in two. "I suppose I owe you an apology."

A sigh slipped from her. "No, you don't."

"Lydia apparently had something to do with the kidnapping, and I wouldn't even—"

"Max, stop." She placed a hand on his. "Let's just see what she has to say, all right?"

Gratitude at her sweet response swelled within him. He shot her a look that he hoped conveyed his feelings and nodded. "All right."

Chapter 19

Erica leaned into Max. Her head hurt, but that didn't bother her nearly as much as her heart. The betrayal and sheer fury she felt toward Denise rocketed through her. Max's arm around her shoulder helped. It felt right.

She'd started to tell him so when they walked into the observation room but she didn't have the chance. Katie's partner, Gregory Lee, entered the room and stood beside Max.

Erica trained her attention on the scene in front of her.

Lydia sat at a table on the other side of the glass. Katie had several photos spread out on the table, and a young woman in her midtwenties stood nearby behind a video camera. "Rolling," she said.

Katie said to Lydia, "I want you to tell me when you see the woman who paid you to watch Molly. The woman who threatened you and stabbed you."

.Lydia took a deep breath and nodded. "Okay."

Katie laid the pictures out one by one. When she placed Denise's picture in front of Lydia, her gasping cry was all the answer Erica needed.

"We got the right person," Max said.

"Did you doubt it?"

"No, but better to confirm it than not."

Katie said, "You know her."

Lydia nodded and squeezed her eyes shut. "Yes."

"Two more questions, Lydia."

"What?" Lydia kept her eyes shut.

Katie said, "Open your eyes and look at me."

Lydia did. Tears shimmered on her lashes, and Erica felt Max tense and lean forward. He wanted to rescue his sister. She thought he might get up and rush into the room. Instead, he clasped his hands behind his head and let out a slow breath.

When he dropped his hands, Erica reached over to curl her fingers around his. He shot her a grateful look. Her heart ached at the pain in his eyes, but she was proud of him for realizing Lydia needed to face this on her own. When she came out on the other end, Max would be there for her. But this—she had to do this herself.

Katie asked, "Do you want a lawyer?"

"No, I don't want a lawyer. I don't need one."

"Because it's your right to have one."

Lydia slapped a hand on the table and leaned forward. "I don't want one."

"Fine. Did you help the woman you identified as Molly's kidnapper? Did you help her take Molly that day?"

"No!" The horrified cry burst from Lydia. "I wouldn't do that!"

Katie continued her line of questioning, and Lydia never wavered from her insistence that in the beginning she didn't know what Denise had done.

Max asked, "Gregory, can you get me in there?"

"Why?"

"Because Katie's not asking the right questions."

Gregory studied him for a moment, then said, "What questions do you think need asking?"

"Let me talk to Lydia, Greg."

Gregory nodded. "I'll ask her."

Within minutes, Katie walked into the observation room. Max said, "Let me talk to her."

"Why don't you tell me what to ask her?"

"I'll get more out of her. If she had anything to do with the kidnapping, I'll get her to tell me."

Katie studied him. "I'll have to clear that with my captain."

"Sure."

Erica studied Max. "I'm sorry, Max."

He met her eyes. The grief and defeat she saw there nearly broke her heart. She stepped up to him and wrapped her arms around his middle. His chin dropped to rest on her head. "I really didn't think she'd have anything to do with it."

"I know." She paused. "What are you going to do if she has to do some jail time?"

She heard him swallow and then pull in a deep breath. "I don't know, Erica. I truly don't know."

Erica nodded against his chest. "I'll be there for you if you want me there."

For a moment, Max didn't move, then he gripped her upper arms and set her away from him. At first, Erica thought he was upset with her and pushing her away. But he simply leaned his forehead against hers and said, "Thanks. I'll let you be there—if it comes to that." A short pause. "And even if it doesn't I still want you there."

Erica kissed him lightly and stepped away from him when she heard the door open.

Katie said, "He said you could 'visit' her. The visit will be recorded. Lydia knows this."

"Fine."

Lydia jumped up and rushed to Max as he entered the interrogation room. "Get me out of here. I didn't have anything to do with that kidnapping."

"Then why do you have a thousand dollars hidden in a shoe box in Bea's house?" he countered.

Lydia's eyes went wide. Her lips formed an O but no sound came out. Max nodded. "I found it. I had to convince Bea you were in serious trouble before she'd give me the box."

Lydia's gaze shot to the door as though Denise stood outside ready to pounce. "*She* gave it to me," Lydia whispered. She shuddered. "I was working for her, helping her, I just didn't know I was helping a kidnapper." She gave a humorless laugh. "I was going to quit being such a brat to you. My eighteenth birthday was an eye-opener for me. Believe it or not, rehab taught me a few things about what it means to have family who loves you. I finally saw you cared, that everything you did was out of love." She smiled at his raised brow. "Don't think it was as easy as I just made it sound, but…"

Stunned, Max asked softly, "What happened, Lydia? I don't understand what you're saying."

Lydia sighed and looked at her brother. "I was going to surprise you. Show you I could change, stay clean. Make you proud that I had a job, that someone would trust me with her child…" Her teeth caught her lower lip and she gave a quivering sob, but Max watched her gain control.

"Oh, Lydia…" he sighed. He didn't bother to remind her she could have come to him.

"I promise," Lydia said. "I didn't know she wasn't Denise's daughter. Not then." She turned to the mirror. "Erica's watching, isn't she?"

"Yeah."

To the mirror—to Erica—Lydia said, "Denise told me her husband was trying to take her daughter away from her and she had to keep the little girl hidden. She told me he hit her and their daughter, and that she was leaving him. I wanted to help her. She told me I had to be willing to commit myself to four weeks of almost total hiding. At the end of the four weeks, I could keep the thousand dollars. I agreed. I didn't know anything about the kidnapping. The only television I had was for videos for Molly."

"So you didn't see the news?" Max asked.

"No. Not until almost three weeks after the kidnapping. I ran out to get some more pull-ups for Molly. Instead of going to the grocery store I went to the gas station around the corner. I saw Molly's face on the television and heard how she'd disappeared from her zoo trip and her mother was anxiously waiting for her to come home." Lydia's hands shook as she swiped her hair back from her face and shot another glance at the mirror. "You got up there and pleaded to your daughter's kidnapper to bring her home. You cried and you told Molly how much you missed her. That's when I realized the truth. I ran back to the apartment to grab Molly. I was going to take her home."

"But?" Max asked.

"Denise must have seen something in my face. She grabbed a knife and stabbed me."

He winced. "I thought that stabbing was related to a drug deal gone bad."

Lydia turned back to her brother. "I know. And I let you think that. I couldn't tell what I knew because Denise said she had evidence that would send me to jail. Evidence of drug use, evidence that I'd been the one to kidnap Molly. Everything. I couldn't say a word or I'd go to jail." She swallowed hard. "Who would believe a junkie over a successful businesswoman?"

"And the best friend of the grieving mother," he muttered.

Lydia nodded. Katie stepped inside the room and asked, "How did the clothes show up in the crack house three years later?"

Lydia bit her lip and swiped a hand over her face. "I was so tired of running. Denise kept people after me all the time, warning me to keep quiet, saying that she was watching me. I figured it was only a matter of time before she just had someone kill me. So—" she shrugged "—I put the clothes and hair bow in a bag and gave them to Red to give to the cops if anything happened to me."

"They were found in the crack house."

"I know. I saw that. She probably sold them to another junkie for a few ounces of crack." Her eyes hardened. "Shows you just can't trust people."

Max said, "No, you can't trust the *wrong* people. Some people you can trust."

"Why were you at the mall that afternoon when you ran from us?"

Lydia rubbed her red-rimmed eyes. "Red said Denise called her and told her to tell me that she'd give me enough money to leave town and never come back." She swallowed hard. "After Red called, I set up the meeting where there were a lot of people because I didn't know what she'd try. I was going to take the money and run." Lydia lifted her chin and tears glinted. "I'm sorry, Max, but I was just tired. Beyond tired."

"I know. I just wish you'd have trusted *me*."

"Well, it was a setup. I caught a glimpse of her gun and ran."

After a few more minutes, Max left Lydia and made his way back to the observation room. He'd done his best to help her. Now they just had to wait to learn if the charges would be dropped or if the D.A. would push to prove Lydia was involved intentionally rather than accidentally.

Erica looked worn out. He said, "I think we have the whole story now."

She nodded. "Denise had that bee venom all ready to use on me when she had the chance, didn't she?"

"Looks that way."

"And I told her exactly where I'd be. All she had to

do was head over to the mall and call in a bomb threat, lose herself in the crowd and…" She blew out a sigh. "Well, I set myself up with that one, huh?"

"You didn't know."

She grimaced.

A knock sounded, and he turned to see Brandon and Jordan at the door. Brandon said, "Sorry to interrupt, but we've got some news. We've found Peter." Max lifted a brow, his silent question clear. Brandon said, "He's alive. Barely. They've taken him to the hospital."

"What happened?" Erica whispered.

"Looks like a hit-and-run sometime yesterday. He'd been lying in a ditch for at least one night. A jogger found him this morning and called 9-1-1."

Max's heart thumped in sympathy for Erica. In spite of her brother's issues and shortcomings, he knew she loved him. "I still don't understand why he was at the mall when Denise attacked Erica."

"I don't know. We may never know until he wakes up."

Max said, "I feel sure Denise had something to do with it." He looked at Erica, then at her brother and Jordan. "It's obvious now that Peter didn't have anything to do with trying to harm Erica. Maybe he was trying to warn her. There's one way to find out if it was Denise who hit him. The evidence will be there."

Katie said, "I just got word that Denise's bumper showed recent damage. There was some material caught in the fender. If CSU finds Peter's DNA on there, Ms. Tanner has another count of second-degree aggravated assault coming against her at the very least. Attempted murder is what it should be." She looked at Erica and Max. "That woman is going away for a very long time."

Erica gave a slow nod, deep sorrow rooting itself in her heart. A sense of betrayal like none she'd ever felt before, not even when her husband left her, swept over her again. She could almost understand Andrew's need to escape the situation they were in—how many times had she wanted to run away and forget everything? But for Denise to have done this…

"She needs help," Erica whispered. "I don't know if jail is right for her." She looked at Katie. "Will you see if you can get her some psychiatric help?"

Katie lifted a brow. "Yes."

"I mean, she needs to pay the consequences for her actions, but—" Erica sighed "—she just needs help. Okay?"

"Sure."

Erica tugged on Max's arm. "Let's go see Peter."

Fifteen minutes later, Erica stood at her brother's hospital bedside. "You were trying to warn me about Denise at the mall, weren't you?"

"Yeah."

"I'm sorry, Peter." She reached over and gripped his hand as he slipped off to sleep again. "I'm sorry for a lot of things."

Just as she decided he hadn't heard her, a slight squeeze assured her he had. Relief rolled through her. She glanced at the clock.

Soon, she would hold her baby in her arms once again.

Chapter 20

Erica was sitting in the airport waiting area, hands clasped between her knees. Max sat beside her, his left leg jiggling. Lydia paced in front of the window. So far, no charges had been brought against her.

Although Red wasn't exactly a sterling reference, she'd confirmed Lydia's story about how Molly's outfit had come to be in the crack house. She'd left it there after the raid and hadn't thought anything else about it. She'd also confirmed how happy Lydia had been when she'd secured the babysitting job with Denise. And how she'd changed shortly after that.

Erica was glad. Lydia hadn't had anything to do with the kidnapping, and she seemed willing to work on her relationship with her brother. She'd tested clean, and Erica knew Max was glad, but she also noticed he didn't drop his guard with the girl, either. Not yet, anyway.

Her nerves had taken a beating all last night and this morning. Now she was waiting on Molly to come off the plane with her escort.

Her phone rang and she jumped. She saw it was Katie. "Hello?"

"Hey, Erica. I know you're at the airport waiting on Molly, but I thought you should know Denise didn't make it."

Erica's breath whooshed from her lungs. Sorrow and anger swirled inside her. She closed her eyes and felt Max settle a hand on her shoulder. She said, "Thanks for letting me know."

"Sure. Let me know how everything goes, okay?"

"Yes. I will."

They hung up and she looked at Max. "Denise died."

His jaw tightened and he nodded. "I don't know whether to say I'm sorry or not."

"I don't know, either. I'm sorry for our lost friendship. I'm sorry I didn't see her pain. I'm sorry for a lot of things." She stared toward the door she knew Molly would walk through. "I'm not sorry I'm getting my daughter back, though." Her chest tight with anxiety, she took a deep breath and let it out slowly. "How did you manage to keep the media out of this?"

Max shot her a smug smile. "The press loves a leak."

She lifted a brow. "Huh?"

"We fed them false information. We booked Molly on two flights and told the press she was coming in at the Columbia Airport."

"You're amazing."

His eyes lit up at her words, and he leaned over to

lay a kiss on her lips. "I think you're pretty special, too. We have a lot to talk about."

Her heart thundered in her ears. "Like what?"

"Like us."

"There's an us?"

Another kiss, this one long and lingering, took her breath away. She could feel the flush on her cheeks. He grinned and said, "There's definitely an us."

"Okay, I'll go with that."

He sat back and settled his right ankle onto his left knee. "Good."

"Is she here yet?" a familiar voice asked.

Erica twisted to her left to see her mother standing there uncertainly, her father right beside her mother. Erica blinked at them.

Her mother offered a wobbly smile. "Max called us."

At first Erica couldn't find any words. When she'd made the decision to let the past go, she'd wondered if she would be able to do it. Now, seeing her parents' pleading expressions softened her heart. She nodded. "I'm glad you're here."

Her father's jaw loosened and his eyes crinkled at the corners. "Thank you, Erica. We are, too."

She waved at the empty chairs beside her. "Have a seat. Her plane is going to land any minute." She looked at Max. "Thank you."

"Sure."

The four sat down. "Where's Brandon?" her father asked.

"He's here somewhere." Before it could become awkward, Erica asked, "Did you go see Peter?"

Her mother nodded. "Yes, we did."

"How is he today?"

"Recovering." Erica shot another glance at the time on her phone. Her mother reached over and clasped her hand. "I'm so sorry it was Denise."

Tears threatened, but Erica refused to let them fall. She'd cried enough last night. Her headache had eased with a painkiller prescribed by the doctor, but a crying jag this morning had brought it back full force. She didn't want to cry now and chance starting it up again. "I am, too. I never would have thought in a million years she would have been the one."

"She tried to frame Peter," her dad said. The anger under the words took her by surprise. She thought her parents had given up on her brother.

"Yes, she stole his car and tried to make it look like he was the one trying to kill me."

Her dad nodded. "He told us he was trying to warn you at the mall. He'd gone to the hospital to see Denise's father and overheard her apologizing for taking Molly."

"What?" Erica gasped.

"Peter said he couldn't call you immediately, but was trying to get away from someone he was with so he could let you know. He said later he kept dialing your number, but you didn't answer. He called your office looking for you, and Rachel told him where you were."

"And he came to the mall to warn me."

"Only he was too late."

Erica swallowed hard. "If only I hadn't ignored his calls." She shook her head. "Denise betrays me and tries to frame Peter to make it look like he was the one who took Molly. Unbelievable."

"Almost worked, too," Max said to her parents.

"Only Erica's unwavering belief in her brother convinced me of his innocence."

When she'd gone to see Peter at the hospital last night, he'd awakened briefly. He'd looked at her and recognized her, and whispered something about having tried to warn her, but Erica didn't know what to make of his words. They were the only ones he'd managed before lapsing into unconsciousness.

The doctor had come in and said how lucky he was to be alive.

Her parents were here. Her brother was going to be okay. And her daughter was finally coming home.

Max paced and checked his watch, paced some more and checked the flight board. Officers stood by, and security was tight. All was as it should be.

The news ran clips of Molly's pending arrival in Columbia. Max smiled. He loved it when a plan worked out. He knew the media would swarm Erica's house when they realized they'd been duped, but for now, they'd have this time together. A private reunion with just family.

And him.

He hoped someday that *he* would be family to Erica. Some day soon.

He hadn't even met her little girl and already he had visions of being a father to her. It scared him to death, bringing out insecurities he thought he'd dealt with ages ago.

But even all that couldn't drive him away.

"What are you thinking?" Erica murmured as she stood next to him to look out the window.

He wrapped an arm around her shoulder, and took a deep breath. "I can't believe how much I've come to care for you in such a short time, Erica. I don't even know how to describe it."

She smiled, a serene look in her eyes lighting her entire face. The shadows were gone, and anticipation had taken their place. "I know what you mean. I feel the same way."

"I want to take you out on a real date. I want us to get to know each other without all the craziness of danger and worry."

"I do, too." A frown puckered her forehead.

"What is it?" he asked.

"What about my work at the shelter? Are you going to be all right with that?"

He sighed. "I won't say I'm crazy about the idea, but I'm not totally opposed to it anymore. I may just have to hire a bodyguard to keep you company on the days you work there."

She laughed. "Silly."

He shrugged. "We'll work it out." He leaned down and gave her a kiss, and then nodded toward the arrival board. "Erica, she's here."

Erica held her breath as she waited for Molly's sweet face to appear. It seemed to take forever, but suddenly there she was. Tears clogged her throat and her breath hitched.

A young woman in her late twenties held Molly's hand. Erica wanted to rush forward and scoop the little girl up and never let her go again.

But she couldn't do that. Because her daughter didn't know her.

Erica approached slowly. Max stayed behind her. Everyone around her faded away except her precious baby girl. Erica dropped to her knees in front of her.

"Hi, Molly," she said.

"Hi." Molly cocked her head. "Who are you?"

"I'm…" She couldn't say *your mother*. That wouldn't be fair to Molly—it would just confuse her, maybe even scare her. Erica shut her pain down and finished with, "Erica."

A brilliant smile lit Molly's face. "I know you."

Erica gulped. "You do?"

"Uh-huh." Molly nodded her red curls. "I dream about you."

Erica felt a tear slip down her cheek and swiped it away. "You do?"

"Yes. You always smile in my dreams."

Erica felt a smile slip across her lips. What a wonderful gift the Lord had given her. Molly remembered her.

Then Molly frowned. "Where's my mom?"

Erica held out a hand and Molly looked uncertain for only a moment. Then she took it. Erica nearly lost her breath at the fact that she was touching her child for the first time in three years. "Molly, I have some very sad news for you. Your mommy…died."

Molly's eyes went wide and tears hovered. "She did?"

"I'm very sorry, sweetie."

Molly scrubbed her eyes. "But I already don't have a daddy."

Erica gulped. "Well, if you would like to think

about it, maybe one day you could think of me as your mommy."

"I don't know." Her frown deepened and her bottom lip poked out. "I want my real mommy."

Erica backpedaled. "Well, you think about it. Will you do that?"

Molly sniffled. "Okay."

"I know this is very hard for you, Molly, but I think you're going to like living with me...." She turned and held out a hand to Max. "With us."

"Live with you?" Uncertainty flickered and she shook her head. "I want my mom."

Tears fell and Erica wiped them away, her heart breaking at her child's distress. "I'm so sorry, honey. I really am."

Molly scrubbed her eyes and shifted her gaze to Max. "Who're you?"

"I'm Max."

"Max." Molly nodded. "I like that name. It starts with *M,* like mine."

"So it does."

Erica knew Molly would have to process everything and would need professional counseling to come through this, but right now the little girl seemed to be handling everything pretty well. She decided to keep moving forward. "You want to meet some more people?"

Molly stayed quiet and shy while Erica introduced her to her grandparents and Uncle Brandon. Then Molly looked at her. "There're too many people. Will you hold me?"

With near reverence, Erica picked her little girl up and held her next to her heart. "You're very precious, you know that?"

"I'm tired." She laid her head against Erica's shoulder.

"Then let's go home." Erica almost couldn't breathe, her joy was so intense.

Max settled his hands on her shoulders and leaned in to press a kiss to her temple. "Come on. I'm driving."

"I'll ride in the back with Molly."

Molly lifted her head and eyed Max. "Do you like dogs?"

"I sure do."

Her eyes widened. "Do you have one?"

"No, but I'm getting one next week. Would you like to name him?"

"Her."

"That's what I meant. Would you like to name *her?*"

A grin slid across Molly's lips and she gave a shy nod. "I'd call her Penelope."

Erica smothered a giggle at Max's wide-eyed expression. But he didn't miss a beat. "I think that's the perfect name for a dog."

"What kind is she?"

"What kind do you want?"

"A golden retriever, of course."

"Of course."

Erica's heart swelled with love and prayers of thanksgiving as the two kept up their conversation all the way to the car.

Epilogue

Max held the large fork and carving knife as he looked around the dining room table. Love for his family squeezed his heart. Or what would soon be his family, once he married Erica.

He was having the Thanksgiving he'd always wanted.

Erica, happy and flushed from her work in the kitchen, grinned at him. Molly leaned against her mother, her smile coming more often over the past couple of days—especially since the addition of Penelope, better known as Nellie. The two-year-old golden retriever sat at the back door and watched over the proceedings with a proprietary air. Max had adopted her from the humane society the day after Molly's arrival. He'd never forget the look on Molly's face when he'd brought the dog over. One of stunned disbelief and overwhelming joy. The dog had already been house trained and fit right in with her new family. She was even starting to answer to Nellie.

Erica's parents sat across from Brandon, who had surprised everyone and agreed to come to dinner.

"I…uh…guess I should say something profound, but my stomach is growling so loud I don't know if you would hear any of it," Max said.

"So cut the turkey already," Peter teased. Max thought he looked exceptionally good for a recovering addict.

"Yeah, come on, Max. We're starving," Lydia chimed in. She, too, had bright eyes and a smile on her face.

Max took a deep breath. "Let's pray and I'll get started."

They bowed their heads, and Max said, "Lord, we come to You as we are. Broken and sinful, but with the hope that You can take what we are and make it into something beautiful. Thank You for this day of giving thanks. Thank You for the reminder that we need to stop and take inventory of all that we have been blessed with. Thank You for this food, thank You for life, thank You for family. But most of all, thank You for Your son, Jesus. Amen."

"Amen," Molly echoed.

Laughter filled the room and with joy in his heart, Max began to carve the bird.

Hours later, Erica and Max sat on her porch swing, a space heater aimed at their feet and a blanket wrapped around their shoulders. The moon peeked between the clouds, and Erica breathed a sigh of contentment.

"Today was amazing," Max said.

"It was a good day, wasn't it?"

"I think it's probably the best one I've ever had."

Erica leaned her head against his shoulder and said, "Molly really seemed to bond with Lydia."

"I wonder if she remembers her a little."

"Maybe. Her counselor said she's doing really well."

"I heard her laugh while y'all were making the sugar cookies."

Erica smiled. "I opened the flour and squeezed the bag a little too hard. That flour shot out like a volcano erupting."

They shared a laugh and a sweet kiss.

Max pulled back a little. "So… I have a question for you."

She looked up at him and lifted a brow. "What's that?"

He slid off the swing and knelt on the floor of the porch. Erica's eyes went wide. He took her hand in his and cleared his throat.

"Erica, we've been through a lot, and maybe this is a little fast, but I've fallen hard for you. I love you like I've never loved anyone before. I want to spend the rest of my days with you, in sickness and health. I want to walk together with you through whatever the future holds. I want you to be the mother of my children. And I want to be Molly's daddy." He reached up and swiped a tear she couldn't blink back. A shuddering breath escaped her. "I was wondering if you would marry me. Soon."

Erica swallowed hard. He was right…it was fast. But she knew she wanted to spend the rest of her life with this man. She knew beyond a shadow of a doubt. "I love you, too." She gave a shaky laugh. "I would be honored to be your wife, Max."

He reached into his pocket and pulled out a small, shiny diamond ring. He slipped it on her trembling finger and then placed a sweet kiss on her lips.

"You two sure do that kissing stuff a lot."

Molly's voice interrupted the tender moment. Erica laughed and pulled away from Max to find Molly and Lydia watching them. Lydia's eyes sparkled with mirth.

Erica held out her arms and Molly moved into them. "Well, you better get used it." She grinned at Max. "Because it's going to happen a lot more."

Max grinned, then reached over to tickle Molly until she screamed with laughter. Lydia joined in until they were all breathless. Nellie just watched them, tongue lolling to the side. Her golden eyes seemed to laugh at their silliness.

Lydia leaned back on the porch swing and shifted so she was in front of the heater. "I like this," she said softly.

Max gave his sister a gentle smile. "Yeah. I do, too."

"We're a family, right?"

Max pulled Lydia up and then wrapped his strong arms around them all. "We're definitely a family. It took a little bit to get us here, but now that we've found each other, we're together forever. Deal?"

"Deal!"

Erica relished the unanimous shout and sent up her own silent thanks to the One who'd brought her family home—and Max Powell into her life.

* * * * *

Laura Scott is a nurse by day and an author by night. She has always loved romance and had read faith-based books by Grace Livingston Hill in her teenage years. She's thrilled to have published over twenty-five books for Love Inspired Suspense. She has two adult children and lives in Milwaukee, Wisconsin, with her husband of over thirty years. Please visit Laura at laurascottbooks.com, as she loves to hear from her readers.

Books by Laura Scott

Love Inspired Suspense

Justice Seekers

Soldier's Christmas Secrets
Guarded by the Soldier

Callahan Confidential

Shielding His Christmas Witness
The Only Witness
Christmas Amnesia
Shattered Lullaby
Primary Suspect
Protecting His Secret Son

True Blue K-9 Unit: Brooklyn

Copycat Killer

True Blue K-9 Unit

Blind Trust
True Blue K-9 Unit Christmas

Visit the Author Profile page at Harlequin.com for more titles.

SECRET AGENT FATHER

Laura Scott

So we say with confidence,
"The Lord is my helper; I will not be afraid.
What can man do to me?"

—*Hebrews* 13:6

This book is dedicated to my sister Joan—
thanks for reading my books. I love you!

Chapter 1

"I made a terrible mistake," her sister Trina said in a low voice, her expression bleak. "I need you to take Cody."

Shelby Jacobson shivered from the desperation in her sister's tone as much as the sharp March wind blowing off the rocky shores of Lake Michigan. Her gaze fell upon her four-and-a-half-year-old nephew, huddled with Trina. Beneath the hood of Cody's coat, his bright green eyes were wide and frightened within his pale face.

Instinctively she knelt down before him, holding out her arms. Cody broke away from his mother, flinging himself at Shelby, burying his face against her chest. She crushed him close, frowning at Trina over his head.

"Of course I'll take him. But why? What's going on? Why did you drag me out of bed and ask me to come down to the marina at four-thirty in the morning?"

Trina didn't flinch under her glare, but Shelby saw a flash of unmistakable regret flicker across her sister's eyes. Trina thrust a piece of paper into Shelby's hand, along with a cell phone. "Here. When you get to the car, call Alex. Once he knows about Cody, he'll protect him. Whatever you do, don't go back to your place, that's the first place he'll look."

Shelby glanced at the note in her hand, her frozen mind trying to untangle Trina's request. She'd assumed, from Trina's frantic call, that her sister and husband had had another fight. But this sounded much more ominous. "I don't understand. Who will look for us? And who's Alex?"

For a long moment Trina stared at her, and then motioned to Cody, still buried deep in her arms. "Alex was my contact. He's also Cody's real father. Let's go. We don't have much time."

Stunned, Shelby gaped at her sister. What? Her contact? Cody's real father? What about Trina's husband, Stephan Kirkland? She cast her memory back in time. Trina had married Stephan a few months after Cody had been born. Of course, she, like everyone else had assumed Cody was Stephan's son.

"Does Stephan know?" Shelby bit back the urge to ask about Cody's biological father, conscious of little ears.

Trina nodded, but kept looking around the deserted marina as if expecting someone to show up. "Stephan isn't listed as Cody's father on his birth certificate. And he can't help. But Alex can. Keep Cody safe, Shelby. Promise me you'll keep him safe."

"Safe from what? Did something happen? Why

would you have a 'contact'? Are you some sort of undercover agent?" Zillions more questions whirled in her mind.

Trina waved an impatient hand. "No, I'm not an agent. And none of this matters right now. We have to hurry. Cody's in danger. All I need from you is to keep my son safe. Will you do that for me? Please?"

It wasn't like her sister to beg. "Of course." Shelby loved Cody more than anyone on this earth. He attended Shelby's Little Lambs Day Care Center for preschool and stayed overnight at Shelby's more often than not. The thought of Cody being in danger made her feel sick to her stomach. She couldn't bear it. Was her sister overreacting? Trina tended toward the dramatic. "I'll keep him safe, but I'm sure we can work this out together. We can go to the police for help."

Trina shook her head. "No. You have to leave now. Don't trust anyone, especially the police. Promise me you'll call Alex. That number is a secure line and you need to use that phone. Tell him it's been *twelve nights* since I've seen him last, that way he'll know I sent you. Don't call *anyone* but Alex. Understand?"

"No, I don't understand. Why can't *you* call Alex? Why can't we all go together?" Stubbornly, she stayed where she was, refusing to budge even though Trina's tension was palpable.

"I am coming with you. But if we get separated… don't come after me. Grab Cody and run. Let's go, we need to hurry."

Giving in to her sister's urgent fear, Shelby quickly shoved the phone and scrap of paper into her jacket pocket, and hoisted Cody up into her arms. Deeply thankful that Trina was coming with them, she turned to head back toward the brightly illuminated parking lot. Trina fell into step alongside Shelby, her gaze still intently sweeping the area.

"Please tell me what's going on," Shelby begged. "Why are you and Cody in danger?"

"It's safer for you if I don't explain," Trina whispered. "I've made a terrible mistake, but Alex will know what to do. He knows what's going on."

She wanted to ask more, but decided to wait until they were safely on their way. They were over halfway to her car when Trina sucked in a sharp breath.

"What?" Shelby shifted Cody's weight in her arms, trying to look past his bulky coat to see whatever had caused Trina's sound of distress.

"Run, Shelby! Don't stop for anything. Do you hear? Don't stop no matter what happens." Trina paused momentarily to brush a hand over her son's head, then veered to the right and sprinted in the opposite direction from the parking lot, heading back toward the wooden walkways leading to the rest of the boats suspended in their raised slips for the winter.

"No! Wait! Don't go. Come with us—" Too late. Shelby's eyes widened in horror, her feet glued to the dock as she saw a figure dart into view from behind one of the outbuildings heading straight for Trina. The figure lifted his arm and a sharp retort split the air.

A gun! He was shooting at Trina!

Instinct pulled at her to help her sister, but she remembered what Trina had told her. Shelby clutched Cody tight and surged into high gear, running for the safety of her car as fast as she could with the added burden of Cody's weight in her arms.

Cody began to cry. She whispered words of comfort between panting breaths. They were near the parking lot. She wanted to glance back to see what happened to Trina, but didn't dare. Had the gunman followed Trina? Or was he right now coming up behind them? She strained to listen, but could only hear the whistling wind.

Braced for the pain of a bullet, she bit back a sob and shifted Cody to the side, groping for her keys. Jamming her thumb on the key fob, she unlocked the door and scooted Cody into the passenger seat. She slid behind the wheel, twisting the key in the ignition. She yanked the gearshift into Drive, while she craned her neck around, to search for her sister.

Along the shore, two figures continued to run. The smaller one stayed several yards in front of the larger one. Shelby gasped, when the larger figure pointed his weapon at Trina. Another gunshot ripped through the air.

The smaller figure went down. And didn't move.

"No!" Sobbing, Shelby gunned the engine and swerved out of the marina parking lot, nicking the edge of a nearby light pole. Fear that the gunman would now turn his attention toward her and Cody fueled her panicked desire to get away. She fumbled in her coat pocket for the phone Trina had given her. She dialed 9–1–1, telling the operator that someone was badly hurt down at the lakeshore.

When the dispatcher pressed for more information, she sobbed, "Just go!"

Her careful wording hadn't fooled the little boy beside her. Tears streamed down his face. "Aunt Shelby, is Mama hurt?"

She swiped the dampness from her own eyes and struggled with what to tell him. He was only four-and-a-half years old. He should be home asleep instead of running for his life from a man with a gun. Her heart hammered in her chest. She took a deep breath to steady herself. She needed every ounce of courage she possessed. His safety depended on her.

"Yes. But the police are on their way to help her." She prayed it wasn't already too late.

Dear Lord, protect Trina. Please keep her safe.

Solemn green eyes regarded her steadily, breaking her heart. "Did the bad man get her?"

The bad man? A chill slithered down her spine and she clenched the steering wheel to keep her hands from shaking. She wished, more than anything, that Trina had told her exactly what was going on. "Did you see the bad man, Cody?" Could this be why his life was in danger?

He nodded, silent tears streaking down his cheeks.

No! Was this Trina's mistake? Allowing the bad man to see Cody? Her stomach clenched with fear. She pulled her nephew close within the circle of her arm. He buried his face in her side and she held him tight.

"It's okay, Cody. I love you. Everything is going to be just fine. We're safe. God will protect us." She kept her foot hard on the accelerator, speeding through the early morning darkness, taking various turns and changing direction often, in case the gunman had friends who might come after her. At this hour, the streets were empty. After she was certain no one had followed and that she and Cody were safe, she headed toward the main highway.

Don't go to your apartment, that's the first place he'll look. Call Alex. Don't trust anyone, even the police. Only Alex. Understand?

Careful not to jostle Cody, she pulled the slip of paper from her pocket, and divided her attention between the road and the scribbled note. The handwriting wasn't Trina's, but a deep, bold stroke of a pen, with the name Alex McCade and a local phone number.

She had no idea who Alex McCade was—other than Cody's father—but Trina seemed to think he would keep them safe. Trina had sacrificed herself to help them escape, so she had no choice but to trust Trina's judgment. With renewed hope, she glanced at her nephew, nestled against her side.

"Don't worry, Cody. Everything is going to be fine. We're going to find a man who can help us."

Alex McCade prowled the length of his room, rhythmically squeezing a palm-sized foam ball in his right hand. The throbbing pain in his arm often kept him up at night, until he thought he might scream in sheer frustration, but he wouldn't give up his efforts to rebuild the damaged muscles. The bottle of narcotics sat unopened on his nightstand. No matter how intense the agony in his arm, he refused to take them.

After a few minutes of pacing, the wave of pain receded to a tolerable ache. With a sigh, he paused before the sliding glass doors to stare outside where dawn peeked over the horizon.

Deep in the north woods of Wisconsin, there were no city lights to distract the eye from the wonder of nature. A blanket of fresh snow from the most recent March snowstorm covered the ground and coated the trees, illuminating the area around his sister's rustic bed-and-breakfast with a peaceful glow. A perfect, secluded area to recover in.

His sister, Kayla, had welcomed him with open arms. Things were quiet here, she didn't do as much business during the long winter months.

The muscles in his right forearm seized up, the intense agony making him gasp. The foam ball fell from his numb fingers and he clutched above his wrist with his left hand, massaging the injured muscles into relaxing again. Every time he exercised his damaged arm, the same thing happened. The muscles would spasm painfully, forcing him to abandon his exercise regimen.

Helplessly, Alex stared down at the numerous surgical scars that crisscrossed his right arm from wrist to elbow. He didn't want to admit the plastic surgeon who'd spent long hours reconstructing his damaged muscles and tendons might be right. That his gun hand might never return to one-hundred percent. He should be grateful that he hadn't lost the arm completely, yet it was difficult to remain appreciative when his career, his reason for living, teetered on the brink of collapse.

The muscles in his arm loosened and he breathed a sigh of relief. Bending down, he picked up the foam ball and this time, kept it in his left hand. To strengthen the muscles, he opened and closed his fingers, squeezing tight. If he couldn't use his right arm, he'd build up his left. Anything to get him off medical leave and back on duty.

He needed to finish the case that continued to haunt him. For personal reasons of his own, he'd dedicated his life to being a DEA agent. For this case, they'd joined forces with the coast guard, in an effort to identify the mastermind behind the drug trafficking from Canada through the Great Lakes down to Chicago. Working undercover, he knew he was close to cracking the case before he'd been jumped by two men with knives. During his attempt to get away, they'd slashed his arm to ribbons and it had been too late to replace him. His coast guard partner, Rafe DeSilva, was doing his best to pick up the thread of the investigation.

Five years of work might be lost forever if he couldn't get back in the field soon.

He desperately needed to bring the brain behind the drug smuggling operation to justice. To do that, he needed to train the muscles in his left hand to become his dominant one. He didn't want to sacrifice his career for nothing.

His private secure cell phone rang. Startled, he dropped his foam ball in his haste to reach for the phone. Gritting his teeth, he forced himself to use his left hand as he warily answered. "Hello?"

"Is this Alex McCade?"

The female voice didn't sound quite right, considering the number indicated the call was from Trina Kirkland, his contact within the Jacobson Marina and shipping business. "Who's this? Who gave you this phone?"

"Trina gave it to me. I'm supposed to tell you it's

been twelve nights since she saw Alex last. She also said Alex would help us—me." There was a brief pause and he heard the woman's voice break as if she were struggling to hold back tears. "Please tell me you're Alex McCade."

"Yes, this is Alex." Whoever this woman was, she knew the code phrase he had always used with Trina. What had happened? What had gone wrong?

"I need your help. It's a matter of life and death."

Life and death? His gut tightened with anticipation. Followed by a wave of guilt. He was currently on medical leave. If she was legit, he'd need this woman to talk to Rafe. He shoved the helplessness aside. "I'm going to put you in touch with Rafe, he's with the coast guard."

"No!" Her voice rose to a hysterical pitch. "Trina told me to call you. Only you. No one else. There was a man with a gun. I need your help, please!"

Alex blew out his breath, sensing the woman was teetering on the edge and one wrong word would send her tumbling over. His gut also told him she wasn't involved in the criminal activity surrounding the shipyard. He couldn't deny the possibility of a setup, but too much caution could be dangerous. Trina must have given her phone and the code phrase to this woman because her life was in jeopardy. The panic in this woman's tone was too good to be faked.

"What's your name?" he asked.

There was a brief hesitation. "Shelby."

"Where are you right now?"

"Near a town called Shawano."

Shawano was almost two hours away. Perfect. He'd have plenty of time to arrange a backup plan in case this woman wasn't who she claimed to be. "Okay, I'll give you directions to a truck stop in another town. From there, call me again to get further instructions."

He rattled off the directions, satisfied when she repeated them back correctly.

"So you'll meet us—me at the truck stop?" she asked.

"Not exactly." He knew if he mentioned his plan to have Rafe check her out first, she'd get upset again. Rafe would be discreet. She'd never know he was there. "I need to make sure you're not followed."

"Oh. Okay."

"Trust me, we'll be in touch soon." He hung up and immediately called Rafe.

"Yeah?" His partner sounded half-awake.

"I need backup. Can you be here in an hour?"

"What's up?" Rafe sleepy voice disappeared.

"Something has happened to Trina."

"Trina?"

Rafe's voice had sharpened and Alex knew his partner was finally awake. "Give me a few minutes and I'll call you back."

Alex picked up his foam ball and squeezed rhythmically with his left hand as he waited for Rafe to return his call. What had happened to Trina? He hoped she was all right. He couldn't help feeling that he should have been there with her. He hated being on the outside of the case, instead of working it from center stage. It was already mid-March and the ships would hit the water the first of April. He only had two weeks to get his left arm in shape to be his dominant hand.

For now, once he'd determined the woman, Shelby, was legit, he'd have no choice but to turn her over to Rafe.

* * *

Driving on the highway toward the truck stop with a clear destination in mind helped Shelby keep her rioting emotions under control. She could do this, one step at a time.

While Cody slept, Shelby battled grief as her thoughts dwelled on Trina. She knew, with gut wrenching certainty, that her vibrant, live-life-on-the-edge sister was dead. When they were younger, opposite personalities kept them from being close. Shelby was Christian and had never embraced her sister's freewheeling lifestyle, but in the past five years Cody had managed to bring them together.

Shelby was grateful for that time when they'd been closer, but the truth was she hadn't really known Trina, and now she never would.

Their father would be devastated by the loss. He thought the sun rose and set on Trina. He'd always ignored her mistakes, the bad choices that had time and again landed her in trouble. Shelby sniffed loudly and blinked back tears. Trina had gotten in trouble again, but this time she'd made the right choice. Trina had sacrificed her life for her son.

How would the little boy deal with losing his mother on top of meeting a father he didn't know? Now that she knew Stephan wasn't his father, she understood why Cody had spent more time with her than Trina and Stephan over the past few years. It was no secret her sister and her husband were having marital problems. Stephan and Cody had never been particularly close. Now Cody's whole life had been turned upside down.

And he was in danger. She could only hope and pray he didn't realize how much.

Cody stirred, waking up after his short nap. Sleep had been the best thing for him after all the trauma of the morning's escape from the marina. Pushing her steep exhaustion aside, Shelby smiled at him reassuringly. "Hey, are you hungry?"

He rubbed his eyes with his fists and nodded.

There was another small town coming up and she'd noticed a sign for a fast food place. "We'll pick up some breakfast in the next town, all right?"

After making a quick bathroom stop inside, they placed their order in the drive-through lane. Shelby fastened Cody back into his toddler seat, and watched him munch on his breakfast sandwich through the rearview mirror. She wasn't sure how much of Trina's conversation about him being in danger he'd picked up on, so she tried to distract him. "Guess what? We're heading into the north woods."

Cody's eyes widened, his interest piqued as she'd hoped. "Are we gonna see bears?"

"Nah, they're hibernating for the winter. But we might see deer." She took a sip of her coffee, hoping the caffeine would jump start her system now that the adrenaline rush had worn off.

"What about wolves? Or coyotes?"

Shelby shook her head, grinning wryly at Cody's fascination with wild animals. "I don't know, maybe."

Cody loudly slurped his chocolate milk through a straw. Steady green eyes regarded her in the mirror. "Aunt Shelby?"

"Hmm?"

"Am I gonna live with you now, forever?"

Shelby sucked in a harsh breath and tightened her grip on the steering wheel. *Yes,* she wanted to shout. *Yes, you'll stay with me forever.* But the words clogged her throat. Did Cody sense the truth about his mother's death? Did he know he was in danger? What was the best way to have this conversation?

Lord, give me some guidance here. How should I tell him? Please, Lord, help me find the best way to explain this.

"I don't know, Cody. Maybe." She took a deep breath and let it out slowly. "First we're going to visit your other dad."

"My other dad?" Confusion wrinkled his brow.

"Yes. You're a very special boy, Cody, because you have two dads. The dad you've been living with and your other dad."

"After the visit, then I'm gonna live with you?" he persisted.

She wanted him to. Very much. Not right after the visit, as Cody had said, since they were still in danger. But once all of this was over... Still, she had no way of knowing if Alex, his biological father, would have other plans. Stephan wasn't listed as Cody's father and he'd married Trina after Cody's birth, which meant Alex would have the edge, if he wanted custody. The idea made her stomach hitch. She didn't know anything about Alex. Would he be a good father? Maybe she should find a way to disappear, keeping Cody with her forever.

As much as she wanted to do just that, her conscience wouldn't let her. The thought of the bad man knowing Cody saw him scared her to death. Would the man know Cody was with her? Was that why Trina had told her not to go back to her apartment over the day care center? She couldn't take a chance. No matter what the future held, Cody's safety had to be her first concern.

And regardless of who Alex was, he had a right to know about his son.

"I don't know, Cody. I hope so. We'll see."

Instantly his face crumpled. "I don't wanna go back to the marina! I don't like it there. I wanna stay with you."

"Shh. Hey now." Shelby reached her arm back around the seat to rub his leg. Trina and Stephan had lived near the marina. It didn't make sense that he was so afraid of going back there. "Cody, don't cry. I love you. I'll stay with you no matter what. I promise." She wished she could pull him into her arms, inhaling the sweet scent of his baby shampoo. But they needed to get to the truck stop as soon as possible. "I love you," she repeated. "I'll stay with you always. Okay?"

Cody swiped at his eyes and nodded, stifling his tears.

It was a rash promise but she didn't care. Because even if Alex claimed custody of his son, she wasn't leaving Cody. Alex would just have to deal with her being an important part of Cody's life, whether he liked it or not. She was not letting this boy go without a fight.

At the truck stop, she called Alex again on Trina's phone.

"I'm sure I wasn't followed," she told him. "No cars stayed behind me and I passed the exit, before doubling back."

"I'm sure you weren't followed, either."

She frowned, wondering how he could be so certain, but listened intently as he gave her specific instructions on how to get to the bed-and-breakfast where he was staying.

"I'll see you soon." Shelby snapped Trina's phone shut.

The sun was high in the sky when she turned onto Oakdale Road. Covered with freshly fallen snow, there were no recent signs of a snowplow. She hoped her lightweight, fuel-efficient car wouldn't get stuck.

She pulled into the bed-and-breakfast driveway, winding through the trees until she saw the house. She gaped in surprise at a huge log home lined with numerous windows. A massive deck encircled the house giving rooms on the second floor access to the outside. The grandness of the place intimidated her. This was a bed-and-breakfast in the north woods? She'd expected something smaller. Quaint. Cozy.

With a sigh, Shelby hefted Cody into her arms since he was without snow boots. Her jeans were quickly covered in snow up to her knees as she trudged up to the house.

A tall, rugged, dark-haired man answered her knock and seemed surprised to see her standing there with a child. His piercing green eyes weren't at all welcoming.

"Alex McCade?" She shifted Cody's weight on her hip.

"Yes." A deep frown furrowed his brow.

"I'm Shelby."

He hesitated, his eyes darting to the boy before he opened the door wider. "Come in."

A welcoming scent of pine surrounded her as she stepped into a warm great room with a huge stone fireplace lining one wall. Through an arched doorway to the right, Shelby saw several tables draped with bright red and white checkered tablecloths. For a bed-and-breakfast, the place was notably vacant.

She stomped her feet on the braided rug, trying to dislodge as much snow as possible. Cody wiggled impatiently in her arms, so she set him on his feet beside her. Now that she was face-to-face with Alex McCade, she couldn't seem to find the right words to tell him about his son. Especially since his tall, broad presence was more than a little intimidating. She cleared her throat. "My name is Shelby," she said again. "And this is Cody."

Cody suddenly clutched her leg, hiding his face against her jeans as he wailed. "No! I don't wanna visit my other dad!"

She winced and tried to untangle Cody from her leg, casting Alex an apologetic glance. "I'm sorry, I didn't mean for you to find out like this."

For a heart-stopping moment, the man stared at Cody. Then his cold, furious gaze cut to hers. "Is this some sort of sick joke?"

Swallowing hard, she thrust her jaw defiantly. "No, this isn't a joke. Cody is your son and I need your help to keep him safe."

Chapter 2

His son? Alex stared at the woman, seconds stretching into a full minute. His heart froze in his chest. His stunned gaze fell to the child clutching the woman as if his life depended on her. The woman moved gracefully as she bent toward the crying child, quietly beautiful in a wholesome way, he noted as he continued to stare in shock.

Rational thought quickly soothed his initial panic. Her claim couldn't possibly be true. Tall and reed thin, with long curly blond hair and bright blue eyes, she looked familiar. But not to the point where he could have possibly fathered a child with her.

"You're lying." He glared at her, as if willing her to tell the truth. "Was this why you called? To make these ridiculous accusations? I thought you needed help?"

"We do need your help. Cody's in danger. But I

wouldn't lie. Not about this. I'm sorry, I know this must be a terrible shock to you." The troubled expression in her eyes bothered him, as if she really cared what he thought and how he felt. "You have to believe Cody is your son."

He didn't have to believe anything. Alex's steely control over his anger slipped. "Look, I don't know what game you're playing, but I'm not amused."

"No game." The woman sighed and placed a protective arm around the boy. "Let me start at the beginning. My name is Shelby Jacobson and this is Cody. We live in Green Bay and…"

"Wait a minute." The pieces to this jumbled puzzle were finally sliding into place. He should have realized it sooner. Shelby Jacobson was Trina's sister. He knew Trina and Stephan had a son but he didn't know Shelby had a child, too. Not that he'd paid much attention to Trina's younger sister, since Shelby wasn't involved in the marina or the shipping business. She ran some sort of Christian day care center. "You're Trina's sister. That's why she gave you her phone to call me, right? Did she tell you she was in trouble?"

Shelby nodded, looking relieved. "Yes. But we're all in trouble, now. Trina promised you'd keep us safe. And she said you'd tell me what's going on. Trina mentioned you're her contact. What is she involved in? What's going on at the marina? Exactly what is the source of the danger?"

He curled the fingers of his injured hand experimentally. The pain was better now. He wasn't completely useless but he'd probably need to call Rafe if they were in danger. "I'll answer your questions the best I can but right now, you might know more than I do."

She opened her mouth to say something, but he quickly interrupted. "Don't worry, you're safe here," he assured her gruffly. "I'd never turn away a woman and her child, no matter who the father is."

Her gaze narrowed with annoyance, but he pivoted and gestured toward the great room. His eyes fell once more on the boy, who stopped crying long enough to stare at him with wide green eyes, identical to his own. A sick feeling settled in his gut. Irritably, he thrust it away. "Come in and take off your coats."

"Thank you," Shelby murmured helping Cody remove his bulky jacket before shrugging out of hers. She tossed them over a nearby chair and then crossed over to the wide sofa facing the tall fireplace.

Alex sent Rafe, his coast guard liaison, a quick text message telling him that he'd be in touch soon. Rafe was on standby, after having checked out Shelby at the truck stop to make sure she hadn't been followed, but Alex wouldn't require backup yet. He needed time to figure out what happened to Trina that forced her to give her sister the code phrase and her phone.

The boy climbed up next to Shelby on the couch and pressed against her. She put a protective arm around his shoulders. The two shared the same golden shade of blond hair and the same stubborn chin.

His sister Kayla came into the great room, sending him a wary glance before greeting Shelby. "Hi, I'm Kayla. I don't want to interrupt, but I just finished making a batch of chocolate chip cookies." She flashed

Cody a warm smile. "Are you interested in sampling a few?"

Cody eagerly looked up, then hesitated and shook his head, scooting closer to Shelby. Alex frowned. What was the boy so afraid of? He tried to wipe the scowl from his features. "Kayla's cookies are the best. And you'd better get a couple, before Clyde finds them."

Cody threw him a puzzled look. "Clyde?"

"Our new cocker spaniel puppy, although no matter how many times we tell him that he's a puppy, he still thinks he's a boy, spending his entire day trying to eat people food." Alex wrinkled his face in mock disgust as he sat in a nearby chair.

The lure of a puppy who liked people food was too much to resist. Cody's gaze shifted between Alex and Shelby, his tiny brow furrowed as if leaving Shelby's side was a monumental decision.

"It's okay, Cody. I promise I won't leave without you. Go ahead and see the puppy." She let him off the hook, seemingly relieved at having him out of the way. Alex understood she was scared and wanted answers. But what exactly did Shelby have to gain by claiming the boy was his son?

She'd claimed they were in danger, but he needed to know exactly what happened, what had brought them here. After all, Trina had been his inside contact, not Shelby.

"Okay," Cody agreed readily enough but moved reluctantly away from her.

Kayla held out her hand. Cody trustingly took it. "You know, I have a daughter about your age. Her name is Brianna and she's spending the day with her grandmother. Maybe if you're still here later this afternoon, you'll get to meet her." Kayla chatted to the boy as she led him into the kitchen.

Shelby turned toward him with a look of abject horror etched on her face. "You have a *daughter* about the same age as Cody?"

Alex hissed a long breath between his teeth. "Kayla is my sister, not my wife. And let me make one thing perfectly clear. You and I did not create a child together."

Her eyes widened in frank dismay. "Of course we didn't. Cody is Trina's son."

For a moment he was taken aback. Then he scowled. "You mean he's Trina and Stephan's son."

"Trina told me you were his biological father." Shelby twisted her hands in her lap although he admired how she kept her voice steady. "Cody was born September tenth, roughly four years and six months ago. And Trina gave me this." She reached into her pocket and pulled out a crumpled slip of paper.

Alex took the scrap of paper from her and stared at his own handwriting in shock. This was the initial note he'd given Trina all those years ago, after their night together.

"She told me that once you knew about Cody being your son, you'd help keep him safe."

Unable to sit still, Alex jumped up to pace the length of the room. How was this possible?

One night. They were only together for one night. He swallowed hard. "Okay, but if that's true, why wouldn't Trina have told me that she was pregnant? Why marry Stephan?"

"I don't know. Trina didn't confide in me, either."

He jammed his fingers through his hair in frustration. Alex met Trina shortly after arriving in Green Bay. He'd been trying to dig up information on a tip about possible drug trafficking in the area. Trina seemed to know all about the boats entering and leaving the harbor so he had asked her out a few times to see if she'd let anything slip.

He hadn't meant for things to go so far. He wasn't proud of his actions, and had distanced himself from her after the night they'd spent together.

"I knew Trina had a child, but when Trina married Stephan a few months after the boy was born, I assumed the child was his," he admitted in a low tone. "Frankly, I was relieved that she'd moved on to someone else after our night together." And he'd never made the mistake of getting too close to anyone on the job ever again. "So why have you decided to spring this news on me now?"

"Because Cody's in danger. And Trina obviously thought you needed to know he was your son, in order to protect him. Early this morning, Trina called and asked me to meet her down at the marina. She asked me to take Cody and made me promise to call you. She was going to come with us, but then..." her voice trailed off.

A chill snaked down his spine and he stopped in the center of the room, slowly turning to face her. On the phone she'd mentioned something about a man with a gun. "And then what? What happened?"

Shelby hesitated, worrying her lower lip between her teeth. He glanced at her upset expression, feeling an uncharacteristic spurt of sympathy for her, before abruptly turning away. *Don't go there,* he warned himself. He'd help Cody and Shelby but becoming emotionally involved was out of the question.

"On the way to my car, Trina spotted someone. She told me to run and she took off, heading back toward the marina. I caught a glimpse of a man with a gun. I—I grabbed Cody and ran."

"And Trina?" Alex forced himself to ask, although he could guess what happened next by the stricken look in Shelby's gaze.

"I think he killed her." Shelby's voice was barely above a whisper. "I dialed 9–1–1 but..."

Alex winced, unable to bear the frank pain in her eyes, crossing over to where Shelby sat on the edge of the sofa. He couldn't imagine how terrified she must have felt—witnessing an attack on her sister.

"She risked her life to save us," Shelby continued, her eyes welling with tears. "She drew the gunman away, sacrificing herself to save her son. Your son."

Awkwardly, he sat beside her and placed his injured arm around her shoulders. For a moment she held herself stiff, but then sank against him, burying her face in his chest. Muffled sobs reached his ears and his shirt became damp with tears, but still he held her close. He murmured soothingly even as his hand delved into the softness of her hair. The sweet, spicy scent of it teased his nostrils. Holding her soothed him, too. Trina's death was a shock. She'd put her life on the line for them, to help bring the drug smugglers to justice. Who had killed her?

"I'm sorry." Shelby sniffled loudly and pulled away from his embrace. "It's just that every time I think of trying to tell Cody that his mother might never come home, I get all choked up. How do you tell a four-year-old something like that?"

Stunned, the full implication of her statement hit him like a snow-laden log falling on his head. If Trina was dead, and if he was the boy's father, then he was the child's only living parent. Ten minutes ago he hadn't known he had a son, much less one he might be solely responsible for. "Wait a minute, maybe there's some mistake...."

"I don't think so." Shelby misunderstood his murmured comment and took a deep shuddering breath. "I saw the guy aim at her and shoot. She fell to the ground and didn't get up."

Alex fought back a surge of panic. A father? No. This couldn't be happening. He wasn't father material. Look at the role model he'd had. His old man drank too much and hadn't hesitated to lash out if he and Kayla said the wrong thing. Alex had vowed he'd never have children.

Yet, Cody had his green eyes.

Taking a deep breath he concentrated on identifying one problem at a time. It had been dark and Shelby only thought she saw her sister get shot. Even if she fell to the ground, Trina may have survived. Trina knew how to take care of herself.

He focused his attention on the problem at hand. Shelby and Cody needed protection from whomever had attacked Trina. Trina had been leaking information to the coast guard and DEA for the past two years, playing a very dangerous role. Someone on the drug smuggler's payroll must have caught onto her. She may have gotten careless, digging too hard to find proof that Alex was targeting the wrong suspect. Whatever she'd found, he could only imagine she'd been shot to keep her mouth shut. He couldn't help but wonder what she'd learned, and if her theory had been right. She'd vowed her father was innocent, but Alex had never been totally convinced.

Drugs were coming in on Russ Jacobson's ships and Alex believed that Jacobson had to know what was going on right under his nose. In Alex's opinion, Jacobson himself could be the mastermind behind the entire drug smuggling operation.

But did that mean Russ Jacobson was capable of having his own daughter killed? It was a stretch, but without proof one way or the other, he had no way of knowing for sure.

"Tell me what's going on," Shelby pleaded.

"It's complicated," he warned. "But first, are you sure the person with the gun was a man? Did you see him clearly?"

"No, I couldn't see him much at all, but I'm pretty sure he was a man." Shelby stared at him, her brow furrowed. "And in the car when we were driving away, Cody asked me if the *bad man* hurt his mom."

"What? You mean *Cody* actually saw the guy?" This news changed everything. The danger was worse than he'd imagined if Cody was a witness to the potential leader behind the smuggling.

Alex eased away, trying to unobtrusively disentangle his hand from her hair. The silky strands seemingly had a will of their own as they clung to his fingers. He glanced toward the kitchen where the boy had disappeared. "I need to talk to him."

"Oh, no you don't." Shelby's tone was sharp and she

tugged on his arm when he moved to get up. He hid a wince as a tender nerve zinged with a shaft of pain. "Not until you tell me what's going on. Besides, Cody has been through an awful ordeal. He practically saw his mother being murdered. I don't want him to relive the horror all over again so soon."

"But if he's seen the bad guy, maybe we can get a description or at least something to go on." Alex understood her reluctance to expose the boy to more distress, but this was a possible murder investigation. Not to mention, a potential lead to the organizer behind the drug smuggling ring. Trina's murder was obviously linked to his case. Or rather, to Rafe's case.

"Maybe you can talk to him later," she hedged. She stood up and walked closer to the fireplace, as if needing the warmth. "I brought him here so that you'd keep him safe. We need to protect him, not traumatize him."

Alex frowned, understanding her logic to a certain extent. But decided to let the subject go for now when Kayla and Cody emerged from the kitchen trailed by the clumsy puppy.

"Shelby, look at Clyde," Cody said happily. "Isn't he great?"

"He sure is." Shelby's face softened into a warm smile and Alex couldn't dismiss her obvious love for the boy.

In a daze, Alex did the mental math and came to the conclusion that the timing was right for him to have fathered Cody, although for all he knew Trina could have been sleeping with both him and Stephan at the same time. He'd request a DNA test at the very least, so that he would know for sure.

During the time he'd been undercover as a longshoreman, he hadn't seen Trina's son at all. Wisely, she'd kept him far away from the unsavory characters who had often hung out at the docks.

One look at Cody now, though, told him almost as much as a DNA test. At first he was so focused on Cody's blond hair, he hadn't really looked at the rest of his facial features. He could see that aside from the hair and the stubborn chin, Cody was the mirror image of himself at that age. Kayla had a box full of their baby pictures in the attic to prove it. The kid's green eyes haunted him.

Not the kid, he admonished himself. *My son. I'd better get used to the fact that Cody could really be my son.*

Shelby knelt beside Cody and scratched the pup behind the ears. "So how were the cookies? Did Clyde get any?"

Cody giggled as he petted the puppy. "No. Dogs can't eat people food. It's bad for them, 'specially chocolate. The cookies were good, but not as good as yours," he loyally added.

"I can show you to your rooms." Kayla's intensely curious gaze bounced back and forth between the three of them. "That way you'll have some time to freshen up or to take a nap, if you prefer, before dinner."

"Oh, well—" Shelby's hesitant gaze swung around to collide with Alex's.

Alex raised a brow at her dismay. Clearly Shelby hadn't thought any further than tracking him down. Logically, he knew he should turn both of them over to Rafe. But now that they were here, he'd rather keep them close at hand. At least, until he'd gotten a chance to talk to Cody.

"Kay's right. You're both safe here, so there's no point in you leaving to go somewhere else. Especially when this place has more than enough room." He flashed a crooked smile, waving a hand at the various rooms overhead. "There's plenty of privacy, I'm the only guest at the moment."

Shelby drew in a long breath, reaching up to rub at her temple. "All right, then," she agreed slowly. She stabbed him with a fierce glance. "But we still need to talk."

Alex hesitated, glancing down at Cody who was watching them both curiously. "We will, but for now, why don't you get settled into your rooms. I have some phone calls to make."

"Me, too," she said with a frown.

"That's not a good idea. You can't tell anyone you're here or what you've seen," he warned. "I'll explain more later."

He could tell she wasn't happy with being put off, but she also clearly didn't want to say much in front of Cody. Obviously she took her role of being the boy's protector very seriously.

Slowly she nodded. "All right." She turned to Cody. "Should we check out our rooms, partner?"

The boy nodded, although his attention was focused on Clyde who jumped up on him, trying to lick him in the face. Within moments the two were rolling on the floor with Cody giggling madly over the puppy's enthusiastic affection.

Alex felt his chest tighten at the sight. He glanced

up to find Shelby staring at him intently. For a long moment, they exchanged a look full of understanding. Hers reinforced that she would protect Cody at all costs. His admitted the need to take things slow, so he didn't scare the boy.

He watched them walk up the stairs, grappling with the knowledge that he could deny the truth all he wanted, but he was likely Cody's father.

What he was going to do about it, he had no clue.

Shelby's earlier fear slowly began to fade as she gazed at her surroundings, while Kayla gave them the nickel tour. They mounted the staircase to the second story. The log home was even more impressive inside. A cathedral ceiling towered overhead giving an expansive view over the great room from the loft encircling the second floor. When Kayla showed them two adjoining rooms, Shelby saw that her earlier assumption was correct. Each room contained patio doors leading out onto the snow-covered deck.

"The shared bathroom is through this door here." Kayla crossed the room to demonstrate. "And you can leave the connecting door open, if you prefer."

"You have a beautiful home." Shelby admired how the furnishings in the room had a rustic look, from the overstuffed chairs to the pine, sleigh-shaped bed frame. For the first time since leaving the marina in a mad rush, fully expecting the gunman to come after them, she felt safe. Secure. Because of Alex?

Kayla's mouth formed a sad smile. "Thank you. My husband had a hand in building it himself, before he died."

"I'm sorry." Shelby inwardly winced at her blunder. She couldn't imagine how difficult it would be for a woman to raise a child alone after her husband's death.

"That's all right." Kayla straightened, shaking off the despondency. "He died nearly two years ago, but he was a wonderful man. And I'm not totally alone, his mother helps me by watching over Brianna when I'm busy working. Well, here I am jabbering in your ear, when all you want to do is relax for a bit. Dinner will be ready about six. If you're hungry before that, just come down to the kitchen. There's always plenty to eat."

"Thank you." When Kayla left, Shelby closed the door behind her and glanced over at Cody. He didn't usually take naps, but his eyelids drooped as a result of his interrupted night. She wasn't feeling too perky herself and the white down comforter on the bed looked soft and inviting. "So, partner, how about we lie down for a few minutes?"

"I don't wanna lie down." A wide yawn belied his words but he pried his eyes open, fighting fatigue the way kids tended to do. "Are we gonna live here now? I like Clyde."

Shelby shook her head, eyeing the puppy that had followed them upstairs, claiming Cody as his new-found friend. Clearly, every child should have a pet. She made a mental vow to get Cody a dog of his own once this mess was over. Would Alex mind? No, she wasn't going there. If she wanted Cody to have a puppy, he'd have one.

"We can't live here, Cody. In the spring and sum-mer, these rooms are rented out to guests. We're just lucky there isn't anyone here now." Inspiration struck. "Would you like to take a nap with Clyde?"

"Yeah!" Cody ran into his room, the puppy close on his heels. Her ruse worked, forestalling further questions about his father or their possible future together. She wouldn't be able to dodge the little boy's questions forever.

But first and foremost, Cody needed to be safe. Once they were out of danger, she intended to ask Alex to grant her sole custody. The apprehensive expression in his eyes, when he'd looked at Cody, convinced her that he wasn't overly thrilled to be a father. Which was fine with her. She couldn't have loved Cody any more if he really were her son.

Cody would feel better, once he knew what to expect in the future.

Shelby left open the adjoining door between their rooms, so that she'd hear Cody when he awoke. She slid between the sheets, sighing gratefully as the down mattress cushioned her tired and aching body. Sleep should have come easily.

Instead Alex's face swam in her mind, interrupting her search for blessed oblivion. She couldn't believe she'd cried on his shoulder. She hadn't leaned on a man in a long time, and Alex wasn't exactly the best candidate. He was too intimidating by far. And besides, maybe he wasn't married, but he'd clearly been irresponsible all those years ago.

Instantly she felt ashamed. She couldn't pass judgment on him for having an intimate relationship with Trina, since she wouldn't have Cody in her life if he hadn't.

But she didn't get the sense he held the same Christian beliefs she did. She'd found God as her savior after an awful experience in college, where she'd narrowly escaped being sexually assaulted. She'd found solace in God and her church, and the people there had helped her again after she'd suffered a brutal attack at the shipyard a few years ago. She'd overcome her fear of men slowly but surely, with help from the Lord. Creating her Little Lamb's Day Care Center had helped her find a greater purpose in life. She hadn't planned to have children of her own—she wasn't sure she'd ever trust a man enough to risk her heart—but she'd love to raise Cody as her son.

Shelby knew she was getting ahead of herself, since she didn't really know what Alex's plans were, so she tried not to dwell on him. Or his relationship with her sister. She trusted him only as far as his ability to keep them safe.

Nothing more.

Tossing and turning in the unusually soft bed, her unanswered questions swirled through her mind. What had Trina been involved with? What was the source of the danger? Who had Cody seen?

She couldn't help a tiny flash of guilt. Maybe she should let Alex question him, get some answers. But she knew all too well what it felt like to be a victim. She didn't want to cause Cody to have nightmares like she'd had. The poor kid needed time to assimilate what had happened.

And really, how much detail would a four-year-old be able to give in a description, anyway?

She wondered what was going on back in Green Bay.

She didn't talk often to her father, but surely he'd find out soon about what happened to Trina. She'd have to call him. And what about Stephan? Had Stephan discovered the truth about Cody's biological father last night? Was that the reason Cody was in danger?

No. She couldn't believe Stephan was the *bad man* that Cody had mentioned. Up until now, Cody had called Stephan *dad* even if they were never really close.

Too many questions and she grew irritated with Alex for not giving her nearly enough answers.

She must have fallen asleep because she abruptly woke up, blinking groggily in the darkness, instantly aware of her strange surroundings, wondering what had woken her so suddenly. In a rush she remembered the bed-and-breakfast, and Alex. Outside, dusk had fallen, telling her she had slept longer than she'd planned. Quickly pulling on her clothes, she poked her head through the connecting doorway, her gaze searching for Cody.

His bed was rumpled, but empty.

She paused to listen for sounds of him playing with the puppy downstairs, but everything was quiet— though not for long.

The sharp retort of a gunshot from somewhere outside ripped through the silence of the night.

"No!" Shelby ran downstairs, barely pausing to grab her coat from the chair before she threw open the door. Her mind raced with terrifying thoughts of what she might find as she barreled out into the frigid moonlit night desperate to find her nephew.

Chapter 3

Shelby peered through the night, forcing her eyes to adjust to the darkness. The snowy ground showed a trail of footprints. She thrust her arms into her coat sleeves even as she slipped and stumbled on the icy trail of trampled snow leading back around the house. The darkness swallowed her. Concern for Cody overpowered her usual fear of the night.

"Cody!" Shelby began to shout as she dodged between trees. Her voice sounded distant through the roaring in her ears. She noted another building—a pole barn, hidden in the woods to the left of the house. A shaft of light shone through the small side door left ajar. "Cody?"

Another gunshot ripped through the air, louder this time. With a sob of horror, Shelby burst through the door. She glanced around wildly. Alex stood in the cen-

ter of the room holding a gun, wearing a pair of ear-
muffs.

Alex pulled them off the moment he saw her.

"Shelby? What's wrong?" In an instant, he crossed
over to her, lightly grasping her arm.

Helplessly, she shook her head, choking back tears
and gasping for breath. Her heart pounded frantically in
her chest. "I—I woke up and Cody wasn't in the room.
And th-then I heard gunshots."

Chagrined, he glanced over to the target he'd clearly
been using. "I'm sorry. I should have realized you'd
worry."

"The last time I heard gunfire, my sister was shot."
She couldn't help pinning him with an accusatory look.
A burst of anger quickly replaced her gut-wrenching
fear. She tore from his grip, curled her fingers into a fist
and smacked him square in the chest. "What on earth
possessed you to shoot off a gun?"

He frowned and glanced down at the weapon in his
hand, as if noticing it for the first time. "I needed to
work on my arm. It's not what it should be. Considering
you came here for protection, I thought I'd better practice. I'm sorry. I wasn't thinking about Trina."

She stared at the long paper targets hanging over
sheets of plywood propped in front of several bales of
hay stacked in the back of the shed, forcing herself to
think logically. Alex wasn't the bad guy here. He was
Trina's contact which meant he must be a good guy.
And he was Cody's father. He was just trying to protect them.

Shelby drew a deep, shuddering breath. For years,
she'd avoided men, but suddenly now here she was, to-

tally dependent on Alex for safety. The idea was extremely disconcerting.

She let go of her anger, knowing her overreaction wasn't his fault. Since his goal was to protect them, how could she argue?

She glanced at Alex, and he shook his head at the unspoken questions in her eyes. "Let's go back to the house," he suggested. "So you can see for yourself that Cody's fine."

Shelby slowly nodded, following him outside down the path she'd taken a few minutes ago.

When a low hanging branch tangled in her hair, she tried to yank free, muttering under her breath.

"Here, let me help." Alex came up behind her and deftly unhooked the naturally curly lock of hair from the branch. His nearness made her shiver and not necessarily with fear. She stepped away. She shouldn't be tempted to lean on Alex, not when she'd fought so hard to remain independent.

"Thanks." Her breath shortened and she hunched her shoulders, careful to duck far below the trees. His calm presence managed to distract her from her fear of the dark.

Alex must be a cop. That would explain why Trina sent them to him for protection. Her preoccupation with her sister caused her to stumble over a fallen branch, half-hidden beneath the snow. Alex caught her by the arm.

"Watch your step." Alex frowned when she instinctively pulled away from his touch. He glanced down at her sodden feet. "We need to get you a pair of boots. Kayla's already loaned Cody a pair of Brianna's."

"We left Green Bay in a hurry." Shelby grit her teeth together to stop them from chattering. Alex's domineering personality put her on the defensive. She wasn't used to anyone questioning her parenting skills. "Besides, we didn't have as much snow there as you do here."

"I'm sure Kayla has a pair that'll fit." Alex kept his hand under her elbow as they climbed up the few steps to the house.

Shelby refrained from answering. Safe inside the well-lit house, she breathed a sigh of relief. She'd conquered the darkness, at least for a few minutes. Feeling foolish for her rush of panic, she removed her coat and her sodden tennis shoes. Her jeans and socks were damp, but she ignored the discomfort, simply walking toward the sound of voices coming from the kitchen that had died down in their absence.

When they entered, Cody ran up to her. She caught him close in a quick hug, which he tolerated for a half a second before squirming away. She reluctantly released him.

"Aunt Shelby, were you practicing shooting with my other dad outside? When I get older, he said he's gonna teach me how to shoot a real BB gun."

"Oh, really?" Calmer now, Shelby sent Alex a narrow look. Just who did he think he was making a promise like that, without even asking her? No matter what biology said, he was *not* Cody's only parent, and he had no right to make decisions like that without consulting her. She didn't approve of guns and she especially didn't approve of teaching children how to shoot them. Shelby held on to her temper with an effort, turning her attention to Cody. "Who's your new friend?" she asked, gesturing to the girl standing near the stove with Kayla.

"That's Brianna. She's five. Clyde's her puppy, but he likes me better."

Shelby rolled her eyes at the rivalry in his tone. "I'm sure Clyde likes you both the same. Are you hungry, or did you eat dinner without me?"

"No, of course not," Kayla said. "Brianna, you and Cody need to set the table."

"Okay," Brianna agreed as she dashed toward the cabinets on the other side of the kitchen, dragging Cody with her.

"I'm sorry," Kayla murmured, her gaze apologetic. "I didn't realize you'd heard the gunshots until I saw you running for the door. I wanted to come after you, but I couldn't go outside like this." She pointed down to her feet, covered only in thick socks.

Shelby tried to smile. Cody was safe and that was the important thing. "It's okay. I'm just not keen on guns."

"Guns are only a problem when they're misused." Alex spoke testily. "Don't worry, I keep trigger locks on all my weapons."

All his weapons? How many did he have? Shelby wasn't about to stand around, debating the pros and cons of gun legislation with him. Not on the same day when she'd watched someone shoot her sister. In fact, she was glad Cody was doing all right in here, and hadn't reacted to the noise of the gunshot with the heart-wrenching fear she'd felt. Maybe he hadn't seen as much during their frantic dash to the parking lot as she'd thought. Gathering every ounce of patience, she steered the conversation toward a safe topic. "So, what's for dinner?"

"Venison stew," Kayla replied.

"Venison?" Shelby tried to hide her dismay.

Kayla chuckled. "That was my reaction too, at first. But trust me, you'll like it."

"Don't tell me it tastes like chicken."

Kayla laughed. "Why don't you two go have a seat in the great room?" she suggested. "I'll call you when everything's ready."

Back in the great room, Shelby noticed that the fire had died down. She reached for a log, intent on adding to the dying embers, but a masculine arm snatched it from her grasp.

"Here, let me. You need to change into some dry clothes."

Annoyed, Shelby wondered if all men liked to pretend they were in charge of the world, or if this was a characteristic unique to Alex McCade. She might be afraid of the shadows, but years of living alone had taught her to fend for herself in her own way. She valued her independence and preferred to keep it that way. Dire circumstances had brought her here. She needed Alex to keep Cody safe. She did *not* need him to boss her around.

She sat on the edge of the sofa, propping her feet on the stone hearth of the fireplace. "I don't have anything else with me. Besides, I'm fine."

"I'm sure Kayla will lend you a few things."

"I'm fine," she repeated stubbornly. She didn't want to put her hostess out any more than she already had.

"I know you're upset with me," Alex murmured in a low tone. "I promise I'll try to answer your questions. But I don't want to talk in front of the kids." Alex waved in the general direction of the kitchen, where Cody and Brianna were still helping Kayla by setting the table.

Shelby lifted her gaze to his. He wasn't looking at her, though, but stared thoughtfully into the fire. When he wasn't ordering her around, he was very attractive, not that she had any business noticing. He wasn't at all her type, even if she wasn't interested in men, which she wasn't. Considering her past experiences, she didn't trust men on a personal level and that included Alex. "They won't hear us if we're quiet. Be honest with me. Are you in law enforcement?"

"Sort of." He shrugged and glanced at her. "I work for the government."

Her eyes widened. "FBI?"

He shook his head. "DEA. Shelby, you'll need to keep everything I tell you confidential. Your life and Cody's depends upon it."

She swallowed hard at the seriousness of his tone. "Okay."

Alex took a deep breath and let it out slowly. "How much do you know about your father's shipping business and the marina?"

"Not a lot. Most of my time is spent running my day care center." Shelby wrinkled her forehead, realizing she'd have to call her assistant soon to let Debbi know she wouldn't be there on Monday. "Trina and Stephan manage the marina."

"I know. Trina was helping us, providing inside information."

Shelby frowned. "Like what?"

"Details that may be pertinent to us finding the drugs being smuggled into the U.S. from Canada through the

Great Lakes. Names of ships, routes, etcetera. We're trying to find the identity of the mastermind behind the drug smuggling operation. We knew there were several insiders, including one in customs, but we needed to find the guy in charge."

"Drugs? On my father's ships?" She stared at him in shock. "You can't be serious."

"Shelby, I saw the shipments firsthand. I was working undercover as a longshoreman, reporting to Bobby Drake, the warehouse foreman and your father's right-hand man. During the time I spent on the docks, I discovered drugs coming in on your father's ships over and over again. That much is fact. What we don't know is who's responsible."

She sucked in a harsh breath. She'd had no idea. "You think my father is involved, don't you?"

"I saw him on the docks a fair amount. He kept his hand in every aspect of his business. Russ Jacobson was especially interested in the cargo on the ships that traveled from Sault Saint Marie to Green Bay, with the final destination being Chicago. The same ships where we found drugs."

"No!" Shelby jumped to her feet, her hands fisted at her sides. "I'm telling you, Alex, my father isn't involved in drug smuggling."

"Shh." He frowned at her, and then glanced over his shoulder toward the kitchen where the kids were playing with Clyde. "Calm down. Trina felt the same way you do. Yet we have no choice but to treat everyone as a suspect, until proven otherwise. You wanted to know the source of the danger, well this is it. Whoever hurt Trina must have figured out she was feeding us information."

"Dinner's on," Kayla called.

Alex glanced toward the kitchen. "We'll discuss this more later."

Shelby didn't want to discuss it later. She wanted to talk about it now, so she could show Alex he was wrong. Yet in spite of her instinctive defense, she felt uneasy. She wasn't an idiot. Her father's shipping company dominated the Great Lakes shipping business. How could drugs be on his ships without his knowledge? She shoved aside the shimmer of doubt. She didn't know how her father had missed what was going on, but she was relieved to hear Trina believed in their father's innocence, too.

She was tempted to insist he tell her more, but bit her tongue, in deference to Cody. The poor child had been traumatized enough. He didn't need to hear his aunt arguing with his *other dad*.

"Yes. We will talk more later." Her gaze warned him that she expected answers. He returned her look with a bland one of his own.

Kayla called out to them from the kitchen. "Are you coming?"

They both hurried into the kitchen. Instead of eating in the formal dining room usually reserved for guests, they crowded around the oak picnic table in the kitchen. There should have been plenty of room, especially when Cody insisted on sitting next to Brianna. Yet Alex seemed to take up more than his share of space. His presence was disturbing and not just because she usually avoided being so close to a man. For some strange reason, his woodsy aftershave teased her senses.

"Excuse me," she muttered when their elbows bumped for the third time. She scooched over a few more inches. Any farther, she'd be sitting on the floor.

"Switch places with me, I'm left-handed." Alex lifted his plate and stood while she slid into his spot so that he could sit at the end.

He was still too close. His right hand rested on the table and Shelby could see a few of the reddened scars above the denim cuff of his shirt. What had happened to him? Mesmerized by the dark sprinkling of hair on his forearm, she didn't realize she'd eaten half her stew until Kayla snickered at her from across the table. Flustered, she stared at her bowl. Had the meat tasted different? She couldn't say one way or the other.

"What do you think?" Kayla asked.

She flashed her a sheepish smile. "You're absolutely right, Kayla. The venison stew is wonderful."

"Thanks. Alex is a hunter and he shot the deer himself, last year." Her voice rang with pride.

"Can I learn how to hunt deer?" Cody piped up from the other side of the table.

"No."

"Sure."

Both Shelby and Alex answered simultaneously. She threw him a dark look. Alex had the grace to look away guiltily.

"I don't think you'll be old enough to hunt for quite a while yet, Cody," Shelby amended, noticing the confusion in the boy's eyes. She mentally cursed Alex for interfering. She'd been making decisions regarding

Cody's upbringing for years, how could he expect to suddenly step in and take over?

Because he's Cody's father. Shelby's appetite vanished and she stared down at her half-eaten food. The thought of losing Cody to Alex twisted her stomach into a hard knot. She loved Cody. She couldn't love him more if she'd borne him herself. What if Alex took him someplace far away where she'd never see him again?

Her fork clattered to her plate from fingers gone numb.

"Shelby? Are you okay?" Alex sent her a glance so full of concern she nearly blurted out the truth. Only a deep sense of self-preservation made her hold her tongue.

"Sorry. I'm just clumsy I guess." Shelby tried to smile, but her face felt as if it might split in two with the effort.

Drugs coming in on her father's ships. Cody's bad man. Trina's death. Suddenly it was all too much. Obviously she needed Alex, in order to keep Cody safe, but a tiny part of her just wanted to grab Cody and run away from it all. But that was the problem, wasn't it? All alone with Cody would she ever be able to stop running? She couldn't condemn Cody to that kind of life. He was safer here with Alex. For now.

How she made it through the rest of dinner, she'd never know. Afterward she excused herself from helping with the dishes and retreated to her room long enough to use Trina's phone to place a call to their father and then to Debbi, her assistant manager of the day care center. Shelby didn't intend to break her promise to

Alex, but needed to at least find out about Trina. Maybe her sister had miraculously survived.

Punching the numbers on the phone pad, she dialed her father's number. A woman's voice drifted over the line after the third ring.

"Hello?"

Shelby swallowed her annoyance when her father's wife answered the phone. She didn't particularly care for the woman who'd become their stepmother. "Hi, Marilyn. Is Dad around?"

"Shelby? Your father's worried sick. He's been trying to call you for hours. What is wrong with you? You should be here with him. Don't you care about him at all? Where are you?"

Shelby winced at her shrill voice. "Please, Marilyn, stop yelling at me. Just put Dad on, would you?"

"Fine. Be that way."

Marilyn dropped the phone with a clatter making Shelby pull the instrument away from her ear. After a few minutes, her father's booming voice came over the line.

"Shelby? Where have you been? I've been calling your place all day."

"Sorry, Dad." Shelby tried not to back down from his accusatory tone, but it wasn't easy. Her relationship with her father wasn't great. When her mother was still alive, they'd been a close-knit family. Every Sunday, after church, they'd have family game night. She'd cherished those times. But things had gotten worse after her mother died. Her father had changed. Ever since her mother's death he'd been trying to toughen her up, trying to make her into something she wasn't. Someone like Trina. Most of the time she avoided her family, preferring her friends from church to the rowdy crowd who hung around at the marina. Her father never hesitated to vocalize his disapproval.

"I've been worried about you. Do you have Cody?"

"Yes, Cody's with me. We're safe. Everything is fine," she hastened to reassure him.

"So you haven't seen Trina, then?"

She hesitated, not wanting to lie, but not wanting to break her promise to Alex, either. "Not in a while," she hedged. To the best of her knowledge, no one had known that she was meeting Trina down by the marina. Cody had often stayed with her when her sister was working.

"Then you don't know." He let out a heavy sigh. "There's been a terrible accident, Shel." For a moment, he sounded like the father she used to know. The one who taught his young daughters how to sail on the waters of Lake Michigan. "Your sister…" He struggled to get the words out. "Someone shot her. She's dead."

Shelby closed her eyes against a wave of grief, even though she'd suspected the worst all along. To hear her father state the truth so bluntly was harder than she'd anticipated. "What—what happened?"

"I don't know." The helplessness in his tone was so uncharacteristic that Shelby wished she were with him. "I can't think of anyone who'd want to kill her. Of course I called the mayor, asking him to make Trina's murder a priority. It pays to have friends in high places. So far, Lieutenant Holden thinks it's a robbery, since all of the jewelry Trina had been wearing was stolen, including her wedding ring."

Her father sounded lost and forlorn, reinforcing what Shelby had known all along. He couldn't possibly be involved in something so heinous as drug smuggling, and he certainly played no part in Trina's death. A part of her wanted to blurt out the truth, how she'd seen the dark figure shoot Trina, but she held her tongue. For Cody's sake. "I'm sorry, Dad."

"Where are you? You said you have Cody with you? Because Stephan has been wondering where he is."

"I have Cody and we're staying with a friend." She frowned. "I know Stephan and Trina were having problems, and that Trina had moved out, but I'm sure this is still very hard on him."

"Yes. I was hoping they'd work things out." He sighed heavily. "Why don't you come home? I need you, Shelby. Trina—the police haven't released her body yet, so we haven't scheduled the funeral."

The funeral? A fresh wave of tears threatened and Shelby blinked them back with an effort and rubbed the scar at her temple.

Of course she and Cody would be expected to attend the funeral. But would that be good for Cody? Was it safe enough for him to attend? She honestly didn't know. "I'm sorry, but I can't come home right now, Dad. Please don't worry, we're fine. And I promise I'll stay in touch."

"See that you do." Russell Jacobson's tone hardened. "I know your church views prevented you and your sister from becoming close, but our family needs to stick together in times like this."

His words were sharp, an arrow piercing her heart. Her father had taken this attitude, acting as if her Christian path was somehow the wrong one, maybe because she'd found so much comfort in her church community, rather than with her family. "We weren't that close, but I loved Trina. And I love you, too. I'll call you later, Dad."

She snapped the phone shut before he could say anything more. A battery of emotions assailed her: grief, fear, anger, despair, loneliness. And of course, above all, guilt. Her father had a knack for making her feel guilty, even for events beyond her control.

Brushing away the evidence of her tears, Shelby stood, took a deep breath and squared her shoulders. Trina trusted her to keep Cody safe and that was exactly what she'd do. From here on out nothing mattered except the small boy who hadn't deserved to be dragged into harm's way.

Shelby crossed the room to the patio doors that led to the snow-covered deck surrounding the house. Troubled by her conversation with her father and her concerns about Cody's future, she gazed into the darkness outside. She didn't dare go home, not if that meant Cody would be in danger. But she knew her father was worried. With a sigh, she rested her forehead against the cool glass.

Dear Lord, guide me. Show me the way.

Shelby needed to seek God's guidance. Because no matter what she wanted, she had to do whatever was best for Cody.

Feeling calmer, she lifted her head and took several deep breaths. For a moment, she basked in the wonder of God's beauty, the snow-covered trees surrounding Kayla's log home and the occasional star twinkling in the velvet sky.

A bobbing light captured her gaze. She sucked in a quick breath and swiped at the fog on the glass. Intensely, she peered at the wooded area to the left side of the house.

The light was gone. She blinked, wondering if she'd imagined it. Maybe the events of the past twenty-four hours had gotten to her.

Shelby stood, indecisively. Maybe her tired mind had played tricks on her, but what if someone really was out there? She couldn't ignore the slim possibility.

She needed to find Alex.

Chapter 4

"Alex!" Shelby's serious tone made him spin away from the fireplace in the great room to look up at where she stood, leaning over the rail in the loft. "I think someone could be outside."

"You saw someone?" Immediately his senses went on alert.

"I saw a light. But it was gone so fast, it might have been my imagination." Shelby ran down the steps to meet him in front of the fireplace, her blue eyes round with alarm. "Is it even possible that Trina's shooter found us? Where's Cody?"

"Playing video games with Brianna." He wasn't surprised her first concern was for the boy. He couldn't bear the thought of either Shelby or Cody being in danger. He pushed aside his fear for their safety to think logically. A light in the woods? Could be a poacher with a flashlight. Or possibly Rafe? He'd asked Rafe to stake out the truck stop to make sure Shelby hadn't been followed. Had Rafe come out to the B & B to provide backup? Maybe. Maybe not. He'd need to investigate, to confirm. "I'm not sure how the shooter could have followed you here. It's probably nothing. Stay here. I'll check things out."

She caught his arm, preventing him from leaving. "Alone? Maybe I should go with you."

Did she think he couldn't handle himself? He frowned. He'd protect her with his life, if necessary. "You stay here, with Kayla and the kids. I'll be fine."

With excruciating slowness, her slim fingers loosened their grip on his arm and dropped away. The bare skin of his forearm tingled from her touch. Maybe his injured arm was overly sensitive from the damaged nerves.

Ignoring the strange sensation, he grabbed his coat and shoved his feet into sturdy snow boots. He grimaced, realizing he'd left his handgun in the shed after Shelby had gotten so upset.

He went into the cold night. The darkness was absolute. Black clouds obliterated most of the stars that might have illuminated the sky. He stood on the porch for a moment, his back against the wall of the log cabin, while he scanned the area.

Nothing seemed off-kilter. He dug his cell phone out of his pocket and texted Rafe.

R U outside the B & B

No in town

He stared at Rafe's response and debated whether he should explain about Shelby seeing a light or not. Shelby was tense, skittish. Could be she only thought she saw a light. Or more likely, saw a flash of headlights from the highway.

Need backup?

Rafe texted again.

No stay put.

Icy snow crunched beneath his boots as he made his way down the porch steps and around the side of the house. He didn't turn his flashlight on right away, preferring not to announce his presence if someone was out there. He took his time, stopping frequently to listen and look.

No telltale signs of lights anywhere.

Moving quietly, he made his way around to the left side of the house, along the path they'd taken earlier from the shed. He edged along the aluminum side of the shed. His gun was inside, but he didn't want to alert anyone by going in. He peered around the corner. For long seconds, he didn't move.

Nothing.

No owls hooting as they hunted for prey.

No white-tailed deer making their way through the trees searching for food.

No wolves roaming the night.

The lack of wildlife, or at least the sounds of wildlife, nagged at him. Sometimes animals could sense a pending storm. The thick clouds overhead reinforced that theory.

But sometimes they also sensed the presence of an intruder.

He slipped through the woods, finally turning on the flashlight and making a broad sweep around the house until his wounded arm ached with cold. There was no evidence of strange footprints in the undisturbed snow.

Shelby must have seen headlights through the trees, nothing more. He made another sweep around the house, and then convinced there was no immediate threat, he headed back inside.

Shelby glanced up at him expectantly from the corner of the sofa, one of Kayla's colorful quilts wrapped around her.

"Didn't see a sign that anyone has been here other than us," he said, as he toed off the snow boots. He crossed to warm his right arm by the fire.

"I know what I saw," she protested, her voice low and husky.

"I believe you." And he did. But Shelby was a city girl and this was the forest. They were far away from the civilization she was accustomed to. "Could have been a poacher, or maybe lights from the highway. We know you weren't followed here, so try not to worry. I'll keep you and Cody safe. No one will get past me to harm you." He couldn't hide the husky note of protectiveness in his voice. "I'll bunk here on the sofa tonight, just to be sure."

She captured her lower lip between her teeth, but didn't say anything as her faintly questioning gaze clung to his.

Mesmerized, he couldn't look away. Shelby was beautiful, in a softer, more unpretentious way than her sister. She was hesitant and shy where Trina had been bold and vivacious. Yet every minute he spent with Shelby, he found himself drawn to her. There was something about her that made him feel possessive. Protective. Alive.

And when she gazed at Cody, the love shining from her eyes made him ache with longing.

The crackle and pop of the logs in the fireplace only added to the charged atmosphere. He swallowed hard, inhaling the warm scent of cinnamon and spice that seemed to cling to her.

Focus, McCade. Concentrate on the case.

He cleared his throat. "Don't worry. I can get backup here quick, if we need it."

She frowned a little. "Backup? Like other DEA agents?"

"No. Like Rafe, my liaison with the coast guard. The DEA teamed up with the coast guard in order to break the drug smuggling ring." He glanced at her, hoping she wouldn't get upset about using Rafe for help, the way she had on the phone, but she didn't.

"How long have you worked for the government?" Shelby asked.

His entire adult life. He'd joined the DEA to help fight the war against drugs. Because he'd lost his best friend in high school, Toby, to a horrible drug overdose. But she didn't need to know all that. "Long enough. In one way or another, I've been working on this case for well over five years."

"Over five years?" Realization dawned in her eyes and she sucked in a harsh breath. "Cody."

He winced at the reminder. He wasn't used to explaining himself, but for some reason, he was tempted to do just that. He didn't want Shelby thinking the worst of him.

"I swear to you, I didn't know he was my son."

She shrugged and tucked a strand of hair behind her ear. "I know. The look on your face..." She trailed off. Then her expression closed up. "Your relationship with my sister is none of my business."

"We didn't have a relationship." His tone was blunt. "I—made a mistake. It was—well, we weren't in love or anything. I didn't see her again until several years later. After she agreed to help us." And by that time, their conversations had been short and terse, only about the case and nothing more.

She plucked at the threads on the quilt and then raised her guilty gaze to meet his. "Speaking of Trina, there's something you need to know. I called my father, using her phone."

"You what?" He ground his teeth together, trying to rein in his temper. "I told you not to tell anyone you were here, remember?"

"I didn't." She lifted her chin defiantly. In that moment, she reminded him of Trina. "I called my assistant at the day care center to let her know I wouldn't be in on Monday. And I called my father. But don't worry. I didn't tell anyone where we were or even who I was with. But my father confirmed Trina was shot to death at the marina." Her voice broke.

"I'm sorry," he murmured. He felt bad for Trina.

Someone had figured out she was leaking information. But who?

"Thank you. The police are investigating," she went on. "My father is on friendly terms with the mayor and he's pressing for a quick arrest. Apparently Lieutenant Holden thinks Trina's death was the result of a simple robbery."

"Holden? Eric Holden?" he interrupted.

"I guess. Why?"

He knew Rafe had worked with Eric Holden, and knowing Holden was involved in Trina's case made him feel better. As far as he could tell, Holden was a decent cop. In general, the Green Bay police department hadn't welcomed the interference of the coast guard and DEA. Eric had been the most accepting of the bunch, even if he hadn't fully bought into the theory of a Canadian drug running operation until they'd provided proof.

Would Holden give Rafe details about their investigation into Trina's death? Worth a try. He'd call Rafe first thing in the morning.

"Do you know him?" Shelby asked with a puzzled frown.

"I know about him from Rafe, but he doesn't know me. I worked deep under cover. And despite the standard line he gave your father, we both know Trina's death had nothing to do with a robbery. Trina must have stumbled into the truth behind this drug running operation. It's all linked to how the case started unraveling months ago." Three months ago, to be exact, when he'd been jumped and stabbed and set up to take the fall.

She reached up to massage her temple. "So now you know why my father couldn't possibly be involved in your case. Trina was his favorite. He loved her. If you could have heard him, you'd understand." She swallowed hard.

Alex didn't know what to say. A sense of unease washed over him. Trina had always claimed her father was innocent too, but he just couldn't be certain. It all seemed far too coincidental, how Russ Jacobson liked to be visible down at the shipyard. His interest in the ships coming from Sault Saint Marie to Green Bay and then to Chicago. The same ships where the drugs had been found.

Was he truly capable of killing his daughter, or ordering her death? The man behind the drug running scheme took innocent lives every day by exposing people, especially kids, to drugs. Not to mention, nearly killing him. He flexed his injured hand in surprise. Shelby's need for protection helped him to forget the pain.

Or maybe she just helped him understand there was more to life than just this case.

He shook his head at his foolish thoughts. For him there was only the case. Nothing more.

Shelby was right. The few interactions he'd witnessed between Russ and Trina indicated a deep fondness between father and daughter. But that didn't prove anything. When torn between love for his daughter and greed, who knew what he'd choose? And maybe there was someone else involved. Someone calling the shots, over Russ's head, or behind his back. There was a missing link, and he needed to find it to put this all together.

The sound of voices carried from the kitchen. Kayla's rooms were on the main level, tucked behind the kitchen and away from the guest rooms. Alex easily picked out Cody's excited tone rising above the din, asking if he could sleep with Clyde. Within moments, the boy laughed gleefully as he dashed through the great room, Brianna and puppy hot on his heels.

Cody saw him standing there and tried to stop but there must have been water on the floor so he slipped and skidded headfirst into Alex, cutting him off at the knees and nearly bowling him over.

As he regained his footing, Alex suddenly knew. The missing piece of the puzzle was his son.

"Sorry," Cody mumbled, when he disentangled himself from Alex and scrambled to his feet.

"No harm, no foul." Alex kept his tone light but inside, his emotions whirled. He desperately needed to question the boy, but the protective instincts vibrating from Shelby prevented him from pushing the issue. Besides, he couldn't help worrying about Cody, too. Could he afford to let his need to protect his son keep him from pursuing every lead on this case?

Cody wrinkled up his forehead. "What does that mean?"

Alex blinked, focusing on his son's curious face. "What? No harm, no foul? That just means I won't hold it against you, since you didn't hurt me."

"Oh." Cody still looked puzzled, and for the first time Alex wondered about the man who'd helped raise his son. What kind of father had Stephan Kirkland been to Cody? Did he spend Saturday afternoons pitching baseballs to the boy? Did they go hunting and fishing? Or to the movies together?

Did Cody miss him?

"Never mind." Shelby stood, shooting him an exasperated glance. "Cody, you need to go upstairs and get ready for bed."

"Okay. Brianna said I can sleep with Clyde tonight." The kid had a one-track mind and he'd focused it on the dog.

"How nice of her." Shelby flashed his niece a warm smile. Alex found himself wishing she'd smile like that for him.

"Brianna!" Kayla called from the other room. "You're supposed to be brushing your teeth."

The kids scampered in opposite directions and Alex turned to Shelby. "I have to talk to Cody. I need to know who he saw."

She stared at him for several seconds. "I know. But not yet." Fierce, she stood her ground. "I already told you, he's been through enough. Let him get a good night's sleep and then we'll see how he does."

"He's four years old. What if a good night's sleep makes it hard for him to remember what happened? Don't you realize he might be the key to cracking this case?" Alex raised his voice, unable to hide his frustration. He understood her protectiveness, he felt the same way, but honestly, how could a few questions hurt?

Shelby raised a hand to her forehead, grimacing as if she had a pounding headache. "Yes, I do. And I told you, we'll talk about it tomorrow. What more can you do tonight, anyway?"

He wasn't used to anyone questioning him, but at this point, he hated to admit she was right. Maybe it would be better for Cody to have a good night's sleep. "All right. Tomorrow then. No more stalling."

"I'm not stalling." Impatience laced her tone. "I want to know who is after him as much as you do. But I'm concerned about Cody's mental health, too. How much can a child take without breaking? What if all of this haunts him for the rest of his life?"

For a long moment, they stared at each other, on opposite sides of a line drawn in the sand.

Alex sighed in frustration. He strove to hang onto his temper. "I don't know," he allowed. "I don't want Cody hurt any more than you do. But I can't help if I don't know what the danger is."

"I thought you'd already had a list of suspects? Including my father." Shelby arched one brow. "If I recall correctly, you've accused Cody's *grandfather* of a despicable criminal act."

Stunned, he stared at her, unable to come up with a response to that. His son irrevocably tied his life to Russ Jacobson's. Lashing out at Shelby's father wouldn't win him any points. "I won't question Cody without your permission, okay? We need to work together on this."

Shelby eyed him warily for a tense moment. And then her shoulders slumped as if she'd been carrying the weight of a huge burden. "You're right. We need to work together."

He wanted to go to her, to ease the tension from her muscles. To pull her into his arms, offering comfort. Her features were fragile, as if another wrong word would make her break. She turned away, putting distance between them. "I'm going to put Cody to bed."

"May I join you?"

His question halted her midstep and she swung around to face him. "What?"

"I'd like to help put Cody to bed." Why was she staring at him like that? He tucked his hands into the pockets of his jeans. What did putting a kid to bed entail? Tucking him in? Reading a bedtime story? He hadn't done fatherly things with Brianna, and now he wished he had. He might be out of his league with this fatherhood stuff, but something made him stand there while Shelby stared at him in frank dismay. Maybe Cody didn't feel comfortable with him yet, so he'd act more like a father, starting now.

He couldn't protect Cody if his son didn't trust him.

"I—guess." Her stark frown of disapproval was not reassuring.

Alex almost let her off the hook, but held his tongue. With obvious reluctance, her back stiff and unyielding, she kept pace with him as they climbed the stairs together.

Inside his room adjacent to hers, the boy giggled as the puppy growled and pounced when his foot moved beneath the covers. The sound of Cody's childish laughter made Alex grin.

Shelby went over to Cody's bed and sat on the edge beside him. "Did you brush your teeth?"

Cody nodded vigorously. "Yep. Kayla gave me a toothbrush. How come dogs don't have to brush?"

"Because they have special treats that help keep their teeth clean." Shelby gently pushed the puppy aside, so she could pull the covers up to his chin.

"Why can't we use treats instead of toothpaste?" Cody persisted, more, Alex thought, to keep her talking than because he wanted to know. Either way, Alex noted Shelby never lost patience with Cody's stream of questions.

"Because people treats have sugar in them and sugar is bad for our teeth." She leaned over to hug and kiss him, even as he opened his mouth for another question. She forestalled it by placing a finger over his lips and giving him a no-nonsense look. "It's time for bedtime prayers."

As if someone flipped a switch, the boy quieted down. He pressed his tiny palms together and closed his eyes. "Dear God, please help me to be good and to follow Your path. Please bless Mommy and Daddy and Aunt Shelby and Clyde." There was a pause, and then he added, "And please bless my other dad, too. Amen."

"Amen," Shelby echoed softly.

Alex stared down at Cody, his throat was thick with emotion. Never in his life had anyone prayed for him. He hadn't grown up going to church. Had he missed out on something important?

"Good night, Cody," Shelby was saying. "Remember, I'll be right next door if you need anything."

Alex darted a glance over his shoulder and saw that indeed, she'd left the door open between their adjoining rooms.

"Okay. Can I leave my light on?" Cody's gaze hesitantly darted to Alex as if worried he would refuse.

He stepped forward, seeking and finding the light switch in the bathroom. "How about if we leave the bathroom light on, but close the door a bit, like this?" He demonstrated what he meant.

Cody earnestly nodded his approval. "That's good."

Alex wondered if Cody had always been afraid of

the dark or if this was something new. A surge of protectiveness enveloped him. For the first time, he understood Shelby's resistance. At that moment, he knew he wouldn't hesitate to stop anyone who threatened to harm his son.

"I love you, Cody," Shelby said, leaning over to finally give him a hug and a kiss. "Always and forever."

"Me, too." He hugged and kissed her back. Then looked up at Alex expectantly.

Awkwardly, he leaned down to smooth a hand over Cody's fair hair, in lieu of a kiss. "Good night, Cody."

"G-night." Cody pulled Clyde close within the crook of his arm. The puppy didn't seem to mind, lifting its head to lick the boy's cheek.

Shelby stood and together they left the room. She headed over to stand at the railing overlooking the great room. Alex sighed out his pent-up breath. He spoke without thinking. "That wasn't too hard."

She arched an eyebrow at him. "No, I suppose not."

He let out an exasperated sigh. "Why do I have the feeling you don't approve of me as Cody's father?"

Shelby flushed, but thrust out her chin stubbornly. "Because I don't. You have no clue what being a father really means."

Okay, she had him there. His role model was a workaholic father who spent zero time with his kids. And when his dad wasn't working, he drank. He'd taken the brunt of his father's fits of anger to shield Kayla. Until he grew strong enough to defend himself.

But over these past few months, he'd bonded a bit with his niece, Brianna. So he knew a little about kids. Or at least, he'd learned to be comfortable around them.

Maybe he'd never been a full-time father, but Shelby's attitude bothered him. She'd known him for less than a day. Was she really willing to write him off so quickly? Alex hid his consternation under a cool look. "I'm a good uncle to Brianna, so it's not as foreign as you think. I'm sure Cody and I will figure it out together."

The color left her face as if he'd slapped her. Then he understood. Shelby was afraid he'd take custody of the boy, cutting her completely out of his life. What had she said? Something about Cody pretty much living with her for the past three years? Before he could hasten to reassure her, she spun on her heel and headed for her room, closing the door behind her with a sharp click.

He stared at the door, imagining she'd have built a barricade by hand, brick by brick to keep him far away from Cody.

And he didn't much care for the feeling of being left alone on the outside looking in.

Shelby washed her face, wishing she'd kept her mouth shut with Alex. She stared at her reflection in the mirror. What was wrong with her? Where was her Christian attitude now? God would not approve of her picking a fight with Alex McCade.

Alex was Cody's father. A tiny, selfish part of her knew she wasn't being fair to Alex because she didn't want to lose custody of Cody.

But Cody certainly deserved a father. Alex was a decent man who truly cared about his son. She needed to let go of her fears.

Before climbing into bed, she sank to her knees, bowing her head in prayer.

Forgive me, dear Lord. Help me to follow the path You have chosen for me, now and always. And please, Lord, give me the strength and the wisdom to put my trust in Alex. And to help him form his relationship with his son. Amen.

Feeling more at peace after opening her heart and her soul to the Lord, she crawled into the sleigh bed. Tomorrow would be a better day. She needed to work things out with Alex, no matter how difficult, for Cody's sake and for her own. She didn't want to be the person she'd been today—so anxious and frightened that she couldn't stop herself from lashing out.

No matter how tense and confused Alex made her feel on a personal level, she trusted him with her life. And Cody's.

A muffled noise woke her from a deep sleep. She blinked, straining to listen.

The sounds were coming from Cody's room.

She threw the covers aside and scrambled from her bed. Heart in her throat, she darted through the connecting doorway.

Cody sobbed, thrashing his head back and forth on the pillow. The puppy whimpered in tandem beside him. Her chest tightened and she pushed the covers away, gathering Cody into a warm embrace. His arms clutched her and he continued to murmur through the sobs.

"Shh. Cody, it's okay. I'm here." She rocked with him cradled against her chest. The puppy settled down, his tail thumping against the bed.

"Mama." He sobbed the word against her neck.

"I know, Cody. I know you loved your mama." She hesitated, and then gently told him, "Your mom is in heaven now, with God. She's looking out for you. I'm here with you, Cody. I love you very much. You're safe now." Shelby battled tears as she rubbed a hand over his back.

"Why did she talk to the bad man?" Cody asked, his plaintive voice muffled against her skin. "Why?"

Shelby froze. Was he aware of what he was saying? "You saw your mom talking to the bad man?" she asked, holding her breath, afraid of the answer.

He nodded, his sobs quieting. "Outside. At night. I saw them through the window."

Who had Trina talked to? And why? "Where was your dad?"

He shrugged. "I dunno. But I don't wanna have any more bad dreams."

"I know, sweetheart. I'm here with you now." She didn't have a psych degree, but she instinctively knew not to push him. The poor child had enough to deal with at the moment. "I love you, Cody. I will always love you."

"I love you, too." Chubby arms clung tightly around her neck and she shifted so that she could lean back against the headboard of his bed, keeping Cody nestled in her arms. Clyde edged closer, and pushed his nose under her hand, licking her fingers. She pulled the puppy into a three-way embrace.

She closed her eyes, reveling in the peace and quiet of the night. She didn't want to think right now. She just wanted to hold on to Cody and pretend that as long as she kept him close, he'd be safe. They'd both be safe.

Chapter 5

Shelby was half-asleep when she heard a soft knock.

"Cody? Are you all right?"

It took several seconds to pull herself together. "He's fine," she called out in a low, soft voice. "Just a bad dream."

Cody stirred a bit, but didn't awaken.

Alex opened the door and stepped farther into the room. His hair was tousled, as if he'd just gotten up. His concerned gaze fell on Cody. "I heard noises. Everything okay?"

"Fine," she whispered. She lifted a finger to her lips, indicating they should be quiet, but Cody stirred again and this time he groggily lifted his head.

"Is it morning?" he asked, his tiny brow puckered in a confused frown.

"No, it's still nighttime," Shelby reassured quietly. "Go back to sleep, Cody."

He yawned, and pried his eyes open. "What if the bad dream comes back?"

"Think of God and the angels up in heaven," she suggested. "I promise they're watching over you and they'll keep the bad dreams away."

When he didn't look convinced, she added, "I'll stay here until you fall asleep."

"And I'll be right downstairs, too, Cody," Alex added. "If you need anything, just holler."

"Okay." Cody snuggled down against the pillows, his little arm curling around Clyde. The puppy laid his head right next to Cody's.

Alex smiled and Shelby was surprised by the flash of tenderness in his gaze. Despite her earlier resentment, she was glad he was so concerned.

He backed out of the room, his gaze on hers and she waited a few minutes, until Cody's breathing relaxed, before she gently disentangled herself from the bed and followed Alex into the hallway.

She was amazed he'd heard them from downstairs. Had he heard her get up? And if so, just how much of their conversation had Alex overheard?

Alex stood, waiting for her in the hallway. She took a few minutes to compose herself, as she gently closed Cody's door behind her.

By silent agreement, they walked down the hall away from Cody's room, pausing outside the door to her room.

"Did he have a dream about the bad man?" he asked.

His question didn't surprise her. But still she hesitated, wondering how to respond. She knew he wanted a description of the man Cody saw, but what if Cody couldn't really give them one? The only new information she'd learned was that Cody had watched through the car window as his mother had talked to the bad man. And that bit didn't exactly provide clues he could use on the investigation.

"Yes, but he didn't remember much. Only that he was afraid." Shelby tried to keep her gaze trained on Alex's face so he wouldn't sense the half truth. Right now, Cody needed his rest, and she was afraid to ask more questions while that night was fresh in Cody's mind. She tightly gripped the doorknob behind her, anxious to escape into the safety of her room. "I'm sorry he woke you."

In the dim light from the fire in the fireplace below, she saw him shrug. "I don't sleep well anyway, so it doesn't matter."

"Why not?" The question slipped out before she could check herself. She bit her lip, knowing his issues were none of her business. "Sorry, that was incredibly rude."

"That's okay." He lifted his arm and pulled up the sleeve of his soft denim shirt uncovering the angry looking surgical scars. "Pain tends to keep me awake."

Even in the dim light from downstairs, the scars looked horribly painful. She resisted the urge to touch them, wishing there was something she could do to help ease the hurt. "Isn't there something you can take?"

His lips thinned and he shook his head. "No."

A charged silence fell between them. Suddenly she realized he was close. Far too close. And it was dark. Old fears bubbled to the surface. She took a step backward and bumped up against the door. She felt trapped.

Panic surged and she struggled to keep her breathing even, though it seemed something had sucked all the oxygen from the air around them.

"I have to get to bed. Good night, Alex." Twisting the knob in her hand, she opened her door.

"Wait." Alex clasped her hand and held fast, preventing her from leaving. "Don't leave."

The way his fingers clamped around her wrist sent a cascade of dark memories crashing into her mind. "Let me go," she hissed, yanking her hand from his grasp.

Instantly, he released her. She stumbled back against the door, trying to get as far away from him as possible, her chest tight with fear.

"I'm sorry." He stared at her, his brows pulled together in a dark frown.

As quickly as they caught her off guard, the horrible memories receded, followed by a wave of shame. What was wrong with her? This was Alex. He'd come up to protect them, not to hurt her.

"It's okay," she regained her footing and tried to sound normal even though her hands were shaking. "I'm fine. You just surprised me, that's all." She winced at the lame excuse and forced a smile. "I'll—uh—see you in the morning."

"Shelby…" he began, but then caught himself and stopped. He held her gaze and took a deliberate step back, giving her more room. "You're right. It's late. Get some sleep. We can talk in the morning."

"Sure." She gave a jerky nod, her heart still rapidly beating in her chest. "Good night."

"Good night, Shelby." His concerned gaze stayed on hers as she shut the door between them.

Mortified by her overreaction to Alex's touch, she crossed the room and knelt at the side of the bed. After closing her eyes, she took a deep breath and reached out in prayer.

Dear Lord, I know You sent me to Alex to keep Cody safe. I know You're watching over us. Please give me the strength I need to conquer my fears. Amen.

Alex silently trod down the stairs to the main level, pausing long enough to replenish the wood for the fire. For a long moment, he stared into the dancing flames, reliving that awful moment when Shelby had physically recoiled from his touch.

He felt sick knowing how badly he'd frightened her. He'd never physically hurt a woman in his life. Certainly he'd never threatened a woman on a personal level.

But there was no mistaking the stark fear in her eyes when he'd caught her arm in an attempt to prevent her from slipping away.

He sank onto the couch, using the heels of his hands to rub his eyes. Shelby hadn't seemed threatened by him earlier in the day. He shouldn't have grabbed her arm like that. He hadn't realized she'd think he would force her to stay with him.

His stomach churned. She was afraid of men. Deeply afraid, in a primal way he'd never imagined.

He knew she'd been attacked by a man several years ago, one night down at the shipyard warehouse. Did that night haunt her still? After all this time?

If so, it was his fault. Maybe if he'd acted quicker, he could have prevented Shelby from being hurt. At the time, as he'd watched the attack take place, he'd wanted to go after the guy who'd hurt her, but he couldn't afford to break his cover.

Bitter guilt surged and he shot to his feet, pacing the length of the room, trying to get a handle on his simmering emotions. He'd done the best he could.

But his best hadn't been nearly good enough.

Once he'd calmed down, he stretched out on the sofa, grabbing Kayla's quilt to ward off the chill.

Sleep didn't come easy. Somehow he knew he needed to gain Shelby's trust. He couldn't stand to think she'd ever be afraid of him.

He cared about her, more than he should. He wanted the right to keep her safe.

Even though he knew she could never really belong to him.

The next morning, Alex fought the effects of his sleepless night, stumbling to the kitchen before anyone else was up to make coffee. He would need gallons of it to get through the day.

He stared broodingly at the pot as it slowly dripped. When it was finished, he poured himself a mug and carefully carried it in his left hand back to the living room.

Using his left hand still didn't come naturally. He needed to return to the shed and do more left-handed target practice. His aim was getting better, though not quite good enough that he'd trust himself in the field. To protect Shelby and Cody, he'd need to be in top form.

And time was slipping away. Russ Jacobson's ships would be back in the water in less than two weeks. Which meant more drugs making their way into the hands of innocent kids. Whoever was responsible would be using this time to take care of all obstacles, road-blocks and witnesses, like Cody. He found the foam ball and began working the stiff muscles in his left hand.

When he heard Kayla moving about in the kitchen, he knew he should go in to help. But he wanted to see Shelby. To talk to her.

To reassure her that he'd never hurt her. He only wanted to protect her, and his son.

Soon he heard Cody's giggles and the clickity-click of Clyde's toenails on the hardwood floor. Seconds later, Clyde dashed down the stairs with Cody on his heels.

"The puppy needs to go outside," Alex warned.

"I know." Cody didn't seem to have suffered any ill effects from his nightmare as he let the dog out. The kitchen was empty, and he realized his sister must be with Brianna.

"You're taking really good care of Clyde," he said to Cody, trying to strike up a conversation so his son would feel more comfortable around him.

Cody's smile brightened his tiny face. "Can I feed him, too?"

"Sure. I'll have to help you with the bag of dog food, though." Alex lifted the thirty pound bag and carefully poured the contents into the dish Cody held. "See? We make a great team."

"Will I be as strong as you someday?" Cody asked, when Alex had set the bag down.

"Absolutely. I bet you'll even be stronger than me." He couldn't help wondering if Cody's desire to be strong had anything to do with what the boy had witnessed two nights ago with Trina. But he didn't ask. This wasn't the time or the place. Besides, he wanted Cody to be comfortable, not afraid.

"Where's your aunt Shelby?" He glanced up toward the loft.

"She's coming. I'm hungry."

He glanced around the kitchen. "Well, I could try making breakfast," he started. But just then Kayla hurried out.

"I'll make breakfast. Cody, do you and Brianna want to help me make French toast?"

"Yeah!" Cody exclaimed, following Kayla and Brianna over to the cupboard where Kayla kept the powdered sugar.

Considering they'd only arrived yesterday, it was good to see the boy was already making himself at home. Kids were often more resilient than adults gave them credit for.

He heard Shelby coming down the stairs, so he went out to meet her. Her footsteps faltered on the stairs when she saw him. She smiled but her smile didn't quite reach her beautiful blue eyes.

Swallowing the lump of bitter regret in his throat, he tossed the foam ball onto the sofa and stood. He slid his hands into his front pockets to appear nonthreatening. "Good morning. Did you sleep all right?"

"Of course." The dark circles under her eyes belied her words and likely matched his own. "How about you?"

"Sure." If she could stretch the truth, so could he. "Ah, do you have a minute? I wanted to talk to you for a moment, about Cody."

"All right." Although she nodded, her eyes remained wary. She sat on the edge of the sofa, as if prepared to bolt.

He regretted their argument yesterday evening and wanted to find a way to reassure her about his intentions regarding Cody. He reached over and picked up a photograph off the end table. He handed it to her. "Here. Kayla found this in the attic."

Shelby's mouth dropped open as she looked at the small boy who was the mirror image of Cody, aside from the color of his hair. "Is this you?"

"Yeah. When I was about Cody's age."

"The resemblance is amazing." She raised her gaze to his. "Is this your way of telling me you believe you're Cody's father?"

Trust Shelby to get right to the point.

"Yes. I'm convinced." He took a seat across from her, still giving her plenty of space. "That's what I wanted to talk to you about. I don't know what the future holds for us, but I wanted to let you know, I do want Cody in my life, but I'll never keep Cody away from you. I've seen you interact with him and it's clear how much you love him. And he loves you, too. I would never take that away from either of you. You will always be an important part of his life."

"I—thank you."

For a moment his chest tightened when her eyes shimmered with tears.

"I'm the closest thing he has to a mother and he's been traumatized enough. Last night, he cried out for his mother during his nightmare. I tried to explain how she's up in heaven with God and the angels, but I don't know if he really understands."

He remembered Cody's prayers, but had thought that was just a childhood routine. "Do you really believe that?"

She looked shocked. "Of course. Don't you?"

He had vague recollections of going to church as a child, but that was long ago, before his father had started to drink. "I don't know. Maybe."

She appeared troubled by his response. "I plan to continue to raise Cody as a Christian." It wasn't a question, and the way she angled her chin made it a gauntlet she'd thrown between them.

He wasn't sure what exactly that entailed, but he figured having Cody brought up with church beliefs couldn't hurt him. "That's fine."

Her shoulders relaxed a bit and he could tell she'd been prepared for an argument. "Cody's asking questions about where he's going to live. I know right now the focus needs to be on keeping him safe, but eventually we'll need to make some plans. He needs stability. Cody deserves to have answers, not more evasions."

"I know." He honestly wasn't trying to avoid the future, but there were more important things to worry about at the moment. "Does Stephan have any parental rights to Cody that I need to know about?"

"No. Trina didn't list him as Cody's father. And she had Cody before they were married. I'm certain he never formally adopted him."

The news should have been reassuring. But he couldn't completely get rid of a sense of panic. There was nothing standing in the way of him being Cody's father. What sort of father would he be? He wished he knew. "All right. We'll figure something out. Right now, the priority is to keep you both safe. I'm hoping to talk to Cody later today, if that's all right with you."

She hesitated and then nodded. "Yes. It's fine."

He glanced toward the kitchen where Kayla and the kids were having breakfast. "Let's get something to eat, shall we?"

In the kitchen, Kayla was in command, wearing a plain white apron tied around her waist as she manned the stove. The griddle sizzled as she cooked another batch of French toast. For a split second, Alex could easily picture Shelby standing there, making breakfast for him and Cody. The thought jarred him.

Where had that bizarre image sprung from?

He'd never looked for any type of permanent relationship before because in his experience, even those women who claimed they didn't want kids wanted more than he was willing to give. So why was he even thinking about it now? Especially with a woman like Shelby? A woman whose picture was likely in the dictionary as a definition of home and family.

She believed in God. Raising Cody as a Christian.

He didn't know the first thing about being a father. And he knew even less about how to raise a child to be religious. Who was he trying to kid? Being an uncle to Brianna wasn't the same as being a full-time father.

"Good morning," Kayla greeted them. "Grab a plate and help yourself."

"Thanks." Shelby poured a cup of coffee, and then turned to him, holding out the pot with a questioning gaze. He swallowed hard and nodded, holding out his empty cup for a refill.

Knocked off balance by the domesticity, he took a

hasty sip and scalded his tongue. Served him right for imagining the impossible.

Forcing himself to use his left hand, he ate several slices of French toast, chuckling a bit when he noticed the powdered sugar smiles on Cody's and Brianna's faces.

"Kayla, I need to buy some clothes for us," Shelby said as she finished her meal. "Is there a place nearby you can recommend?"

Alex frowned, remembering that she mentioned yesterday how they didn't bring anything with them. "Do you have cash?"

She flushed with embarrassment and averted her gaze. "No, I'm afraid not."

"Shelby, I don't want you to use your credit or debit cards," he told her sternly. "Anyone with a little access could easily track you here."

She paled and glanced at his sister. "I didn't think of that. Kayla, would you be willing to loan me some money?"

Alex grit his teeth at the way she was avoiding him. Why was she acting like he was some sort of piranha? He pulled out his wallet and pulled out some cash, wishing he had more to give her as he tossed the money on the table in front of her. "Here. I have plenty. Let me know if you need more."

"That's too much," she protested, staring at the bills as if they might bite.

He slid a glance at Cody, who was earnestly talking to Brianna between mouthfuls of food. "Apparently, I have a few years of child support to make up for."

Her brows drew together in a hurt frown, and he

wondered what he'd said to cause that reaction. Whatever the problem, she reluctantly picked up the money and stuffed it in the front pocket of her jeans.

"There's a large discount department store in town." Kayla piled her own plate full of food and sat down with them. "I'd offer to go, but I have a leak under the kitchen sink that needs to be fixed."

Alex raised a brow. "I'll take a look at the leaky pipe, Kay."

His sister's gaze dropped to his injured hand and he tensed when she shook her head.

"I've learned to do a lot of things since my husband died, including fixing minor plumbing problems. Maybe you should take Shelby and Cody to the store so they don't get lost."

"We'll be fine," Shelby protested.

"I'm not an invalid." He didn't bother hiding his annoyance. "I'll fix the leaky pipe, and then we'll all go to the store together."

There was a long pause before she finally relented. "If you insist. I guess I could pick up a few things, myself." Kayla finished eating as Shelby stood and began clearing the dishes. "Leave them, Shelby. Would you mind going out with the kids to bring in more firewood from the woodpile?"

"Sure, after I finish with the dishes." Shelby cleared off the rest of the dishes, neatly stacking them next to the sink, until Kayla stopped her.

"Please? I hate bringing in the firewood and Brianna loves to do it," Kayla said. "I'm sure Cody will get a kick out of helping, too. They could use a break from being indoors, give them a chance to play in the snow. If you'd supervise, I'd be grateful."

"All right then." Shelby finished clearing the dishes and then took the kids and the puppy into the great room, so they could put their coats and boots on.

Alex stayed where he was for a minute, wrestling his frustration under control. How was he going to get back into the field if he couldn't fix a leaky pipe? "I'm not helpless," he told Kayla.

Kayla finished her food and took her plate to the sink, her back stiff. She filled the sink full of warm soapy water and began scrubbing. There was a distinctive dripping sound as water fell into a bucket beneath the sink. "I never said you were. But if you slip and hurt your hand worse…"

"Kay." He stood and crossed over to her, turning her shoulders so that she faced him, ignoring the sudsy water that dripped to the floor. "If I can reinjure my hand by fixing a leaky pipe, my career is over."

"So what? Would that be the worst thing in the world?" she burst out in exasperation. "Alex, you have a son now, a responsibility—" Her voice cut off and she sighed.

"Kayla," he began, but she quickly interrupted.

"I promised myself I wouldn't harp, but Alex, be reasonable. You know as well as I do your career isn't conducive to raising a family. And now that you know about Cody, you can't simply abandon him. He needs you."

"Give me some credit, Kay. I know I have a son and believe me, he is my primary concern. But don't you see? To keep him safe, I need to finish this case. And the only way to get back to work is to strengthen my left hand."

She let out a heavy sigh. "Can't your partner, that coast guard guy, handle the case? You've already been stabbed. You're lucky to be alive. Isn't that enough?"

"No, Rafe can't finish this case alone. He needs me. And I need to be able to close this case." And afterward? He didn't even want to think about what might happen then. What would he do? How would he find a way to keep drugs off the streets? And how would he learn to be a father to Cody?

Kayla rolled her eyes in disgust. "Fine. Go ahead and put your life on the line, then. Cody's already lost his mother, who cares if he loses his father, too?"

Please bless my other dad.

Cody's prayer reverberated through his mind. But he steeled his resolve. He couldn't give up the case. Not now. Not until they'd brought the mastermind behind the drug smuggling operation to justice.

"Go help Shelby with the firewood," Kayla said in a resigned tone. She clearly didn't want to discuss the matter any further. "I'm sure the kids will be no help, since they'll be covered in snow."

Before he could move, Shelby burst through the doorway, her eyes wide with alarm.

"Alex! I need you to come outside right away." Her hands were shaking and her face was chalk white.

"What's wrong?" He crossed over to her in two steps.

"I found footprints and a tiny pile of cigarette butts in the snow behind the woodpile. I—I think someone was out here, watching us."

Chapter 6

"Show me," Alex commanded. Shelby didn't bother to argue, quickly leading the way outside, clenching her teeth together to keep them from chattering.

"Right here," she said, pointing to a small area a few feet behind the woodpile, between two rather large oak trees. It wasn't exactly the same place she'd seen the light, but it was close. "I know you're going to think I'm crazy but I found them because of the smell."

He sent her a questioning look. "There's only a couple of cigarette butts here."

She lifted a shoulder, helplessly. "I still smelled them."

This wasn't the time, or the place to explain how the slightest scent of cigarette smoke made her gag, ever since she'd been attacked by the shipyard by some man who'd reeked of cigarettes.

Sometimes, she could still smell the stench of stale

cigarette smoke in her dreams. Today when she'd gotten close to the woodpile, she thought she was imagining things.

But then she found footprints. And cigarette butts.

Alex approached the area, crouched down and looked at the telltale evidence preserved in the snow, his expression intent. He glanced up at her when the kids came running outside to get another armload of firewood.

"Shelby, get the kids back inside the house. Now."

She understood his concern and turned, pasting a smile on her face. "Cody, Brianna. It's time to go inside."

"No! We don't wanna go in!" Cody's tone was belligerent.

"Cody, don't argue," she said in a sharp, no-nonsense tone. The one she used to make him understand she was not kidding. "Inside the house. Now."

For a moment he stared at her defiantly, but when she kept her expression seriously stern, he grudgingly complied. Brianna followed without a protest.

"Take Clyde with you," Shelby added. She was thankful when Kayla met the kids at the door, to help with their wet clothes. Alex's sister cast a worried glance in their direction, but Shelby didn't know how to reassure her.

What if Cody's bad man had found them? The idea that she might have put Kayla and Brianna in danger by coming here made her feel sick to her stomach.

Fighting to control the panic that threatened to overwhelm her, she turned back to Alex. He was working as if she weren't there, following the path of boot-prints as they wove their way through the trees, toward the back of the far side of the house. The opposite side from where the shed was.

He stopped in another clearing and looked up at the house. She followed his gaze, trying to gauge the layout of the upper story. She hoped it was one of the empty rooms, and not hers or Cody's.

The wind kicked up, dark clouds swirling overhead, bringing a threat of more snow. The sky turned an eerie gray-green. She shivered, from cold and fear.

"Come inside," Alex said in a low tone as he headed toward the front door.

The house was blessedly warm and they could hear Kayla's voice in the kitchen as she entertained the kids. Sounded like she was trying to find dry clothes for Cody to wear.

Alex swiftly shed his outer gear and went straight up the stairs to the second story living quarters. Full of curious dread, she followed him.

He stood in Cody's room, gazing out the patio doors. When she came up beside him, she could easily see the indentations in the snow where the cigarette smoker had stood and watched the house.

Watched Cody.

Shelby glanced at Alex as he abruptly swung away from the window. He muttered something unintelligible under his breath and reached for his phone.

"Rafe? I need backup, ASAP."

She imagined his coast guard contact had readily agreed because Alex listened and then said, "Get in touch with Holden first, ask what's going on with Trina's murder investigation and then get here as fast as you can," before snapping his phone shut.

"Do we really need him to come here?" she asked, wishing they could handle this on their own, without involving anyone else. "Can't we all just leave?"

Alex scowled and shook his head. "I can't be responsible for keeping everyone safe. I haven't been officially cleared to return to duty. I should have turned you and Cody over to Rafe from the beginning."

"I'm glad you didn't."

He pinned her with a narrow gaze. "Really? Because I got the distinct impression last night that you couldn't get away from me fast enough. It's obvious you don't trust me."

"I trust you." She was surprised to realize it was true. Despite her irrational fear last night, when she'd felt crowded and let her haunted memories of the past get the better of her, she did trust Alex. Far more than she trusted anyone else.

Including the unknown Rafe.

He let out a harsh laugh. "Yeah, right. Why would you trust me? You told me you saw a light last night, but I didn't take the threat seriously enough."

"You investigated," she protested.

"Yeah, I did. And I checked behind the woodpile and didn't see these footprints, so they must have been made after I came inside. But still, when I didn't see anyone outside, I should have called Rafe for backup."

She didn't know what to say to that. If Rafe had been there helping Alex, would they have found the guy? Maybe. But maybe it would have led to another confrontation where someone got shot, or even killed. There was no way to know.

Self-recrimination blazed in his eyes before he turned away. "My negligence nearly got you and Cody killed."

She didn't believe that, not for a moment, but she also couldn't deny how seeing those footprints in the snow along with the two cigarette butts had shaken her deeply.

"How did he find us?" she asked, bewildered.

"I don't know. But it doesn't really matter, since we're not staying here." Alex turned and stalked toward the door. "Pack up whatever you have and borrow stuff from Kayla if necessary. Rafe should be here within the hour."

Alex had arranged what he could as far as next steps in his escape plan. When those preparations were finished, he began working on Kayla's leaky pipe, since standing around and waiting was driving him crazy.

Rafe arrived fifteen minutes later. Alex heard Rafe and Kayla talking in the great room. No doubt his sister was filling Rafe in on the details of what had happened before Rafe came to find him.

"Alex. Is it true?" his coast guard partner demanded.

"What? That I blew it last night?" He snorted and nodded. "Yeah, I'm afraid it is."

Rafe sent an exasperated glance. "Not that. The boy. Cody. Is he really your son?"

He concentrated on wielding the bulky pipe wrench with his left hand, ignoring the zinging pain that traveled up his right arm. He thought about how he'd planned to have a DNA test, but it wasn't necessary. He knew, with deep certainty, Cody was his son. He finished opening up the elbow pipe and lowered the wrench, sitting back on his heels. "Yes. It's true. He's a good kid, but a scared one. He saw something the night before Trina was shot."

"Something? Like what? Didn't you talk to him?"

"He's only four, Rafe. I can't very well interrogate him." Odd how he sounded like Shelby when she'd staunchly defended Cody. "He's been traumatized, practically saw his mother being killed. Besides, it's not as if the court is going to take action on the word of a child eyewitness."

"Maybe not the court, but it would give us something to go on," Rafe responded. "We need answers and we need them quickly."

"I know." He went back to work on the pipe. "I will talk to him, later. Right now, I want you to get a security system installed here at the B & B."

"A security system, are you crazy? Your sister and her daughter can't stay here," Rafe argued hotly. "Not until we've cracked this case."

"I know, but I want it installed anyway, for when they can return."

Rafe looked like he was going to argue, not that Alex could blame him. What good would a security system do if Kayla's business involved inviting strangers into her home on a regular basis? He didn't care. He didn't want an intruder on the grounds catching him or Kayla unaware ever again.

"Okay, consider it done. Anything else?" Rafe asked.

He'd made a lot of arrangements, but he wasn't sure

Rafe was going to approve. Especially since he wasn't quite ready to turn over Shelby and Cody into Rafe's protection. He lifted the heavy wrench again. "I've made some initial plans," he admitted.

"Like what?"

He glanced at Rafe and in the split second he'd taken his eye off the pipe, the wrench slipped from his grasp. Since he was leaning on it with all his strength, the tool skipped off the pipe and crashed back down on his injured right hand landing directly on the deepest and longest surgical scar.

Blood spurted from the wound and a shaft of pain stole his breath, as if he'd been hit by a cargo flat full of steel. For a moment he was paralyzed by the pain.

When the dizziness passed, he scrambled to his feet, holding his injured arm and swallowing the waves of pain that rolled up his arm. Blood sprayed everywhere, and he vainly attempted to use his other hand to keep it from going all over Kayla's floor.

Cody chose that moment to charge into the kitchen, skidding to a stop, his eyes wide with horror as they fixed on Alex's bloodstained arm.

Alex found his voice. "It's okay, Cody," he hastened to reassure him, forcing a grim smile. "I'm fine. This is no big deal, it's just a scratch."

To his utter surprise, Cody let out a shrill scream. Before Alex could stop him, he turned and ran from the room.

Shelby gasped when she heard Cody scream. She ran into the dining room, snagging him as he darted past. When he saw it was her, he clung like a monkey around her neck.

"Cody, honey, what's wrong?" She gathered him close, running a soothing hand over his back as he trembled and sobbed against her. "Shh, don't cry. You're safe. Don't worry, everything is going to be okay."

Alex came rushing out, a towel wrapped around his right arm. Deep grooves of pain lined his mouth, but he leveled his concerned gaze on Cody.

"Is he okay?" Alex asked.

She shook her head, feeling helpless. What had gotten Cody so riled up? He'd seen small injuries before at the daycare. They'd never upset him like this. "What happened in there?"

"I'm not sure." Alex tightened his grip on the towel.

Shelby held Cody until he stopped crying, realizing the young boy's emotional status was more fragile than she'd realized. He needed to talk to a professional child psychologist, the sooner the better.

Kayla walked up behind her. "You'd better let me take a look at that," she said, indicating his injured arm.

Alex frowned and shook his head. "Later. I think Cody freaked out because of the blood."

Why would Cody react so strongly to the sight of blood? She continued to hold him close, murmuring words of encouragement even as her mind raced over the possibilities.

He couldn't have seen blood from Trina being shot, because his mother and the gunman had been too far away. She hadn't even seen any blood, and she was the one who saw Trina drop to the ground.

Which meant Cody had to have seen blood at another time. Like when he saw his mother talking to the bad man. Had he witnessed a physical confrontation? Trina hadn't seemed injured when she'd handed over Cody at the marina, so perhaps she'd hit the bad man so she could escape.

Alex's green gaze was watching her intently and she wondered if he'd come to the same conclusions she had. She narrowed her gaze, vowing to monitor Alex's questions for Cody very carefully. Yes, they needed the information, but there had to be away for getting it from Cody without upsetting him further. If the poor child reacted like this to the sight of blood, then he'd been far more traumatized by what he'd seen than she'd imagined.

"I'm going to take him upstairs for a minute," she murmured, hitching Cody higher in her arms so she could carry him through the great room.

She half expected Alex to stop her, but he didn't. She could feel his gaze boring into her back as she headed upstairs to the sanctuary of their rooms.

After she'd gotten Cody calmed down and had washed the tears from his face, they returned to the kitchen where Rafe, Kayla and Alex were gathered around the large picnic table. She was relieved to see that a bulky white bandage covered Alex's injured arm.

"I don't understand why I have to go anywhere," Kayla was saying in a stubborn tone. "I'm fine with you taking Brianna someplace safe, with Ellen, my mother-in-law, to watch, but there's no reason for me to leave, too."

Alex opened his mouth to argue, but Rafe beat him to it.

"No. Absolutely not. You will be safe. I won't allow anything else," Rafe commanded, anxiety making his thick Hispanic accent stronger.

"You won't allow it?" Kayla narrowed her gaze. "You don't have control over what I do."

"The decision has been made," Rafe brushed aside her protest as if it was nothing more than a bug to be squashed. "You, Brianna and her grandmother will enjoy an extended stay at a resort offering an indoor water park for entertainment."

"Why drag Ellen into this?" Kayla asked.

"Because your mother-in-law was watching Brianna the day Shelby arrived. If someone had followed her, we can't assume they didn't see Ellen dropping Brianna off later that day. I don't want to take a chance on her safety."

When it looked like Kayla was going to argue some more, Shelby stepped in, catching Kayla's gaze with hers. "Please go somewhere safe. For me? I hate knowing I put you and Brianna in danger by coming here."

"It's not your fault, Shelby." Kayla's stout defense touched her heart. "But if you think I should go, I will." Her eyes widened and she glanced at her brother. "Maybe Cody should come with us?"

Considering the magnitude of Cody's breakdown, Shelby didn't think leaving him alone with Kayla and Brianna was a good idea at all. "I don't think so..."

Rafe and Alex exchanged a look and they both simultaneously shook their heads. Alex spoke up. "No, Cody needs Shelby."

She was pleased he'd understood. Obviously Alex really did have Cody's best interests at heart.

"I've made arrangements for Shelby and me to hide out in a small hotel several miles from here," Alex said, changing the subject. "Rafe, I want you to take Kayla, Brianna and her grandmother to the resort and then come and meet up with us afterward."

Rafe nodded. "All right. But I think we need to get rid of Shelby's car, in case someone used it to track her here. I can't figure out how else they found her. I tried checking it over, but without the proper instruments, a tracking device could be anywhere. I thought I'd have some friends of mine pick it up and take it back to Green Bay."

"Sounds reasonable." Alex raised a brow. "Can I borrow your Jeep? There's a storm headed this way."

"Sure."

They finalized their plans. Kayla offered the use of her SUV since Ellen had agreed to pick up her and Brianna to head to the resort. When they had every angle covered, they ate some quickly prepared sandwiches, more for the kids' sake, before splitting up.

When Cody realized the puppy wasn't coming with them, he threw a rare temper tantrum. Shelby concentrated on calming him down, and she couldn't help wondering if she'd made the right decision. Was she being selfish? Would it be better for Cody to be at the water park resort with Kayla and Brianna?

"Did you know that Clyde is going to have a new batch of brothers and sisters soon?" Alex asked, crouching down so he was at eye level with Cody.

Magically the boy's tears vanished. "Really?"

Alex gave a solemn nod. "Yep, the puppies are due

in early May. Maybe we can get one of the puppies for you. Would you like that?"

Cody's eyes widened in awe. "A puppy? For my very own?"

Shelby wanted to protest that Alex had no right to promise such a thing, yet hadn't she already thought of getting Cody a puppy once this was over? Still, this was the sort of thing both parents should agree on. Alex had no idea she'd planned on allowing Cody to have a pet.

"You have to be a good boy and listen to your mother—er—your aunt Shelby. Do you understand?"

Cody nodded vigorously and the crisis was adverted.

Irrationally annoyed, the brief conversation replayed over and over in her mind as she buckled Cody's toddler seat into the back of Rafe's Jeep.

"All set?" Alex asked softly.

She nodded and pushed her uncharitable thoughts away. Why was she upset? This was what she'd wanted, for Cody and Alex to have some sort of relationship. She'd asked for God's help. He'd answered. She should be glad.

She then buckled Cody in, making sure he had his animal kingdom figures to help keep him entertained on the long ride, before she climbed into the passenger seat. The time was only about three in the afternoon, but the clouds were so dark and thick overhead that the hour seemed much later.

She swallowed hard, trying not to succumb to the impending sense of doom. Being close to Alex in the car was a bit unnerving. She wasn't afraid of him, but it felt strange for her and Cody to be alone with him. Still, she couldn't deny she was relieved they were leaving the bed-and-breakfast and those disturbing cigarette butts, to find anonymity in another hotel far from here.

"Do you really think the bad guy put something on my car?" she asked.

He glanced at her, his brow furrowed in a deep frown. "I'm not sure how they found you, Shelby. Could be they somehow tracked either Trina's phone or your car. Or maybe you were followed and we just didn't catch on. But either way, we should have our bases covered now. You didn't bring Trina's phone, right?"

"I turned it off and left it back at the B & B like you told me to do."

"Good. I'm sure we'll be fine."

He sounded so certain, she believed him. Slowly she unclenched her twisted hands, willing herself to relax.

Alex had only driven for ten miles when large, fat, wet snowflakes began to fall. The slick roads forced him to slow his speed considerably.

"Do you think we'll get to the hotel before dinnertime?" she asked, not because she was hungry but because traveling with a child Cody's age meant keeping track of meals.

"I hope so." Alex's attention was riveted on the highway. She could see from the compass in Rafe's Jeep they were heading northeast.

The snow fell harder, covering the roads with an icy slush, forcing Alex to slow his speed even further. He glanced in the rearview mirror frequently.

"Is there someone behind us?" Shelby asked, craning her neck around.

"Yeah. For the past two miles." Alex did not look happy and he gripped the steering wheel tightly. "As soon as I find a cross street, I'm going to pull off so we can lose him."

Her stomach clenched. Another coincidence? She hoped so.

"What is he doing?" Alex suddenly ground out.

Before she could ask what he meant, she saw the black truck swerve into the oncoming lane of traffic, pulling up beside them even though they were in a no-passing zone, heading into a sharp curve in the highway.

"Hang on!" Alex shouted as he hit the brakes.

Too late. The black truck smashed into them, sending the Jeep skidding across the slick road, crashing up against the side rail of the highway.

"No!" Shelby cried. The metal rail gave away, allowing the Jeep to barrel down into the steep ravine below.

Chapter 7

Alex fought to stay conscious, even though his head pounded from the impact of the air-bag deployment. The Jeep finally came to rest against a band of evergreens, miraculously intact. For long moments he couldn't move. The abrupt silence after listening to the Jeep crash against the rocks and trees was just as deafening.

"Shelby?" He leaned over to put a hand on her shoulder, fearing the worst. Relief overwhelmed him when she stirred and lifted her head. There was a small cut on her forehead, but her eyes were clear.

"I'm fine. Cody?"

Cody, who didn't have the benefit of air bags to protect him from the crash. Alarm gripped him by the throat and he struggled to release the latch of the seat belt so he could turn around to check his son.

A soft keening cry from the backseat nearly made

him weep in relief. Shelby got her seat belt undone first and crammed her body through the narrow opening between the seats to reach him.

"Shh, Cody. It's all right. We're fine. God was watching over us. He kept us safe."

Alex paused at her words. Maybe she was right. Maybe God had been watching over them. This accident could have ended much worse.

Except it wasn't an accident. The black truck had stayed on his tail, no matter how hard he'd tried to put distance between them. And when the truck had pulled up alongside, Alex had glimpsed the driver through the tinted windows the moment the guy had jerked the steering wheel, sideswiping them.

There was no doubt in his mind that the driver of the black truck had hit them on purpose. Alex would have bet his pension on it. Spurred by a new sense of urgency, he unlatched his seat belt and took stock of their situation. Thankfully they'd taken Rafe's sturdy Jeep. If they'd been in Shelby's small compact car, they wouldn't have stood much of a chance. He swallowed hard, trying to see out the cracked window.

The snow had cushioned their fall, minimizing the damage but they weren't out of danger yet. The driver of the black truck could be right now coming down the ravine to finish what he'd started.

"We can't stay here," he rasped, using all his strength to pry his dented driver's door open.

Shelby had gotten Cody out of his seat and was holding him protectively in her arms. "Alex, it's cold and wet out there. He'll freeze."

He shared her concern. Cody's body mass was so

small he was at a much higher risk for hypothermia. Yet if they stayed here, they were too much like a beacon, drawing the driver of the truck directly toward them.

"I'll come up with something," he promised before he jumped out into the snow and made his way to the back of the Jeep.

Rafe worked for the coast guard. And he loved to camp and fish. Surely he had some leftover gear in the back they could use. The back window was broken open and he leaned in, thrilled to discover his gut instincts were right.

Rafe had plenty of stuff tossed back there.

As he rummaged through the gear, picking and choosing what they needed the most and discarding the items that held little value other than weighing them down, he listened to Shelby talking in a low voice to Cody.

No, not talking. Praying.

"Heavenly Father, we thank You for keeping us safe in Your loving arms. Please continue to give us Your strength and guidance, Lord, as we seek shelter from the storm. Amen."

Cody's young voice echoed, "Amen."

Humbled, he finished rifling through Rafe's things with a renewed sense of purpose. They could do this. After all, God was watching over Shelby and Cody.

And maybe, even though he hadn't prayed or stepped inside anything resembling a church in years, God was watching over him, too.

Alex climbed back into the Jeep with his loot of supplies. He knew Shelby had doubts about the wisdom of leaving the vehicle.

She phrased her next words carefully. "Won't it be better to stay here, until we're rescued?"

"We don't want just anyone to find us," he answered, with a meaningful glance at Cody. Her eyes widened when she absorbed his hidden meaning. "Don't worry," he interjected when she opened her mouth. "We won't have to hike too far. As soon as we're safely hidden, I'll get in touch with Rafe."

"Cody is too young to hike," she protested.

"I'm going to make a sling, like this, and carry Cody against my chest. Rafe has a survival blanket which helps contain body heat. With the survival blanket and sharing my body heat, he'll be as snug as a bug in a rug."

He was encouraged when she forced a smile and nodded. "Sounds like a plan."

Considering it was the only plan he had at the moment, he didn't respond. Hiking through the snow while carrying Cody's additional weight would not be easy. He'd made the sling out of the nylon tent, but Shelby would have to carry a pack of supplies, too. When he handed her the gear, she didn't voice a single complaint.

Soon they were ready to go.

Outside, he scanned the area, searching for any sign that the driver of the black truck was making his way to find them. But the swirling snow had a negative impact on the visibility and the only sound he could hear was the whistling wind.

As much as he would have preferred taking the easy route using gravity to head farther down the ravine, he forced himself to take a parallel path from the Jeep, going back in the direction from which they'd come.

He wasn't crazy, he simply hoped to buy a little time, in case his worst fears were correct and the driver was brave enough or foolish enough to search for them. With any luck, by the time the guy found the Jeep, partially hidden in the evergreen trees, the wind would have obliterated their tracks in the snow. The driver would assume that since they had Cody, they'd head down the ravine, continuing north.

It wasn't a perfect plan, but the best he could drum up at the moment.

As if sensing the seriousness of the situation, Cody kept quiet in his makeshift sling. Alex tried to keep his gait as smooth as possible, clasping one arm securely around the boy to avoid jostling him too much. He led the way, but had insisted he and Shelby be tied together with rope found in the back of Rafe's Jeep, since they could barely see a few feet in front of their faces.

He'd figured they'd only gone about a mile when the rope tugged sharply. He stopped and turned around to find Shelby on her hands and knees in the snow. He staggered toward her, a sense of hopelessness washing over him.

How much more could Shelby take? They'd barely gone a mile but in these adverse conditions, it seemed like ten. He was breathing hard and he was accustomed to physical labor. How much longer could they battle the storm? They needed shelter. Soon.

He helped Shelby to her feet, and clasped her hands, peering at her through the snow. "Are you all right?"

Her mouth trembled but she nodded. "Fine," she whispered.

Encouraged, he gave her hands a gentle squeeze before letting go. He turned about to face the invisible path he'd chosen.

As he walked, his boots sinking as far as his knees in some places, portions of Shelby's prayer echoed in his mind and he found himself repeating them over and over again.

Heavenly Father, show us the way. Give us Your strength and guidance. Keep us safe.

Shelby clenched her teeth together, trying to keep them from clattering. Alex was amazing. He'd managed to rig up the tent he'd used to carry Cody into a temporary shelter between two large fir trees. Then he'd spread out another tarp over the snow-covered ground to minimize the chill. She was grateful he'd kept the survival blanket around Cody. With the shelter overhead and the trees around them, they were safe from the snow and the wind, but she was still wet and cold.

He'd used his cell phone to contact Rafe. At first she'd been worried the storm would ruin their connection but texting worked perfectly. They'd arranged for Rafe to contact them again, once he was in the general location, so Alex could risk marking their location with a flare.

"Here, you hold Cody for a while," he said in a low voice, noticing her shivers despite her attempts to hide the extent of her discomfort.

"No, I don't want him to get chilled." She stuck her icy hands under her armpits, shivering at the coldness. "He'll be warmer with you."

"He'll be okay. He's drier than we are and with that survival blanket around him, his body is literally radiating heat." She was grateful Cody appeared to be sleeping, a natural sleep, not one from dangerous hypothermia. Alex glanced at her. "You'll need to take him soon anyway, when Rafe arrives."

"I'll wait until then." When the feeling in her fingers returned, she clasped her knees to her chest, hugging them close. She wanted to ask if Rafe would get here soon, but there was no point in asking the impossible. In this weather, it could easily take him hours.

She closed her eyes, giving in to her numbing exhaustion.

"Shelby," Alex said, shaking her to get her attention. "Stay awake. Here, come over next to me, I have enough body heat for the both of us."

Gratefully, she scooted closer, leaning against him. He wrapped his arm around her, hugging her close. He was right. She could already feel some of his warmth seeping through her jacket.

"Don't go to sleep," he commanded softly, still keeping his voice low so as not to disturb Cody. "Talk to me."

"Talk? About what?"

"Anything." He rubbed her arm, helping to warm the side of her that wasn't pressed against his warmth. "Tell me about yourself. What made you decide to open a day care center?"

Since that was actually a fairly long story, she decided to give him the abbreviated version. "I majored in education in college with a minor in business. I taught fifth grade for a while, but it wasn't exactly what I was looking for. After Cody was born, it seemed natural to open a day care center."

"Natural? What do you mean?"

"Teaching was all right, but I wanted more. I discovered I'm able to make a bigger impact in my children's lives through the day care center."

"I'm sure you've made a huge impact on Cody's life," Alex murmured. "He's a great kid."

"Thank you." She smiled, finding it was easy to talk in the cozy darkness. If not for being so chilled, she'd be comfortable here with Alex. "Yes, I like to think I'm making a difference. Trina and Stephan were very busy managing the marina. I often kept Cody overnight in my apartment above the day care. I used to wonder why they didn't spend more time with him, but now that I know Stephan knew he wasn't Cody's father, it makes sense. Although I still think Trina should have been more of a mother to Cody. I guess she was trying to make Stephan happy, too."

"Stephan wasn't—mean to him, was he?"

"No," she hastily reassured him. "More like indifferent in a way. I just thought they were always too busy to make time for him."

"So you really have been like a mother to him." He paused and then added, "Didn't you ever think about having a family of your own?"

"I'd love to have children some day." She couldn't hide the longing in her tone. She stared into the darkness, thinking it was funny how she wasn't afraid to be with Alex like this. "But I guess you've probably realized I have issues. With men."

"All men?" he probed gently. "Not just me?"

"All men." She felt bad he'd taken her aversion personally. "Unfortunately, I was attacked twice. The first time was a near miss in college." She had no idea why she was telling him all of this, when she normally preferred not to talk about the attacks at all.

"What do you mean by a near miss?" This time his tone was lined with steel. "Did some jerk hurt you? Did he—?"

"No." She couldn't let him think the worst, and tried to downplay what had happened, as if she hadn't been completely terrorized at the time. "He didn't want to take no for an answer, but I managed to get away, mostly unscathed."

"Mostly unscathed." There was a strange undertone in his voice, one she couldn't quite pin down.

"A few bruises, nothing more." She turned her head in the darkness, trying to see him, wishing she could read the expression in his eyes.

"Bruises." There was a tense silence. "And the second time?"

"I was attacked down at the shipyard."

She thought he tensed beside her, but when he didn't say anything, she continued.

"A man came up behind me and grabbed me. I thought he was going to drag me into the warehouse, but he hit me over the head. I woke up in the hospital, and they said I was only physically attacked, nothing more." At the time she'd feared the worst, that she'd been sexually assaulted while she was unconscious. But even without that violation, the two attacks had sometimes blurred into one awful nightmare where she'd been unable to get away. Her fear colored her interactions with every man she'd dealt with ever since.

There was another long pause. "Did they arrest the man who hit you?"

"No." She'd often wondered if that was part of the reason she remained so haunted by the attacks. She'd sought solace in God, but there was still a part of her that was worried the man who'd attacked her would find her again.

"You reported the jerk in college, didn't you?"

She couldn't answer. Because she had, but the entire event had turned into a fiasco to the point where she was made to feel like the guilty one. After all, she'd agreed to meet him in his dorm room. And he had claimed that she led him on, then changed her mind. The bruises on her chest and arms hadn't convinced the authorities to press charges.

That experience, along with the attack at the shipyard made her want to protect Cody from being a victim, too.

Alex's phone beeped, indicating a new text message. He looked at the message, and then shut the phone.

"Rafe is on the road where we went over. Take Cody so I can set the flare."

"All right." She gladly took the burden of Cody's weight. The boy roused a bit with the movement.

Alex pulled the flare out of his coat pocket and made his way to the edge of their enclosure.

"Shelby?" She glanced up at him. "We're not finished with this conversation."

Before she could respond, he disappeared into the cold.

She huddled with Cody, missing Alex's warm presence. Somehow, being with him, the two of them caring for Cody, felt right. Sharing her secrets with Alex hadn't been as difficult as she'd imagined.

She was starting to care for him.

And that thought scared her more than being caught in the middle of a snowstorm.

Alex didn't completely relax until he'd gotten Shelby and Cody safely tucked into Kayla's SUV which Rafe had brought to pick them up.

That had been a close call. Too close. If they hadn't had Rafe's Jeep, complete with the camping supplies in the back, there was a very good chance they would have died from hypothermia exposure before Rafe had been able to rescue them.

Had that been the truck driver's plan?

Alex had to believe it was. He'd given Rafe all the details leading up to their crash and Rafe agreed that, somehow, the smoker who'd been watching outside the bed-and-breakfast had followed them.

The roads were still in bad shape, so it took them longer than planned to reach the small motel, located in the middle of a dinky town that was nothing but a speck on most road maps.

"I'll order something to eat," Alex said, after they'd secured two connecting rooms. "At least there's a small café attached, or we'd really be in trouble."

Shelby nodded, looking relieved to have decent living quarters after the time they'd spent in a makeshift tent. He guessed she was still chilled when she'd immediately crossed the room to crank up the heat.

"Keep the connecting door unlocked, would you?"

he asked. "Rafe and I will be right next door. We'll let you know when the pizza arrives."

"Sure," she said with an exhausted smile.

"Maybe we should take shifts staying on guard tonight," Rafe suggested in a low tone after they'd left Shelby and Cody alone. "Just in case."

"You're probably right, although I don't see how we could have been followed," Alex said with a sigh. "There wasn't another soul behind us once we got off the main highway. This town isn't exactly a hot spot."

"I know, but I still don't like it that you were followed at all," Rafe said with a scowl.

He didn't like it, either. "You arranged to have Shelby's car returned to Green Bay?"

Rafe nodded. "Everything worked out fine. Two friends of mine picked up Shelby's car. Kayla, Brianna and Ellen are safe at the resort. I was heading back to Green Bay myself when you called."

"I'm going to get cleaned up a bit," Alex said. "By then the pizza should be here. If you want to take shifts, tonight, that's fine with me."

"I'll take the first shift, since you look like you could use some sleep."

Alex doubted he'd be able to sleep, no matter how exhausted he was. Those moments the black truck had rammed into them would be forever etched in his mind. What if something had happened to Cody? Or Shelby? The thought of either of them being injured, or worse, made him feel sick to his stomach. They'd only been part of his life for a couple of days, but suddenly he couldn't imagine living without them.

He cleaned up in the bathroom and when he emerged

ten minutes later, he could smell the enticing scent of pizza. Rafe and Shelby were speaking in low tones in the room next door.

When he stepped through the connecting door, he abruptly stopped, surprised to see Rafe, Shelby and Cody, all sitting with their heads bowed, as Rafe prayed.

"Dear Lord, thank You for providing us food to eat and shelter from the storm. We are grateful to have You watching over us and providing for us. Amen."

Awkwardly, he stood and waited for them to finish before coming farther into the room. He and Rafe had been partners over the past few years while working this case, but it wasn't as if they'd spent a lot of time together, considering he'd been deep undercover as a longshoreman. He'd seen the simple gold cross Rafe wore like a talisman around his neck, but Alex had figured it was more for decoration rather than as a true symbol of Rafe's religious beliefs.

Obviously, he'd been wrong.

After they finished the pizza, Alex cleaned up the mess while Shelby tucked Cody into bed. Rafe went outside to do a perimeter check around the hotel area to make sure there was nothing suspicious. Alex stood in the entryway between their rooms, watching as Cody finished up his prayers.

He gestured Shelby over when she doused the lamp next to the beds, leaving just the bathroom light on.

"What is it?" she asked.

"Shelby, while Rafe is outside, I want to talk to you. It's important." Alex pulled up two chairs, so they could sit down.

"All right," she agreed, her expression wary. "What is it?"

He took a deep breath, trying to think of a way to tell her. He wanted to say something sooner, when she'd bared her secrets about the attacks but Rafe's arrival had interrupted them.

There was just no easy way to break the news. "I was there that night," he finally said. "At the shipyard. When you were attacked. I happened to be coming toward the warehouse, when I heard something. When I turned to look, I saw the guy grab you."

"You saw him? You can identify him?" The hope in her voice only made him feel worse.

"I wish I could, but his back was toward me and since he was dressed like every other longshoreman with a knit cap pulled over his head, I couldn't tell who he was. But I created a diversion, which was when he hit you and left you there. Once he'd gotten away from you, I called the police. I went over to make sure you were okay, staying by your side until I heard the sirens. I left before the police arrived, so I wouldn't risk blowing my cover."

She gaped at him. "You didn't tell the police what you saw?"

He slowly shook his head. "No. I'm sorry, but I couldn't be seen cooperating with the police. Not when I was trying to behave like the kind of guy who wanted to be included in the action of the drug running operation."

"I see." She dropped her gaze to her hands, twisted tightly in her lap.

"Shelby, I'm so sorry. Please try to understand. If I'd had information that would help the police catch the guy, I would have left an anonymous tip. But I didn't see anything that would help me identify him."

"I understand, really." Shelby's attempt at a smile was pitiful.

"Why did you go down to the warehouse that night?" he asked, puzzled. It had only been a fleeting moment in the middle of his case and he hadn't immediately recognized Shelby as the woman who he'd helped back then.

"I was looking for Trina and my father said she was down at the warehouse."

The warehouse where there were likely hidden drugs. Why would Russ Jacobson send Shelby to the shipyard where rough longshoremen hung out? He stared at her, trying to remember what she'd looked like back then. "You wore your hair shorter, didn't you?"

"Yes. And it was much lighter from being out in the sun."

Realization dawned and he wondered why he hadn't thought of this earlier. "I bet the guy who attacked you mistook you for Trina!"

Chapter 8

Shelby stared at Alex, her mind whirling. It was difficult to comprehend that Alex had been there the night
of her attack, risking his cover to help her. The idea that
he was there, looking out for her while she was unconscious, was oddly reassuring.

But was he right in that the attacker thought she
was her sister? Shelby forced herself to go back to that
night in her mind, dragging long buried memories to
the surface.

*She was walking toward the warehouse located at
the farthest end of the shipyard. The area was not well
lit, several of the overhead lights were burned out.
She'd thought she was alone.*

*The hint of cigarette smoke made her wrinkle her
nose. A male voice had called, "Trina?"*

She shook her head as she started to turn around to

see who'd called her Trina. But the smell of cigarettes got stronger. Hard fingers dug into her arms. Before she could scream, something hard had struck her in the temple. Darkness surrounded her.

She winced a bit, remembering the pain in her head when she'd finally awakened in the hospital, surrounded by medical personnel. The police had been there, asking her over and over again if she'd seen the man who'd attacked her.

She hadn't. But she'd remembered the stench, the thick odor of cigarette smoke. And the bitter taste of fear as she wondered if he'd done anything else to her. Ever since that night, she'd been afraid of the dark, had asked for God's strength to help conquer her fears.

Up until tonight, she hadn't remembered her attacker had called her by her sister's name.

"Shelby?" Alex took hold of her hand, breaking her from her reverie. "Are you all right?"

For a moment she stared at their entwined hands, before raising her eyes to meet his compassionate gaze. "You're right. He did mistake me for Trina at first," she finally admitted. "But I responded seconds before I started to turn around. Just as I caught a glimpse of him, he attacked."

His fingers tightened around hers and the expression in his eyes was full of agony. "I'm sorry I couldn't stop him, Shelby. I'm so sorry."

She tried to smile. "It's okay. The point is that I don't think he attacked me because he thought I was Trina. Quite the opposite. I believe he attacked me because I *wasn't* Trina. Because when he realized who I was, he didn't want me anywhere near the warehouse."

He sucked in a harsh breath. "That makes sense. The minute he knew you weren't Trina, he had to get rid of you to stop you from stumbling into something you shouldn't." His gaze was thoughtful. "I wonder if a big drug shipment was scheduled to come in that night?"

She didn't like the sound of that. "You're telling me they trusted Trina with drug smuggling information?" she asked, appalled. "That they considered her part of that business?"

"I'm afraid so." Alex's expression was one of chagrined guilt. "You need to know, it was Trina's idea from the very beginning. She was trying to gain their trust, so she could get information about the identity of the drug smugglers. She felt it was the only way to prove your father was innocent."

She wrapped her arms around her stomach, feeling sick. When Alex had told her Trina was feeding the DEA and coast guard information, she hadn't realized exactly what that role had entailed. But the image he painted was all too real.

Trina had been acting like an undercover agent, much like Alex had been.

And now Trina was dead.

"So that's why they killed her," she whispered.

Alex's expression turned grim. "Yes, that's the only explanation that makes sense to me, too."

The sound of the hotel room door opening prevented them from saying anything further. Rafe stepped inside, stomping the snow from his boots.

"I don't think it's snowing much, but the wind is still blowing pretty hard," Rafe informed them. "I made a huge path around the hotel and I didn't see a single soul who was brave enough to be hanging around outside in this weather. I made note of the cars parked here at the hotel, and I'll run them through the computer. But even without that, I think we're safe for the night."

"Thanks, Rafe," Alex said. He turned to Shelby, gesturing to the connecting room. "You'd better get some rest. It's been a long day. We'll come up with some sort of action plan first thing in the morning."

"All right. Good night, Rafe, Alex." She closed the connecting door most of the way to give her some privacy, leaving it unlocked in case of an emergency.

Knowing they were safe at last, sleep should have come easily, but it didn't. Instead she kept thinking about the night she was attacked, the moment she'd turned to look at who'd called her sister's name.

A blurred face hovered on the edges of her memory, but no matter how hard she tried, she couldn't get that momentary glimpse of the man's face to focus.

When Shelby woke up the next morning, the sun was shining brightly through the windows. Rubbing her gritty eyes, she realized with relief the snowstorm was over.

Her gaze sought Cody, but his bed was empty. She scrambled out of bed to search for him, her heart racing.

Of course, she needn't have worried. The connecting door between the rooms was standing ajar and she soon discovered Cody was bonding with Rafe and Alex, putting a pretty big dent into a box of doughnuts, no doubt purchased from the café next door.

"I never get to eat sweets for breakfast," Cody was saying, his mouth full of Boston crème. "Aunt Shelby always says we hav'ta eat healthy." He made the last word sound like something disgusting.

Miffed, she turned away. Ridiculous as it was, she resented having to be the role model parent, while Alex showered Cody with all the fun stuff.

"We would be eating healthy, too, Cody, if we had a stove to cook on," Alex said. "Don't expect this every day. We're only having doughnuts for breakfast as a special treat."

She paused, mollified by his words.

"'Cause we got in a car crash and fell down the hill?" Cody asked.

"Yes, exactly," Alex agreed. "And because you were such a good boy as we walked through the storm to find shelter."

"How come we didn't see any wild animals?" Cody wanted to know.

A wry smile tugged at the corner of her mouth as she listened to Alex's drawn out response. He didn't seem to mind playing the role of father to Cody, and she was happy they were adjusting so quickly to spending time together.

But as she was about to turn away, she hesitated. If she left Cody alone with Alex while she cleaned up, would he take the opportunity to question the boy about what he'd seen the night Trina died?

Alex had promised he wouldn't question Cody without her permission. She'd trusted Alex to keep them safe, and maybe it was time to trust him to keep his word. She silently closed the connecting door and used the few moments of privacy to freshen up in the bathroom.

When she returned twenty minutes later, feeling much better, she joined the men in the next room.

"What's the plan?" she asked, saying a quick prayer of thanks before she helped herself to the last doughnut. She was very grateful to have something to put in her stomach. "Where are we going from here?"

Alex's expression was serious, as he turned to her. "Do you think it would be okay for Cody to watch cartoons for a while?" he asked.

The doughnut sank like a rock to the bottom of her stomach. Whatever they needed to discuss, Alex didn't want Cody around to hear it.

"Sure. Are you finished eating, Cody?"

"Yeah." He wiped his hands on his pants and she hid a wince.

"All right, let's go find the cartoon channel for a while, okay?" She led Cody back to their room and turned on the television for him. When he was settled in, she returned to Alex and Rafe.

"He doesn't usually watch much TV so I don't know how long the cartoons will hold his attention," she warned.

The two men exchanged a solemn glance. "Sit down, then. There's some new information that you need to know."

Truly worried now, she sat. "What is it? What's going on?"

Alex leaned forward. "We got some information from Logan Quail, he's the DEA agent that was sent in to help replace me when I was shot."

She frowned. "I thought you said it was too late, that no one could replace you?"

"No one could replace Alex's undercover role," Rafe

corrected. "Or his knowledge of the case after all this time. But we did get Logan to help keep an eye on things. He's not undercover in the shipyard as a long-shoreman, but he has managed to get a job in the local packing plant nearby."

She supposed that did make some sense. With Alex recovering, the DEA needed to have someone stationed in Green Bay.

"Logan called first thing this morning with some disturbing news," Alex continued. "Your father's fore-man has been found dead."

"Bobby Drake is dead?" She paled. "What happened?"

Rafe shrugged. "Looks like it could be suicide, but we won't know until the ME finishes his report. Suicide or murder, either way, we suspect his death is related to the case."

Alex glanced at her. "And just so you know, there's another weird piece of the puzzle. Your stepmother moved out of your father's house."

"Marilyn?" She raised a brow. "Moved out? Are you sure? I just spoke to her the other day."

"When?" Alex's tone was sharp.

"The first day I arrived at the bed-and-breakfast. Don't glare at me like that, I told you I called my father. Marilyn answered the phone."

Alex scrubbed a hand over his face and softened his tone. "You're right, that is strange. Rafe, tell her exactly what Logan said."

"Logan heard that Russ Jacobson had stormed into to the police station, claiming that Marilyn was missing. A good portion of her personal items were gone,

too, but he claimed that she wouldn't have left him voluntarily." Rafe spread his hands wide. "After reviewing
the evidence, the police felt differently."

Her poor father. She and Trina hadn't gotten along
very well with their stepmother, but they'd accepted
her into the family, regardless. Now she'd moved out?
It didn't make much sense.

"That doesn't sound like Marilyn," Shelby mused.
"To leave like that. I mean, she and my father have been
married for nearly five years. She wasn't my favorite
person in the world, but as a couple, they seemed to get
along well enough. And she certainly enjoyed spending his money."

Alex's expression grew grim. "Shelby, you need to
know there have been a lot of rumors over the past few
months. About your stepmother's infidelity."

Her eyes widened. "You mean she's cheating on my
father?"

Rafe shrugged. "Maybe. It's only a rumor at this
point, but it does appear incriminating that she suddenly
moved out of your father's house. Some people have
suggested she was having an affair with Bobby Drake."

"I thought you said he was dead?"

"He is, but it's possible he killed himself over her.
Could be she broke off things with him and took up
with someone else."

"Bobby Drake doesn't seem to be her type," she protested. "She likes spending money."

First her father had lost Trina and now his wife. How
was he holding up? She remembered how different he'd
sounded on the phone, as if the weight of the world

rested on his shoulders. "I should be there for him," she murmured.

"It's too dangerous to go back," Alex reminded her gently. "Right now, keeping Cody safe is our main concern."

He was right, she knew it. But the thought of her father dealing with all of this alone ripped her heart into tiny pieces.

"There's a death notice in this morning's paper for Trina," Rafe said, breaking into the prolonged silence. "Her funeral service is scheduled in three days, for this upcoming Thursday."

"I really want to be there for the funeral," she said.

"I don't think that's a good idea—" Alex started, but she quickly cut him off.

"It's important," she insisted. "For me, my father and for Cody."

Especially for Cody, who deserved the chance to say goodbye to his mother one last time.

"Don't," Rafe said, grabbing Alex's arm to prevent him from following Shelby as she stalked off to the connecting hotel room. "You're not going to talk her out of this one, my friend."

Alex sat down with a heavy sigh, wishing there was some way to make Shelby see reason. "Why is she being so stubborn? It's too dangerous to go back, even for a funeral."

"Would you miss Kayla's funeral?" Rafe asked reasonably.

No, he wouldn't. "That's different," he protested

weakly. "There's not someone after me. Besides, Kayla and I are very close."

Rafe raised a brow. "And you don't think Shelby feels the same way about Trina? Or that Cody deserves the opportunity to say goodbye to his mother?"

Alex groaned and buried his face in his hands. "Okay, fine. Great. If Shelby and Cody are really going to return to Green Bay for the funeral, you have to help me dream up some plan that will keep them safe."

"That will be a challenge." Rafe scratched his jaw. "Maybe we need to come up with a different approach. Maybe instead of avoiding the place, we should head there right away. Today."

"Are you crazy?" Alex nearly shouted. "No. Absolutely not. Risk Cody's life? And Shelby's?"

"Calm down and think this through logically," Rafe said in a stern voice. "Trina's shooting triggered a domino effect. Shelby and Cody were traced to Kayla's bed-and-breakfast. Then Bobby Drake's death. Now this stuff with Marilyn." He shook his head slowly. "Marilyn's disappearing act might be nothing, but I think we're missing putting pieces of this puzzle together because we're hiding out instead of being in the thick of things in Green Bay."

Alex clenched his jaw. Rafe was right. If not for Shelby and Cody being in danger, he wouldn't think twice about heading back to Green Bay. Except for one tiny problem. "Have you forgotten I'm not cleared to return to active duty?"

Rafe glanced down at his injured right arm. "How accurate are you with your left hand?"

"Not accurate enough," he responded tersely, opening and closing the fingers of his left hand, wishing for the impossible. "I can hit a large target from a distance of fifty feet without a problem, but anything requiring more finesse or a longer distance..." he shrugged. "I wouldn't bet anyone else's life on my ability, that's for sure."

Rafe pursed his lips thoughtfully. "If you can shoot from a distance of fifty feet, you can easily play bodyguard for Shelby and Cody once they're safely tucked inside a hotel. That gives me and Logan some time to dig under some rocks to see what we can uncover."

Exasperated, he stared at his partner. "That's it? That's your plan?"

Rafe scowled. "Do you have a better one?"

Alex closed his eyes and told himself to get a grip. No reason to take out his lousy mood on Rafe. It wasn't his partner's fault that the thought of Shelby and Cody being exposed to danger made him sweat. "No," he said finally. "I don't have a better one. But if anything happens to Shelby or Cody..." He couldn't finish the thought.

"You need to have a little faith, my friend," Rafe said quietly.

"I have faith in you," Alex protested.

"Not me. Faith in God. You need to reach out to the Lord, putting yourself in His hands."

His gaze caught on the cross Rafe wore around his neck and knew his partner was serious. Never in a million years would he have imagined having this conversation with Rafe. "Is that what you do?" he finally asked.

"Absolutely." Rafe leaned forward, his expression

earnest. "And you can, too. Shelby would be more than happy to offer you guidance if needed."

He knew that much was true. And he suddenly felt sick at the possibility Rafe might be developing personal feelings for Shelby. After all, they shared the same beliefs.

"You like Shelby, don't you?" he asked.

"Of course I like her." For a minute Rafe looked puzzled and then suddenly he threw his head back and laughed. "Relax. I admire Shelby but I'm not interested in her on a personal level."

"Good." He couldn't deny the overwhelming sense of relief. As much as he knew he didn't deserve a woman like Shelby, he found he didn't want to imagine her with any other man, either.

Rafe's cell phone rang and he glanced at the screen. "Logan," he greeted the caller. "What's going on?"

Alex tensed, knowing Logan Quail wouldn't have called without a good reason. He watched Rafe expectantly, as his partner's face turned stone cold.

Shelby chose that moment to return. "Cody's getting bored."

"In a minute," Alex said, waiting for Rafe to finish. When his partner hung up the phone, he asked, "What's going on?"

Rafe glanced at Shelby and then back at Alex, letting out a heavy sigh. "Someone threw a firebomb at Shelby's car."

Chapter 9

Shelby let out a shocked gasp. Alex stared at Rafe in horror. "Where was her car parked?" Was her house gone? Her day care center? He braced himself for the worst.

Rafe gave a curt nod as if he'd anticipated the question. "Not directly in front of her day care center, thankfully, but close enough to cause damage."

"Damage? What kind of damage?" Shelby swayed and Alex jumped up to lead her toward the nearest chair before she collapsed. "The children?" she asked in an agonized tone.

His chest squeezed painfully. Today was Monday, so Shelby's day care was likely full of kids.

"Logan is on the scene and he'll keep us updated," Rafe said, downplaying the topic of potential casualties. "The timing of the firebomb happened when most of the kids were outside in the backyard."

"But the infants don't go outside in the winter." Shelby's eyes filled with tears. "I'll never forgive myself if something happens to one of my children. Never."

Alex gently squeezed her hands trying to offer strength and support. "Shelby, this isn't your fault. No one will blame you."

What was going on? Why the sudden act of violence? At this late stage in the game, especially after Trina's death, it didn't make sense.

Unless there had been a tracking device on her car. And this was some sort of bizarre warning.

Shelby looked like she was in a daze repeating, "My children, my children," over and over again.

Helpless, Alex speared Rafe with a hard look. "Do you really think it's still a good idea for Shelby and Cody to go to the funeral?" he demanded.

"Alex," Rafe started, but he was quickly interrupted.

"Listen to me. Why would someone toss a firebomb at Shelby's car, huh? No rational reason other than as a dire warning to stay away. A warning we'd be idiots to ignore. The last place she and Cody should go is back to Green Bay."

"Maybe the firebomb was meant to destroy the tracking device? Or what if it *was* an effort to keep Shelby and Cody away? Because whoever threw it knew you'd react like this?" Rafe pointed out with infuriating logic. "And if that's the case, you'd be playing right into their hands by refusing to let them attend the funeral."

"I don't care." His gut clenched with the thought of anything happening to Shelby or Cody. "They're not going."

"Yes, we are." Shelby seemed to snap out of her

trance to join the conversation. "Cody needs closure. Somehow, someway we need to find a way to take him."

He wanted to yank his hair out of his head in frustration. But he already knew from experience that yelling and arguing wasn't going to work. "Think about it, Shelby," he pleaded. "Please, think this through."

"I am trying to think it through," she said, looking suddenly exhausted. "I know we have to keep him safe, yet I also don't want Cody to have emotional issues for the rest of his life. Maybe it would be best to take Cody to see a child psychologist before making a final decision. I don't want him to be in danger. If the psychologist doesn't feel it's important for Cody to be there, to say goodbye to his mother, then I won't take him."

Rafe's phone rang again. "Logan? What's the status?" Rafe listened for a moment, and then his face relaxed. "No injuries," he repeated aloud for their benefit. "Thanks for letting us know."

Alex chest expanded with a wave of overwhelming relief.

Shelby closed her eyes and dropped her chin to her chest. "Thank You, Lord," she whispered.

Alex silently echoed the heartfelt prayer. If Rafe was right, someone had gone to great lengths to scare Shelby away.

Because of Cody?

Alex knew he couldn't hold off any longer.

"Shelby, it's time." At her blank look, he clarified. "I need to talk to Cody. We need to know what he saw."

Shelby wanted to protest, but she couldn't deny the truth. Her children at the day care center had been put at risk. Because of her. Because of the bad man Cody had seen.

As much as she didn't want Cody to relive those awful memories, she didn't seem to have much of an alternative.

"He'll be upset," she said in a low voice. "Remember how he reacted to seeing blood?"

"I know," Alex agreed softly. "I don't want to hurt him any more than you do. Let's think about it for a bit. There must be some way we can uncover his memories without causing too much harm."

"Art therapy is often used for troubled kids," Shelby said slowly. "I'm not an expert, but we learned a little about it in college."

"Worth a try." Alex turned to Rafe. "Can you find some art supplies?"

"Sure."

"Could we take Cody outside for a while?" Shelby asked. "He lost interest in the cartoons fairly quickly and I think the fresh air would do him good."

"I'll make another sweep of the area before I go to the store," Rafe offered.

"I'll go with you," Alex said. When he stood she caught a glimpse of a handgun tucked into the back waistband of his jeans, mostly hidden behind his denim shirt. "Give us a few minutes before you get Cody's coat and boots on, all right?"

She nodded, disturbed at the very real evidence of the danger. Was she being stubborn, insisting on going to Trina's funeral? Maybe. Yet she couldn't tolerate knowing that this was Cody's last chance to say goodbye to his mother. She wanted to do what was right for him.

Cody was thrilled with the chance to go outside to

play in the snow. She waited for Alex to return before getting Cody dressed in his winter gear.

"Would you like to build a snowman?" she asked, pasting a bright smile on her face.

"Yeah!" Full of energy he dashed outside. She quickened her pace to keep up.

"Do you want to help?" she asked Alex, as he followed more slowly, alertly scanning the area.

"No, I'd rather watch."

She understood he meant keeping an eye out for anyone suspicious and turned her attention to Cody. The back part of the hotel had a large area of the parking lot no one had bothered to snowplow. Putting aside her worries, she threw herself into making this fun for Cody, showing him how to start the base of the snowman. The snow was wet and heavy, perfect for packing. Cody helped with more enthusiasm than skill.

When she and Cody struggled to get the second snowball placed on top of the first, Alex jumped in to help. She noticed Cody brightened the moment Alex began paying attention to him. He constantly looked to his father for approval.

Their snowman was a bit lopsided, but she didn't care. And neither did Cody.

"Our snowman needs a hat," Cody declared.

"Here, Cody, use mine." She was surprised when Alex stepped in to offer his own. And when Cody couldn't reach, Alex lifted him up so that Cody could place the hat on the snowman's head.

Watching father and son interact caused a lump to form in the back of her throat.

When she glanced back at Alex, she caught a hint

of longing in his eyes. As if he'd regretted not joining them in building the snowman from the beginning. For a moment she saw a glimpse of what their life could be like, if both of them raised Cody together.

A true family.

The idea caught her off guard. Yet the more she thought about it, the more she realized it really wasn't so surprising. She'd grown closer to Alex during these past few days than she'd ever been to any other man. And wouldn't it be wonderful for Cody to have two parents who loved him?

She told herself to get a grip. Alex didn't embrace her Christian lifestyle. She'd gotten the impression he might be open to the idea—he'd agreed to have Cody raised with Christian beliefs—but she couldn't share her life with someone who didn't share her faith.

She started toward him, but then Rafe returned with the art supplies, and the moment was gone.

"Good job." She applauded Cody when he found matching rocks for the snowman's eyes and a pinecone for the nose. She held him up so he could complete the snowman's face himself.

"Who's ready for lunch?" Rafe asked, as he hauled several sacks of food and art supplies from the SUV.

"I am!" Cody shouted, squirming out of her grip and running toward Rafe.

"We'll talk to him after lunch," Alex said softly.

She nodded, knowing she'd run out of time and excuses.

Watching the way Shelby played with Cody as they built a big, if lopsided, snowman, Alex realized she was a natural when it came to taking care of children.

Owning and operating a day care center was probably part of the reason, but everything Shelby did with Cody revealed the depth of her love for the boy.

She was Cody's surrogate mother, in every way. He admired everything about Shelby. The way she bravely faced her past. The way she helped Cody. The way she cared about the people in her life.

He found himself hoping she included him in her sphere of caring. Because his feelings for her were growing into something more intense than mere friendship.

Even though this wasn't the time or the place for anything more.

As they ate peanut butter and jelly sandwiches and apples for lunch, he couldn't get the image of her carefree laughing face out of his mind. For those brief moments outside, she'd seemed happy.

But not anymore. The tiny brackets around her mouth told him that she was dreading the moment he began questioning Cody.

He wasn't feeling too great about it himself.

Typical Shelby, though, she didn't whine or complain, but got right to work as soon as she'd finished clearing away the lunch mess.

"Cody, look at what Mr. Rafe brought for you." She spread out the large sheets of paper on the small hotel table and opened up the container of crayons. She spilled them all over the table, so it would be easy to pick out whichever colors he preferred. "Would you like to draw pictures?"

"Yeah!" Cody knelt on one of the chairs, so he could reach the table. "Are you going to draw with me?"

"Of course." Shelby sat across from Cody, her expression thoughtful. "What should we draw?"

Alex stayed back with Rafe, allowing Shelby to take the lead. Obviously he didn't have the same experience she had with kids.

"How about a snowman?" Cody asked.

"No, we already made a snowman outside." Shelby pretended to think. "Maybe we should draw the marina?"

Even Alex could tell Cody had tensed up. "I dunno," he hedged.

Shelby leaned forward, brushing a hand over Cody's blond hair. "Cody, do you remember the night you saw the bad man?"

His green eyes widened until they seemed to take up his entire face. "Yes."

"Would you be able to draw a picture of the bad man for us?" she asked, gently. "Please? It's very important."

He stared down at the blank piece of paper in front of him, and Alex knew if Cody refused he wasn't going to force the issue. They'd simply have to figure out what happened some other way.

"Okay," he said, picking up the black crayon.

Alex held his breath as Cody began to draw. Shelby worked on her own picture, choosing to draw sailboats on the water, but kept her attention on what Cody was doing.

"What is that, a car?" she asked when Cody put down the black crayon.

He nodded. "I saw the bad man through my window."

Alex glanced at Shelby in surprise, but she was holding Cody's gaze. "You were in the backseat, here?" she asked, pointing to the picture.

"Yep. The bad man was yelling at my mom." For a moment his lower lip trembled and Alex had to stop himself from rushing over to stop Shelby's art therapy session.

"You're safe here with us now," Shelby said softly. "Your other dad and Mr. Rafe are here to keep you safe."

Cody glanced at Alex and Rafe, as if to reassure himself they were indeed there to keep him safe from harm.

"What did the bad man look like?" Shelby asked, pulling Cody's attention back to the picture. "Was he taller than your mom or shorter?"

"Tall. Really, really tall." Cody picked up the brown crayon and began drawing a man. He made a rectangular body, with stubby arms and legs sticking out of it. The figure was tall, much taller than the car.

"That's a great picture," Shelby said, admiring his work. "What color hair did the bad man have? Yellow like yours? Or dark like your dad's?"

Cody scrunched up his face. "I dunno. Mostly bald." He left the figure hairless and finished putting in the man's face, eyes, nose and mouth, and the mouth was frowning.

Then he picked up the red crayon and drew a wide red streak down the side of the man's head.

Alex sucked in a quick breath.

"Why is he bleeding?" Shelby asked in a calm tone.

"Mom hit him with a long skinny thing," Cody's voice was so quiet she could barely hear him. "He fell down and then she jumped in the car and drove away."

Alex closed his eyes, his stomach churning with guilt

and regret. Cody should not have been forced to witness such violence. No wonder the poor kid had nightmares.

And it was all his fault. When Trina had offered to give inside information, he should have told her no. Should have encouraged her to stay far away from the shipyard.

Finding the mastermind behind the drug running operation shouldn't have cost Trina her life.

Shelby tried to keep calm, even though her stomach churned with nausea as she stared down at Cody's drawing.

"You're safe here with us," she reminded him, when he'd stopped working on his picture. "What else is in the picture? What was next to your car?"

Cody scrunched up his face for a moment, then picked up a navy blue crayon. "Big ships," he said, drawing a large rectangle to one side of the picture.

"Like in the shipyard?" Shelby asked, as she worked on her own drawing. She found herself drawing the marina, the morning the gunman had found Trina. Was the man with the gun the same person Cody had drawn with the blood streak on his face? It seemed likely, but she wasn't sure.

He nodded but didn't say anything, simply drawing more ships.

When Cody finished his picture, he shoved it away. Since he seemed to lose interest in the paper and crayons, she decided not to push. He'd opened himself up enough, she didn't want to add to his distress.

"There's a Disney movie on the television," Alex offered in a low voice. "Maybe he'd like to watch?"

"Sure." She knew they wanted to have Cody pre-occupied while they discussed the details they'd un-covered. She took Cody into the connecting room and found the movie. He'd burned off enough energy build-ing a snowman outside, that she thought he might fall asleep while watching.

"Mostly bald," Alex repeated as she walked back to talk with the two men. "That should help us narrow our list of suspects."

She sat down with a sigh. "Maybe, but to Cody's mind, mostly bald could be short hair, like a military cut, too."

Alex grimaced. "And really, really tall doesn't mean much either, other than that the guy was taller than Trina."

"Let's re-create that night," Rafe suggested, look-ing at both Shelby's and Cody's pictures. "Cody drew large ships, as if he was in a car parked at the shipyard."

Alex leaned forward eagerly. "Cody is in the back-seat of a car, while Trina goes to meet someone. Some-thing happens and she's forced to defend herself, maybe with a baseball bat or a tire iron, hitting the bad guy. He goes down and she jumps into the car to escape. But she doesn't go back to her place because she thinks she'll be followed."

Shelby joined in the theorizing. "And she doesn't come to my place for the same reason. She calls me and insists I meet her at the marina because Cody's in danger. I drive down there and she's standing in the shadows of our father's yacht, the *Juliet*."

"How does the gunman know she's there?" Alex asked, when Shelby paused. "Does he have a tracking device on her? Or does he know her well enough to know she wouldn't go home or to Shelby's place?"

"Trina said something interesting when I met her down at the marina," Shelby said slowly. "She told me she'd made a terrible mistake. And that I needed to call you, Alex. No one else, not the police, not anyone but you." She stared for a moment at Cody's drawing. "So what was her mistake? Trusting the wrong person? Stephan?"

Alex exchanged a concerned look with Rafe. "Stephan isn't mostly bald," Alex pointed out. "And I would think if Cody had seen his stepfather, he would have said something to that effect, rather than calling him the bad man."

"Okay, that makes sense." Shelby nodded with relief. "But then who did Trina trust that turned out to be a terrible mistake?"

"Your father?" Alex said. "He's tall and mostly bald."

She narrowed her eyes. "Same argument as with Stephan. Cody knows his grandfather. He wouldn't have referred to him as the bad man, either."

"Maybe you're both wrong on that," Rafe spoke up. "Maybe the guy Trina was fighting with was wearing some sort of face mask obscuring his features?"

"No, I'm sure Cody would have said something about a mask." Shelby looked down at the drawing again, trying to imagine what Cody might have seen. "If they were arguing at an angle, or if the man's back was to Cody, it's possible he didn't get a good look at the man's face at all."

"He drew a frown," Rafe said tapping the guy's face on Cody's picture.

"The frown could be something he added because he heard them yelling." Shelby grimaced. "That might be simply the way he portrayed the man's anger onto the drawing."

Alex let out a heavy sigh. "So you're telling us Cody's description is basically useless? That we can't really narrow down any of the suspects unless they happen to be the same height or shorter than your sister or have a head full of hair?"

As much as she hated to admit it, she couldn't lie. "I think if it was dark, and Cody didn't get a good look at his face, then no, we can't narrow down any of the suspects. Stephan has always worn his hair long, and he's only a couple of inches taller than Trina, so we can probably take him off the list."

"But not Bobby Drake. Bobby was six feet tall and wore his hair in a crew cut," Rafe said.

Alex captured her gaze with his. "And not your father."

Chapter 10

The minute the words left his mouth, Alex wanted to call them back. Especially when Shelby paled, bit her lip and looked away, a hint of angry desperation in her eyes.

What was wrong with him? Why couldn't he keep his big mouth shut? There was no reason to blurt out his true feelings like that.

Of course Trina and Shelby wanted to believe their father was innocent. Yet no matter how much she and Trina had protested, he just couldn't quite believe their father was innocent. His background research had shown how Jacobson had taken the shipping business from a struggling operation to amazing success within the first five years he'd owned the place. There was no denying Jacobson clearly possessed a keen mind for business. And that was exactly why Alex simply couldn't believe Russ Jacobson didn't know about the drugs coming in on his ships. A man that involved in his company had to know what was going on.

There was a long moment of silence while Rafe shifted uncomfortably in his seat.

"We have a long list of suspects," Rafe said finally. "And I'm sure there are plenty of other people we haven't even considered."

"Trina seemed wary of involving the local authorities, Shelby commented in a low voice. "She specifically told me not to trust anyone, even the police."

"Exactly my point. There could be someone working on the inside," Rafe agreed. "There were many cops who had made it quite clear they didn't like the DEA homing in on their turf."

Shelby lifted her chin and regarded him steadily. "I think Rafe is right. We can't do anything from here. We need to be closer to the action. We need to head into Green Bay, the sooner the better."

Alex clenched his jaw, biting back a protest. Because she was right. Not that he had any intention of exposing Shelby or Cody to danger. No way was he going to allow them anywhere close to the so-called action. But he and Rafe needed to be closer to the scene. And besides, if she was really going to take Cody to Trina's funeral, then they'd need to figure out where the funeral home was located and how they were going to cover the various entrances and exits to keep everyone safe.

The idea of allowing Shelby and Cody out of his sight even for a second made him sweat. He wasn't going to let it happen unless he was absolutely certain they'd be protected.

"Logan is picking me up in an hour," Rafe announced. "Why don't you let us go into the city first? That way we can find a place for you to stay that's relatively close to where Trina's funeral will be."

Alex jumped on the opportunity to put off heading into Green Bay one moment earlier than they needed to. "Sounds like an excellent plan. I'll call you in the morning before we leave."

"Wait a minute," Shelby protested. "Do we really need to wait until tomorrow? I want Cody to see a child psychologist as soon as possible. I'd like a professional opinion on whether or not he should attend his mother's funeral. And to do that, we need to get to Green Bay, sooner rather than later."

Alex raised his eyebrows in surprise. Still, maybe she was right. There was a good possibility the child psychologist would tell Shelby the funeral wasn't a good idea.

At least he could hope.

He quickly amended their plans. "It's better if we go in the morning, but I promise we'll get to Green Bay early enough so you can take Cody in to see someone."

Her expression mirrored her relief. "Thank you."

Cody chose that moment to join them, rubbing his eyes sleepily.

"I'm hungry," he announced.

"I'm sure you are, partner." Shelby glanced at him. "Normally he gets a snack in the afternoon to hold him over until dinnertime."

"Logan's pulling up to the hotel now," Rafe said when his cell phone went off. "I asked him to bring some things for Cody. Clothes and snacks."

"Wonderful," Shelby said warmly. "Thanks, Rafe."

"You're welcome, *amiga*." Rafe flashed a bright smile. "Why don't you and Cody come out to meet Logan?"

"Okay." Shelby quickly gathered their coats and bundled up Cody before following Rafe outside.

Alex stood near the window, watching them. Cody scooped up some snow and threw a snowball at Rafe. There wasn't much power in the attempt, but Shelby laughed and Alex's gut tightened with awareness.

They didn't seem to be in any hurry to come back inside.

He couldn't deny he was out of his element when it came to being a father figure to Cody. He'd never spent much time around kids, until his most recent injury. His niece, Brianna, was a cutie and he'd enjoyed spending time with her over the past few months, but he didn't know the first thing about raising a child. Much less how his sister managed to do it on her own in the two years since her husband had died.

Shelby was a lot like Kayla. She would do just fine raising Cody on her own, too.

Wait a minute. He thrust his hands through his hair and spun away from the window. Was he seriously considering giving up custody of his son to Shelby?

The very thought tightened the knots in his stomach. He wasn't sure he knew how to be a good father, but the thought of giving Cody up didn't sit well, either. Yet shouldn't he worry about what was best for his son? Cody obviously considered Shelby to be his surrogate mother. And sadly, he was young enough that in a few years, his memories of Trina would likely fade away. Shelby would soon be the most important person in his life.

But didn't a boy need a father, too?

Maybe, but Shelby was a wonderful woman. It was very likely she'd meet a man one day. Someone like Rafe, who would be a great father to Cody.

A far better father than he could ever be.

Every cell of his being rejected the idea of Shelby finding someone else. But if he proved that her father was guilty, she wasn't going to forgive him anytime soon. And if that was the case, he knew he would give up custody of his son to Shelby.

He pulled his scattered thoughts together, when the group came back in, filling the small motel room.

"Logan," he greeted the tall, brown-haired agent who'd been sent to replace him. Logan Quail wore cowboy boots and a Stetson cowboy hat, but his voice only held the barest hint of his Southern roots.

"McCade. How's the arm?"

Alex shrugged, opening and closing the fingers of his damaged right hand. "It's still attached, I guess. I've been working on shooting left-handed."

If Logan was concerned about Alex's ability to get back into the field, he didn't show it. "Good. Things are heating up, big time. I think the case is about to be blown wide open."

A surge of adrenaline flowed through his veins. Along with a healthy dose of wariness. "I'd love to put this case to rest, but it would help to know where the source of the danger is coming from."

"Don't I know it," Logan agreed. He glanced at

Shelby, who stood near Rafe. "How well do you know your stepmother?" he asked.

Shelby frowned. "Marilyn? Not very well. She's not my favorite person. Trina and I always believed she married my dad for his money."

Logan and Alex exchanged a look. "What makes you say that?"

Shelby shrugged. "She doesn't have just one materialistic bone in her body, she has several. From the moment she married my father, she has spent his money as if it washed up on the lakeshore along with the dead fish. Why all this interest in Marilyn?"

Logan threw a questioning glance at Alex, and he gave a subtle nod, indicating Logan could speak freely around Shelby.

"I did a little digging on Marilyn Hayes Jacobson," Logan said slowly. "She died about six years ago."

Shelby's jaw dropped. "What do you mean, she died?"

Logan's expression was grim. "A woman by the name of Marilyn Hayes with your stepmother's social security number has been dead for the past six years."

Alex narrowed his gaze. "So whoever this woman really is, she re-created herself six years ago? That's about the time we began hearing about the potential drug smuggling operation coming through Green Bay."

"I know." Logan looked at Shelby, who sank into a nearby chair as if her knees had gone weak. Shelby was strong, but Alex wondered just how many more shocks she could take before crumbling. "I'm sorry to dump this on you so abruptly, but I figured you needed to know, especially considering your father's company is knee deep in this mess. We're still trying to figure out exactly who Marilyn really is, but the fact that she's using a fake name and social security number is enough to put her at the top of our suspect list."

Alex couldn't deny the timing was right. And considering how Shelby and Trina weren't close to their stepmother, she wouldn't hesitate to eliminate one of them if they got in her way.

"So if Marilyn is at the top of the suspect list," he mused aloud, "that means Cody's bad man is likely working either for her or with her as a partner in crime."

Shelby's mind reeled at the news regarding her stepmother. Or maybe her soon to be ex-stepmother, if Marilyn had really moved out of her father's house.

Once Alex and Logan left, her room had seemed far too quiet. She stayed with Cody, until Alex poked his head through the connecting doorway and asked if she wanted to go down to eat in the diner.

"Yes, getting out of the hotel room for a while would be wonderful."

The diner wasn't very crowded, so they pretty much had the place to themselves. Once Cody had finished his chicken strips, he went over to the race car driver video game in the corner. He sat in the seat, clutching the steering wheel, making *vroom, vroom* noises.

Alex stood and crossed over to put a few coins into the slot. "Push this button, here," he directed. "This starts the game. Now you can really drive the race car."

She couldn't help but smile when Cody shouted with glee as he maneuvered the video game. Alex came back to take the seat across from her. "He's having fun."

"I know. Thanks." She toyed with her water glass. "Alex, you said you wouldn't mind if we raised Cody as a Christian, right?"

He slowly nodded. "Yes, that's right."

"But yet, you're not a believer." It wasn't a question.

He hesitated. "You're right, I wasn't raised to be a believer. But I have to admit, that first night when Cody prayed for me, I was surprised and humbled to be included in his prayers. And then when we had to walk through the storm to find shelter, I prayed for the first time in my life."

She sucked in a surprised breath, her heart filling with joyful hope. "Really? Then God answered both of our prayers, guiding us to shelter."

Alex's smile was crooked. "I have to agree, since I couldn't see much of anything with the snow and the wind in my face and yet managed to find exactly what we needed."

She was so happy to hear Alex wanted to have faith. "I'd love for you to join my church. We can do bible studies and meet so many great people." The possibilities were endless.

Alex's smile faded. "Maybe," he said cautiously. "But if I am able to go back to work, I won't be around much."

Her hope collapsed like a deflated balloon. "What do you mean? You're Cody's father. Of course you have to be around for him."

He sighed. "Shelby, my work with the DEA is important to me. My best friend in high school died of a drug overdose. I've dedicated my life to keeping drugs off the streets. If my aim with my left arm becomes good enough that I can stay in the field, I will."

"And what about Cody?"

He dropped his gaze. "I'll grant you sole custody of Cody."

She stared at him, hardly able to believe what she was hearing. Surely she must have misunderstood. "You'd give him up completely?"

"Yes, I would. If that's what was best for him."

That night, Shelby couldn't fall asleep. Alex wasn't the man she'd thought him to be, if he could actually consider giving up his son.

Certainly being a DEA agent was admirable. And his reasons for dedicating his life to eradicating drugs from the streets were honorable, too. To lose someone you cared about to drugs was horrible. But surely there were other ways to help his cause? A path that didn't push him toward giving up custody of his son.

She closed her eyes on a wave of regret. Her dream of becoming a family with Cody and Alex was nothing more than foolish fantasy.

But this wasn't about her. It was about Cody. And Alex. Even without the family she'd always wanted, they needed each other.

Lifting her heart and her mind to God, she prayed. *Dear Lord, help me understand Your will. I love Cody so much and I've begun to care for Alex, too. Guide me toward Your path, Amen.*

When her troubled soul was soothed by prayer, she drifted off to sleep hoping Alex was praying for guidance, too.

The next morning, Alex agreed to drive into Green Bay. She was relieved to know Cody would soon get the help he needed, but she couldn't deny a flicker of fear.

Trina had been murdered only three days ago. And since that time, someone had not only followed them, but had tried to kill them. She wasn't sure what awaited them in Green Bay.

Heavenly Father, keep us safe in Your care.

When they'd finished breakfast in the diner, they packed up Kayla's SUV and headed into Green Bay.

"You're awfully quiet this morning," Alex said, casting a glance in her direction.

She tried to smile. "I've been thinking a lot about what you said last night."

He gave a slight frown. "I thought you'd be happy to know you'll have custody."

"I love Cody and would gladly take custody of him. But I also believe a child should have two actively involved parents." She paused before asking, "What if you can't go back to the DEA? What then?"

Alex didn't answer for a long moment, his gaze glued to the road. The sun was shining brightly and the temperature had warmed up enough that much of the snow from the storm was already melting. "I don't know."

His response wasn't reassuring. "But you would stay part of Cody's life?" she persisted.

"I'd try," he finally answered.

"Praying for guidance may help," she said slowly. "I'm certain God would show you the right path to take, much like He did during the snowstorm."

He shot a surprised glance in her direction, as if the

thought had never occurred to him. After several long seconds, he gave a slow nod. "Maybe I will."

Satisfied that she'd done the best she could, Shelby turned her attention to Cody. Earlier that morning she'd used the hotel phone to call Debbi, her day care center assistant, to find out the extent of the damage from the firebomb. Debbi had confirmed they would have to be closed for a few days until the front window glass was replaced. So far, only one parent had taken their child out of the program. Shelby could only hope it wasn't the first of many.

Debbi had also given her the name of her brother-in-law, Dr. Kade Zander who happened to be a child psychologist.

"He's generally pretty booked," Debbi had told her, "but as a favor to me, Kade said he'd make room for Cody whenever you need him to come in."

Shelby had been thrilled and had requested Kade's phone number. When she'd talked to him, he'd agreed to see Cody at noon that day, over his lunch hour. Shelby had been grateful for the favor. She really wanted a professional's opinion on what was best for Cody.

After a few hours of driving, Alex pulled up to a large, well-known hotel, located not far from the church where Trina's funeral services were to be held.

"I hope you're not upset, but I reserved a two-bedroom suite for us," he said. "There's a living room and small kitchen area in the center and I thought it would be good for Cody. And then the two bedrooms are on opposite ends of the suite."

She was glad he'd thought about Cody's needs and her privacy. "A suite should be fine, if we can afford it."

He gave her an odd look. "We can afford it. Logan booked the room under his name, so we don't have to worry about anyone finding us here."

She hoped he was right. The room wasn't ready yet, so Alex drove them to Dr. Zander's office.

"I'll pick you up in an hour," he said. "In the meantime I'm meeting with Rafe and Logan. We'll pick up some groceries after lunch."

"All right." She took Cody's hand as they went inside. The waiting area was full of toys and he didn't need any urging to find something to play with.

Dr. Kade Zander met with her for a few minutes first, and she immediately liked the gentle, soft-spoken doctor. She'd explained what Cody had been through and her dilemma about taking him to the funeral, especially her fears related to his mental health balanced against the need to keep him safe.

"Closure is very important for young children," he admitted. "My first instinct is to agree he should go, if you think it's safe enough. Let me meet with him first, to see how traumatized he's been."

"I understand," she agreed. Would the funeral be safe? She found it hard to imagine that someone would try to harm Cody in the middle of a public funeral. Surely there were precautions they could take.

Dr. Zander took Cody back into another playroom, and Shelby settled in to wait. She leafed through various parenting magazines, even though she was dying to know what was going on in the other room.

The forty-five minutes seemed to drag by slowly, but when Cody came back out, he appeared to be his usual happy self. The doctor gestured for her to come over.

"Cody is adjusting fairly well, but I do think going to the funeral will be good for him," he told her. "He misses his mother, but I get the sense she wasn't always the most dominant person in his life. He talks about you a lot."

She couldn't help but smile. "I spend a lot of time with him. Between the hours he's at the day care center and the times he spends at my apartment, we've become very close."

Dr. Zander nodded. "It's apparent he loves you very much. Death is a difficult concept for children to understand. Telling him that his mother is in heaven certainly helps, but he sometimes makes comments about his mother coming back, so I do believe attending the funeral will give some closure, if precautions can be taken to make sure he's safe. I'd be happy to see him on a weekly or biweekly basis if you think it would help going forward."

"I would like that," Shelby confessed. "I've been so worried I'm making things worse for him, rather than better."

"You're doing fine," he reassured. "Considering everything that has happened, I think Cody's doing remarkably well."

"Thank you." Relieved she'd been on the right track, she offered her hand. "I feel much better now."

"My opinion is only based on my expertise regarding a child's emotional health," he warned gently. "It's your decision if the potential physical danger is worth the risk."

She nodded, her relief fading. "I know."

He seemed satisfied with that. "I've been recommending your day care center to my clients," Dr. Zander said, clasping her hand gently yet firmly. "I believe faith is very important in raising children."

"Debbi and I certainly appreciate it." She couldn't help thinking about the damage from the firebomb. It wasn't her fault, but the end result was the same. She couldn't blame parents for taking their children out of her center to attend someplace else. "Thanks again."

Alex was waiting outside when they left the office building. "Are you hungry?" he asked. "I don't want to go anywhere public, but we could pick up something at a fast food place to take back to the hotel."

"Sounds good."

Alex pulled into a parking lot of a restaurant offering buckets of fried chicken. Shelby volunteered to stay in the car with Cody. Directly across the street was a small pub, and when a familiar woman stepped outside, glancing around furtively before rushing over to her car, Shelby sucked in a harsh breath.

"Marilyn!" She couldn't take her eyes off her stepmother. Marilyn seemed to be in a big hurry, and somewhat upset, her eyes red and swollen when she jumped into her car and quickly drove away.

Had Marilyn been inside, meeting someone? A man? Cody's bad man?

Alex opened the door and handed her the food. She took it, but when he slid in beside her, she grabbed his arm. "Alex, I just saw Marilyn. She left that pub across the street, looking upset. What if she was meeting someone?"

He glanced in the direction she indicated. "I don't believe it. Look who's coming out now."

She glanced over and saw a tall man walk out into the sunlight. In a heartbeat, she recognized him. "Mayor Flynn."

"Yeah. He's tall and mostly bald, just like Cody's bad man."

Chapter 11

A sense of excitement hummed in Alex's bloodstream, like it always did when he was on the verge of breaking open a case. This was the part of his job he liked, bringing the bad guys to justice. He stared at the mayor, watching as the guy walked toward a shiny black Lexus.

"Do you think Marilyn was meeting the mayor?" Shelby's voice sounded incredulous. "That she's cheating on my father with him?"

"That's one explanation," he murmured with a frown. "But you mentioned she looked upset, so we shouldn't be hasty, jumping to conclusions." He turned on the SUV engine and pulled out of the parking lot, heading in the opposite direction.

"But he can't be—" she stopped and glanced back at Cody and Alex knew she didn't want to say too much in front of the boy.

He didn't respond, his mind whirling with possibilities. They knew Marilyn wasn't who she said she was, but for Mayor Flynn to be Cody's bad man seemed a bit of a stretch. As mayor, James Flynn's life was very much in the public eye. Yet at the same time, he could use his power to influence the local police investigation.

Like telling everyone Trina's murder was likely a robbery gone bad. And pushing for a quick closure on the case.

Still, to be fair, Cody's description covered a wide range of people. Too many to be of much help, really.

"Isn't City Hall on the other end of town?" Shelby asked, her brow puckered in a tiny frown.

"Yeah. If they were having an affair, it's possible they'd traveled all the way over here to minimize their chances of being seen."

"If I hadn't insisted on bringing Cody to Dr. Zander, we wouldn't have seen them," she said in a quiet tone.

He couldn't deny the truth of her words. In the rearview mirror he could see Cody sitting in the backseat. "Did Cody see him?" he asked, lowering his voice too, so Cody wouldn't hear.

"I don't think so," Shelby said with a grimace. "And I didn't think to point him out."

"There's no guarantee he'd have recognized him, anyway," Alex assured her. "And we could show him a picture. The mayor's photo would be easy to find on the Internet."

"Which may not help, since we don't know if Cody got a good look at his face," she reminded him.

"I know." He returned to the hotel as quickly as possible, knowing he needed to get in touch with Rafe and Logan about the latest turn in events.

"Dr. Zander believes Cody can benefit from attending Trina's funeral," Shelby said, breaking the silence. "If you think it's safe enough to go."

He glanced over at her. "Really? And if I don't think it's safe enough?"

For a moment, she looked uncertain. "If you say it isn't safe, we won't go. I trust your judgment. But Alex. I really want to attend, especially if going will help Cody deal with the loss of his mother. His emotional health is important, too. The funeral is going to be crowded with lots of people attending." The all-too familiar stubborn glint was in her eyes. "This is really important. Can you look me in the eye and tell me there's absolutely no way you, Rafe and Logan can't ensure Cody's safety?"

Alex let out a deep, heavy sigh. He couldn't look her in the eye and say that, because she was right. The crowded funeral wasn't exactly the time he would choose to take out a young witness. Yet on the other hand, the thought of his son being in danger, no matter how remote, made him cautious. His earlier enthusiasm for the case evaporated, leaving a vague, nauseous feeling in its place.

"We'll see what we can do," Alex reluctantly promised.

When they finished their lunch, Shelby took Cody into their bedroom. She didn't close the door and Alex could hear her asking if Cody wanted to watch a movie or read some of his picture books.

He called his partner, updating Rafe and Logan on the newest development with Mayor Flynn and Marilyn, along with Shelby's plan to attend Trina's funeral.

When he finished with his phone calls, he stayed on the sofa, eavesdropping on Shelby's conversation with Cody.

"I know my mom is in heaven, but why can't we visit her?" Cody asked.

"Heaven is where God lives, Cody. People on earth like you and me can't go up to visit. When we die, our souls go up to live with God in heaven. And that's where your mom's soul is right now."

"So she can't come down to visit me, either?" Cody asked.

"No, sweetheart, I'm afraid not. But you can still talk to your mom, just like you talk to God when you pray."

"Is she going to be lonely up there, all by herself?" Cody asked.

"Oh, no, Cody, she won't be by herself. Heaven is a wonderful, beautiful, peaceful place with lots of people your mom knew and loved when they lived on earth. Once souls get up in heaven, they don't want to come back."

Alex smiled a bit at the thought of Trina being in heaven. Listening to Cody and Shelby's conversation about God and heaven made him remember the night he'd waded through the snowstorm, carrying Cody and leading Shelby with a rope, praying for the first time that he could remember.

Shelby thought God had answered their prayers and looking back, he could only agree. There was certainly no other logical explanation as to how he'd managed to find the shelter of those far trees. He couldn't see but scant inches in front of his face. One minute he was walking blindly, wondering how much longer Shelby would be able to keep up and the next, he'd stumbled onto the shelter.

Some people might argue luck, but at that moment, he'd known that he hadn't found the shelter of those trees on his own. He'd had help.

Guidance from God.

Shelby had suggested he seek help in figuring out his future through prayer, but somehow he didn't think it would work the same way. Just because God had answered one prayer, did that mean He would answer more? Feeling a little foolish, he closed his eyes and opened his heart.

I'm new at this stuff, Lord, but I need Your help to know what I should do with my life. Since Toby's death, I've vowed to do my best to keep drugs off the streets. But being a DEA agent isn't the best career for a man raising a son. Shelby will be a good mother for Cody, of that I have no doubt. But I'm not sure how to be an equally good father. I need direction, Lord. Show me the way.

He opened his eyes and glanced around. Okay, it was silly to think that God would simply drop some sort of note out of the sky telling him what to do with the rest of his life. But deep down, there was a strange sense of peace.

Shelby came out of the bedroom, half-closing the door behind her.

"Is he sleeping?"

She smiled and nodded. "Yes. Fell asleep while I was telling him my favorite Bible story."

"I don't know any Bible stories," he confessed. "But I did what you suggested. I prayed for guidance as to what I should do with my career and my future."

Her expression brightened and he was amazed at how beautiful she was. "I'm glad. I just know God will help you decide what's best."

He gestured for Shelby to take a seat beside him. "Is it really that easy?" he asked. "To become a believer?"

She laughed, a light musical sound that warmed his heart. "Yes, it's really that easy. Having faith and praying are a big part of what is important."

"I'd like to learn more," Alex admitted slowly.

Shelby reached over to take his hand in hers, curling her slight fingers around his. He caught his breath at her soft caress. "I'd love to help you in any way I can," she murmured.

The way she stared at him, so intently, made him feel short of breath, as if there wasn't enough oxygen in the room. Holding her hand like this, as if they were the only two people in the world at this moment, gave him the insane urge to draw her close, enveloping her in a tight embrace.

And the way she was looking at him, shyly curious, made him wonder how she'd respond to his touch.

Considering her past experience with men, he knew he had to go slowly, lest he frighten her. She'd allowed him to help warm her up while they were in the shelter of the snowstorm, but at that moment, their embrace hadn't been personal.

"Shelby," he whispered, reaching up to brush a stray

curl off her cheek. Her skin was satiny smooth and he was amazed to see his fingers were trembling. He wanted to tell her how special she was but didn't know how. Gently, he cupped her cheek with his hand, brushing the silky softness with the pad of his thumb.

Her eyes widened at the caress. But she didn't pull away. Just the opposite. She tilted her head, leaning into his palm.

His breath strangled in his throat and he captured her gaze with his, lowering his head, slowly, so as not to scare her, wanting nothing more than to steal a kiss.

His cell phone rang. No doubt Rafe or Logan with news on the Mayor Flynn angle. He froze, torn by duty and desire.

Duty won. Regretfully he dropped his hand from Shelby's face and turned away, reaching for his cell phone.

Wishing he'd met Shelby at another time or place.

The skin of her cheek still tingled long after Alex's hand had dropped away. She sat on the sofa, unable to move, her emotions in turmoil as Alex spoke to Rafe.

He'd been about to kiss her. She'd known it the moment he'd looked deep into her eyes. And even more shocking, at least to her, was that she'd wanted him to.

She licked suddenly dry lips and tried to understand what was happening to her. She avoided men, had resigned herself to living her life alone, without male companionship. Yet with Alex, she couldn't remain indifferent.

She cared about him. More than she ought to. Because while she knew she could trust him, while she firmly believed Alex would never physically hurt her, she wasn't so sure she could trust him with her heart.

"Stephan Kirkland called Shelby?" Alex interrupted her thoughts when he swung around to face her. It took her a moment to realize he and Rafe were discussing her. There was another pause as Alex listened to what Rafe was saying. "I don't like it, Rafe," Alex said with a scowl. "I don't want her anywhere near the guy."

She frowned at his commanding tone. She knew Alex wanted to keep her safe, but he couldn't shut her off from the rest of the world forever. And besides, Stephan might not be Cody's father, but he'd still raised the boy for the past four years. He had a right to know what was going on. And she knew it would be safe to see him—he was too short to be Cody's bad man. "I'd like to meet with him."

Alex's gaze drilled a hole into her for a long moment, before he swung away. "I need time to think about it," he said in an abrupt tone. "I'll get back to you." Clearly irritated, he snapped his phone shut.

"Did Stephan say why he wants to meet with me?" she asked, when he didn't offer any further information.

"He claims he wants to talk to you about releasing custody rights to Cody." Alex's scowl deepened as he continued to pace the center of the room. "But I'm not buying his story. I don't trust him."

The vehemence in his tone surprised her. "I thought we basically ruled Stephan out as Cody's bad guy?"

"No one is ruled out," Alex responded flatly. "If Stephan was safe, why didn't Trina send you to him?"

He had a point. She remembered specifically asking Trina about Stephan and if he could help. "Well, she also told me not to trust anyone, even the police, so apparently she didn't want me to take Cody to anyone but you. That doesn't mean Stephan is guilty."

Alex spun around to face her. "Can you repeat exactly what she said?"

It was three days ago, but Trina's words were indelibly imprinted on her brain. "She told me she had made a terrible mistake and asked if I'd take Cody and keep him safe. She told me to call you, because you were Cody's real father and once you knew about him, you'd keep him safe. I asked her if Stephan knew, and she nodded and told me she had never listed Stephan as the father on Cody's birth certificate. She said, 'He can't help,' meaning Stephan. Then she told me not to trust anyone, especially the police."

"Especially the police?" He stared down at his cell phone for a moment, as if it were some sort of foreign object. "If the mayor is involved, he could easily have a cop on the inside working for him," he murmured. "And someone inside the police force would have the ability to trace Trina's cell phone to Kayla's bed-and-breakfast."

"It's all my fault," she whispered.

He shook his head. "No, it's mine. I should have realized the possibility earlier. Especially after hearing from Rafe that Holden didn't have any suspects or a clear motive for murder, and that he was getting pressure to close the case quickly."

"No clear motive?" Had everyone gone crazy? "What about giving inside information to the DEA? Surely that's motive."

Alex glanced away. "We haven't said anything about

that. Right now, it's better for us if the police do conclude robbery. Once we know who's behind the drug smuggling, then we can gather the evidence needed to pin Trina's murder on them."

Troubled, she dropped her argument. Because what he said made some sense. If there was a dirty cop inside the police force, they would want Trina's murder covered up too, so pushing for a more thorough investigation wasn't going to help.

She rubbed the aching area on the side of her temple. "So we can't trust the police. I get that part. But Stephan wouldn't hurt Cody. And Cody would have recognized him if Stephan had been the one arguing with Trina. So there's really no reason I couldn't meet with him."

Alex clenched his jaw. "I don't like it."

She tried to hide her uneasiness. "He might know something, Alex. He was married to Trina, after all. Granted, they were having marital troubles, but for all we know, Trina's mistake involved trusting the police, not anything specifically about Stephan."

"I still don't like it," he muttered. But the resigned expression in his eyes convinced her that he'd already given in. "You're not going alone. I'll be with you and we're going to meet with him in a very public place."

"You?" Once again, she was surprised. "Won't going out in public risk your cover?"

A grim smile tugged at his mouth. "If you'd seen me as a longshoreman, you'd know how different I look now. I grew my hair long and dyed it dishwater blond. With a scruffy beard and dark brown contact lenses, even Rafe had trouble recognizing me. Besides, my cover is the least of our worries. The fact that I was jumped and stabbed three months ago indicates my cover has already been blown."

Understanding hit hard. "You're in danger, Alex. They wanted to kill you, too."

He didn't disagree. "I'll call Rafe so he and Logan can help prepare for this meeting with Stephan. Unless you've changed your mind?"

"No. I haven't changed my mind."

Shelby could tell Alex wasn't happy, even though he hid his feelings behind a brisk no-nonsense attitude. He and Logan had picked a busy restaurant as the place for Shelby to meet Stephan. Logan was seated not far from their table while Rafe had stayed back at the hotel with Cody.

She and Alex were already seated in a booth when Stephan arrived. Trina's husband looked awful, as if he hadn't gotten any sleep since Trina's murder.

"Thanks for meeting me," Stephan said, sliding into the empty space across from them. Shelby was pinned in the corner of the booth, between Alex's large frame and the wall of the restaurant. He glanced nervously at Alex. "Who's your friend?"

"I'm with the federal government and Shelby's in our protection," Alex told him. "That's all you need to know."

Stephan didn't seem too surprised to see a federal agent sitting beside Shelby. He ignored Alex and turned his attention to her. "How's Cody?"

"He's doing as well as can be expected," Shelby answered.

Stephan nodded grimly. "I wanted to know what

your plans were. I know he's not my son, but I need to make sure someone is going to take formal custody of him."

"Have you always known he wasn't your son?" Shelby asked.

Stephan slowly nodded. "Yeah. I was upset at first, but I loved Trina. And we'd both made mistakes that were better left in the past."

"You didn't offer to adopt him?" Alex asked.

"No. Trina didn't suggest it, so I didn't offer." Guilt flashed in Stephan's gaze and she realized now why Trina had been happy to let Cody stay overnight with her so many times. Stephan was bothered by Cody's presence. "He's not a bad kid," Stephan continued, "but I didn't want to be responsible for someone else's son."

Shelby could feel Alex tense up beside her, and she hastened to interject. "I'm going to request custody of Cody."

Stephan looked relieved. "Good. I'm glad to hear that. It's always been obvious to me how much you love him."

"When was the last time you saw Trina?" Alex asked, changing the subject.

Stephan sighed and scrubbed his hand over his face, clearly exhausted. "The police have already taken my statement, why don't you ask them?"

"Because I'm asking you." Alex's voice reminded her of steel wrapped in velvet. "Did you know about the drugs coming in on Jacobson ships?"

Stephan didn't look surprised. "Yeah, I suspected there was something going on and stumbled upon the truth. I brought it up with Trina and she told me undercover agents were working on it, so I should keep my mouth shut."

Shelby saw the flash of anger in his eyes. "Is that why you moved out?"

Stephan flushed guiltily and averted his gaze. "Yeah. I mean, I didn't like the ways things were going. Trina was different, acting weird and frankly, I didn't want to be dragged into danger."

"Did Russ Jacobson know about the drugs?" Alex persisted.

Stephan shrugged. "I didn't say anything to him, but I don't know how he couldn't. He knows everything that goes on in the shipyard."

Shelby couldn't believe Stephan had known about the drugs coming in on her father's ships. Seemed like everyone had known but her. Yet no matter what, she still couldn't believe her father was guilty. There had to be some logical explanation. "When was the last time you saw Trina?" she asked.

"The night before she died." Stephan's expression was haggard. "I kept my mouth shut about the drugs, but that night I found a hidden stash in our bedroom. I was shocked and angry. I'd trusted Trina and didn't want to believe she and her father were both a part of what was going on."

"Then what happened?" Alex asked, when Stephan paused.

"I showed her the drugs and she went a little crazy. She told me that she had to leave, right away. She needed to take Cody over to Shelby's place." Stephan swallowed hard. "That was the last time I saw her alive."

Shelby felt sick but forced herself to ignore the sensation as she glanced at Alex. "But she didn't come straight to my place."

"What time did she leave?" Alex wanted to know.

"After midnight, maybe close to one," Stephan admitted.

"She didn't call me until four in the morning," she said, glancing at Alex. "Someone must have confronted her after she left Stephan, but before she called me. Why would she go to the shipyard with Cody in the backseat of her car?"

"Good question." Alex turned toward Stephan. "Did you see anyone else that night?"

"No. But I did call the police. I couldn't trust Trina to do the right thing, so I made the call." Stephan's face twisted with remorse. "Only I was too late. Maybe if I'd have called earlier, the minute I suspected something was going on, Trina would still be alive today."

"And you told all of this to the police?" Alex persisted.

Stephan gave a grim nod. "I had to. They were looking at me as a suspect. Only once they found out about the drugs, they closed her case. The official theory is that someone shot Trina because she stole their drugs. And they believe the shooter took all her jewelry as partial payment for the missing heroin."

Chapter 12

Alex took Shelby's hand in his, giving it a warning squeeze when he saw the flash of anger in her eyes. "I'm sure the drugs didn't belong to Trina," he said quickly before she could respond. "I think someone found out Trina was leaking information to us, and they hid the drugs in her room to cast suspicion on her."

Stephan paled. "Is that what happened to her? She was killed because she wanted to help by giving information to the Feds?"

"I'm afraid so." Alex didn't like Stephan much. And he really, really didn't like the guy's attitude toward Cody. So what if the boy wasn't his biological son? After spending the past four years with him, Stephan should have cared about Cody a little. Instead, he was trying to dump the kid onto Shelby before Trina had been given a proper burial.

A stab of guilt tightened his gut. Hadn't he been tempted to do the same thing? Hand Cody over to Shelby because she'd made it clear how much she loved him? He swallowed hard and pushed his personal feelings aside to turn his attention to Stephan Kirkland and the matter at hand.

"I thought she might be guilty." Stephan looked shocked. And slightly embarrassed for thinking the worst.

"She wasn't," Alex said. He leaned forward, planting his elbows on the table. "Okay, here's how this is going to work. You are not going to tell anyone about this meeting, understand?" Alex pinned Stephan with a fierce gaze. "If anyone asks, you have not seen me or Shelby. Especially Shelby. You can say you've been trying to get in touch with her but she's not returning your phone calls. Got it?"

Stephan gave a terse nod.

"And if you're smart, you'll start looking for another line of work."

"What do you mean?" Stephan asked, shooting worried glances between Shelby and Alex. "Why do I have to look for another line of work? The marina isn't involved in anything illegal, right? The drugs were only in the shipyard."

Shelby stared at Stephan in shock. "Is that why you married my sister? For the marina?"

"No, of course not." Stephan flushed beet red and Alex suspected Shelby's question was closer to the truth than Stephan wanted to admit. "But I've dedicated my life to the marina. I'm not just going to walk away. Besides, if Russ Jacobson is going down, my skills will be needed to keep the marina running smoothly."

Alex shrugged. He'd done his duty. Stephan's decisions were his own. "Don't say I didn't warn you."

Stephan glanced at Shelby. "So you'll keep Cody? Is there any paperwork I have to sign? Do you want to stop by to pick up his things?"

"There isn't any paperwork. Trina told me that she didn't list you as Cody's father, so you're off the hook," Shelby said in a low voice.

"And no, she's not going to stop by. He doesn't need anything from you," Alex added dismissively. "I'll provide whatever Cody needs."

Stephan narrowed his gaze. "He's your son," he accused.

He didn't bother to deny it. "Get out of here," he said, gesturing toward the door. "And remember, not a word about this meeting to anyone."

"Don't worry, I don't want to be involved in this mess any more than I already am," Stephan said with a trace of bitterness as he slid out from the booth. "Take care, Shelby."

"Goodbye, Stephan."

Alex glanced over at Logan, who'd finished his meal. At Alex's nod, Logan tossed a handful of bills on the table to cover his tab and strode after Stephan, following him outside.

"Heroin," Shelby whispered in a tortured tone. "I can't believe heroin is being smuggled on my father's ships."

He understood what a shock it must have been, to hear the awful details of what had happened to Trina right before she was killed. If he could have sheltered Shelby from the harsh reality of drug smuggling, he would have. But it was too late now. "Try to remember how Trina was working to help us," he murmured.

"I know," she said in a strangled tone. She clasped her hands tightly in her lap. "Can we leave? I want to see Cody. I need to see Cody."

"Stay here for a few more minutes," he warned when she pushed against him, indicating she wanted to get out. "When Logan returns it will be safe for us to leave."

He could tell she was barely hanging on to her composure as they waited for Logan. When Alex saw his partner signal from the other side of the door, he slid out of the booth and offered a hand to Shelby.

She accepted his hand, her cold, clammy fingers tightening around his in a death grip. She stumbled a bit as she followed him out of the restaurant. Feeling helpless, wishing there was something he could do to make her feel better, he led the way outside.

Shelby might be in shock now, but this was nothing compared to what she was going to go through if it turned out her father really was the mastermind behind the drug running operation.

"Alex, my man, we have new intel on Marilyn, the mystery woman," Logan said when he finally met up with them back at the hotel room.

Several hours had passed since they'd finished their meeting with Stephan Kirkland. Shelby seemed to be avoiding Alex, choosing instead to focus her energy on entertaining Cody with simple card games.

Alex wished he knew what she was thinking, but he

was unable to read any hint of the thoughts going on behind her shadowed blue eyes. He dragged his gaze back to Rafe and Logan, who were both watching him curiously.

"You have an ID for her?" he asked. He was almost grateful when Shelby's head snapped up to glance in their direction. He'd been concerned when she'd remained so distant and withdrawn.

"Yes, we do. Her real name is Roberta Gerard and she's originally from New York," Logan announced reading from his notes. "Roberta's quite the interesting lady. She was married to a Joseph Allenburg, a rich old guy who was thirty years her senior. When he died rather unexpectedly, Roberta was arrested for suspicion of murder. But she was eventually released, all charges dropped when the autopsy revealed Joseph Allenburg died of natural causes."

"So she makes a habit of marrying older men, but doesn't necessarily do anything to hasten their demise," Rafe mused.

"That we know of," Alex muttered darkly. He wouldn't put anything past her.

"That's not all," Logan spoke up. "Her criminal record before that marriage, which lasted about two years, also includes being arrested for prostitution, possession of heroin and selling drugs." Logan shrugged. "Could be she decided marrying old men was an easier way to make money. Or she's more involved in the drug smuggling than we realized."

"So it's possible she's in on the whole thing. The timing fits. She came to Green Bay right about the time when drugs started showing up on the ships. Maybe marrying a rich guy like Russ Jacobson was icing on the cake." Alex glanced at Shelby who had grown pale as they discussed possible theories. "So who is she working with? Is it a mere coincidence that she left Russ the same day Bobby Drake showed up dead? And why was she meeting Mayor Flynn at the pub, looking upset?"

"We can try showing Cody the mayor's picture, see if he recognizes him," Logan drawled. "If he's the bad guy, then we'll know how she's involved. The two of them could be in on it together."

"Yeah, or else she was involved with Bobby Drake and is worried about her own fate now that he's dead. Or she could be involved with someone else that we haven't thought of yet." Alex let out a deep, heavy sigh. "All right. Let's show Cody the picture. See what happens."

Rafe and Logan glanced at each other and nodded. Rafe pulled out a newspaper article. "I have a photograph right here. It's a close-up of the mayor's face."

Alex took the photograph and smoothed it out on the table. Shelby and Cody had just completed their game of Go Fish. "Cody? Would you come here for a minute?"

"Sure." Cody eagerly scrambled to his feet. Shelby followed, her expression grim.

He understood her trepidation and tried to smile reassuringly. He pulled Cody onto his lap and tapped the picture on the table. "Do you know this guy?"

Cody scrunched up his face and shook his head. "No."

Alex frowned. "Are you sure?"

Cody nodded. "I'm sure. Will you play cards with us?" he asked, his attention clearly not on the photograph.

"Ah, maybe in a little while." He glanced at Rafe and Logan who both shrugged. Cody either hadn't seen the bad guy's face or the mayor wasn't involved.

But that didn't leave Marilyn off the hook.

Alex threaded his hands through his hair in sheer frustration. There had to be a way to break this case open. There just had to be.

"Cody, why don't you go play in your room for a while?" Shelby said softly.

Alex glanced over, noticing Cody looked like he might argue, but the boy finally did as he was told. He slid off his lap, landing on the floor. She waited until he was in the other room before turning toward him. "If you suspect Marilyn is involved, doesn't that mean my father is innocent?"

"I don't know, Shelby." He stared at her for a moment. The threads of this case were so tangled, he couldn't be absolutely sure of anything. "Maybe. For your sake, I hope he is innocent. Obviously he's not Cody's bad man. And I will admit, I can't imagine Russ Jacobson giving the order to have his own daughter murdered."

"Exactly." Shelby's tone was full of satisfaction. "It's very easy for me to believe Marilyn is guilty. I never liked her much anyway. And the more I think about her being involved with Cody's bad man, the more I'm convinced my father could be innocent."

Alex wished he could agree. "Or maybe your father discovered she was involved in the drug smuggling but kept quiet because he loved her."

Shelby's eyes narrowed. "Why do you insist on be-lieving the worst about him? I thought we just agreed he'd never harm Trina?"

Alex glanced away. His gut instincts weren't easy to explain. He just didn't have a good feeling about Jacobson.

Rafe spoke up. "I think we have to consider that Cody's bad man might have been working on his own, crossing the line when he attacked Trina."

Alex followed the line of Rafe's logic. "Which means, it's possible Jacobson is the ringleader, and knows who's guilty of killing his daughter. If that's true, then maybe Trina's death means the plan has changed and now he's going to pin the whole operation on the murderer." Abruptly, the puzzle pieces fell nicely into place. "Taking Marilyn down with him."

He heard Shelby suck in a harsh breath. He wanted to go to her, to put a supporting arm around her shoulders. Yet despite their almost kiss earlier that afternoon, he knew his presence wouldn't be welcome.

Not anymore.

Everything had changed after the meeting with Stephan. For the first time, Shelby was being forced to seriously consider her father's guilt. Even Stephan had believed Jacobson to be involved in the drug smuggling. And there was nothing Alex could say to soften the blow.

She might claim her father wasn't a murderer, but in his opinion, anyone helping to put drugs into the hands of children was exactly that. A murderer. His best friend Toby's death was only one example. There were hundreds and thousands more.

Alex curled the fingers of his injured hand, flexing the damaged muscles. He planned on bringing the man responsible to justice. He'd do whatever was necessary to break the cycle of drugs and death. Even arrest Shelby's only living parent.

Yet he also knew, no matter how unfair it was, that if he did so, Shelby would always look at him as the man who'd arrested her father and Cody's grandfather.

Seeking justice could mean losing the woman he was beginning to fall in love with.

Shelby sat by Cody's side long after he'd fallen asleep. Despite her own bone-weary exhaustion, her mind kept replaying the conversation with Stephan over and over in her mind.

Finally she knelt beside her bed, and opened her heart and her mind to prayer.

Heavenly Father, help me to see the truth, Your truth. If my father is guilty of this horrible crime, give me the strength to do whatever is necessary to keep us all safe. Please, Lord, guide Alex, too. Help him to keep his mind open to all possibilities. I trust You, Lord, to show him the way. Amen.

With her heart and her soul at peace, she finally slept.

The next morning, she awoke early, feeling well rested and anxious to do something. Being in the hotel suite with Alex and Rafe made her feel safe. But since Trina's funeral wasn't until tomorrow, she feared the day would drag by excruciatingly slow.

Silently, so she wouldn't wake Cody, she washed up in the bathroom and then paused near the doorway leading into the general living area. She could hear two male voices talking. She knew it was wrong to eavesdrop, but couldn't help herself when she heard her name.

"Shelby's never going to forgive me," Alex said.

"You underestimate her faith, my friend," Rafe countered. "She knows you don't mean her any harm."

"Yeah." Alex let out a harsh sound. "But that doesn't exactly change the outcome, now, does it? I'm hurting her even though I don't mean to."

"If her father is guilty, he's the one at fault," Rafe pointed out. "Not you."

"It doesn't matter much either way. I'm still the guy who's going to help bring him down." Alex's agonized tone wrenched her heart.

Shame washed over her, causing her to turn away from the doorway. She'd been so upset about the recent turn in events that she'd misled Alex into believing she blamed him. And she knew very well that none of this was his fault. She'd come to him for help and he'd gone above and beyond, especially during the snowstorm. It was her own problem if her father happened to be involved.

She took a step toward Alex, wanting to go to him, to reassure him that she didn't blame him at all, when Cody cried out in his sleep.

"Mama!" Shelby hurried to his side, where he thrashed around in the bed. "Mama!"

"Shh, Cody. It's okay. I'm here with you," she crooned, gathering him close so he wouldn't hurt himself with his flailing arms and legs.

He continued to cry, so she rocked him in her arms, murmuring words of comfort. She wasn't surprised when the door opened farther and Alex stood in the doorway.

"Is he all right?" Alex asked, his expression mirroring his concern.

"He had another nightmare," she explained, although no doubt Alex figured that one out for himself. "I'm sure he'll be fine."

He hesitated in the doorway, as if loath to leave them alone. "Do you really think attending the funeral will help?"

"According to Dr. Zander it will. But you know as well as I do, there are no guarantees. And I need to know you'll think of a way to keep him safe."

He nodded, and stood awkwardly for a moment. "Is there anything I can do?"

Her heart squeezed for a moment, as she saw a hint of longing reflected in his eyes. Alex wanted to be a father to Cody, but he didn't know how. She'd gladly let him step in right now, but Cody's emotional state was still fragile, and he didn't know Alex well enough to find comfort with him.

"Is there something for breakfast?" she asked.

"Instant oatmeal, since Cody claimed apple cinnamon was his favorite."

"We'll be out in a few minutes," she promised.

Alex nodded and finally moved away from the doorway, leaving them alone. Once she'd gotten Cody calmed down from his dream, she helped him brush his teeth and change his clothes.

Alex, Logan and Rafe were all in the kitchen area when she emerged from the bedroom. They greeted both her and Cody.

When they finished eating breakfast, she urged Cody to watch cartoons for a bit, sensing the men were on a mission. Sure enough, once she'd cleared the table of their dishes—it still made her chuckle to watch all of the men eating Cody's oatmeal—they took over.

Rafe took a sheet of Cody's drawing paper and quickly drew bold strokes across the page. "Here's the intersection the church is on. And here are all the door-ways leading in and out of the building."

"There are too many entry points," Alex said, groan-ing and throwing up his hands in frustration. "How are we supposed to keep an eye on all four?"

"We don't." Rafe's calmness only seemed to grate on Alex's nerves. "Shelby and Cody will only go in and out of the main entrance, here. From this vantage point across the street, you can keep an eye on both of these doorways." Rafe marked them in blue. "Logan and I will be inside with Shelby and Cody. No one is likely to make a move on her or the boy in the middle of a crowded funeral."

Alex scowled. "You don't know what this guy is ca-pable of doing. What if he knocks her unconscious and drags her out the back?" Alex seemed bent on poking holes in their plan.

"You mean after he's managed to get past both me and Rafe?" Logan asked with a loud snort. "Don't think so."

She moved closer, realizing she was a big part of this plan. "I can tell you what the inside of the church looks like," she offered.

Rafe flashed his blindingly white smile. "Thanks, *amiga,* but I know what the inside of this church looks like. We checked it out earlier this morning."

"Of course you did," she murmured, blushing a bit. "Sorry, I should have known." She glanced at the drawing in the center of the table. "Why have you decided to keep Alex outside?" she asked, curiously.

The three men exchanged a long look.

"We feel it's safer for Alex to stay outside," Logan offered.

She paled and glanced at Alex who was scowling again. "Safer?"

"Shelby, we've decided it's best if Rafe accompanies you and Cody to the funeral," Alex explained.

A cold chill snaked down her back and she crossed her arms over her chest to hide how she was feeling. "I don't understand. You went to the meeting with Stephan with me. What's the difference?"

"For one thing, I haven't been fully cleared to get back in the field, and there's no guarantee that my shooting will be accurate enough," he said. "And besides that, being attacked proves my cover was blown. Even though I look much different now, I don't want the members of your family, or even Mayor Flynn for that matter, to get a good look at me." Steel determination lined Alex's gaze. "I'll be stationed outside as backup, well within reach if you need anything."

"As a member of the coast guard, I'm the most recognizable of the bunch," Rafe added. "The plan is for you to introduce me as your new boyfriend. I'm going to stay glued to your side and Cody's the entire time."

"And Logan?" she asked, looking at the newest agent.

"He's going to mingle as one of Trina's friends," Alex said. "We're hoping your father doesn't notice him much. We figure there are bound to be people there, friends of Trina, who your father won't know."

She blinked, trying to take it all in. They'd planned

all this out in such a short time. Yet while she was sure the plans were solid, she hadn't realized how much she'd been counting on Alex to be there with her. "Is it really necessary to introduce Rafe as my boyfriend?" she said finally. "I don't like lying, no offense, Rafe."

Rafe chuckled. "None taken. How about you simply introduce me as the new man in your life? Technically, that's true. I'm one of three new men in your life." He waved his arm wide, including the others.

She supposed stretching the truth that much wouldn't hurt. "All right."

"Okay, now that we have that settled, let's get back to the entrances." Alex tapped on the paper in the center of the table, frowning. "I don't know. I still don't like it. Let's just say that somehow you both lose Shelby in the crowd and someone comes behind her with a gun. If they force her out the back doorway, we wouldn't know until it was too late. It's too big of a risk."

"Remember, he'd have to get past both of us," Logan said with a long-drawn-out sigh. At Alex's dark look he shrugged. "But okay, let's say you're right. Rafe and I both lose Shelby at the exact moment someone approaches her from behind. What if we put together some sort of time frame? Say an hour? If Shelby and Cody don't come out through the main doorway in an hour, you go in after them."

"An hour? Are you kidding me?" Alex pushed away from the table in a fit of disgust. "By then, they could easily be dead."

Chapter 13

Alex knew he was probably overreacting, but he didn't like the idea of Shelby and Cody being exposed to danger. He couldn't seem to shake the bad feeling that nagged at him, ever since he'd put the pieces of the puzzle together about Shelby's father.

He was keenly aware of the way Logan and Rafe exchanged a concerned glance when they thought he wasn't looking. They no doubt thought he was too emotionally involved to be of any use to them.

Maybe they were right. He dragged a hand through his hair. It was difficult to remain cool and objective when Shelby's and Cody's lives were in danger.

"Forget the time-frame angle. If we lose sight of Shelby, we'll send you a text message," Rafe said, breaking the strained silence.

Since he couldn't come up with anything better, he

nodded. "Fine. A text message will have to be good enough." It wasn't as if he didn't trust Rafe and Logan, but he'd prefer to be the one inside, next to her.

Shelby glanced at him too, her gaze full of concern. As if she was worried about him, rather than the other way around. He had to get a grip, or he wouldn't be any good to anyone.

He hid the depth of his fear behind an indifferent mask. "What time does the funeral service start?"

"Visitation starts at four in the afternoon," Rafe announced, reading from the obituary he'd picked up. "Followed by a brief prayer service at five-thirty."

"I'd like to stay for the prayer service," Shelby said.

He nodded. "I know. Should be fine."

"We could get the local authorities involved, requesting extra security for the back exits," Logan said, staring at Rafe's sketch.

"No." Alex's bold refusal caused more raised eyebrows. "No local cops. We can't rule out the possibility of someone working from inside."

"Do you really think so?" Logan asked.

"Someone tracked us to Kayla's bed-and-breakfast. The only two calls that we made, outside of Rafe, was the call I made to the local police and the one Shelby made to her father."

"I called the day care center, too," Shelby reminded him.

"Cartoons are over," Cody called out, interrupting them from where he was seated in the living room. Alex glanced over to see the boy was jumping up and down on the sofa.

"Cody, get down from there." The boy stared at him

defiantly, continuing to jump, adding fuel to Alex's temper. "I said get down!"

Cody's eyes widened with fear and he immediately stopped, his face crumpling as he started to cry. Alex mentally winced, knowing he'd been too harsh. For a moment he'd sounded just like his father.

A really bad comparison.

"Cody, that's not how we sit on the furniture," Shelby said in a soothing voice, as she crossed over to Cody, gathering him into her arms. "If you fall off, you could hit your head."

Alex hated knowing he'd scared Cody and stepped forward. "Do you want to see my scar?" he asked, kneeling down by the sofa where they were seated. "I was jumping on my mom's bed and hit my head on the edge of the frame. Got five stitches right here," he tapped the diagonal scar half-buried in his right eyebrow.

Cody's expression cleared as he gently fingered the mark on Alex's forehead. "Did it hurt?"

Alex nodded. "Not anymore, but at the time I cried and cried." He almost added more detail about the blood, but then remembered Cody's extreme reaction to his injured hand. "That's why I corrected you. I didn't want you to be hurt like I was."

Cody jammed his fingers in his mouth and nodded.

Crisis averted, at least for the moment. But those moments when he'd lost his temper, sounding too much like his father, bothered him for a long time afterward.

Alex couldn't seem to relax, even after he'd escorted Shelby and Cody to the local department store so they could pick up the proper clothing to wear for Trina's funeral. The brief outing had helped to get Cody out of the hotel suite for a while, but Alex had been tense and nervous the entire time.

Long after Shelby and Cody had gone to bed, he sat in the kitchenette area, too keyed up to sleep.

When Shelby opened the door from her bedroom, he glanced up in surprise. "Can't sleep either?" he asked in a low voice.

"No. Figured I'd try some herbal tea," she said, clenching the sash of her robe tightly at her waist. "Would you like some?"

He grimaced and then nodded. "Sure. Why not?"

She heated two mugs of water in the microwave. After putting a tea bag in each, she carried them to the table. "You're really worried about this funeral, aren't you?"

He stared into his cup for a moment. "I shouldn't be worried. The funeral is a public place and it's not likely anyone will try something shady with all those people around."

"But you're still worried," she persisted.

"Yeah. I guess I am."

She reached over to cover his hand with hers. "Maybe you need to try putting your faith in God, Alex. You, Rafe and Logan have prepared as much as you can. I've prayed about this too, and I believe we are meant to attend Trina's funeral. From here on out, the future is God's will."

He offered a faint smile. "Guess I still have a lot to learn about being a Christian, don't I?"

She didn't move her hand and he turned his so that

their palms were meshed together, their fingers inter-
laced. "You're doing fine. All you need to do is believe
in our Lord."

"Yeah." He took a sip of the tea, which wasn't as bad
as he'd anticipated. "I think the hardest part is realizing
I'm not the one in control."

"We certainly control our actions and our thoughts,
but I believe everything outside our control happens
for a reason," Shelby gently pointed out. "Helps to talk
about it and to pray."

"I'll keep that in mind." He took another sip of his
tea. She'd finished hers, setting her empty mug aside.

"Good night, Alex," she said tugging on her hand
and rising to her feet.

He didn't immediately let go of her hand, but stood
and leaned close, brushing a gentle kiss along her cheek,
so he wouldn't scare her. "Good night, Shelby."

Shyly, she reached up and brushed her mouth against
his, a soft caress that was over before he knew it yet still
made his breath catch in his throat. The kiss was over
far too soon. "See you in the morning," she murmured.

He let her go, even though he wanted very much to
hold her close. But he told himself to be patient. Shelby's kiss had been her way of telling him that she wasn't
afraid. At least not of him.

And her trust was definitely worth waiting for.

Shelby was glad when the time came to prepare for
Trina's funeral. Sitting in this hotel room was already
driving her crazy.

After they'd gotten safely through the funeral, she
and Cody would go back to the hotel with Alex, while

Rafe and Logan did their best to uncover the mastermind of the drug smuggling operation. Apparently they'd discovered some secret gambling debts Mayor Flynn was hiding and as a result, he'd moved back up a few notches on their suspect list.

She took a deep breath when Rafe pulled into the church parking lot. "Are you ready?" he asked, flashing his bright smile.

"Yes." She glanced back at Cody, who'd been uncharacteristically silent on the way over, since she'd explained what to expect at church and the somberness of the occasion. "Are you ready, Cody?"

He nodded.

She reached for the door handle, and then stopped and looked at Rafe. "Wait. I need to know your last name, so I can introduce you to my father."

"DeSilva. My name is Rafe DeSilva."

She repeated the name, committing it to memory. She stepped from the car and opened the rear door, for Cody.

"I'm scared," he said, his lower lip trembling.

"Oh, sweetheart, church isn't scary. We're going into God's house. He's going to be watching over us the whole time."

He seemed to hesitate, but then allowed her to unlatch his toddler seat so she could lift him from the car. Instead of setting him on his feet, though, she kept him in her arms.

"Everything okay?" Rafe murmured.

"Fine." She reminded herself that Dr. Zander thought it was good for Cody to have closure, so she walked into the church, feeling a sense of peace the minute she entered the sanctuary. The place was already crowded and several people approached her, offering condolences. Once Cody seemed to adjust to his surroundings, she set him on his feet.

She finally caught sight of her father and he quickly made his way over. "Shelby." He leaned down to kiss her cheek, and then ruffled Cody's hair affectionately. "How's my favorite grandson?"

"Hi, Grandpa." Cody's apprehension seemed to vanish.

"It's good to see you, Dad." Shelby wet her suddenly dry lips and pulled Rafe forward. "I'd like to introduce you to a very special friend, Rafe DeSilva. Rafe, this is my father, Russ Jacobson."

Rafe held out his hand and her father took it solemnly. "Rafe DeSilva. I recognize that name. Didn't I just read something about you in the paper?"

Rafe nodded and slipped a steadying arm around Shelby's waist. "Yes, sir. I'm with the ninth district coast guard. You might have read about how we rescued those ice fishermen off the bay a few weeks ago."

Shelby thought her father appeared taken aback by that news. "You're with the coast guard?" he asked.

A chill snaked down her spine and her smile slipped. Rafe must have noticed because he gave her a reassuring squeeze. "Yes, sir, for the past seven years," Rafe said proudly.

Her father didn't seem at all happy. "How did you and Shelby meet?"

"My nephew attends her day care center."

Shelby was glad they were standing together, so they'd have their story straight. She didn't understand how Alex could work undercover.

If she didn't know better, she'd think Rafe was thoroughly enjoying himself. "It took me a while, but I finally convinced Shelby to go out with me. God was watching over me, I think."

Shelby returned his smile, pretending that her father's discomfort didn't bother her.

"Hmm." Her father continued to look uneasy, but just then a group of relatives arrived, his cousins that she didn't know very well, so she moved away and took the opportunity to kneel beside Cody, straightening his shirt beneath his vest. "How are you doing?"

"Okay." His gaze was serious. "Is it time to say goodbye now?"

Assailed by a barrage of doubts, she hesitated. Maybe she shouldn't push him. "Is that all right with you?"

He nodded.

"We'll say goodbye together, then." She took his hand and ignoring Rafe for a moment, led Cody over to the front of the church. She knelt beside the casket and Cody followed suit.

She clasped his hand. "Dear Lord, we ask You to keep my sister and Cody's mom at Your side in heaven. We will miss her here on earth but we know she's in a much better place with You. Please help us to be strong. We loved her so much," her voice broke and she fumbled for a tissue. "Rest in peace, Trina," she said softly.

"I'm glad you're in heaven now," Cody whispered. "Goodbye, Mama. I love you."

When she and Cody finished praying for Trina, she led him away so others could approach. She was surprised when Rafe was the next in line, kneeling to offer a brief prayer for Trina as well, before coming back to join them.

She blew her nose and he enveloped her in a warm hug. It was nice, but at that moment, she missed Alex. Reminding herself that Alex's safety was more important than her needs, she took hold of Cody's hand and led him through the crowd toward the back of the church.

Suddenly she heard Cody gasp.

She froze, glancing around in alarm. "What is it?" she asked.

"I saw him." Cody's eyes were brilliant green orbs, dominating his small face.

"Who?" she asked, even though she was very much afraid she knew.

"The bad man." Cody pointed through the milling crowd with a small chubby finger. "Over there."

Rafe swiftly swung Cody into his arms, so that his face was next to Rafe's. "Where? Show me the bad man, Cody."

Cody clutched Rafe tightly around the neck. "I don't know. I saw him, over there somewhere."

"But not now?" Rafe persisted, slowly moving from side to side so Cody could get a good look around. She scanned the crowd herself, looking for anyone who might match Cody's description.

"He's gone," Cody whispered, burying his face into Rafe's neck.

"Don't worry about it," Rafe soothed, rubbing a hand over Cody's back. "If you see him again, let me know, okay?"

Rafe carried Cody in his arms until he relaxed and

wiggled to be let free. Rafe set him on his feet and Shelby kept Cody's hand in hers, unwilling to let him get too far.

Logan approached. "All right?" he asked.

Rafe nodded. "Cody thought he saw the bad man, but he's gone now."

Logan scanned the crowd. "There are a lot of people who could fit the description. I saw the mayor talking to Russ Jacobson. Neither one of them seemed very happy."

"Maybe my father is still upset about Marilyn," Shelby pointed out.

"Could be," Logan drawled. "I overheard the mayor and your father saying something about Bobby Drake. I got the impression that Marilyn had gone to the mayor about Bobby's death, but I can't say for sure."

She felt sick at the thought of Marilyn cheating on her father with a rough guy like Bobby Drake. "Where is she?"

Logan shrugged. "Haven't seen her around at all, which is odd considering she and Jacobson aren't divorced yet. I'd expect her to be here."

Shelby thought Marilyn's absence was strange, too.

"My pager is going off," Rafe said. "I'm not on call except as emergency backup, so I have to answer this. Don't go too far," he warned moving a few feet away for privacy.

Stephan chose that moment to approach and Logan drifted away. "Shelby, your father wants to talk to you when you have a minute." Stephan glanced down at Cody. "Alone."

"Why?" She tightened her grip on Cody's hand. She wasn't going anywhere without Cody.

Stephan shrugged. "He didn't say, but I get the feeling he's not too keen on your new boyfriend."

If Stephan wondered where Alex was, he didn't mention anything. A gnawing concern filled her stomach. Was Alex right that her father had been protecting Marilyn all along? It was possible now that Marilyn had left him that her father was looking for a way to tell the authorities without condemning himself.

And if so, she knew she'd offer to help.

Rafe was still on the phone, so she glanced around looking for her father. When she saw him standing beside the front door, he caught her gaze and gestured her forward. Hesitantly, she glanced over at Logan, who stood only a few feet away, chatting with someone she didn't know.

Swinging Cody into her arms, she walked toward her father. She didn't doubt that Logan would keep an eye on her. And Alex was outside, watching the main entrance. All she needed was a few minutes alone with her father.

If he was in trouble, she'd beg him to turn himself in.

Alex slouched against the side of the building across the street from the church, stamping his feet in the cold and remembering only too well why he hated stakeouts.

Interestingly enough, he'd noted that Marilyn hadn't bothered to show up at the funeral. In his mind, that only added to his suspicions. The mayor was there, along with several members of the Green Bay police including the Chief of Police, Benjamin Wallace. Seems like Jacobson had an important standing in the community.

From where he stood watching the various men walking into the church, many of them could have fit Cody's description of the bad man.

The main doors opened and he saw Russ Jacobson emerge from the building. Alex frowned and glanced at his watch. Odd, that Jacobson would leave his daughter's funeral early. Especially before the prayer service.

His heart froze in his chest, when the door opened again and Shelby walked outside, holding Cody in her arms. Without any sign of Rafe or Logan, she fell into step beside her father, following the winding sidewalk, as if she didn't have a care in the world.

Chapter 14

Alex clenched his fingers into fists, a ball of fear clogging his throat. What was she doing? Had she lost her mind? Any minute he expected her to stop, turn around and go back inside, but instead Shelby, Cody and her father took the pathway leading all the way down to the street, talking earnestly.

He had no idea how Shelby managed to get out of the church without either Rafe or Logan noticing her departure. He quickly texted messages to each of them, as he ducked over to the building next door, trying to follow the rambling path Shelby and her father made.

Jacobson gestured toward the marina located just a few blocks down the street with one hand, and he imagined the old man was trying to convince Shelby to go with him, but Shelby stopped walking and shook her head, holding Cody to her side.

"That's it, Shelby," Alex muttered to himself, as he stayed in the shadows, out of sight. "Don't trust him. And don't leave the area around the church."

But then she moved forward, walking up to meet her father, and the three of them took the sidewalk that led down to the marina. He wished he could tell what Shelby was saying to her father as they walked, their heads bent toward each other deep in conversation, but he couldn't.

Maybe she was trying to convince her father to give himself up to the authorities. The very idea made him sweat. She might not understand the magnitude of danger, but he did.

He didn't trust Russ Jacobson. Not even knowing he loved his daughter and grandson.

Turn around, Shelby. Go back to the sanctuary of the church, he silently pleaded.

He took several deep breaths to calm his racing heart. She wasn't far from the church and Logan and Rafe would be there soon. Remembering what Shelby had said about putting his faith in the Lord, he murmured a quick prayer as he followed them down to the marina.

Heavenly Father, please keep Shelby and Cody safe.

Shelby and her father paused near the main building of the marina, deserted for the most part this time of the year. There was only a sliver of moon in the sky as darkness fell. Alex took a chance, crossing the street to get closer to the marina. When he reached the building, he stayed along the side, creeping closer until he could overhear what Shelby and her father were saying.

"Okay, Dad, you've told me your concerns about

Marilyn. And I'm sorry she cleaned out your joint bank account."

"I was a fool," Jacobson muttered.

To her credit, Shelby didn't comment. "Marilyn wasn't just unfaithful, though, was she? Come on, Dad. I want to hear the truth from you. The truth about the drugs."

"Drugs?" Jacobson's voice sounded surprised. "Shelby, how in the world do you know about the drugs?"

"I tried to tell you, I know what's going on. And furthermore, we're pretty sure Marilyn is involved in the drug smuggling, too. But Dad, it's not too late. You still have a chance. You need to turn yourself in and tell them everything!" she pleaded urgently.

Alex risked a quick glance around the corner to see Jacobson shaking his head.

"No, Shelby," he said firmly. "Not yet. I need more time to clear my name."

"There isn't enough time," Shelby insisted.

"You should listen to your daughter, Jacobson." A deep voice came out of the darkness, from farther behind them. Alex froze for a moment, until the figure came closer. A tall man dressed in a dark blue cop uniform stepped out of the shadows, and when he saw the man's face, he felt a wave of relief.

Lieutenant Eric Holden, Rafe's contact within the Green Bay police department.

"Shelby, take Cody and get out of here, now!" her father commanded.

Shelby reached for Cody, but before she could move, Holden leveled his weapon, aiming directly at them. "Nobody move."

Alex stared in shock. What was Holden thinking? He should know better than to aim his weapon at civilians.

"Step away from your father, Shelby," Holden continued, his gun never wavering. "I don't want you or Cody to get hurt."

"I'm the one you want, leave her alone," Jacobson said, in a voice accustomed to being obeyed.

"Dad? I don't understand—" Shelby glanced between the two men, obviously confused. Eric Holden took a few steps toward her and she didn't move away from the man who represented the law.

"I'm sorry you had to see this, Shelby," Holden said in a placating tone. "Especially on the night we're honoring your sister's memory. But I have to tell you, your father is under arrest for drug smuggling and murder. Your father's wife, Marilyn, is dead. And we have irrefutable proof, Jacobson, that you killed her. You might as well turn yourself in. There's no escape, not anymore."

Shelby gasped, her eyes widening in horror. Alex watched the scene unfold. This was the moment he'd been training for, taking out the mastermind behind the drug smuggling operation. But something wasn't quite right. He held his weapon firmly in his left hand, in case Shelby's father decided to make a run for it.

His gaze dropped to Cody. The stark horror etched on his son's face made him freeze. His son was staring at Eric Holden, as if he were seeing a ghost.

Or the bad man of his nightmares.

And suddenly he knew. The bandage on the side of Holden's temple confirmed it. He was the one who had attacked Trina. It had been him all along. No wonder they couldn't crack the case. Holden, Rafe's contact, was running the drug smuggling ring. And from the looks of things, he was right now setting up Shelby's father to take the fall. For Marilyn's murder. And for the drugs. The same way he'd arranged for heroin to be found in Trina's bedroom.

Just like he'd arranged for Alex to be attacked, when he'd gotten too close to the truth.

"Grandpa!" Cody shouted, darting away from Holden and running toward Jacobson.

"Cody, no!" Shelby cried out trying to follow. But it was too late. Jacobson grabbed Cody, hauling him out of harm's way, but Eric Holden grabbed at Shelby. She slipped away, running toward the docks, hiding in the shadows of the boats that were suspended high above the water.

Alex was tempted to fire, but didn't want to let Holden know he was there. When Russ Jacobson ducked around the far corner of the building, carrying Cody out of harm's way, Holden disappeared, taking off after Shelby. The stalemate was broken by the knowledge that Shelby would want him to see his— their—son.

Alex peered through the night, his heart thundering in his chest, trying to figure out where he'd gone. He was faced with an impossible decision. Staying here to ensure his son's safety or going after Shelby.

After long tense seconds, he headed around the opposite side, to meet up with Jacobson and Cody.

Silently praying. *Lord, keep Shelby safe.*

* * *

When Eric Holden had nearly grabbed her, Shelby had almost collapsed in fear. In order to save Cody, she'd kicked off her useless pumps and ran.

Visions of the gunman chasing Trina flashed in her mind. Maybe this was God's plan all along, for her to live her final moments the way Trina had before she'd died. Trina had given up her life when she'd drawn the gunman away from Cody. And Shelby was willing to sacrifice herself to do the same.

Her father's yacht, the *Juliet,* offered some protection as she darted into the boat's shadow. Tonight, the darkness wasn't something to fear. It offered protection.

She held her breath, straining to listen. She'd noticed Cody's reation to Lieutenant Holden, so she knew he must be Cody's bad guy. He'd murdered Marilyn and Trina, too. She'd be more afraid if not for the fact she knew Alex had likely followed them down to the marina.

Alex would protect his son.

Strangely enough, she wasn't as worried about herself. Her normal fear of the dark vanished. She knew God was with her.

She inched down around to the front of the boat. The sound of metal scraping against metal made her hold her breath, unsure which way to move. She waited, her eyes searching the darkness, struggling to come up with a plan.

She needed to head farther north, to put more distance between Eric Holden and Cody. Surely Rafe and Logan would have arrived to help by now.

All she needed was a little more time.

Her feet were freezing without shoes and just when she'd decided to run, a figure loomed out of the darkness.

"Gotcha," Eric said, an evil, leering grin on his face.

In a desperate move, she darted to the left, but he moved faster, grabbing her and hauling her against his hard chest. The acrid scent of cigarette smoke made her gag.

The memory of the night she was attacked swelled in her mind. She could see his face from the corner of her eye and knew. This man smelled and sounded the same. Holden! Eric Holden had attacked her two years ago.

"Don't try anything," he warned, his voice low and gravel-rough near her ear. "I have a gun." He put the cold steel to her temple, as if she needed the harsh reminder. "And this time, I'll finish the job right."

"You'll never get away with this," she said, trying to remain calm. "The DEA is on to you."

Holden momentarily tensed, his tight grip painful around her neck before he finally relaxed. "I have the law on my side. Your lovely sister figured that out pretty quick. She thought she could get away from me, the little fool."

"You killed her."

Holden didn't deny it. "That brat of hers saw me from inside the car, when she fought me off with the tire iron. I would have tracked her down and killed her for that alone. I was so close to getting away clean, but it doesn't matter."

"Why did you kill Marilyn?" she asked.

"She's nothing but a drug addict, weeping and wailing after I killed Bobby Drake. When I realized she was on the verge of ratting me out, I got rid of her."

"She met with the mayor before she died. She probably told him all about you." It was a shot in the dark, but she knew her arrow had hit the mark, when he tensed up again.

"She couldn't have said anything. She didn't know I was involved until I killed her."

He acted like he was invincible. Shelby held herself still, swallowing her fear.

"I can get rid of you, the brat and your stupid father, and still come out of this looking like a hero. I'll set up your useless DEA agent as the guilty one. I'm a cop, I know how to plant evidence, making sure everyone will believe me."

Was Holden delusional? Did he really think he could keep killing people and get away with it? She noticed he didn't mention Rafe and Logan, and prayed that meant he didn't know about Alex's backups. Instinctively she knew she needed to buy more time. Time for Rafe and Logan to find Alex. For the three of them to get to Cody and her father. Between the three of them, they'd take Eric Holden down easily.

She wanted to live, to have a chance at a future with Alex and Cody. She'd just begun to realize how much she cared for Alex. If necessary, she'd sacrifice her life to save them both. She prayed it wouldn't come to that.

"Come on," he said harshly. Keeping his arm locked around her neck, her back against his chest and the gun pressed against her temple, Holden dragged her to the main building of the marina. She stumbled as rocks stabbed at her feet.

"Listen up, Jacobson," Holden called as he approached. "I have your daughter. Bring me the boy or I'll kill her."

Her father came out from around the corner of the marina building, holding his hands up high. She was relieved Cody was nowhere in sight. "Don't shoot. Please, don't shoot," Jacobsen pleaded.

"No!" Shelby struggled to get free, but Holden's arm tightened painfully around her neck, cutting off her airway. Red dots swam before her eyes. For a moment she feared she'd choke to death right then and there.

And while she didn't mind going home to her Lord, she did wish she'd taken the time to tell Alex how much she cared about him.

How much she loved him.

He eased up on the pressure, and she drew lifesaving oxygen into her lungs.

Soon, she'd make her move. He'd likely kill her but that didn't matter.

Dear Lord, keep Alex and Cody safe.

"What are you waiting for?" Jacobson asked in a low, harsh tone. "Shoot him already."

Deep in the shadows, Alex trained his gun on Eric Holden's face, holding his left arm steady by propping it against the building. From the corner of his eye, he noted Rafe had taken hold of Cody, trying hard to keep the boy quiet. Rafe had a wound on his head from when he'd been knocked unconscious, no doubt by Holden before he'd made his move, and he was still unsteady on his feet. Logan had gone back around to the opposite side of the marina, planning to trap Holden so that he'd have no place to run.

A bead of sweat ran down the length of Alex's spine. The situation couldn't possibly be any worse. He had a clear view of Holden's head, a shot he would normally take without thinking twice. But not now. Not like this. And absolutely not with his left hand, considering how Holden had Shelby pressed in front of him, his gun plastered to her head. Any sudden move on Alex's part might cause Holden to pull the trigger, killing her.

Alex gripped the gun, swallowing hard.

"Where's the kid?" Holden shouted. "I'll shoot her if I don't see that kid in ten seconds!"

From the corner of his eye, he saw Cody struggling in Rafe's arms. There was no possibility of risking Cody for Shelby, but Holden didn't know that. Time was running out. He knew with grim certainty Holden would shoot.

He thought about how God was watching over them. Guiding him. He took a deep breath and held it, focusing his energy on his target.

Suddenly, Shelby grabbed at Holden's arm clamped around her neck. She dug her fingernails into his flesh and sank her teeth into his arm, as well. The bold move caught Holden off guard, and he howled with rage, moving the gun away from her temple for a few precious seconds.

Praying with every fiber of his being, Alex squeezed his finger on the trigger of his weapon. Holden jerked, and his hold on Shelby broke. She dropped to the ground at his feet, covering her head with her hands. Holden aimed wild, getting a couple of shots off, aiming all over the place, including straight down at Shelby. Alex saw her body jerk and knew she'd been hit.

His gaze trained on Holden, Alex fired again and again.

Holden stumbled backward, a shocked expression on his face moments before he finally hit the ground. Alex realized he'd finally hit Holden in the center of his forehead.

If only it wasn't too late.

"Shelby!" Alex rushed over to Shelby's side, dropping to his knees, his worst fears clawing to the surface when she didn't move. His heart thundered in his ears, filling his head with a strange roaring sound. He couldn't be too late. He couldn't! He pressed his fingers against her neck, feeling for a pulse. Nearly fainted with relief when he found the thin, thready beat. "Shelby? Please don't die. Please don't die."

Urgently, he ran his hands over her body, searching for any sign of an injury. Maybe she was suffering from shock? But then his fingers stumbled upon something wet, warm and sticky.

Blood. From a small wound in the lower part of her abdomen. He balled up a fistful of her jacket, pressing it against the oozing wound.

"Call an ambulance!" he shouted, using all his weight to stem the flow of blood. "Hurry!"

"Aunt Shelby!" Cody cried. Rafe must have let him go, because the boy came running over, tears streaming down his tiny face. "Aunt Shelby!"

Alex held out a hand to his son, catching him up against him, holding him close with one arm even as he held pressure on Shelby's wound with the other. "She's alive, Cody. She's going to be okay." He wasn't sure which one of them he was trying to convince.

"Daddy," Cody wailed, burying his face into Alex's neck. "Don't leave me, Daddy!"

His heart squeezed painfully in his chest as his son called him Daddy for the first time. He turned and pressed a kiss to the top of Cody's head.

"I won't leave you," he promised. "Your aunt Shelby is going to be all right, and I will never leave you."

Cody's arms snaked around his neck, clinging tightly. Alex closed his eyes as a sudden, overwhelming surge of love enveloped him.

He couldn't face losing them. Either of them. Cody or Shelby.

His family.

What had made him think he could let either of them go? As Alex held onto the two most important people in his life, he knew he'd never voluntarily walk away from them again.

He could be a father. Not just because he loved them. But because he'd accepted the Lord. With God's love and guidance, he was certain he'd be a good father to Cody. And a faithful husband to Shelby.

If she'd have him.

"Stay strong, Shelby," he whispered, as the reassuring sounds of sirens filled the air. "Hang tight, my love. Help is on the way."

Chapter 15

Alex was forced to move out of the way, placing Shelby's care in the hands of the paramedics once they arrived.

"Nice shot," Logan said, nudging Holden with his toe.

Alex shrugged, holding Cody against his shoulder and barely sparing his fellow DEA agent a glance. "I missed the first few times. God helped me in the end."

Logan raised a questioning brow. "You didn't miss," he said. "He was wearing body armor. I found three slugs, one in the chest, another one in the gut and the last one dead center in his head." He flashed a crooked grin. "Congratulations, I'd say you have your shooting arm back."

Alex simply shook his head. He knew that without the Lord's help, this night may have ended very differently. "Doesn't matter, I'm finished with the agency."

Logan looked surprised, but he didn't say anything.

After being treated for a minor injury on his right hand from one of Holden's wild shots, Russ Jacobson walked over. He eyed Alex suspiciously. "Did I hear my grandson right? Did he call you daddy?"

Alex smoothed a hand down Cody's back and nodded. "Yes, sir. Cody is my son."

A fleeting expression of sorrow darkened the old man's gaze. "Never did understand why Stephan and Trina acted the way they did, letting Cody stay all the time with Shelby. And there isn't a bit of Stephan in the boy."

The sight of the paramedics lifting Shelby onto a stretcher diverted Alex's gaze. "Excuse me," he muttered, before hurrying over. "Wait. Where are you taking her?"

"The closest hospital." The paramedic barely glanced at him, shoving Shelby inside the back of the ambulance and closing the door before Alex could try to jump in beside her.

"Come on," Russ came up to rest his hand on Alex's shoulder. "They're not going to let you and Cody ride along. I'll drive."

"McCade, where are you going?" Rafe asked testily from his seat near a second ambulance. He held an ice pack to the wound at his temple. "You can't leave until the scene has been cleared and all our statements have been given."

"They can come to the hospital to take my statement," Alex told them. "And I'm not with the agency anymore, I quit."

Rafe and Logan gaped at him, as he followed Russ Jacobson to the church parking lot where he'd left his car.

Cody held tightly to Alex, as if he were afraid all
the people he loved might leave him. He decided then
and there to make another appointment with that child
psychologist Shelby had found. Cody would need all
the help and support he could get.

There was a strained silence in the car, as Shelby's
father drove to the hospital.

"I'm sorry about Marilyn," Alex murmured.

Jacobson's mouth thinned and his expression was
full of pain. "Thanks. Me, too. No matter what she was
guilty of, she didn't deserve to die."

Alex winced, thinking about all the lives that had
been lost. Trina, Bobby Drake and Marilyn. He prayed
God would spare Shelby.

"So how long have you known about…" Russ Jacobson's voice trailed off as he glanced at his grandson.

"Not even a week," Alex said, not wanting to remind
Cody of the night Trina had died.

"Hmm." Russ glanced at him. "And Shelby?"

Alex couldn't help but smile. "About the same time
frame."

"So she's not seeing that coast guard guy?" Russ
demanded.

"No, sir. Rafe was there to help protect her."

"From Holden?"

"From anyone who might want to hurt her." Alex
frowned a bit. "I'm sorry to say, I suspected you might
be in on the drug running operation."

Russ's mouth thinned. "I guess I can't blame you.
I've been a fool. I discovered the drugs and was working
closely with Holden to try to find out who was stash-
ing them on my ships. I suspected Marilyn might be

involved but Holden convinced me she was only hiding that she was fooling around with Bobby Drake. I never suspected he was the one behind the drugs all along."

"Don't feel bad, he had us fooled, as well," Alex said grimly. "He was Rafe's liaison inside the Green Bay police department. He had access to a lot of inside information."

Russ Jacobson pulled into the parking lot of the hospital. He shut off the car and turned toward Alex. "What's your name, son?"

It felt strange to be considered this man's son, but he held Jacobson's gaze steadily with his. "Alex McCade. I used to be undercover for the DEA."

"But not any longer?" Jacobson asked.

"No. I love your daughter, sir. And if she'll have me, I promise to take good care of my family."

Russ Jacobson held out his hand and Alex took it. "I'll hold you to that promise," Jacobson warned. "My daughter and my grandson deserve the best."

"I know." Alex reached for the door handle, anxious to find out news about Shelby. "Let's go."

Once inside the hospital, they'd discovered Shelby had been taken straight to surgery. Alex finally convinced Cody to eat something, buying cheese and crackers from a nearby vending machine. When the doctor, who looked barely old enough to have finished medical school returned to the waiting room, Alex warily rose to his feet.

"Miss Jacobson's surgery went fine," he informed them. "We're going to watch her overnight in the ICU but only because the wound was so close to her spleen. We need to make sure she doesn't have any more bleeding. If all goes well, she'll be transferred to a regular room in the morning."

Alex closed his eyes on a wave of relief. "Thank You, Lord," he whispered.

"When can we see her?" Russ asked.

The young man glanced at his watch. "She'll be under the effects of anesthesia for about an hour or so. The nurses are getting her settled in the ICU as we speak. Generally visitors are limited to immediate family."

Alex opened his mouth to protest, but Jacobson beat him to it. "He is immediate family," he said in a firm tone. "And this boy is her son."

"No children," the doctor began but when he saw Russ's steely gaze, threw up his hands in defeat. "Just a quick visit then, no more than ten minutes."

"Thank you. We appreciate everything you've done," Alex said, smoothing things over.

"All in a day's work." The young surgeon shook both their hands and then left.

When they were finally allowed in the ICU, one glance at Shelby had Alex sucking in a harsh breath. She was hooked up to several IV pumps and a heart monitor was lit up above her bed. She looked so pale against the white sheets.

Holding Cody, he leaned over to take her hand, a lump forming in the back of his throat. "Shelby? Can you hear me?"

Her eyelids fluttered and she blinked, finally opening her eyes to look at them. "Cody?"

"He's right here," Alex said, holding Cody so she

could see him. "See, Cody? I told you Aunt Shelby would be okay."

"I love you, Cody," she murmured, trying to smile.

"I love you, too." Cody's lower lip trembled. "Get better soon, okay?"

"I will." She glanced up at Alex. "Thank you."

He wasn't sure what she was thanking him for, and he leaned over to take her hand in his. "Shelby, everything is going to be fine. Holden is dead. He can't hurt anyone ever again."

She nodded, her eyelids fluttering closed.

The nurse hurried forward. "I'm sorry, but she really needs to rest. You'll have to come back in the morning."

Alex nodded and gently pulled his hand from her grasp. His eyes were suspiciously moist when he turned away.

"So, Cody, how would you like to come and stay with your grandpa tonight?" Russ asked when they'd left the ICU.

Cody tightened his grip on Alex's neck.

"If you don't mind, sir," Alex said. "I'd like to spend some quality time with my son."

Russ's smile was sad and Alex felt a little guilty, knowing the man was going home to an empty house. "Guess I can't blame you for that," Russ murmured.

Alex asked Russ to drop them off at the hotel, knowing that Rafe and Logan would know where to find him.

Exhausted, Cody protested going to sleep alone in his bed. Knowing the child had been through a lot, he kept Cody in his arms, as he sat back against the pillows on the bed.

And Alex found he didn't mind one bit, holding his son while the child slept.

* * *

Shelby's left side felt as if it were on fire. The doctors were pleased with her progress, though, explaining how lucky she'd been that they were able to save her spleen and that other than the blood she'd lost, she'd be fine.

"What does a spleen do, anyway?" she asked.

He launched into a lengthy explanation that quickly flew over her head. He'd ended the litany by explaining that without a spleen, she'd be on pills the rest of her life. She silently thanked God for sparing her life.

She was glad to be sent to a private room the following morning. From what she could tell, the other patients in the ICU were far worse off than she was.

Her father showed up early that morning. "Hi, Shelby," he greeted her, giving her a hug and a kiss. "I'm so glad you're doing better."

"Me, too." She smiled, determined to ignore the stabbing pain in her side.

"You must have been so frightened," he said, with a dark frown.

"Not really," she told him. "I know you never liked me to talk about my faith, but I wasn't afraid because I knew God was with me."

Her father stared down at her for a long moment. "You sound just like your mother when you say things like that."

"Mom?" Shelby was surprised. "I guess I do remember going to church with her, especially before she died."

Her father let out a heavy sigh. "I'm sorry, Shelby. I know I've been unfair with you, especially when you found strength in God. But your mother kept believing in God's love, right up until cancer stole her last breath."

Understanding dawned. "So that's why you didn't want to hear me talk about faith."

He hung his head. "I was wrong, I realize that now. I should have been smarter, but instead I made even more mistakes. Like marrying Marilyn. A woman who was helping Holden bring illegal drugs into the country on my ships."

She didn't know what to say to that, especially since she'd never liked Marilyn much. "It's not too late, Dad. God is always there, waiting for you."

He nodded slowly. "Maybe you're right. I think I'll have a talk with the church pastor about it. But for now, I'd better get going. I have to make some arrangements for Marilyn's funeral."

"Do you have to?" She struggled to sit up. "Wait a few days, I'll help you. You shouldn't have to go through that alone."

"Relax, Shelby." He placed a reassuring hand on her shoulder, easing her back against the pillows. "I'm not mourning Marilyn, not in the way you're thinking. But I need to do this, to close this chapter of my life, once and for all."

"Oh." She felt bad for her father, but she was also impressed. He was handling the truth much better than she'd ever expected.

"Take care, Shelby. I'm sure your young man will bring Cody over to see you soon."

"I hope so. I miss him."

"Who? Your young man? Or Cody?"

She blushed, knowing she'd meant both. "Cody, of course. I'm sure he must be traumatized with everything that's happened."

"You're a good mother to Cody," he said. "The way you are with him, well, you remind me of your mother. In many ways. I love you, Shelby. I know I haven't always shown it, but I do."

"I know, Dad." She felt her eyes prick with tears. "I love you, too."

He left and she must have dozed because Alex gently shook her arm a short time later.

"Shelby? Wake up. Cody wants to say hi."

She shifted on the bed, wincing a bit when her stitches pulled. She focused on the tiny face peering at her from beside her bed. "I'm awake. Hey, partner. How are you?"

"Aunt Shelby!" Cody tried to climb up the side rails into her bed, holding one of the figures from his animal kingdom in one hand. Alex caught him under the arms, and swung him back down to the floor.

"Oh, no, you don't. You need to talk to her from here," he said, giving Cody a stern look.

"But, Dad," Cody protested.

"No buts," Alex interrupted. "You don't want to make her tummy hurt, do you?"

"No." Cody reluctantly gave in.

Shelby watched the two of them interact with a sense of shock. Cody had called Alex *Dad*. It seems they'd grown much closer in the time she'd been stuck in the hospital.

She swallowed hard, realizing God had brought father and son together. They didn't need her anymore. She tried to quell the sense of panic.

"Shelby, are you really doing all right?" Alex glanced at her anxiously. "We've been so worried about you."

"I'm fine, really. And it seems you've been doing pretty well yourself."

"Me?" Alex's eyes widened. "I'm not the one lying in a hospital bed."

"No, but you've obviously spent time with Cody. He listens to you like a father." She hesitated, not wanting to bring up his career, but since they were talking about Cody's future, she steeled her resolve. "Have you thought about the future?"

"I already resigned from my job, Shelby. My boss has agreed to give me a reference so I can get a job in the training facility. You don't have to worry, I won't leave you and Cody alone."

Really? "You won't?"

"No." He glanced down at Cody who was trying to crawl under the bed. "I know this isn't the time, but you need to know, I'm not afraid to be a father to Cody. Not anymore, although I was before. My own father, well, let's just say he wouldn't win any father-of-the-year awards."

She sucked in a quick breath. "Oh, Alex. He hit you?"

He shrugged and the way he avoided her gaze told her all she needed to know. "A bit, but he also drank. A lot. I've resented him for a long time. And I thought about giving up custody because I was a little afraid I'd turn out like he did."

Suddenly, everything made sense. She realized Alex wasn't avoiding being a father to Cody because he didn't love him, but because he didn't want to hurt him. "Oh, Alex. You'll be a great father to Cody." Her voice thickened with tears. "All he needs is love."

Alex nodded. "I know, because God showed me the way."

She couldn't have been happier to hear that.

"And what about you, Shelby?" he asked, gripping the edge of her side rail, tightly. "I know you've been afraid of men, but now that I've found you, I don't think I can let you go."

She blinked and the room spun dizzily. "I'm not afraid of you, Alex."

"You're sure?" He leaned over, reaching out to gently stroke her cheek. "Because if you need time, I can wait, for as long as it takes."

His offer was so sweet. "I'm sure, Alex. In those brief moments I thought I might die, my biggest regret was not telling you how much I love you."

A broad smile bloomed on his face. "I love you, too, Shelby. Will you do me the honor of marrying me?"

Before she could formulate a response, the head of her bed moved upward and Alex reared back in surprise.

"What's going on?" she asked, fumbling for her controls. The foot of her bed began to rise up too, and for a moment she feared she might be a human sandwich. "Cody? Are you playing with the controls?"

His earnest face popped up from the other side of her bed. "My giraffe is stuck!"

Alex lunged to grab the toy wedged between the mattress and the controls of the bed rail. Her knees were almost to her chest and her head was raised up as high as it would go.

"Got it." He raised the toy, the expression on his face so similar to that of Cody's that silent laughter bubbled up inside her chest.

"Don't laugh, don't laugh," she moaned, holding her stomach tightly, even as her shoulders shook.

"Are you all right?" Alex asked anxiously as he pressed the buttons on her bed to put it back to normal. "Should I call the nurse for more pain medicine?"

"No, that's okay." She scrunched up her face but tears leaked out the corners of her eyes. She pulled herself together, taking a shaky breath. "Laughing hurts."

"I made the bed move." With the crisis over, Cody jumped up and down. "Did you see that? I made the bed move."

Alex scooped the boy into his arms, tickling him in the ribs. "You sure did, troublemaker, but you were supposed to be quiet for a few more minutes. At least until she'd given me an answer."

"What answer? What's the question?" Cody demanded.

Shelby gazed at them, her heart filled with joy and peace. The man she loved with her whole heart and the boy she loved like a son. "The answer is yes. Yes, I'll marry you."

"Did you hear that, Cody? We're going to be a family." Alex set Cody on his feet, gazing at Shelby with love in his eyes.

"Really?" Cody glanced at both of them. "A family that lives together?"

"Yes." Shelby reached out to take Alex's hand in hers, interlocking their fingers together. "A family that lives together, forever."

"Faith and love, Cody," Alex said softly, drawing Cody into their embrace. "All it takes is faith and love."

Shelby smiled through tears of happiness. "No fear."

* * * * *

SPECIAL EXCERPT FROM

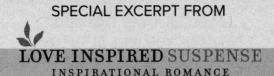

LOVE INSPIRED SUSPENSE
INSPIRATIONAL ROMANCE

When search-and-rescue park ranger Autumn Mercer and her K-9 partner, Sherlock, meet a stranger in the mountains whose brother has gone missing, they drop everything to join the search. But with a storm and gunmen closing in, can she and Derek Peterson survive long enough to complete their mission?

Read on for a sneak preview of
Mountain Survival *by Christy Barritt,*
available March 2021 from Love Inspired Suspense.

After another bullet whizzed by, Autumn turned, trying to get a better view of the gunman. She had to figure out where he was.

"Stay behind the tree," she whispered to Derek. "And keep an eye on Sherlock."

Finally, she spotted a gunman crouched behind a nearby boulder. The front of his Glock was pointed at her.

A Glock? The man definitely wasn't a hunter.

Autumn already knew that, though.

Hunters didn't aim their guns at people.

Her gaze continued to scan the area. She spotted another man behind a tree and a third man behind another boulder.

Who were these guys? And what did they want from Autumn?

Backup couldn't get here soon enough.

The breeze picked up again, bringing another smattering of rain with it. They didn't have much time here. The conditions were going to become perilous at any minute. The storm might drive the gunman away, but it would present other dangers in the process.

She spotted a fourth man behind another tree in the distance. They all surrounded the campsite where Derek and his brother had set up.

They'd been waiting for Derek to return, hadn't they?

Why? What sense did that make?

She didn't have time to think about that now. Another bullet came flying past, piercing a nearby tree.

"What are we going to do?" Derek whispered. "Can I help?"

"Just stay behind a tree and remain quiet," she said. "We don't want to make this too easy for them."

Sherlock let out a little whine, but Autumn shushed the dog.

The man fired again. This time the bullet split the wood only inches from her.

Autumn's heart raced. These men were out for blood.

Even if the men ran out of bullets, she and Derek were going to be outnumbered. They couldn't just wait here for that to happen.

She had to act—and now.

She turned, pulling her gun's trigger.

Don't miss
Mountain Survival *by Christy Barritt,*
available March 2021 wherever Love Inspired Suspense books and ebooks are sold.

LoveInspired.com

Love Harlequin romance?

DISCOVER.

Be the first to find out about promotions, news and exclusive content!

Facebook.com/HarlequinBooks

Twitter.com/HarlequinBooks

Instagram.com/HarlequinBooks

Pinterest.com/HarlequinBooks

YouTube.com/HarlequinBooks

ReaderService.com

EXPLORE.

Sign up for the Harlequin e-newsletter and download a free book from any series at
TryHarlequin.com

CONNECT.

Join our Harlequin community to share your thoughts and connect with other romance readers!
Facebook.com/groups/HarlequinConnection

HSOCIAL201